THE WOMEN OF GUINEA LANE

Gabriel Fielding

Hutchinson
London Melbourne Auckland Johannesburg

© Gabriel Fielding 1986

First published in Great Britain in 1986 by Century Hutchinson Ltd
Brookmount House, 62–65 Chandos Place, Covent Garden,
London WC2N 4NW

Century Hutchinson Publishing Group (Australia) Pty Ltd
16–22 Church Street, Hawthorn, Melbourne, Victoria 3122

Century Hutchinson (NZ) Ltd
32–34 View Road, PO Box 40–086, Glenfield, Auckland 10

Century Hutchinson Group (SA) Pty Ltd
PO Box 337, Bergvlei 2012, South Africa

Phototypeset in Linotron Times 11/12pt by
Input Typesetting Ltd, London

Printed and bound in Great Britain by
Anchor Brendon Ltd, Tiptree, Essex

ISBN 0 09 163980 8

*I dedicate this continuing story to
Edwina Eleanora,
for her skill as my first and most perceptive editor;
for her constancy.*

Acknowledgements

The critical help I have had from friends old and new has been of inestimable value:

Harold Harris, Tony Whittome, Maggie Hivnor, Dr Michael Fielding Barnsley, Dr. Herbert Eastlick, Dr. Eli Bessis, William Ausmus and Miss Alice Quinn.

I am glad to be able to thank, most especially, my friend, Frances, for her timely encouragement.

1

He waited impatiently on the platform of a station near the Uxbridge terminus of the Piccadilly line. He wished he looked more obviously medical so that people might know there was a real reason for his not being in uniform.

The Northolt fighter 'drome was nearby, manned these days by a Polish squadron with some of whose pilots he shared drinks in the evenings at the Shakespeare. Now, in the bitter morning air, they were revving up their engines on the grey perimeter, getting ready for some interception or 'show' later on, when they would accompany the Allied bombers as far as the Belgian coast. Though he did not know their unpronounceable names, they were his friends and he had enjoyed mixing with them; as if their day-to-day courage, their defiance in the foreignness of England, might rub off on him and make him strong.

He strolled about the level asphalt, swinging his crocodile-skin case with its weak lock. Inside it were the tools of his future: the expensive sphygmomanometer, two clinical thermometers in sealed glass cases, a leather folder of scalpels, artery forceps, suture needles and tweezers; two pairs of surgical gloves, gauze bandages of different sizes, a pretty roll of grey wartime cotton wool layered with blue paper, two diaphragm stampers and a stethoscope and two glass and metal syringes.

How cold it was this biting November, how it isolated everyone. People's breath condensed in the air, their footsteps echoed under the shallow roof of the shelter as they walked up and down trying to keep warm. At the signal end of the platform, not far away, there was a girl with a black 'cello case. She wore a tweed coat and headscarf and her face was tightly closed; as closed, he thought, as the case of the instrument she was trying to hide behind.

For several minutes he watched her with a dull interest, wondering how it was he could so easily sense her reserve, her hostility. Her ankles were thin and meagre, he saw, and the end of her nose pinched and pink. She wore no gloves and though she had a deep overcoat collar she had not turned it up.

Now as he looked, he again forgot her because high above the terminus his Polish friends had taken off in their Spitfires: a squadron of monoplanes immersed like small sharks in the deep air, each grey shape rattling the frost with the beating of its pistons as, banking low over the red-roofed suburb, the machines rose and faded into the pale green clouds of southern England.

And now the train came rending down the lines and stopped to discharge WAAFs, RAFs and 'Brown Types' onto the concrete; service personnel who had been up to the West End on overnight passes. He saw them flow past the girl with the 'cello and noticed that she was not opposite a carriage door. She had been forced to carry her instrument down the platform to his own entrance beyond which the City men were already rattling open their newspapers.

He waited for her grudgingly, holding open the automatic doors for her, half hoping she would leave it too late and get left behind or else get her 'cello caught between the doors. As it was, she hurried up to him without even a nod, most of her body hidden behind the case of the instrument. He saw only her mauve hands on either side of its waist.

Someone on the train was pushing the button which forced the doors to close and he was able to restrain them only long enough for her to push past and take her seat on the far side of the carriage. As the train moved out of the station he found a place opposite her. Against the anti-bomb netting glued to the windows he still could not see her face clearly. The light globes down the centre of the carriage were apricot-dim and the haft of her 'cello slanted over her shoulder like a rifle carried at the slope; between her knees the 'cello swayed to the movements of the train.

He was glad now it had not been trapped by the doors;

8

for he was seeing it as a human body and working out the injuries it might have sustained: fracture of the pelvis, a displaced coccyx, haemorrhage into the bladder. It would have required two or three consultants to put it right and these days they were hard to get hold of.

The girl needed to blow her nose, was sniffing unsuccessfully. Why did she not use one of her pale mauve hands to get out a handkerchief? He wanted to offer her his own; the silk one kept for show in the breast pocket of his Donegal jacket: the one he kept for attractive girls to use.

But at that moment the man next to her said something and then held out his own. He whipped it out of the breast pocket of his suit from beneath his British Warm, and she, smiling, took it and nibbled at her nostrils with it.

Her lips parting slyly as if she were not shy or inimical at all, her dark eyelids, closing a little over her darker deep-set eyes, made her suddenly real: no longer a sentinel of the hostile world of embattled London, but delightful; and John felt the pinch of envy.

The man in the short coat and bowler hat, with his blue eyes and tanned cheeks, was talking easily to her now, steadying with a ringed hand her swaying 'cello; establishing something over her: a warm patch in the chill air, a possibility, a semblance of love.

And could she not see as clearly as could John that he was a bounder, an ageing cad as deceptive as his once good clothes now rubbed away to a used smoothness? The very type, he realised, of the stranger who had talked so 'matily' to Victoria that day, fifteen years ago, in Yorkshire, stirring her childish pleasures, giving her promises of confidence, before seducing and later, contemptuously strangling her.

God! he exclaimed to himself. God in heaven! How many of them may there not be about, unkennelled by the war? Free now to do so easily what was so much more difficult in peace? Not killing, except across the Channel in commando raids, or by bombing from the air; but just about everything else that sometimes, with some sneaking part of oneself, one *wanted* to do.

He studied the man again: the flash of the cigarette case, the lick he gave to his cork-tipped Craven A before inserting

9

it between his lips, his eyes fastening themselves on hers so that she hardly looked at anywhere else.

His longings gripping him, he wanted to get up, take a pace forward and tap the girl's knees, tell her: 'This stranger who has just picked you up could be cruel, dangerous. Beneath all the bonhomie, the ease, he could be a woman-hater, studied in the ways and weakness of his prey. When I was twelve years old, just such a man made me notorious, turned my life into that of "The Blaydon Boy".'

But were he to do this, she would at once, and in a way rightly, decide that he himself was the danger. So he sat still, allowing his fury and hunger to settle once again on the stranger in the British Warm.

How maddening it was that because of him he could not approach her, dared not start to tell her about himself and his plans; his dreams of the future and of the dark past too.

As if being alive was not in itself enough, as if whatever caused it was unable to withhold extravagance, he, whilst still so slowly recovering from Victoria's death, had been granted another, a second more immediate one: David's.

And this time at no remove. For though he had never seen Victoria's white body after she had left it, or, rather, had been deprived of it by her murderer, David had died in his wet lap, wet with the rain that was falling on them both. And what was worse, it was he himself who with an innocent but careless hand, had pulled on the rope by the rock face and so brought his brother tumbling to the ground.

He had said his final goodbyes to the staff at David's vicarage that morning: to Mrs Stoker the cook: to good Burley the gardener and handyman; and to the two Anglican nuns whose mission to his elder brother had proved so fruitless.

With the younger of these, Sister Sulpice, the little one with the bad teeth, he had been warm; regret welling up in him that far from ever knowing her again, he had never known her in the first place because she had been too stupid; protected from all but her Maker by the simplicity of her mind.

To pale-eyed Sister Monica he had been cold, shaking

10

her hand briefly, taking one last look into the space between her collar and her veil, the area that enclosed her features.

Did she know, he had wondered? Had she, as her manner seemed to suggest, seen it all from the start? Their mother's lost cause; the steady drip of the whisky; David's final adultery and his betrayal of the cure of souls.

A year earlier, in her unsaid disapproval of his brother on their first meeting, picking the little apples of early Autumn, Sister Monica had looked as sure in her disdain as on this very last Vicarage morning, only an hour ago.

'Well!' she had seemed to be exclaiming; Well!'

And in that one word, that attitude and attention to them all, had been the whole of her measure, her foreknowledge perhaps of what must happen to their sinful priest and to his family; and, come to that, to himself, to John the just qualified doctor. In it, too, had been the single syllable of her obituary for David George Blaydon: 'Well!'

Stepping out from under the Regency porch with its lead flashing grey against the warm bricks, he had passed down the vicarage drive swinging his case and his new instruments as he walked to the station. He had passed the gossipy tobacconist's, the King's Arms, the dispensing chemist where his sister, Melanie, had worked until she married, and had skirted the little twin-celled Saxon church, wanting never to go in there again after that last fearful vigil beside David's coffin with their mother. But, a little way past the stone posts of the entrance to the cemetery, he had been unable to resist the graveside. It had drawn him as do voices heard from over a hill in open country, as music heard across a body of water.

And, reaching the heaped wreaths on the long stone, he had concluded: if I kneel down here, if I order my thoughts, contain them and keep very still amongst these few browning flowers, perhaps I shall hear him speak from below the slate. Perhaps from somewhere there will be just one word, one voice in my mind; his syllable of reassurance and of love.

And he had prayed.

But no, nothing had come from the young face he could

11

still so clearly see; nothing from the white body, the wrapped limbs, the fingers laced across the broken chest. Nothing had come, either, from the hurrying clouds above him or woven itself into the throbbing of the last bombers returning late and singly from raids over France and Germany.

There had been only a sense of waiting, of dispersed attention, of a finger to the lips bidding caution.

That much, he was convinced, there had been. That much, he realised as he brushed the yellow clay from his trousers, had been given to him. And indeed, with bombs and incendiaries falling nightly over so much of Europe, with uncountable, forever unknowable, more innocent anguish everywhere, he had been presumptuous to expect more.

In the darkness of the tunnel the girl with her 'cello stood up. Supported by the man she swayed about in the passageway with her two partners, doing clumsy steps to the clattering of the wheels.

She was still smiling to herself and he, not so very much taller in his black skull of a bowler hat, was amusing himself:

'A spot of lunch somewhere? There's a brasserie in Sloane Square where 'cellos are welcome. So how's about it?'

She wrinkled her pink nose and then added a half-smile to the grimace. This was her reply, and though silly it was affirmative. The bastard had succeeded.

They had passed Acton Town, Earl's Court, Baron's Court, Knightsbridge and were pulling into Hyde Park Corner. The man had succeeded too in getting the girl and her instrument to a place in front of the door. She would be the first out onto the crowded platform.

Wherever, he wondered, as he too got up and followed them out through the doors, wherever were they going? Where was he taking her after the spot of lunch in the brasserie? To some lunchtime concert in the Albert Hall? Then past the empty bandstand beside Churchill's rocket launchers by the trees in the Park and on to some prepared setting in a flat in Earl's Court? Where, evidently, she would gladly be seduced. Where, for all anyone knew he might humiliate her; or worse.

12

2

He ran up the moving staircase past the cigarette, razor blade and beer advertisements and past the bold black-and-white notices of the Government Departments:

IS YOUR JOURNEY REALLY NECESSARY?
CARELESS TALK COSTS LIVES.
OBSERVE THE BLACKOUT.

He hurried past the shopping centre, the expensive fruit stalls, the bookstalls and entrances to the lavatories and up the two final metal flights of steps to the open pavement beside the Hospital.

Behind it and in front of it the red buses lumbered amongst the taxis and the little cars of wartime, gouting grey-blue smoke onto the pavement where he had paused to take a final look at it all. Someone bumped into him and he apologised; but the tweed-clad figure had passed on down the steps and into the Underground.

Good God! Was all London in tweeds or khaki? Harris heather overcoats, peaty Orkneys, schoolmaster checks with patched elbows, coats and skirts from the Scotch House, or Selfridge's large-graph statistical; and the rest, apart from a few British Warms, uniforms: Army, Navy, Merchant Navy, Wavy Navy, WAAFs, Free French, Free Poles.

The canteen, deep beneath the wards and corridors of the old building, was warm and snug. At the tables, by the painted brick of the walls, lounging with their tankards of beer beneath the posters, were four or five top-echelon men; some were six months ahead of him, others as newly qualified as himself.

As he entered, they looked up from their drinks and away again with near indifference. And though jealous of them for their greater success he warmed to them. As young and untried as himself, conventionally friendly towards one another, they had no feelings whatsoever for him; no curiosity. They were absorbed in themselves, their nurses, their prospects; he was sure that in his two years at St Luke's they had never discussed him, knew nothing of his past, of Victoria's murder, of his failure in Ireland; nothing, even, of David's most recent, publicised, death.

He got himself a cup of coffee from Susan Hepton-Mallett, the elegantly tired wife of one of the Consultant physicians, and sat down at a table. Soon he had sufficient energy to break in on the desultory conversation of the others.

'I say, do any of you chaps know anything about the Guinea Lane hospital?'

'Guinea Lane? Did he say Guinea Lane?'

'God!'

'It's EMS, isn't it, Rodney?'

'No, Geriatric.'

'Fevers, *I* thought.'

'Sounds a bit odd,' John suggested, and two or three of them turned to face him: white ovals above starched collars and gentlemanly ties.

'Odd?' Phillips repeated. 'It's Emergency Medical Service. Rural and completely chaotic.'

'Guinea Lane is out-back,' someone added, 'Absolutely out ber-back.'

'Does no one go there?'

'You mean Consultants?'

'Not if they can help it. I say, Jack, doesn't Hugh Hepton-Mallett run a few of his chronic skins out there?'

'I believe so. Mostly suburban eczemas and neurodermatoses.'

'Anyone else?' John asked, 'Do the surgeons use it?'

'One heard something about a couple of women from the Royal Free.'

'*Women*, Rodney?'

14

'Believe so. Someone said they were from one of the Chocolate Colonies.'

'Not black!'

'Christ, no! Australians – ambitious buffaloes from Sydney or somewhere, getting experience.'

John got up and Susan Hepton-Mallett served him a pewter tankard of beer. The pewter was comforting.

'Any gynae?' he asked.

'Wouldn't know.'

John drank, stretched and yawned, simulating the indifference he felt he needed.

'Well, then, does anyone know who got the other house job?'

'Wantage, I believe.'

'Not Jerry Wantage? He's Siamese, isn't he?'

'No, Hindu – Injibob!'

'I heard he was Polish.'

'No, Japanese-Mexican.'

'God, is that possible?'

Phillips turned to him: 'You got the other job, I suppose?'

'I did as a matter of fact.'

'Of course you're from outside, aren't you? Manchester or somewhere.'

'Trinity College, Dublin.'

'Oh Dublin. Did my Midder at the Rotunda. Nice place.'

'Yes, it was pretty busy.'

'No contraception, of course.'

'None. All very Catholic, bags of babies.'

Someone got up: 'I say, Rodney, we were due upstairs about ten minutes ago.'

'We kept them waiting; good way to start.' Phillips turned to John, 'Well, if we don't see you again, good luck!' He paused. 'There *was* something about that place of yours. They've got a rather weird Scot in charge out there.'

'Oh thanks. You don't happen to know in what way, do you?'

'Oh Rodney, do come on!'

'No, just weird – some kind of woman trouble.'

They clattered to their feet and were gone.

*

15

He had intended to wait around a little longer in the hope
that Sidney Grautbaum or one of his other friends would
turn up; but by now he was impatient, eager to be gone
from there and on his way to the Guinea Lane in what,
even before this conversation, he had thought of as the dark
country, beyond the bounds of London proper. And, he
decided, even if Grautbaum or Peel or Shrago did turn up
they would not be able to tell him much more. Most likely
they would be even more comfortless about the Emergency
Medical Service, about the patients out there; and about
Jerry Wantage.

He collected his suitcase from the luggage room and made
his way through the courtyard centred behind the white
Regency walls. He crossed through the tunnel, climbed up
the steps to the pavement and walked down Knightsbridge
towards Harrods and the Sloane Street Underground. It was
brighter now; the barrage balloons were silvering up under
the dispersal of the clouds; a canary sunlight paled the Hyde
Park greensward and painted black the railings in front of
the Albert Memorial.

He swung the crocodile skin case carelessly and attempted
to whistle to himself to strengthen the mood of nonchalance
in which he had set out; the image he had had of a fully
fledged doctor, a physician and surgeon about to start upon
a successful career. But the whistle faded almost before it
had begun.

I am recovering, he thought; that is all. His death, my
David's, was so cruel: that groaning. How could he have
groaned so deeply and for so long? In the rain. It was
scarcely a human sound and it was quite outside any time.
I don't understand the anatomy of it. He was light-voiced,
he had a shallow chest; but it was as if the whole of Europe
was groaning, the whole world! Anyone would be upset,
haunted really: and, of course, lonely. That's the only
reason I'm going on like this; and, somehow, I have got to
stop it.

I shall be better when I get there, when I am able to start
some work. And how much worse everything could be if,
for instance, I'd failed in that last Final in Surgery; but I
got through it. I passed. I have my Membership of the Royal

College and I've got my blue raglan overcoat and some money and the 'wee black bag' that David always laughed about. So what does the past matter to me? Even now I am rising out of it; I am surfacing into clear air.

3

Walking through the main gate of the Guinea Lane, carrying his light suitcase in the right hand and the crocodile bag in the other, he craned out of the collar of the blue raglan to face the winter-bright morning. He squared his shoulders and tensed his spinal muscles to achieve a soldierly walk. Melanie had been right, 'Don't slink, John. Be a fine figure of a man, make people get out of *your* way.'

He looked about him. The hospital was period, pre-war Thirties; low buildings everywhere connected by gravel paths, scattered with silver birches, rowan trees and cemetery spruce. Down one side of the wide compound were the two-storey houses of the married staff facing Guinea Lane, the country road up which he had just walked from the 'bus stop.

Quite far away a nurse came out of one of the wards. She was trim in her red shoulder cape, her dark hair escaping from under her cap, her body delightful. Busy and preoccupied, she came tapping up her chosen path and with a quick smile for him passed into one of the single-storied wards as though again totally self-absorbed.

At intervals in the shrub-planted grass there were irregular cement pools with flowerless saxifrage and aubretia plants round them. The contained water was clear and black, lipping against the weedless rock surrounding it. Here and there, beside the pools, were groups of cement birds of no particular species; they had been cast in different attitudes; some looking up at the sky as though praying, others paddling the scanty grass, still others preening their stony breasts. He looked to see if there were goldfish or water plants below the surface of the ponds, but there were none; so it must all have been a pre-war conceit, some councillor's idea; and now, since the war would never end, it would remain one.

He had reached the main block of the hospital now, another low spread-about building with wide dark glass doors at the top of a shallow flight of steps, and, let into the pink brick above the entrance, a rectangular tablet:

ADMINISTRATION

He walked in beneath it, pushing open the doors with his chest to spare himself the hefting of his luggage again. As the glass and metal swung to behind him he looked as keenly as he could at nothing; since, for what he hoped might be the last time, he was reliving the immediate past and a period behind it which, as yet, was not remote enough. Gingerly as a surgeon moving aside some bodily structure, his mind was touching memory, nudging it to make room for the present he so much needed.

It is back there, he told himself, the sorrow, the confusion. It is with David's vicarage, with all the fearful comfort we distrusted: the Van Eyk triptych: the empty, modish bedrooms; the just-filled grave and that ridiculous kitchen.

And, too, it is Yorkshire, in Danbey Dale; the night of Victoria's disappearance. As she, perhaps quite near by, called out in her terror among the sheep-hung moors.

Seeing this, all of it, in an interval so tight that he had not even reached the glass clock at the end of the corridor, he paused to pray: 'Please let me forget; let me start,' and waited for his heart to slow.

The clock was elaborate, a stylish monstrosity: brass, thistles, glass, tartaned figures on a businesslike face and a complicated pendulum which kept touching shiny terminals let into the back. On a brass plate affixed to the wooden pediment he read:

18

ELECTRIC CHRONOMETER

Conceived and Constructed
by

DAIRMID FAIRBURN GILLESPIE, MRCP (EDINBURGH), DPH

He turned to face someone following him down the length of the passageway, someone very young and a little nervous at approaching him.

'Excuse me. Were you lookin' for someone?' she asked.

'I suppose I was.'

'Are you Doctor Blaydon?'

'Yes.'

'Well – may I help you?

'Of course.' He looked at her properly. She had shining grey eyes. 'I'm sorry, I was thinking about something; daydreaming.'

'Doctor Gillespie – ' she began, 'The Superintendent, he's been looking out for you. He asked as we were to be sure and call him over at his house soon as ever.'

'You mean, as soon as I got here?'

'We thought, Doctor Gillespie thought, you might have been held up and Doctor Whooper – well, she – '

He smiled at her anxiety. It was very disarming and made him confident:

'I suppose you want me to check in, do you? Sign a book or something?'

'Wel, they all do; but usually they like to look around. They seem to want to find it all for themselves and get to their rooms.'

'I see.'

'The others have wanted to meet them others – the medical staff, Doctor Miss Whooper and Doctor Wantage.'

She really did need some total reassurance.

'I know Doctor Wantage,' he said, 'I was at St Luke's with him.'

'Oh, well you'll be – ' Her smile had come and gone so quickly that he might have imagined it.

'Yes, I will be happy; you're right; but tell me, did you

19

say Doctor Whooper was a Miss? Is she on the strength? Permanently, I mean?'

'Oh yes; Doctor Whooper has to be. She looks after infectious diseases which was in the main section when they built and all.'

She had ceased to smile and her silence made him look at her afresh. What an indefinite little thing she was; as though, like many new young creatures, baby mice or seedlings, she hadn't coloured up yet. Her small, hardly-made-up face was ivory sallow, her eyes and her hair, ashen; her hands were as pale as sea creatures in a tidal pool. Strange, he thought, that at so new a coming she was so strong; for despite her nerves she had not swerved at all from what she had to do. Whatever would it be like to make love to her? A little girl? Quite passionless, someone to put to bed and give a glass of milk to.

'Doctor Gillespie,' she was saying, 'said as we were to put you in the staff room until he could get over to show you to the wards.'

He laughed at her, 'To show me to the wards? Or the wards to me?'

'It's both, isn't it?'

'Oh, all right, I agree; but which is the staff room you were going to put me in?'

'This one, Doctor John.'

She opened a door and showed him into a long dun-coloured space. At the far end were bentwood chairs round an electric wall stove, a scattering of sepia carpets, brown wall-radiators and a brown mantlepiece and a long built-in brown sideboard with three or four black telephones on it. At the near end an ochre light filtered in through French windows and fell on seed-coloured curtains and an oak-stained pinewood dinner table with a set of matching chairs.

He put his suitcase and the crocodile-skin bag on the dark polished edge of the floor.

'Is Doctor Gillespie Scottish?' he asked; adding, since she looked taken aback, 'I mean, by any chance?'

'He is from that way. He says it was Kinsale.'

'Oh, where's that?'

'Well, it's in Scotland, isn't it?'

Amused and irritated, he lied: 'I meant, what part?'

'I think it's by Aberdeen.' She paused. 'If you don't mind me asking, how did you know, Doctor?'

'I'm not sure. Perhaps from that ugly clock and the furniture in here. It's all – ' He paused not wanting to discomfort her further, 'It's all in such safe taste, isn't it?'

'It's ever so dull.'

'Exactly. Tell me, does Doctor Gillespie miss Scotland, do you think?'

'He doesn't talk to us about it so much – not now.'

'Then he must miss it.'

'Or else, he doesn't,' she said. 'Before the war they was used to spend all their holidays up that way. But – '

She looked uncomfortable; as if she would like to get away from him.

'But he can't, is that it? Because of the war?'

That means, he thought, that Doctor Gillespie can't grow an annual beard up there on some ghastly island covered with rocks and heather.

'It's not just that – it is in a way.' She was looking at him expectantly. 'Doctor John, I have to be getting back to the office, to ring round the wards and all. I don't know how long it will take to get the Superintendent or Doctor Miss Whooper out, or Doctor Wantage.' She paused as if she did, after all, sense some of his anxiety, 'You'll be all right for a while? There's magazines on the sideboard and the *Daily Express* and the *Mirror*.'

'Thank you. You never told me your name.'

She turned to leave him:

'It's Minna.'

'Minna what?'

'Minna Frobisher: but you could call me Minna.'

Her white fingers on the door, she paused, 'You've had your lunch, have you?'

'No. Why, have I missed it here?'

'Oh dear. It's always served twelve-thirty. Cook is very strict about that. I could get you some sandwiches.'

'No, don't worry; I'm not very hungry.'

'But I could just ring through to their kitchens and they could send someone over.'

He flopped into one of the bentwood chairs.
'And coffee?'
'Yes, Doctor John.'
'That would be nice.'

He was skipping through a *British Medical Journal* when Doctor Gillespie caught him. He hadn't read any of the articles, only repeated the titles to himself and nibbled at an opening paragraph or two. He did not wish at this moment, to have his immense ignorance made any more obvious to him; he did not wish, either, to feel envious of the dedication of others. So, at the sound of the far door closing and of Doctor Gillespie's greeting, he jumped out of the chair with the Journal still in his hand and went forward to greet the older man eagerly as he asked:
'Doctor Blaydon?'
'Yes, Sir; Doctor John Blaydon.'
'Aye! I heard that.'
'I'm sorry, Sir?'
'I heard all about ye, the Blaydon Boy as you were termed in the Press – At the *time*, ye ken? the sorrow; the tragedy.'
'I see.'
The doctor patted his shoulder.
'. . . *All* about it. And 'tis not well-forgotten!'
'You did? How extraordinary. I was hoping that by now – '
Gillespie ignored this, 'You found your way out here all right, then?'
'Yes, but I was delayed at St Luke's a bit.'
'Aye. Minna told me you missed your lunch, too?'
'Yes, I'm afraid so.'
'But you've had your sandwiches?'
'As a matter of fact, I haven't.'
'Good, good! We'd best be making the rounds then. There's a game at Twickenham this day. Kick-off's in half an hour and I want to catch it in the house. Do you play yourself, doctor?'
'Football, Sir?'
'*Rugby* football; or the Soccer?'
'Not since I left school. I was never – '

Doctor Gillespie paused in his rapid, somewhat stiff stride and glanced him up and down out of his sad brown eyes.

'I did not think you played. You've not the build.'

'Nor the guts, I'm afraid.'

'That's bad!' Doctor Gillespie shook his head sympathetically. 'A man misses out a deal if he doesna face the field. Look at *me* now; would I strike you as fit?'

From the side of his head John could see a little group of three nurses striding out of another of the low buildings.

'I should say that you're very fit, sir.'

'You would?'

John gave him the kind of measuring glance that saw nothing of him at all:

'Certainly.'

'Well, you'd be wrong!' Gillespie put a hand on his shoulder and looked him mournfully in the face. 'Aye, totally wrong! I'm *cruppled* with it.'

'Crippled?'

'Aye, *cruppled*. I've two disks out above the sacrum, two median cartilages, bilateral, and I'm rattled with cervical arthritis and a femoral hernia.'

'Femoral? That's unusual.'

'It is that. You're thinking I've a feminine pelvis, Doctor Blaydon?'

'Well, not exactly.'

'Ach! Don't deny it.'

The doctor moved on again and John kept pace with him. He wondered which of the squat buildings they were headed for and what it contained. He was anxious not to think at all about his companion, the sudden and unexpected pressure he was exerting. The wind in the grey sunlight of the hospital compound struck cold. It licked at his shirt front above his waistcoat and he wished he'd kept his blue raglan on.

'You're looking peaked yourself. Are you cauld?'

'Cold? I am, a little.'

'Good! good! Well, now I'll introduce you to the sister in Gynae, and she'll take you to the Abdominal-Surgical, and you'll be passed in that fashion round and about.'

23

'Thank you; could you tell me what my duties are, sir? I mean, this week?'

'Your duties, Doctor? Why, I've given you the sudgery this turn-aboot; the gynaecology and the abdominal and the good specialities of Doctor Miss Graemes and Doctor Mrs Strykes.'

'Specialities?'

'Aye lad! Doctor Graemes' wee pets – the Thyroids. She's probing and researching them fine, as if there were never a war in anyone's head.'

'And Doctor Strykes works with her? With Doctor Graemes?'

'She's just such another. A great pair of colonials they are. Doctor Strykes does all the anaesthetics and she's fetching out some grand advanced ideas I'm told.'

They had reached the glassed entrance to the women's ward, and paused in the sheltered portico.

'And I'm to start in the morning, sir?'

'The *morning*, laddie! You're on call *now* – this minute! There's a war on, ye ken?'

'Yes, and I have a room somewhere, have I?'

'Ye have a bed and a box at the end of the geriatric unit. It's temporary only until I can bide you in one of the married quarters. Doctor Wantage will show you to it before ye sup.'

'And I shall meet Doctor Whooper then, shall I?'

'You will!' The Superintendent closed his jaw tightly and with a timid but hardening persistence, John asked, 'At supper time, sir?'

'Without a doubt.' Again Doctor Gillespie placed a kindly hand on his shoulder. 'And dinna forget she's senior to ye both; answerable, if at all, to *me*. But here's Sister Thorpe to take ye down and meet your patients and show you your list for the morn. Sister! This is Doctor Blaydon. He's our house sudgeon for the quarter, in succession to Doctor Bruce.'

'How do you do, Sister.' He shook the ringless fingers briefly. Then he looked at her more closely.

Her vellum-white face had not a breath of make-up on it, only serious lines. Fine, not too deep lines of consideration

24

crossed the forehead, a little temper or aggravation crease between the eyebrows, a filigree of web around the deep-set, misted irises; and short vertical strokes into both lips, most numerous at the corners of the mouth.

She smiled into his face courteously and with custom, as much as to say, 'Another one! Well, we shall manage together.'

He warmed to her as to someone in the known past, some swift friend of his grandmother's, some historical personage.

She had a little starched cap as crisp as a cockle on her fine leaded hair; below that a white bow tie, starched and stiff as her cap. Her shirt front, short frilled and pleated over the spare chest, was immaculate.

'Perhaps, Doctor Blaydon, you would like a cup of tea in my staff room?'

'Thank you, I certainly would.'

She led him through to her quite spacious room. It was very bare in the three o'clock winter's light; a big black-out frame leaned against the painted wall on which hung photographs of many soldiers in ranks. He recognised the puttees of the Great War, the short moustaches and the haggard look about the eyes.

THE DUKE OF SOMEWHERE'S LIGHT INFANTRY
'A' Company

he read.

There was no carpet on the floor, no cushions on the wooden chairs, only some cretonne curtains on either side of the window and a green fabric lampshade above the circular varnished desk with her books upon it beside the day register.

'And a sandwich?' she asked.

'That would be super.'

'They're only bully beef and there are no pickles.'

'I don't mind. I love it, with or without.'

'Then you've had no luncheon?'

'I was too late.'

'Poor man. Minna could have got you something.'

'Minna?'

'You must have met her. She greets everyone.'

25

'Oh yes, I did. She offered to ring up the kitchen; but Doctor Gillespie caught me before any food arrived.'

'And did he congratulate you?'

'I don't think so.'

'Did he not say, 'Good, good!' when you told him you'd had nothing to eat?'

He laughed.

'It's a little quirk he has. He does so want everything to be like that. So much so that he hardly notices when it isn't.' She passed him another sandwich, 'And so Minna Frobisher was going to have seen to you?'

'I believe so.'

Her frown was swift, 'Most certainly, Minna would have done so if she had said that she so intended. Forgive me, but Minna is rather a pet of mine.'

'There isn't very much of her, is there, Sister?'

'I think you will discover that there is a very great deal. Now do sit down while you munch your sandwiches and I shall tell you something about our patients. Do you take some sugar with your tea?'

'No, thank you.' He drew his chair up to the desk.

'I did notice Minna, you know, Sister.'

'I'm sure you did; but now, down to business. We have twenty beds in this ward and one staff nurse and two probationers to look after them. The young gels are very good, quite in the old tradition of starting under the beds before they get to their occupants. Considering the wartime conditions, we turn our women over fairly fast. They have little chance of a real rest.'

'I see.'

'Have you done much Gynaecology, Doctor?'

'Not nearly enough, I'm afraid. Just the course in Dublin and then again at St Luke's.'

'And surgery, may I ask?'

'Rather a lot of assisting over about four years; but apart from that, only minor stuff in outpatients.'

'Four years? What delayed you?'

'I got the sack from Ireland, when I was coming up to Finals and had to transfer to St Luke's; and I had to start back over from Pathology.'

26

'I'm sorry, but it is no matter and will stand you in good stead with our visiting consultants.' She smiled; 'Are you able to see that really it was very amusing to so annoy the Irish?'

'Not yet.'

'Perhaps you never will.' She looked up at him. 'Are you a grudgy sort of person?'

'I don't think so.'

'You'll find here that our Senior Consultants are most competent and generous.'

'Generous?'

'Not all such are, you know.' She gave him a wintry smile; 'but Mr de Fleur and Mr Brice-Stewart leave much to their assistants. Doctor Bruce, your predecessor, was always saying how glad he was of the experience he gained.'

Oh was he? he thought.

'You'll be working with Mr de Fleur tomorrow morning as ever is, and it's quite a busy list: two hysterectomies, a colpoperineotomy, and three dilatations with curettage.'

'I see.' He put down his cup with a clatter. 'Golly! Did you say *two* hysterectomies, Sister?'

'Sometimes Mr de Fleur will do four, back to back. He is most skilled, Sister Cleary tells me. I have not myself worked theatre for many years of course.'

'No. What times does Mr de Fleur start?'

'Always at nine unless there's been a big raid. Doctor Bruce used to get half his rounds done before breakfast on Mr de Fleur's days. He'd be there awaiting him in the theatre well before they scrubbed up.'

'Oh.'

'He was an early bird, was Doctor Bruce; and you know what they say about *them*, I'm sure?'

'I've no idea.'

'Why, that they catch the worm, of course.' She passed him the plate of sandwiches, 'But you're a tease, Doctor Blaydon. You are teasing me, I fancy?'

'I was.'

'Doctor Bruce did so too, and naturally I encouraged it.'

'Did you?'

'It helps my women. They enjoy a joke before surgery,

and soon afterwards too. They laugh together and that's beneficial. Now, doctor, would you like to have a word or two with your list?'

'Very much.'

'Well, I'll give you everyone's names and the particulars of those you'll be seeing in the theatre tomorrow; you will look in on them before your breakfast, I know? With *those* patients you might like to give a little encouragement this evening?'

'Certainly.'

'Here is a house coat, for I don't suppose you've been given one yet.'

Beyond the double doors of the ward it was warmer; there was the harsh smell of bedpans and cheap scent; stink and Chypre, he thought as he looked down the two rows of beds. In their fluffy jackets of angora, of blue or pink wool, in their black truckle beds tucked neatly under the vermilion blankets and white counterpanes, ten women on each side of the long room turned to look at him. His left hand thrust deep in the starched pocket of the house coat, he stared full at them.

One or two, a dark one with centre-parted hair and a plump pink-cheeked girl, looked back at him; but the remainder were as swift as cats. They looked, they raised their chins to get their eyes full on his face and then escaped to their talk and magazines and books, their crocheting and their dozing. Instant though their glance had been, they had, he hoped and believed, accepted him; though of course it would be impossible to know certainly until he had met them in their minds as he would have to do when he touched their bodies. So far their complaisance was of their nature only and would have been as readily accorded to anyone else.

Women were like that; they adjusted themselves in the first instance to their circumstance; whatever it was. If not outraged by one or other parent, some lover or husband, women were adjusters; they were a silky matrix flowing round the hard edge of fact. They were yea-sayers. It was as if, from the moment of their birth, they looked about

28

them with steady eyes, with readiness, even with initial delight at their surroundings, whatever they might be.

From the night desk at the far end the staff nurse came clipping up to them on her too high heels.

'This is Doctor Blaydon,' Sister Thorpe told her, 'and this, Doctor, is Staff Nurse Edgar.'

She would be no temptation. She was not young, well into her thirties and thin. She looked mildly excited about something and, at the same time, unhappy; totally dissatisfied.

'Doctor Blaydon will be assisting Mr de Fleur in the morning. He will want the case notes from you when he comes over after supper.

'I'll leave them out with Night Sister. I'm off duty at six.'

'Thank you, Staff Nurse. Well, we won't keep you now. I'm going to show doctor our fishes.'

She led him over to the right hand wall to a large table on which stood a brightly lit aquarium, very green and continually bubbling.

'It's an interest for us all in here, and surprisingly healthy.'

'It's very pretty.'

'The children love it on visiting days. The little boys more than the little girls. I wonder why that should be?' She tapped the glass. 'We have some difficulty in getting the ants' eggs for it. How sluggish they are today! What do you suppose could be the matter with them? Are they worried about General Rommel?'

Even as he laughed he wished he hadn't.

'That is what Doctor Bruce thought. He thought the males were particularly afflicted and looked sad.'

'Did he? Why?'

'He was most droll about it. He would say, "A gravid female, bulging with eggs, hovers over the hollow her mate has scraped in the gravel while he circles her, undulating, anxious to play his part. Oh, the displays he gives. Twisting and turning, moving over and under, swimming in ever tighter and tighter circles until – " '

Playing to the gallery, she had turned to face the women in their two rows of beds:

'Why! Until he can contain himself no longer and, *whoosh*!

29

he loses all his seed into the water above the ova she has laid. And so we all know what Doctor Bruce used to call the male, don't we? Now, Mrs Thrim, don't be shy; tell us!'

'It was "Poor Fish", Sister, "Poor Fish"!'

' "Poor Fish" it was.' She led him to the first of the beds. 'And now I want you all to meet our new house surgeon. This is Doctor John Blaydon who is taking over, as from this evening.'

4

On the following Thursday he was awakened as usual by Lynton, the nurse he had seen on that first afternoon as she had pattered up her chosen path and smiled at him in passing.

'Wakey, wakey! Doctor Blaydon. It's on seven and here's your tea.'

'Oh blazes, Lynton. I've been up half the night.'

'You did leave orders that you were to be woke before seven.'

'I know I did. It's Mr de Fleur's day. Evidently he couldn't get in for his list last week.' He turned onto an elbow and looked at the blacked-out window. 'God, what a racket out there! Was there a raid on last night?'

'Yes, that's Bomber Command meeting upstairs, returning from Germany again. They say it could have been another thousand-bomber show and these mornings they always seem to come back this way.'

'Why? Is Hullshold opposite Cologne or Hamburg or somewhere?'

'Who knows? I'm never quite sure where it is.' She put the cup to his lips. 'Now, drink your tea! Did you sleep well – between calls?'

'I don't know. I can only remember being awake. The old ladies were playing up. They seem to get young again at night.'

She sat down on the bed, 'How's your tea?'

'Cold.'

'Poor you. Are you cold too?'

'Not particularly.'

She did look so very nice; that escaping hair he had first noticed in the compound was still escaping from under her little cap this morning. Her health; a quality as perceptible as courage or innocence, surrounded her like a transparent envelope. Clear eyes, firm breasts, flushed cheeks, ready lips and smooth white hands. How remiss of him to have lost that first opportunity by saying, 'Not particularly.'

'Because, if ever you are,' she went on, 'a little chilled, say? I could hop in and we'd soon get warm.'

'*What* did you say? Oh, Lynton!'

'Oh Lynton,' she mimicked. Through the bedclothes she held his right foot with a firm hand. 'Tomorrow then,' she waggled his toes. 'Or next week, when we know each other better?'

'That would be super.'

'Well, anyway, I'm late already.' She got up. 'So there wasn't really time, was there?'

'You could come earlier tomorrow?'

'That's where you're wrong.'

'Why?'

'I'm going up to town.'

'Who with?'

'Staff Nurse Edgar. We've got dates.'

'With who?'

'Hers is a great tall Texan. He calls himself the beanpole.'

'And yours?'

'Oh, just someone! I'll take your cup if I may? I really do have to rush. I'm on with the dragon this 'turn-aboot' and it's one of her bad days.'

'In General Surgery?'

'Yes.'

'Then I'll see you.'

'Perhaps.'

5

He took a cold bath in the staff washroom, dressed from the suitcase he had laid on Gillespie's 'box' the night before and found his way over to the ochre-brown room in the administration building.

The pinewood table was laid for three: a Brown Bess in a knitted cosy, a setting of two stainless steel, plastic-handled knives, one fork, a plain white side-plate with cup and saucer to match, a bowl of curled margarine shells, a pot of Golden Shred marmalade, a pan loaf of brown bread and a covered plate concealing a whitish 'broken' scrambled egg, its congealed albumen sitting in a thin pool of juice.

He ate with gusto; some memory, perhaps of a good day in Sir Patrick Dunne's in Dublin, starting with Limerick bacon and mounds of lacy fried eggs, before getting really busy in Out Patients; stitching delicate skin delicately, unwrapping a previous suture on the seventh or eighth day and finding it clean and tight; syringing the dirty ears of old men out of slums and of young nuns out of clean convents, lancing carbuncles, passing catheters through occluded prostates, watching the tired urine gush into the bowl. All of it satisfying, even happy, because you ceased to lean quite so heavily over youself with the weight of your wishes and fears.

And today, with any luck, could be just such another excursion out of the past, the doubtful future, into the measure of a certain skill, a little contentment.

He mopped up the last of the juice of his 'broken' egg and spread a slice of wholemeal with the jellied marmalade. Where was Wantage, he wondered? Probably sleeping in till the last possible moment. Such a matter-of-fact little blighter; so sure of everything, so 'disillusioned', if such were possible when apparently he had never had any illusions to start with. A communist too, though quieter about it than Grautbaum; even sceptical, like some of the Catholics he'd known in Dublin. And therefore all the more dangerous?

Yes, certainly; for you were less likely suddenly to 'convert back', to lapse, if you were dubious; in matters of faith a little doubt made for constancy.

And Doctor Whooper; what of Doctor Whooper? He had asked Jerry Wantage about her before supper. They had sat smoking together in the bentwood chairs gossiping about people they had known at St Luke's; a laparotomy really, an exploratory conversation to discover, by discussing others, prospects of themselves. Then they had turned to the present and Wantage had said, 'Whooper? Oh, Whooper!'

'Yes?'

'Well, she's a woman.'

'I know; the little secretary told me.'

'Definitely,' Wantage added, 'I mean, she's definitely a woman.'

'That *is* interesting! But couldn't you go a little further?'

'No, I couldn't.'

'Why not?'

'She'll be in any minute. She's never late.'

'Have you had a row with her?'

'God, no! But I think that she and Gillespie – '

Doctor Whooper had come in then and Wantage, who had strange manners, who was not ever rude but who often failed to 'notice', had continued to loll while John got to his feet to see the doctor go straight to her place at the end of the table.

'Oh, Doctor Whooper, this is John Blaydon.'

'I heard.'

She had sat there with her back to them, pressed the bell switch and, once the maid had brought in the tray, had started immediately on her supper.

John caught Wantage's eye; but the other, his coppery little face closed, his jaw well forward, had not returned his glance. Instead he had got up saying, 'Might as well eat,' and together they had trooped over to the table and sat down.

From behind, Doctor Whooper had been only a seated figure presenting the genderless back view of her body in its navy blue coat and skirt. Now, facing one another and seated on either side of her place at the end of the table, preoccupied with silence and hunger, they had not looked at her; and she, quite undismayed, had not troubled to read the case notes she had placed beside her plate.

Apparently she found it unnecessary to pretend anything for them, since, as yet, they did not exist for her. Eating his way through the corned beef and carrot stew, John wondered what he might have to do in order to be noticed by her.

Now, as she came in, wished him 'Good Morning,' and cut into her portion of scrambled egg, he got up, put on his white house coat and hurried over to Sister Thorpe and his morning in theatre with Mr de Fleur.

Mr de Fleur stepped out of a large grime-streaked American limousine with blacked-out headlamps and the word DOCTOR printed tastefully on an enamelled pasteboard behind the windscreen. He was small and dapper. Small surgeons, of course, had to be dapper in gaberdine and cologne, just as the large ones had to settle for tobacco and tweeds. Mr de Fleur, unable to add one cubit to his stature, had polished himself to a West End finish, a fine soft patina that would not alarm the upper-class patients, who, unlike working-class women, might be made to feel uncomfortable, even distrustful, of too blatant a personal hygiene.

He shook hands with John, obviously registering his name as exactly as some new clinical fact, and then hurried him into the theatre block. There, with contained birdlike movements, he took off his grey Homburg with the curled and ribboned brim, his silvery striped trousers, his shining chestnut shoes, and in his silk socks stepped into his boots in the theatre proper, to scrub up.

John, following as quickly and discreetly as he could, took his place at the right-hand lavabo and scrubbed up too.

The scalding water burst from the tap, the liquid green

34

soap ran up his arms as far as his axillae as he scrubbed and scrubbed at his nails, hands, wrists, forearms and elbows; and then, for fear he had missed some small area started on it all again, juggling the shining levers of the taps with the points of his naked elbows and adjusting the pressure with the white rubber toe of his boot.

Through the steam Mr de Fleur spoke as quietly as some well-bred girl at a party.

'No trouble, I suppose?'

'No, sir.'

'Mrs Wilkes, the second hysterectomy – chest all right?'

'Yes, sir, perfectly clean.'

'No one with a cough? No one with an upper respiratory "thing"?'

'Absolutely not. I went over them all.'

'Sister Thorpe said you'd been thorough.' He lowered his voice. 'Between ourselves I would prefer *not* to have Strykes do one of her "blocks" this morning. I'm in a hurry.'

'No, sir. Excuse me, but what is a "block"?'

'Ah, you're new here of course.' He appeared to have lost himself again and John did not like to press his question. Mr de Fleur really was a very busy man even when he was not as busy as usual; and since today he was more busy than usual, he was necessarily extremely and immoderately busy.

Already he had scrubbed up and, like a priest, his arms spread out, his pelvis well back in case his unsterilised underpants should come into contact with anything, he stepped into the green theatre gown held open for him by the white-clad probationer and slid his powdered hands into the gloves opened for him by the hands of Sister Cleary.

For the last time John inspected all his nails closely and discovered a thin dingy crescent behind that of the left thumb where the pulp joined the free edge of the nail. He juggled the jet nozzle directly onto it and scrubbed briskly, digging the bristles into the pink bed of the crevice. Then he went over all the fingers of the hand again and, for good measure, of the right hand as well.

At last he was ready to step into the open gown, the nurse's eyes steady above her mask, her whole stance that of chaste acquiescence; then the ritual of dusting his hands with the bag of chalk before they were slid into their gloves; lastly, the move round to the far side of the bright table; the olive shape of the patient's body which, below the neck, was completely swathed save for one crescent of swabbed yellow skin above the shaved pubis.

He lowered his head while the nurse tied the strings of his mask over the back of his cap, and then stepped forward to take his place opposite the surgeon.

Mr de Fleur was handing something between steel rings to Sister Cleary. It was passed so swiftly that until she placed it on the white enamelled surface of the proffered tray John had no idea what it could be; no notion that the excised uterus with its heavy fibroids had just passed under his nose.

'I think we might close her now. Tension sutures!'

'Tension sutures,' repeated Sister Cleary.

'Yes, sir; shall I do it?'

'Metal sutures.'

'Metal sutures.'

'By all means, Doctor Blaydon.' Mr de Fleur had stepped back and was peeling off his gloves for the nurse to discard. 'All well at your end, Strykes?'

'Great! Inside eleven and a half minutes, I make it.'

Mr de Fleur smiled. 'Minimal shock. We're aiming at the ten minute hysterectomy here, Blaydon.'

'Caught him napping!' put in Doctor Strykes. 'She's surfacing already.'

'Well, wheel in the next as soon as you like. I've a couple at the Westminster when I finish here.'

John pinched in the last tag and passed the clipper to Sister Cleary. God! What a bad start! What an incompetent idiot he must seem. He untied the mask and handed it and the gloves to the probationer and went round behind the anaesthetist's barrier to introduce himself to Dr Strykes.

'I was a bit slow.'

'Too right!' Ella Strykes had a bristly look; she was one of those redheads with freckles and whiskers battling it out on all the free areas of her face. She lifted the mouthpiece from the patient's fat pink cheeks, flicked the eyelids up to see her pupils, and then signalled the bearers to wheel her back to Gynae.

Mr de Fleur's bonzer,' she told John, 'but a goer, so you'd better be on yer tootsies for Mrs Wilkes or you won't get to tie your bows, will you? Right! Roll her in, boys.'

'Prep all checked?' asked Mr de Fleur.

'You could eat jam off her lap, couldn't he, duckie?'

'Oh yes, doctor,' sighed the patient.

'Then nighty night! Off yer go to dreamytimes. Give us a couple of minutes and you can cut, Mr de Fleur.'

Concealed in the stroking fingers as they swept once above the pubis, the scalpel penetrated the dermis and then the yellowish globular fat, finally the peritoneum. John got in the retractor and locked it. Mr de Fleur caught and tied two or three small arteries, checked the caecum, the appendix, and looked at both ovaries; he cut and tied the fallopian tubes and then with a sponge stroked the bladder back from the front of the neck of the uterus. Then he paused, motionless:

'What's that?'

'I think it's a hole, sir.'

'Damn! Someone adjust the light.'

Together they peered at the ragged edge of the little tear, trying to see where it led to. The white light moved, the edges of the perforation enlarged and, through it, the lining of the bladder shone silver-grey beneath its shallow wash of urine.

'Damn again! Retaining catheter, please, Sister.'

'Retaining catheter.'

'Yes, good. I think we'll put it in from this end while we're at it. Less messy. Check the urethra, would you, Doctor?'

'It's through, all right.'

'Good. They have such tiddley ones, the dear creatures. Cobble it up. I hate bladders.'

'Yes, Sir.'

'Go on, man, go on! Don't fiddle. She's going to leak a bit whatever you do.'

'I've put in three.'

'Excellent! There, through the vaginal wall, one two; clamp, sutures please! Ex-cellent. And of course you'll have to watch out for – things.'

37

'*E coli*, Sir?'

'Precisely. Bound to get an infection, poor old girl, bound to. You can clear those up for me, I know. Right, lift it out. Nice healthy ovaries she's left with. Pity really. Still, they've done their job no doubt. Four children, wasn't it?'

'Yes sir, two of each. The eldest boy's about fifteen.'

'Well, well. Now what have we next, Sister Cleary?'

'Mrs Booth, the colpoperineotomy, Mr de Fleur.'

'Thank you, Sister. This lady's husband is in Africa with the Eighth Army, one gathers? A sergeant with the Twenty-First Highland Division, wasn't it, Blaydon?'

'Yes, sir. He's due home shortly. Got a piece of shrapnel in the left perietal. That's why she – '

'Wants tightening up,' finished Mr de Fleur. 'Well, we'll arrange a nice treat for Sergeant Booth, the Soldier's Return; a smooth run-in and a good grip once he's found it. How's she breathing Strykes?'

'Beaut,'

'Away we go, then.'

6

At lunch on a Friday, on that very particular Friday which he was not soon to forget, Dr Whooper said,

'You talk medicine a great deal, Blaydon. So do you, Wantage.'

They didn't look at one another; they continued to eat the carrot and corned beef stew and the sieved boiled potatoes with dull enthusiasm; and Dr Whooper's remark sank into their stiffening silence as it lengthened into the time she took to eat several more mouthfuls; then, without putting down her knife and fork, she asked,

'Are you going to specialise?'

38

'Who?'

'You; Blaydon?'

'I don't know.' He was startled, for he was thinking just then that he would have to, that he would have to know more about something; even some one small branch of a branch of anything, even of some vast part of it all; Gynaecology.

'You don't?' Dr Whooper moved her very clean soiled plate to the tray on the sideboard by the black telephone. 'It's all joost talk, then?'

She sat down and reached for the pot of strawberry jam.

'Not altogether. We might want to specialise, mightn't we, Jerry?'

'Yes.'

'In what, Blaydon?' She had taken a second spoonful of the rationed gelatined jam and was placing it on top of the pile she had made on her ground rice.

'Oh, I don't know. Gynae perhaps.'

'Gynaecology?' she repeated emphatically. '*You*?'

'Yes. Why are you so surprised?'

'That's joost what I'm not.'

'What's so wrong with Gynae?' asked Wantage.

She didn't answer; she had stirred the jam into the tepid ground rice in wavy contours of pink and she was eating it efficiently. So Wantage repeated his question.

'Do *you* suspect anything wrong with Gynae, John?'

'Wrong? No.'

'Neither do I.'

Dr Whooper put down her clean spoon into her nearly clean bowl.

'You two!' she said. 'The pair of you.'

And she went over to the sideboard with the plate and picked up the receiver of the nearest of the three telephones, dialling a number and speaking over her blue-clad shoulder expressionlessly:

'There are only two kinds of gynaecologist.'

Before Wantage nudged him to discretion, John asked, 'What are they?'

Evidently she had not heard him for her voice changed into warmer North Country tones as she spoke into the mouthpiece. 'This is Doctor Whooper. About my appointment for this afternoon: I want to change it to three o'clock. I find I have an engagement at two . . . Aye, that would suit nicely.'

She returned to the table and picked up her case notes from beside her place. She looked through her glasses at them both.

'One,' she said, 'is the effeminate. The oother I leave to your imagination.'

As the door closed behind her they smiled at one another.

'Hostile, isn't she?'

'And ambitious. She's a new kind of person; 'career oriented', as the Yanks say, anti-men; keener on impressing women with her freedom than men with her virtues.'

'Is she one of those, Jerry?'

'What?'

'You know – lesbians.'

Wantage got up on his sturdy little legs and went over to the fireplace, warming his behind at the two orange bright bars of the wall stove.

'There's Gillespie' he said.

'You mean that he and she? How extraordinary!'

'I don't see why. She's a woman.'

'I know, but – '

'Has to be. She was calling for a hair appointment – a perm probably.'

'How do you know? She could have been ringing some gymnasium for a weight-lifting course.'

Wantage did not laugh. 'You *do* hate her!'

'I couldn't, because I don't think she's "there". She's so new to her precious "career" that she's just about had to stop *being* a woman. She doesn't even know the difference between showing authority and being rude.'

'Gillespie finds her feminine enough.'

'Gillespie and Gelda Whooper! What about his wife?'

'Bored, hates footoball. Anyway, she's always away.'

'Doing what?'

'Oh, she throws pots in Chelsea and lectures with the Army Bureau of Current Affairs.'

'Has she got droopy hair parted in the middle?' John

40

asked. 'Long knitted dresses and unshaven armpits? In other words, is she greenery-yallery?'

Wantage was literal. 'I don't know about her armpits, otherwise that's her type.'

'Poor old Gillespie! Is she away now, this week?'

'Probably. He'll bind to you "aboot" it if he can catch you over the weekend.' He yawned. 'How are you getting on with the Virgin Sturgeon?'

'Miss Graemes? Haven't met her yet. What's she like?'

'Difficult.'

'Australian?'

'Not noticeably. Went to some grand finishing school in England, her rich old dad's only comfort. Too bad he didn't live to see her fame – gold medal in Adelaide or somewhere.'

'Is she an orphan?'

'Worse! Mother rejection. You know: ambition, high brains, man-shy – the lot.'

'Fascinating. But how did you find out all this?'

'I read it up one night in Gillespie's office – took a look at his files.'

'Has she any brothers or sisters?'

'She's an "only". Her mummy was on the stage, which could account for a lot.' He looked at his watch, 'I've got to get a move on if I'm to keep my tea-party date. Hepton-Mallett's due in half an hour and I haven't checked his skins yet.'

'Who's your date?'

'One of the night staff. She lives in the compound and makes Yorkshire parkin. Her old man's somewhere on the coast with the balloons. She – '

He broke off and they both ran to the french windows.

'Christ! What a noise! They're back early. Let's have a gander outside.'

Over the asphalt and grass, over the little spruces and the squat wards; over the town and the dull horizon spiked with domestic chimneys and towers, the air was rumbling. Though there was no late Autumn wind down here, the glassy planes of the air were shaking under the impact of hundreds of returning bombers and their escorts as squadron after squadron hung steady high above; beating down the white detritus of the clouds to distant bases.

'It thrills you, doesn't it?' Wantage yelled.

'Yes, it does.'

'Wish Joe Stalin could see it. It may not be the Second Front, but – '

'They're lighter now, aren't they? Lighter than at breakfast?'

'They've unloaded the lot. Tons and tons of blockbusters on Germany.'

'On the Huns,' John added. 'Fire bombs, too. Imagine it! The BBC at six tonight: 'All our planes returned . . . it was reported that the marshalling yards and the town were saturated with high explosive. At least twenty large urban fires were left burning out of control.'

'*Our* turn!' shouted Wantage. 'Remember the East End over two years ago? Makes one feel good, doesn't it?'

'I was in Ireland then.'

'Exhilarating in some way.'

'Their hospitals will be busy.'

'Bloody busy.'

'That is, if they haven't been blockbusted too.'

'*Their* turn!'

'I suppose so; but Jerry! If one had fallen over there – on the women – on Sister Thorpe's unit?'

'So what? We'd be dead. *We* wouldn't be interested.'

'We might be. My brother – '

But Wantage had gone on his rounds. Fortunately he had not heard those words. Had he done so he would only have shouted back, '*He*'s dead, isn't he? Your brother is dead.'

John shivered. The echoing air with the sounds in it of planes already past, of those passing immediately above and of those invisible and still to come, seemed a tree of noise in which also there were voices.

Standing out there on the compound grass which, in the square shadows of the buildings, still had the unmelted grey frost of dawn upon it, each blade encrusted with its crystals, he could hear, if he listened lightly, human voices. Some, he thought, were singing, others calling out something to one another; still others were crying, keening. Not a word

42

was distinguishable, not a single syllable, unless every now and again a syllable *was* clear, so isolated from all others as to remain almost meaningless – a fleck of clarity in the confusion.

Still shivering in his white housecoat, the bone earpieces of his stethoscope gripping his neck, he was prompted to stay out there longer in the rumbling air, to discover, if he might, why it was that when he listened carefully he heard only the firing of the hundreds of piston engines overhead, while, if he did not, those teasing distant voices gradually returned, calling to one another intimately, incoherently as if in foreign tongues.

As he went back into the ochre room, dark now with the low watt bulbs shining on the varnished boards and brown carpets, he heard his name called through the open doorway into the passageway beside Dr Gillespie's chronometer.

He did not answer; he knew she would find him and he liked that, liked to be so much wanted so many times of the day, and very often in the night. He waited by the pinewood table and she came in, little Miss Minna Frobisher. 'Oh, there you are, doctor. I been looking everywhere for you.'

'You didn't look outside. I was watching the show.'

'Doctor Graemes . . .' In her excitement she swallowed. 'Miss Graemes, Doctor Blaydon; she rang up to say she was on her way. You're to meet her at the main gate in fifteen minutes. Well, it *was* fifteen minutes; it will be ten now.'

She was frowning at her wristwatch, a pseudo gold one, very small with a filigree strap that was as wide as the bezel; meant to make the watch look even smaller than it was, more impractical, more feminine.

'If you were looking for me all of five minutes, it will, undoubtedly, be only ten more. Was that a Christmas present last year?'

'My watch? Yes.'

'And you couldn't find me?'

'You hadn't pulled the curtains back. How was I to know you was outside, behind them?'

He stepped over to her. 'Minna, aren't you bothered by the raids? Aren't you interested in them?'

'Once I was.'

'But you aren't now, not now?

'They've been going on for so long. First them and now us; and when I was in school it was leaflets over France and Germany – paper bombs.'

'Let me look at your watch.'

She held out her hand, the sallow wrist on which the hairs were as yet invisible as a child's. Without moisture her whole hand rested in his palm; petal cool. How brave she was; no, not brave exactly, just honest, to accept the raids, the whole war she was living in, without any attitude. Didn't she realise that if even one small bomb fell anywhere near her, or a little fragment of bright steel from our anti-aircraft shells touched and went in through her birchy hair – ?

'Our dad gave it me on his last leave.'

'At Christmas? Surely he must have had leave since then? Oh, I'm so sorry – '

'That's all right. They got him in the desert, a year ago this month it was, outside Tobruk.'

'Tobruk! That's on the coast isn't it?'

'Our dad used to swim in the Mediterranean – between attacks. It was ever so much warmer than Southend – "Got the sand and sweat out of you better than a Turkish bath," he said; and didn't cost you nothing – anything.'

'Free!' he said, as she took her hand away and looked again at the time. 'Well, Minna, I'd better be off to meet Doctor Graemes.'

'Yes, better not be late for *her*.'

'She's a stickler, is she?'

'I don't know what that is. But even Doctor Bruce was – ' She stopped. 'I shouldn't be talking like this. You shouldn't lead me on.'

'I didn't mean to.'

'You shouldn't tell lies, neether.'

'Minna?'

'Yes.'

'Do you like your job here?

'Of course.'

'Well, will you come out with me tonight – for supper somewhere?'

44

'I don't know. The nurses – '

'Don't be frightened of *them*!'

'They pick on me as it is.'

'Then give them stick.'

'All right, I will. What time?'

'Seven, by the main gate.'

'I'll be there – ' as usual she paused by the door, her wristed hand resting on the orange graining, 'It's ever so nice of you.'

'I know. I can't help it.'

'Oh, you never stop teasing. You better not tease Miss Graemes, though. She's awful.'

'What does she look like?'

'Ever so clever.'

'But is she pretty?'

'I don't know. With ladies like her, you don't notice things like that.'

7

Doctor Graemes went straight past him in her off-white Jaguar. She didn't raise a hand to acknowledge his presence, his patience really, for he had been there for all of ten minutes in the thin sunlight filtering through the clouds.

With a nervous curiosity he followed the Jaguar to the cindered parking lot. He hadn't seen her but she wasn't small, he knew. Her head had been well above the steering wheel, and her hair free with no hat or war-time square of silk to cover it.

She came over to him. Above her well-pressed blue trousers her hands were thrust deep into the pockets of a short schoolgirl navy-blue coat. It was made of a soft woollen material and there were thick flaps over the pockets.

'Doctor Blaydon?'

'Yes.'

'I am Doctor Graemes; apparently you had my message? I like my housemen to meet me at the main gate. One does not, even on day calls, want to have the staff ringing round the hospital while one kicks one's heels in the corridors. We will go straight over to Unit Five, I think.'

She had said all this through a loosely wound soft woollen orange muffler which revealed only her white cheek bones and her distant eyes.

'Unit Five?'

She pulled her muffler further from her mouth, allowing her escaping breath, only for a second visible, to melt into the chill sunlit air. Her eyes were distant he saw, because she was abstracted; she was so very much inside her mind; for a moment she was not looking at things, she was hardly seeing them. What fine hair she had; even in this still, breezeless morning, though she had tried to flatten it, flairs of it, individual hairs, even a few pin-thin strands of it, were loose and wandered in the light.

'Unit Five,' she confirmed. 'You have checked my charts this morning?'

'Yes, I talked to all five patients.'

Again the hand came up to the hockey-field muffler so that he should hear what she said.

'That was scarcely necessary. I like my pre-operative cases to be as little stimulated as possible. Absolute physical and mental rest is of cardinal importance. Sister Dyke did not tell you this?'

He did not reply.

'Did not Sister Dyke advise you of this?'

'She may have done.'

'As I hope you know, when my pre-operative thyroids are on Lugol's Solution they should be undisturbed in any way.'

'Two of them were a bit anxious last night. I thought they needed reassuring.'

'That *is* cause for concern, of course.' She paused to look at him. He met her young unserious eyes for a moment

46

before they shifted to his housecoat and, he thought, to his hands.

'And you are not yet a qualified psychologist, I take it?'

'No, Doctor.'

What fine ankles you have. How soft your hair is. Under your delightful eyes, which are a true green with no admixture of olive or blue, there are small crescents, just a line below the lower eyelid, right and left. But how cold you are, how austere.

'You understand, Doctor Blaydon?'

'I do.'

'Which two of my five cases were showing increased anxiety?'

'Mrs Enderley and Maureen Bason.'

'Enderley and Bason – Maureen is not so important of course – Has there been any weight loss?'

'Maureen Bason may have lost a very little – and Mrs Enderley, some.'

Doctor Graemes had paused below the three cement steps that gave on the entrance to Unit Five. Beside the gravelled pathway, one of the smooth cement birds – a stork or a merganser or a very small pelican – was regarding them sightlessly.

For the first time Miss Graemes looked at him long out of her quite beautiful eyes:

'Doctor Blaydon, I require accuracy in all reports. How much weight has Enderley lost?'

'Two or three ounces, I think.'

Her green eyes were still upon him; rather, they were just very slightly over him. They weren't focused on anything external, not on the high clouds beneath which the bombers had passed, not on his hair or his forehead or eyebrows, but on some distant point in her own skull; some infinitely sharp image, some calculation. He wondered if her eyes were unserious because of this, because she did not see any joke in anything, any discrepancy in her life at all. Much as she believed she was dedicated, serious, she was not wholly so. Her virginal abstraction, the student habit of it which had become fixed in the world of men with whom she competed, had distanced her from both genuine gravity and real humour; from love. She had, he thought, contracted 'professionalism', a masculine disorder; an unwillingness to feel.

'Mrs Enderley,' she said now, 'is being disturbed by the Geriatrics the council dumped on us after the parachute mines in October.' Again her abstracted gaze was upon that other point in her mind. 'Was she giving trouble last night? Was that old woman in the end cot shouting for her bed pan?'

'Mrs Gibbons? She was restless.'

'Restless?'

'Well, a damned nuisance actually.'

'What hypnotic is she on?'

'I'm continuing Doctor Bruce's medication; phenobarbitone, two grains.'

'It is not Doctor Bruce's prescription, it is mine. Give her four grains.'

'*Four* grains! That could be risky – her heart – '

'Four grains.'

'But – '

'I shall again see the Superintendent about this absurd situation. They must all four be moved into some other wing – or you must double up the existing beds in the Geriatric unit; in the meanwhile, if any one of the senile cases becomes in the least a nuisance, you are to sedate her effectively. This hospital is not for the terminally old and you are to – ' She paused to glance at the entrance doorway.

'Sister Dyke is coming,' he told her.

Doctor Graemes ignored the Ward Sister's approach.

– 'No matter what the consequences.'

'I don't know that I can *do* that.'

'You will do it if you wish to remain in this area and have my reference on your departure.' She cleared her throat. 'Sister Dyke! I hear that there has again been a quite unnecessary disturbance of my pre-operative Thyroids?'

'It was only for a few minues; the old ladies get a little anoxaemic in the small hours – would you like some tea, doctor?'

'No, not this morning, thank you.'

With her careful walk, quite silent in her white tennis

shoes, themselves a reminder of the Luftwaffe's night raids, and of a kind of secrecy, perhaps of night hours of research, she passed up the steps ahead of him into the small ward where, at the far end, four old ladies in their black, iron-railed cots sat high against their pillows.

She paused at the foot of Maureen Bason's bed.

'Sister, it would be as well if the evacuated patients were completely screened off from the remainder of the ward. I would like this done this morning. How did you sleep, Bason?'

'Quite well, thank you, Doctor,' she smiled at them. 'Lovely really.'

'Then no one was disturbed by the geriatrics?'

'Who? Old Mrs Gibbons? No-oo, she's like our gran. Ever so lively.'

Doctor Graemes was reading the case notes. Her fine right hand with its clear varnished nails plucked at her long muffler, pulled its loop down from her chin so that it hung loosely over her hidden breasts, its fringed orange ends dangling beside her overcoat pockets.

'In the interests of my other cases, my pre-operative thyroids, Miss Bason, I trust *you* to report to me through the Night Sister or the Duty Doctor, if anything or anyone disturbs anybody's sleep or rest.'

'Yes, Doctor.' Maureen Bason smiled at John, 'but I slept lovely last night. I was dreaming, Doctor Blaydon.'

'Were you? Of what?'

'Norman, of course; my fiancé.'

In the bed diagonally opposite, Granny Gibbons laughed. Her childish mouth opened on thin gums and white tongue as, briefly, she cackled out her inaudible joke: 'Ooh! Ooooh! Oooooh!'

The doctor placed Miss Bason's case notes on to the cotton counterpane and Granny Gibbons looked over at the three of them with animal patience. She was chewing on her fallen cheeks, tasting again her laughter, when she called out, 'It'll be all right, dear. It'll be all right on the night!'

As Doctor Graemes went silently to the next bed, Sister Dyke signalled two of her nurses, and folded green screens, like leaves cut and carried by wood ants, rolled down the ward and flowered across it, hiding the four old ladies.

'I don't mind their jokes,' Maureen Bason told everyone. 'Let them have their fun. . . .'

'I wish to speak to you, Doctor Blaydon, in Sister's office. We will not want tea, thank you, Sister.'

She waited until the door had closed and then holding out her ringless left hand pretended, perhaps out of the shyness that comes with a personal truth, to study its palm: 'No doubt you know that I am engaged upon a surgical textbook?'

'Yes, on the pathology of the thyroid?'

'More specifically, on hyperthyroidism – thyrotoxicosis, exophthalmic goitre.'

She pocketed her right hand opposite her left so that she stood very slightly stooped towards him, her shoulders hunched about her white neck. 'If any of the patients, anywhere, should prove to be moribund, I wish to examine them before death – and immediately afterwards.'

'Yes, Doctor.'

'As have my previous housemen, I should be obliged if you would report the onset of clinical death to me immediately – in any wing of the hospital, at any time of the day or night.'

'I see.'

'You will need to keep in touch with the Sisters; particularly the Night Sisters. Also you must report to me the names of those who may prove reluctant to call you in good time.'

'Very well.'

'I am particularly interested in the geriatric cases. Even those without the least trace of exophthalmos.'

'Yes.'

'You have no questions?'

'I was just wondering about Miss Bason. Her case history is rather vague and you said earlier that she wasn't admitted for thyroidectomy.'

'The younger nurses are frivolous. Sister Dyke has her history.'

'Has she – ? Has Miss Bason – ?'

'She has either a vestigial vaginal canal or an imperforate vulva. Apparently, too, she has herself been indiscreet about her condition.'

'I'm afraid so. When would you like to operate? When do you want her on your list?'

'On Monday next, and *first*, please; it could be somewhat lengthy – Doctor Strykes may well want to give a block.'

'Nine o'clock on Monday then? Should she have any special prep?'

'Doctor Strykes will prescribe her own pre-operative sedation. If necessary, I shall make it a two-stage procedure.'

She picked up her thyroid case notes in her ungloved hand, pulled out her fluffy scarf, drawing it round her chin before pausing, quite still, to look at something inside herself; her face smooth with absence, her eyelids widely opened.

He felt a pang at her going, at the tightening of her muffler and her sudden isolation. She had not even thought of her face, he noticed. If she did use the slightest bit of make-up, and he thought she did wear a little something, then, as any other young woman might have done when going off to face more people, she had not troubled even to smooth at her eyebrows or feel at her pale lips with the tip of her tongue.

He longed to find some reason to delay her, to detain her for a few minutes, because of her authority. She was suddenly so truthful, so whole in herself, her pursuit, that he was quite awed by her – no longer surprised by his own subservience, but slightly relishing it:

'You will want regular white cell counts, Doctor Graemes? Of the thyroids, I mean?'

She did not immediately reply. She was looking at the sheaf of case notes in her naked right hand, her eyes sliding fast over her own figures and those of his predecessor, Doctor Bruce.

Without looking up, she said more or less to herself:

'That would be rather pointless, I think, unless you ask specifically for the *lymphocyte* total.'

As if she had served him a cannon ball at tennis he cursed

51

to himself and then started to write things down in his clinical diary.

'*Monocytes*, too, are occasionally significant,' she added. 'I am starting graphs here in the office for each patient in addition to those I have in my own files. So you might like to include in their notes, your own index of the haematology – the blood picture.'

'You mean a weekly count?'

'I mean a bi-weekly count at least. We have a good lab here and two most capable girls who are keen on my programme.'

Again she paused to concentrate and her face relaxed into a happiness of expression that made him think of love; someone considering with joy the beloved.

'You do, of course, realise that with the very possible complications of this disease we get only one second chance at pre-operative stabilisation, consequently at surgery at all, and that, at best, a dubious one?'

'I didn't, as a matter of fact. You mean that the preoperative iodine – '

'I mean that before my next round it would be as well for you to consult your text books, Doctor Blaydon.'

'Yes, Doctor,'

'Eugene du Bois, the American, is quite sound on *Diseases of the Ductless Glands*. You will find his work in the hospital library.'

In bed that night, as hungry for facts as he had sometimes been as a student, he searched in the borrowed book for *Exophthalmic Goiter*, and, under *Etiology*, read:

Exophthalmic Goiter is apparently a disease of civilisation, occurring most frequently among young adults in cities where life is strenuous and especially in people of narrow frame, light skeletal structure and nervous temperament. Women are much more afflicted than men. In a large percentage of cases nervous shock or strain plays an important role and cures are difficult until this strain has been relieved. . . .

He turned to the Treatment:

Treatment – The most important part of all treatment is physical and mental rest. This should, if possible, be obtained away from home in a place where the patient can be isolated from household cares. . . .

So she was right: her concern with minute gains in weight and increases in heart rate was justified.

For these young adults, women suffering from 'a disease of civilisation', her concern was admirable. But her young women, if she was successful, would eventually turn into old women – grannies. What then?

8

He waited by the main gate for Minna. It was like the old days at Trinity, in Dublin, cursing and tense at the front gate for Moira or for Helen or for Dymphna; but it was quieter, no grinding yellow-lighted trams passing up to Stephen's Green, or clanking down the other way towards O'Connell Street and Glasnevin, no perpetually angry Gaels pressing their horns at everything that moved; at the rival world.

Yes, it was quieter, much quieter: England was serious with war: the whole night, the whole countryside round the scattered suburb of Hullshold was hushed with it. No lights showed, no beams from the stealthy cars, no searchlights as yet powdering the clouds of the horizon, no glimmers outlining the blackout frames from houses on the compound or many-windowed wards. Not many voices either, just a throe or two of laughter from nurses walking between units or going to supper; some tentative notes of locomotives coming wavering from far over the river behind the leaning willows; and now and again, as if it had been some solitary bird making wing home, the throbbing of a warplane moving between one airfield and another to rendezvous for the night's raids over Europe.

And he was quieter too. There was a busy silence within him: calculations less expert than Miss Graemes'; small or big decisions having to be questioned as his mother's whippets in Anglesey had questioned the gorse clumps, circling, circling where to enter. There were charts, whole case histories he had taken that afternoon, written beside the physicians' letters that had accompanied the patients from their homes out there in the attendant dark: his own notes jotted down behind the screens that surrounded the beds, and the surgeon's final opinion, her rounded signature at the foot of the copies for the family doctors:

M. CHLORINDA GRAEMES, FRCS

The name made him shiver.

The faces of the patients, too, were beginning to attach to the papers clipped to the folders at the foot of each bed. Mrs Gibbons' face, worn as pumice, shaped grey and pitted with tiny scars and map lines, cheeks as light as pumice so thin and sunken that if she touched their linings with the tip of her tongue it showed sharp as agate through the flesh.

And the riper faces of the women's ward, full with breeding and the assurances of love: their husbands', their children's and their parents'. For in the mid-course of life they were nourished by care on all sides; whereas Mrs Gibbons was only pumice-stone.

And beside hers was that other face which, since her features did not so readily separate themselves from her person, had in it the whole being of Sister Thorpe. The uniform too, derived from he knew not what vagaries of services, was unique to her and he could not visualize her body without it.

Above her left shirt-front, on the starched white pleats of her bodice, was a narrow dark-blue ribbon only an inch in width and about a quarter of an inch in depth. When he had first noticed it, there had hung from it, small as a farthing, a silver-coloured medallion fastened with a silver safety pin. But the next day, and all the days after that, the

54

medal, if medal it had been, was absent; and he was left with the teasing notion that there had been a little cheeked face on it, and no inscription.

Over tea and some broken arrowroot biscuits in her duty room he had peered at the medallion; he had listened to her ineffectively, his interest wandering over her leaded curls beneath her starched cap, her eyes clouded thinly as opals, her shoulders and the narrow ribbon with the little medallion just below it.

'Perhaps, doctor, you have done too much today, for I see that you are not attending to me.'

And he had caught her grave smile as he lifted his gaze to her face:

'I had a bad night, sister.'

'A bad night, or a busy one?'

'A busy one.'

'And there will be many of those. Will you take some more tea?'

Minna was late. He looked at his watch which, in the dark of the night and beneath the unlit globes of the main gate, told him little. Then he saw her; he thought he saw her coming along the opposite pavement, beside the verticals of the black railings round the sewage docks.

'Minna, is that you?'

'Am I late?'

'I don't know.'

'I had to walk slow after the lights inside.'

'You've got on high heels, haven't you?'

'They're Elsie's.'

'Elsie's! I could hear them. Who's Elsie?'

'My sister. She left them when she went into the ATS.' She came across to him. 'Where are we going?'

'I don't know. I thought *you* would.'

'We could cross over by the weir and walk alongside the river to the Chatsworth.'

'That's a pub, is it?'

'They serve a good meal there. They have a real dining room separate from the bars, with individual tables with a flower vase on them each and a candle sometimes. Oh! And a crippled waiter in a black suit.'

'It sounds posh! Is the food really good? Not just Woolton Pie and dried butter beans and baked jam roll?'

'You haven't had your cheque for this month! I know, because I write them out for Doctor Gillespie to sign.'

'You haven't told me about the food.'

'Don't you *like* baked jam roll with custard?

'Yes, do you?'

'Yes. Do you like steak and kidney dumpling with suet?' He was surprised, 'Could we get that?'

'Yes, and Brussels sprouts and boiled onions.'

'Do you like them?'

'Sometimes there's ice cream to follow; or pears and custard. He gets them in London. Mum says he's on the black market. Which would *you* have?'

'Pears and custard. You'd take the ice cream, wouldn't you?'

'I would, if it was strawberry.'

'And if it was vanilla, you'd have the plums and custard?'

'No, *pears* silly! If there wasn't nothing else. Look, the moon's coming up.'

'Yes, the Long Weir was very full. There must have been heavy rain in the Cotswolds. Here, give me your hand; I don't like you to walk so near the edge of the bank.'

'I want to see my head moving under the water. Oh, I forgot – bread rolls too . . . individual ones served separate when you sit down.'

'And butter balls?'

'Stork! But sometimes he gets in some celery sticks. A vase of them which the waiter brings the minute you sit down. Do you like celery sticks?'

'Not much; what do you want to drink, Minna? I mean, would you like a drink first in the bar?'

'Babycham.'

'What's that?'

'It's ever so nice. It comes in little bottles with silver paper round the top and a pink reindeer on the side. They say it's some kind of champagne from America.'

'Is it expensive?'

'For what you get, it is. But *I'll* pay. I want to go halves because of him not signing your pay cheque yet.'

'But I want to treat you this time.'

'Then I'll take you next time; if you still want to?'

'I do. Do you like the river?'

'It's all right.'

'Don't you like it, Minna?'

'It's smelly in the summer.'

'It's only water-weed and dragon flies.'

'People get drownded – drowned – in it.'

' "Drownded" sounds so much worse.'

'You shouldn't laugh at us.'

'So you don't ever swim in it? Not even in the droughts?'

'Oooh, never! Look, the moon's up and they're starting early.'

They stood still beside a clump of bull rushes silvered by the risen moon, their heavy seed-heads reflected black in the blackness of the water. Overhead, in the cleared sky, in the quiet radiance of the moon so silent over the horizon, floating motionless over the chimneys, towers, spires and steeples of the dark land, the unseen air was starting to pulsate, to shake slightly, its motion subtle as a heartbeat.

He felt for Minna's gloved hand. He could see now that she had short-wristed knitted gloves on, the kind he and his sister Melanie had worn in Northumberland to play in the snow. She exchanged the vanity bag she was carrying for his own bare hand, holding it not tightly in the ribbed knitting over her fingers.

They stood there quite alone on the gravelly towpath by the fringes and tassels of the rushes, looking up into the cold heights above as, from afar, the squadrons of the bombers came in high from their quarters, gathering together, assembling, loud and invisible beneath the diamonds of the night sky.

The rumbling grew and faded; was reinforced and bled again by the departure of one wing and the arrival of another, by the recurring whistle of the wingtips of the fighter escorts; by the lumbering of the heavier transports; then, as the slow moon paled, clearing the thicker haze of the horizon, as it lifted against its own light, the armies of

57

the bomber crews departed; the columns of air were stilled and settled.

Their shoes crunching with a small sound the river gravel of the path, they moved on again. Minna's hair was white now as birch bark and beneath it her profile small and sharp against the water. She carried her vanity purse in her gloved left hand, and continued to hold his own in her right.

'They've gone!' he said. 'They're over Surrey by now, or Kent. Some of them could be over the North Sea or the Channel.'

'They make a noise they do. Gives you a headache sometimes. Our Mum gets browned off with it since they took to meeting over Hullshold, especially nights.'

'Have you got one now? A headache?'

'No, not now.'

'Are you happy then?'

'Yes.'

'Why? Because you're going out?'

'It's nice going out with someone for a change.'

'Is that purse your sister Elsie's too?'

'She give it for my birthday. It's pretty really. It's all made of pearls.'

'Real ones?'

'No; just pearls.'

'I know what I wanted to ask you. Do you like going to the sea?'

'You mean Bank Holidays and all? Oh yes, it's a ball at Margate or Southend. In the peacetime we was all used to go; everybody from our street. Dad would get a car from a mate or some fellow up at the garage.'

'I meant, do you like the sea by itself? Do you like to go down to it alone?'

'Me Auntie Millie's got a shally Downchurch way and I wouldn't stay there again for anything.'

'Oh.'

'It's the pubs, mainly.' There's always so many public houses at the seaside. I don't think nobody likes it on their own or why should they drink all the time?'

'You wouldn't like to come to the coast with me? Sometime? On a weekend?'

'I wouldn't mind.'

'I'll try and arrange it.'

'What would we do?'

'Stay in a pub, I suppose. And chat and eat and walk along by the waves – if your mother, if Mrs Frobisher – ?'

'Our mum wouldn't fuss. Since our Dad went she doesn't seem to mind nothing.'

'That's sad.'

'I've told her about you.'

'What did she say?'

'Nothing!'

'Oh *Minna*!'

'What's the matter?'

'What did *you* say?'

'I told her you was lonely.'

'What else?'

'Haunted. I said as you were haunted.'

'Haunted?'

'Well, you are, aren't you?'

'Yes.'

She stopped then. Her gloved fingers tightened for a moment in his own. She asked him:

'Do you see things sometimes that others don't?'

'Go on.'

'Do you see things sometimes that might not be there?'

'I'm not sure.'

She laughed, 'That proves it then, doesn't it?'

'Do you, too? See things?'

'I think so. And hear them.'

'Does it worry you?'

'Course not. But don't tell.'

'Who would I tell?'

'You was right,' she said at dinner at the round-topped table, 'it *was* plums and custard. He said there'd been a run on the pears.'

'Yes, I was right. What are you playing with your stones? *He loves me, he loves me not*?'

She was scornful, 'That doesn't mean anything.'

'Well, what then?'

'The seaside; whether we'll get there. I've got some shells from Downchurch.'

'What kind?'

'Just broken ones I picked out of the sands. I don't know their names.'

'What do they look like?'

'All kinds; there's some like hats, and curly ones, some smaller round ones and some flats; and they're all white. I'm going to do something with them one day.'

'Make a necklace?'

'They're too ugly for that.'

'Why didn't you choose prettier ones?'

'There weren't any.'

'Did you look?'

'Not a lot. That beach by the dunes gives me the creeps. All them shallys with people in them that never seem to get onto their verandahs. My Aunt Nellie is ever so fussy about keeping the sand off of hers. But she and Uncle George doesn't hardly never sit there. He just smokes his shag in the window and watches the ships through his Great War binoculars. He knows all the merchantmen and all the classes of the destroyers.'

'What do *you* like doing, Minna?'

'That's secret.'

'Tell me.'

She looked round at the adjacent tables. Several of the nurses had 'Forces' dates, or housemen from adjacent hospitals. They were all heady with their drinks and expectations.

Minna said, 'Cut-outs and – '

'And what?' John leaned across the HP Sauce bottle.

'Indoor wrestling,' she whispered.

'You mean those big, fat, huge – ?'

'Yes.' She was looking down at her plate with the sucked stones lined up round its rim. Sheepish and defiant at the same time, she raised her face and gazed with her light-filled eyes into his own:

'It's *because* they're big and fat and pink, and there's a lot of them and they shout. That's *why*.'

He said nothing; he was counting his plum stones.

'Any harm in that?' she asked.

'No harm.'

'Well then!'

'We won't be able to go to the seaside after all,' he told her.

'Oh yes we shall. Yours don't count because I done mine first, and they say as we do go.'

'Tell me what kind of cut-outs you collect?'

'Newspaper ones mostly. I've got two books full.'

'But what kind? Strange happenings, supernatural events, film stars?'

'Babies.'

'Photographs of them?

'Yes; they do some smashing ones in the *Mirror*, Thursdays. Last week it was a black one, quarter page. Ever so sweet she is – smiling.'

'Have you got many?'

'I've got ninety-two.'

'And dolls?' he asked.

'Course not. What would I want with dolls?'

'But why? I mean, why do you like photographs of babies?'

'I don't know.'

'Think, Minna!'

'I *am* thinking. It's because of the times: raids and leaflets and silver paper coming down from the bombers. People getting hurt. I like to think there's babies too. They look – '

'Yes?'

'Excited. As if things was all right.'

'Except when they're yelling their heads off,' he said.

'Silly! That's *because* they are all right. Really!'

She got up. 'I've got to go to the "Ladies" now.' Beside him on her high heels she paused to look round at the other tables and whispered, 'There's that Nurse Edgar with the house physician from St Edmund's.'

'Yes, they're drinking Pimm's.'

'Do you like her?'

'She's not bad.'

She leaned down over him, her cheek so close he could smell her baby powder. 'Do you like Sister?'

'Sister?'

'Sister Thorpe, of course!'

She was gone; teetering between the tables, her pearl studded purse in her left hand, her smooth hair taking the dim lights as she disappeared round a hatstand heavy with overcoats to the door marked LADIES.

By the river on the way back to the weir they sat on a damp bench with no back to it. Under the moon the water surface slid past steely dark, thin as a meniscus, seeming to bear reflections away without ever moving them.

'It isn't half cold. I should have worn my camel.'

'Why didn't you?'

'Because this is my *best*!'

'Well, we'd better move on then. You can have my raglan if you like?'

'I want to stay here.'

'With me?'

'It's nice in the cold with nobody else. You could give us a hug.'

'There! Is that better?'

'Ever so. Your coat's smelly and rough – I can feel you breathing. When our dad was back home – '

The Thames was nearly soundless; a little way up it, in a standing patch of reeds, something splashed hurriedly, a scatter of sound from some small animal anxious to get into or out of the water.

'What did you mean about Sister Thorpe?' he asked.

'I just wondered.'

'I know you did; but what?'

'Whether you'd talked with her yet?'

'Of course I have; every day. I have to.'

'Oooh! You *are* slow. I thought as you'd understand me. Why don't you give us a real hug? I'm freezing out here.'

'How's that, then?'

'That's lovely.'

'Minna, please tell me.'

'I wondered if she'd shown you.'

'What? Shown me *what*?'

'She has *me*! She's shown to *me*!'

'You're making me angry.'

'That won't do you no good. She didn't like Doctor Bruce.'

'*Did*n't she?' He sat up in the cold. 'But she's always talking about him.'

Minna laughed. 'That's Sister.'

'Did she "show" him?'

'Course not! Oh dear, I've got to go to the bathroom again. Don't look, will you?'

She walked away over the grass, her high shoes snapping the moonlit frost, leaving dark patches in the silver. He watched until she squatted on her shadow, and then looked away at the unhurried haste of the water as he waited for her to come back to him.

'You won't never tell about it? About Sister and me?'

'There's not much to tell, is there?'

'It's only us two.'

'I said there's not much to – '

'There *could* be though – I think.'

'Listen!' he said.

Beside him she tensed. They stood together holding their hands loosely, her knitted glove ribby against his palm. The squadrons were returning. The clean air was starting to pulsate as they made their way to the water rushing over the weir.

9

They hurried back over the girdered footbridge and the glassy combs of water foaming over the sluices. Though they didn't say it at the time they each felt that they had to get to the safety of the hospital before the bombers finished their passage overhead.

Past the grilles of the sewage railings and the moon-grey

road pooled with the shadows of sycamores they hurried; and, hand in hand, in at the main gate, along the gravelled paths and past the circular ponds with their freizes of motionless cement birds.

'Would you like to come to my room for a bit? he asked. 'Or shall we sit in the duty room with Wantage? I'm on call in ten minutes or so.'

'I'd rather come to your room – if the nurses don't come by there.'

'They don't unless I ask them.'

'It's been nice! Have you got chairs and a table?'

He laughed. 'Only a bed and a box.'

'I was thinking we could play Old Maid or something.'

'We could sit on the bed, I suppose, and turn on the radio. There'll be dance music somewhere. We might get Hilversum or Paris – even Lili Marlene from Hamburg.'

They hesitated at a cross walk, looking at the lightless bulk of the scattered wards, the sprawl of the fever block, the taller shapes of the houses round the compound and their chimneys butting up under the moon. The bombers were nearly gone now, the air still; a few searchlight patches fluttered over the under-surface of the clouds.

'Sometimes there doesn't seem to be no time for anything – nothing.' Minna said. 'If there was, I'd ask you into our place; if Mum wasn't having a sitting.'

'A sitting?'

'A séance. If you listen you can hear our piano music coming through the trees; that's Mrs Webb, the baker's wife who got Mum into it all; she always starts with that soppy tune.'

'Stardust?'

'Yes, *Stardust*. I used to like that one too!'

'I suppose it's since your father was killed?'

'Mum wasn't bothered about religion – till after Tobruk. She got us christened and all; and if Elsie got married out of the ATS there could be a church wedding. Oh dear! I do wish they'd stop that piano playing. I don't even like to walk in home when there's a sitting.'

'Do they try to get in touch with him? With your father?'

'They try to reach lots of people. That Mrs Webb's the

worst; she knows more folk that have "passed on" than there is in Hullshold. And *they* all bring their friends.'

'To the sitting?'

'Yes, the spirits bring their friends, then they bring all *their* friends, so that even Mrs Webb gets muddled. It's worse than silly: it's *bad* for us.'

'You can stay in my room, if you like. You could read some women's magazines and listen to the radio.'

'Where did you get them?'

'The magazines? From the nurses.'

'Which one?'

'*Woman's Own*, or *Woman*; I'm not sure.'

'I meant which nurse.' She was sulky.

'Nurse Lynton.'

'Oh *her!*'

'Don't you like her?'

'She's fast. She's got a bad nature.'

'Minna!'

'All right, laugh! But I *know*. She's got angry cheeks, she has.'

He squeezed her gloved hand but she did not respond.

'*You*'re cross now,' he told her.

'Cross I may be, but cold I am. Take us into your room if you're sure as nobody's going to come.'

'I'm sure.'

They walked down the shiny linoleum under the regulation single bulb that switched itself off just before they reached the entrance. He fumbled for the handle and pushed open the door.

'Wait there while I find the light switch.'

'I don't want to be caught in the corridor.'

'Wait, Minna! There are cables and things on the floor.'

'I'm *in*.'

'Oh, all right.'

'What are all these machines?'

'One's a disused X-ray unit, and then there's the stuff they used for physiotherapy; UVL and infra-red lamps.'

'I don't like them. They look like robots – as if they was watching.'

'They can't be. They're all facing the walls.'

'That's worse – they could turn round in the dark. Give us a hug, will you?'

'I will, when you lie down.'

'Wait till I take my shoes off.'

'There! Is that better?'

'It's lovely. It's like being back in your first home again.'

Her powdered face was on his right shoulder. Her thin legs drawn up round his trousered thighs, and the light from the green limpet shade beaming down on them on the narrow bed.

'You could tell us more of that story about when you was a boy.'

'There's hardly time.'

'There isn't – because someone will be calling for you now.' She leaned across him. 'Where's your telephone?'

'Oh, it's on that box thing.'

'You don't *want* to tell us, is what. You want to hold all to yourself about that girl as got done.'

'Minna, I'm very tired.'

'Course you are with all that hugging of her – of your dead Victoria.'

He pushed her away from him: 'I won't have you speaking of her like that.'

'It's just silly, Doctor John. But don't get vexed with us when we've been so friends!'

'Friends?'

'I don't know. Where did you say your phone was?'

'On the box. There, beside the alarm clock.'

She sat up as if to make sure of it, and then lay down again, wriggling her behind to draw herself closer.

'Who do you like the best?'

'Here, do you mean?'

'Who?' she repeated. 'Not in your whole life, not in that bad time; but since you come to Guinea Lane.'

'You.'

She was silent; but in a moment she wriggled again as if to retain the closeness she had gained and then lost. He thought he heard her sigh in happiness.

'I'm getting sleepy,' she whispered. 'It's heaven quiet

66

when they've gone, isn't it? All them bombers?' She yawned. 'You're on call *now*, aren't you?'

'I damn well am.'

'When they start ringing for you, I could stay here in your bed a bit?' Till Ruby Webb takes herself off from our place?'

'You could get right in if you liked.'

She sat up, 'There goes your bell. It's Sister, isn't it?'

'You're hearing things. The telephone isn't ringing.'

'There it goes again!'

'It didn't *ring*, Minna.'

'I can hear it. There! I told you.'

'You were right.' He looked at her almost expressionless face and picked up the receiver.

'You are bad brought up,' she told him. 'You didn't even take your shoes off.'

'Please be quiet, Minna.' He spoke into the line. 'Yes, Sister, I'll come straight over.'

Minna yawned. 'Well, goodnight then, Doctor. It was all ever so nice of you – real pleasant.'

'Do you want the light on or off?'

'Off please, so's I can see.'

By the door he paused, 'See what? Or do you mean good night-vision like Cats Eyes Cunningham?'

'I mean things; lovely things.'

'What kind? Or are they secret?'

'Trees in summer, white geese swimming. To start with they're just pictures in my head, but after a bit in the dark they get ever so clear.'

'People too? Do you see people?'

'Yes, sometimes I see people as can't see me back; least-ways they don't never show it. So they don't seem to mind me looking, not anything.'

In his interest, he closed the door again and stepped back into the darkened room. 'Do you mean spirit people?'

' 'Course not! They're *messy*. These are whole folk that I see; ever so clear and separate.'

'You mean on their own?'

'Yes, in a way. It's as if they were all alone even when they're together. They seem like foreigners in a park.'

'How strange.'

She sounded more than drowsy; half asleep: 'There must be such a lot – so many just now with that fat Mr Churchill calling for more raids and burnings. What *is* funny is how bright they all are – ever so sure of themselves.'

He waited but she was silent and he grew impatient, wanting to leave and at the same time to stay.

'What else?'

'Just happy; like they were on holiday.' She stirred, pulling a pillow closer and getting settled. 'Sister Thorpe doesn't never say much about such things. So I best go to sleep now.'

'Goodnight, Minna.'

Hardly visible in the bed, only her soft hair showing above the turn-down, she didn't answer.

He switched off the light and closed the door. From the darkness of the corridor he found his·way out into the compound.

10

Sister Thorpe! Sister Thorpe! he said as he walked across the tree scattered compound. What a marvellous evening it has been; as though we had shared a storm together. The rain of bombers has come and gone, the river is still, swift; like Minna's night friends it is living. It is moving without haste, unmindful.

Oh what *did* she mean? I must get to it. There *is* a peace in people seen from a little way off; and this could be why we like to 'catch' them, to spy upon them as we do upon wild animals, wishing to reassure ourselves by seeing them at ease with themselves – making small movements of affection and contentment.

Certainly, families just arrived at some place they have

68

travelled far to reach and long desired to be, 'on holiday' even, have more than cosiness; they have some perfection about them, a reach of completion extending into them. I am sure that is what Minna sees, and now, because of the raids, the perpetual rumble of war, because of the sly invisible bombers, those clouds of iron in the sky, she is allowed to see that other possibility. God *makes* her see it. And who knows why it should be Minna? Or, for that matter, why I should have come across her in this temporary place.

O Sister Thorpe! he repeated; Minna keeps talking about you. She started to mention you when she knew that the telephone was going to ring in my room. And of course you won't be on duty tonight because you were in Gynae all day; and you couldn't be called because as far as I know, nobody is sure where you live.

He stopped then outside the Thyroid bay. He dreaded the time, the minutes he would have to spend in there. So few tenanted beds, since Miss Graemes and Mrs Strykes always reserved four of them for any research cases they might wish to admit at short notice. And now, with the four old ladies screened off at the far end from the five or six pre- and post-operatives in the middle section, the ward had the desultory, attentive air of a base in a cold war.

The thyroid patients tried to be tolerant of the old women behind the screens, but their own condition, their medication, the iodine that had to be so carefully balanced if they were to achieve the needed stability before the gland was subtotally resected, made them more irritable, even, than normal; more frightened, more impatient patients. And as for the women beyond the green screen curtain, they seemed to care for nobody but themselves, were as unhappily self-contained as little children without little children's continual movements of love, their lapses into unselfishness, their generosity.

He went round Doctor Graemes' Thyroids and Miss Bason quickly with Sister 'Balloon'. She had been Wantage's tea-time date for that afternoon and he didn't know her name; but she was smooth and round and he remembered that Jerry had told him her husband was with the barrage balloons on the coast. She was not very attractive and certainly not very young or faithful. He felt quite like a maiden aunt about her – 'No better than she should be!' – 'Old enough to know better', 'Doing night duty and being immoral with the young doctors is *not* helping the war effort' – 'I don't know what our working women are coming to.'

But she was comforting, and in the crocus light of the ward, full of night's hollow shadows and mysterious shapes, the nervous patients warmed to her. Maureen Bason, with her atrophied vagina and absent uterus was pathetic, asking her if she might sometimes call her 'mother'.

'You see, Mum died in the raids; when the Luftwaffe was strafing the East End. So, if you don't mind, Sister? I wouldn't do it in front of Staff or the surgeons.'

'That's all right, Maureen, though I'm only temporary here.'

'Well, I'll say goodnight, Mother. Oh, Doctor Blaydon, I hope I didn't let you in it with Doctor Graemes?'

'You *did*.'

'I know I did! I'll be more careful another time.'

'You're not to think about it.'

'Goodnight, Mother.'

'Goodnight, Maureen.'

They moved behind the screens into the different world of the grannies, all four of them propped high in their cots; two of them with little faces, shrunken and made to look more meagre by their mob caps. The other two, 'past' plump, their fallen cheeks drooping over their lower jaws, giving them grey-white wattles on each side of their chins.

Their four pairs of eyes were simian-bright in the shadows beneath their brows and their voices and coughs shrill as children's. He felt he should be studying their eyes clinically, looking for the least trace of exophthalmos, of whiteness below the cornea; even that he should be running his fingers over the reedy necks to find the hardened or swollen thyroids, so to surprise and gratify Doctor Graemes, to win her approval.

As he nodded to each of them from the ends of their beds he realised with recurrent astonishment that if at any suitable time he wished to discover more about old age, to examine these octogenarians from head to toe, he was allowed to do so. On any free, dull afternoon he could order up more screens, ask a probationer or nurse to prepare a trolley and really study these private, remote bodies and write down anything interesting he might discover.

But he was bored by them. What could there be of interest in such attenuation? The glossy structures of youth, the fecund glands that had informed their passions had dried up like grapes in winter. Beneath the thinning muscles the red bones thinned too, snapping like spillikins at the slightest mishap.

And as for the psychology of their years; what was there to know? Rich or poor, man or woman, white or black, old age struck the world like ice, reducing all to stasis, to immobility. Only below the frozen surface, he believed, in the deeps of memory, moved a few pale impulses amid the darkness of overwhelming resentment.

And in any event, he suspected, even in their prime, even as girls, these urban women would have bored him more than peasants. For they had been given only enough education to muffle their minds, to make them think in clichés, to unload words and phrases that had got stuck in their heads from newspapers and magazines.

But for a very few of their absent descendants; but for the younger nurses, a Sister or so, and one or two of the old guard Consultants, kindly and concerned, no one wanted them. The hospital, for all he knew, the whole world, accepted them as a great port accepts the hulks of ocean-going ships, allowing them berths in forgotten corners where the tides seldom reached.

And tonight, after his evening with Minna, his discovery of her, he found the four old ladies more tiresome than ever. For after dozing for most of the evening they were snapping with ill temper. After yet another day of idleness, of isolation and reasonable food and kindness they were really angry.

In the daytime, on morning or afternoon rounds, he had heard them talking to themselves or to one another. And always they talked of the past, of the time which had accumulated round them in an uncountable number of

71

'whens'; each of them, each failing storehouse of the unique sheaves which made up her life, interested only in that one personal harvest.

To her companions she gave, at most, ear service; a pretence of listening, an initial clacking of the tongue in sympathy or surprise, 'Tk, tk! Well I never!' But soon, he had noticed, as the grievance was elaborated, the listeners would glance at each other with the kind of understanding with which schoolchildren catch one another's eyes in Summers' class rooms.

And each tale teller, old and wily, long trained in the nuances of gossip and complaint, knowing with what impatience her yarn was greeted, soon fell silent; her shrunken cheeks, covering the empty gums, mumbling the end over to herself whilst another hurt, an additional pebble of disappointment, was added to the weight of all her prior sorrows.

After a few 'rounds', a few visits to 'Grannies' End,' as he now thought of it, the dullness of the ward was almost tangible. More than the musty human smell which no amount of pine-tree polish or aniline disinfectant could wholly contain, the loss triumphed.

For that was what the four old women in their black-railed cots seemed most to embody; loss! As if, over their combined near three centuries of living, their dreams of satisfaction, the substance of their expectation in every stage of life, had been whittled away until now, thin as desert bones, as eloquent, they awaited only the darkness; raging to find themselves cheated not of the desires in which they had once rejoiced, but of even the lack of them. For, deprived of the rituals, the sacraments of their simpler forbears, they were a disfranchised generation.

From under their mob caps or rubbed scalps, the hair thinned to finest floss above the pink skin, they glanced complicitly at one another and then openly as children at Sister Balloon and himself.

What was going to be done to them now? they seemed to ask; of what more were they to be deprived? Of their bedpans, their pills, their threadbare sleep? Their jealous companionship, their trickles of vitality, even of the life to which they still clung?

'Where's our biscuits?' Granny Mullens asked.

'And choc'late,' added Mrs Pobgee.

'Yiss!' chorused the other two. 'Where's our cocoa?'

'Now you know you had your bed-time snacks two hours ago.'

'We never, Sister.'

'Nurse Braybrooke served you herself, Mrs Pobgee.'

'She never!'

'You wouldn't eat your biscuits because you didn't like Rich Tea. Remember?'

'I fancy Rich Tea. They're me favourites, they are. It's Digestive *I* don't like, isn't it, Mrs Mullens?'

But Mrs Mullens raised a trembling finger and pointed it at the green screens.

'*We* know what's going on. They're gettin' them that side.' She drew in her breath, leaning forward towards the barrier, and screamed, '*We* know yer! We know yer spoiled baggages over there. You're 'avin' our biscuits and cup on the sly.'

'Surgeon's pets!' added Mrs Pobgee.

'Thy-er-oids!'

' 'Umbugs!'

The accusations winged from the cots; high pitched and threaded with coughs and phlegm.

'Lady doctors' cases!'

'Too good for Gee Pees!'

'Foreigners' glands!'

John tried to intervene: 'I've told you all before,' he said, 'that the screens are there only to give you your privacy. Nobody's doing any better on the other side of them.'

Only Granny Mullens looked at him.

'Who are *you* then? We doesn't know him, do we?'

'No, *that* we don't.'

'Nor don't want to, neither.'

'*We* know Doctor Bruce.'

'You'll really have to stop shouting, Mrs Spark. You're upsetting the other patients.'

'Shoutin'! I'll shout as much as – '

Ancient, three times married, three times widowed, Mrs

73

Spark collapsed onto the hammock of her drawn-up knees, her now phlegmless cough whistling up her tubes.

'I could give her assafoetida,' Sister Balloon whispered, 'Or a rectal?'

'Won't it make the ward stink a bit?'

'They're used to that and it's only for a few minutes.'

'She doesn't mind a rectal?'

'She rather likes it; they all do. It makes them feel mothered again, cared for.'

'Well, give it then. What had we better do with the others, Sister?'

'If you quieten *one*, Doctor, the others seem to settle down.'

'Fine.' He considered. 'I can write you out a little more sedative in case you need it?'

'That would be a help. *You* want your night's sleep, don't you, Doctor?'

'Yes, like Wantage, I'm fond of my bed.'

They smiled at one another in the darkness. Outside, very far away they heard the sirens start up.

11

John made his way between the screens, up the ward and out into the star-dark compound again.

At the end of the corridor leading to the Gynae Unit he paused in the foyer to look through one of the circular glass panels in the double doors.

There had been no one in Sister Thorpe's office, just the green shaded high-candle-power bulb burning in her desk light, the admissions book open on the blotter beneath it. And now, as far as he could see, there was no one in the ward either down at the far end or seated by the night table inside the doors near Sister's aquarium.

Reluctant to enter the sleeping ward until he had someone with him, he peered to left and right along the length of each side wall hoping to discover someone attending to one of the patients: standing beside the head of one of the beds, reassuring or taking a pulse.

He pushed open the door and stepped from the silence of the corridor into the quietness of the long chamber and its sleeping women. The end bed on the far right, he now noticed, was completely screened from the remainder of the room. Above it, the hooded bedlight between the cubicle formed by the walls and curtains cast an additional darker shadow onto the low ceiling.

Whoever was on night duty must be in this enclosure and would emerge as soon as she heard him enter.

Moving on now he paused by Mrs Wilkes' bed and took her charts and notes to the aquarium table to look through them under the low light. Her temperature was still high, he saw, her pulse slightly lower than at the same time the day before, the albumen was still plus plus in her urine and it was time for another sedimentation rate and white cell count. With the date and time of his entry, he ordered them in the day book. On his way out he must remember to look through all the night reports on Sister's desk.

Still no one had come from behind the screened bed at the far end and amid the snores and dream cries of the sleepers he could distinguish no sound rising from it; no quiet voice, no cry of pain nor the clinking of the dressing trolley.

He felt obstinate, stubborn, glanced at his watch and thought that it was very slack of them to treat him like this simply because he was new to the job. It was irregular and unfeminine of these women to allow him to have to fend for himself when he carried so much more responsibility than they did. There certainly should have been someone by now, and where was his cup of tea? Once whoever was on duty appeared from behind the screen he would be cold and clipped with her. Perhaps it was some pretty but slack little probationer who had slipped off for a date with one of the night porters, unless of course she had gone to the lavatory. Could it possibly be Lynton, sweet Nurse Lynton? She was just the type to take such liberties and quite right too for anyone so generally efficient and attractive. And the thought of her 'angry cheeks' and her smooth smooth cleft behind on the lavatory seat delighting him, he got up abruptly from the desk and walked quietly past the sleepers to the final bed.

He pulled aside the wheeled screen and entered the cubicle.

The woman lying before him had massed black hair; it was spread out over the hospital pillow like a mantilla, coarse, uncombed and flecked with small pieces of some gritty substance which, where it had tumbled out onto the white of the cotton, looked black as oyster shell.

Looking down at her, standing quite still in the privacy of the cubicle, he noticed that his knees were not quite steady, that he was frightened. He thought at first that the woman was breathing normally but when he started to count the movements of the turn-down of her sheet he saw that it was moving irregularly with her chest: several highs where it approached the tip of her chin and then for some few seconds no motions at all, a pause in respiration.

Her face, sharp against her untended hair, seemed at first to have no eyes, only the plane of her upturned jaw, that of her chalky forehead and, between them, the flat of her cheekbones; all of her skin, the thin flesh overlying her facial skull was holding solid in the light – lined as it was and slightly dirty, delicate against the iron bars of the bedstead – it was yet more substantial than the pieces of stuff, oyster shell or ceiling plaster, which every now and again slipped from her hair onto her pillow. Her arms, loosely streaked with soot or soil were loosely disposed upon the laundered counterpane. They lay upturned and naked under the light, the elbows not quite symmetrical in the triangles they made with the hidden shape of her waist. On the left wrist the little black-strapped watch cut the grey skin as it rested beside the sharp bulge of her abdomen.

He knew a quick stir of greed at her beauty, so contained and so helpless.

76

As he moved up the side of the bed he turned his own eyes from her watching dark ones to the wine-deep redness of her parted lips. Instantly, with that part of himself which rarely slumbered, he longed to touch them with his hand, to lean down and brush them, kiss them lightly with his own, to see her eyelids close upon him, to hear her breathe and sigh.

The index, middle and ring fingers of his right hand pressed on the smudged wrist hollow below the first metacarpal where the radial artery filled and discharged regularly.

He saw that whilst he had been thinking about her she had closed her eyes; but now, as she felt his touch, she opened them again. Beneath her eyebrows, pencilled and recently plucked, her gaze was steady, as impersonal, as disinterested as if she had been awaiting him, had expected to see him and was neither pleased nor surprised by his visit.

She spoke clearly: *'Herr Doktor? Sind sie mein Doktor?'*

'Yes, I am your doctor.' He was remembering his German.

'You came?'

'Ja.'

How delightful, how pleasing her voice was; not shallow, even a little rough, a sound heard in the woodland, someone young and pleased; heard through many intervening leaves. Was it pleasing, seductive, because she was foreign or was it because it was the quiet voice of someone controlling her pain? Was it the tone of a just bearable suffering, or was it that of a cessation of distress? Had someone given her morphine?

'You are foreign – *Auslanderin*?' he asked. *'Sind sie Deutch?'*

'German, *ja*. From Germany I am; from *der* East, Leipzig near.'

He let go of her wrist. Her pulse was very rapid. He had not much time for anything, for diagnosis.

'What is your name? *Wie heissen sei*?'

'Maria Kleber.'

'Fraulein Kleber?'

77

'Nein! *Frau* Kleber. *Kinder* I have'. She was unsmiling, a little hostile and serious as if she forgave him for some clumsiness.

'You were admitted here by someone? *Kammen Sie heute im das Krankenhaus*?'

'*Ja, Ich – Ich*, I think. Today it was.'

'And from where, Frau Kleber? *Woher*?'

'From my willage, from Leipzig near. *Von meinen Dorf.*'

'Village? I see. And from Germany?'

He placed his hand on her forehead because he could no longer not touch her. He had curved his hand to form a shell of the fingers and the palm to fit the curves of the frontal bones so that she would not be too surprised and mistake his intention. The skin was slippery with sweat and the scalp-line full of grit.

She looked up at him with the acceptance she had shown when first he entered, and, as he stroked back her hair, her lips opened further as she moistened the upper one with the tip of her tongue, running it along the length as does a girl who has just applied lipstick. She raised her right hand a very little from the counterpane and pointed to the centre of her stomach.

'Here,' she said, '*Mein Schmertz ist hier.*'

'There?'

'*Ja, mein* hurt, *mein* pain'

'In your stomach? *Meinen Sie hier unten*?'

'Very bad. *Es tut schreklich weh!*'

He looked away from the secrecy of her face to the sheeted turn-up over her chest. Below her arms lying back again on the counterpane he began to pull the bedclothes down slowly, sliding them over her breastbone and down over the embroidered yoke of her nightdress and her small breasts. The hem of the thin stuff lay high up, crumpled on her rib cage.

Now, as he continued to draw the sheet over the pit of her stomach he was stopped. The underside of the top linen was caught and would not slide down further. Pulling a little harder, beginning himself to sweat, he glanced at her face to make sure he was not hurting her.

Her eyes, deep-set, were very dark again, looking back

at him gravely, seriously as though she thought he had asked her a most personal question, even as if he'd proposed marriage to her or said something else aloud, a prayer perhaps.

'You are all right? *Tu'ich ihnenweh?*'

'*Nein*. No hurt.'

Leaning over, keeping from touching her with any part of himself, he lifted the bedclothes with both hands, one on either side of her waist; he laid them folded beneath her feet and looked down at her body.

A narrow piece of concrete, the butt end of some builder's footing, part of a beam of mortar or a fragment of kerbstone with sea-pebbles in it, stuck out of her swollen abdomen to a height of two or three inches a little to the left of where the umbilicus had been.

A ragged line of blood edged the purpling skin of the occluded wound – the entry, and stained like a flood her black unshaven pubic hair.

He picked up the sheet again with its contained woollen blankets, and raised them over her pelvis. He held them up high and then cautiously eased them and pulled them back until they were nearly level with her shoulders when he laid them down once more.

She struggled to free her arms: '*Ich kann meine Arme nicht bewegen!*'

'You will get cold.'

'*Nein. Bitte machen sie frei.*'

He helped her to replace her arms on the counterpane and she lay still, motionless, only her eyes wandering sideways in their sockets to look over to her left where were the top rails of the green screens.

'Frau Kleber?'

'*Ja.*'

'What happened, Frau Kleber, what happened to you?'

Her eyes still not meeting his, their gaze still engaged upon that other view as though, at a dinner party, she had found his question tedious, she whispered, '*Bomben.*'

'Bombs?'

'*Ja. Die Bomben fielen uberall um mich haruin!*'

'On your home? You mean your house was bombed?'

79

'*Ja.*'

'Today? Your house was bombed today?'

'*Nein*, at night it was – *es war im das Nacht.*'

'By the British? – *Wahren es die Engländer?*'

'Ich weiss nicht!'

'The Americans – *Die Amerikaner?*' he asked.

He could smell her breath now, young and nearly sweet.

He straightened himself, stretching a little in the confined lighted space and then looked at the few case notes lying in their folder beside his feet.

For a moment he scarcely knew what more to ask her.

'Sister Thorpe? Have you seen *Schwester* Thorpe?'

She was exhausted and did not reply. Beneath her plucked eyebrows and the coarse black weave of her hair she had closed her eyes again. As he watched, her jaw slackened and she began to snore lightly.

He rolled back the near screen on its rubber wheels and walked out into the ward.

Where was the night sister? Why had Sister Thorpe's office door been opened and the light on in there as though whoever had occupied it had intended to be absent only for minutes? Why were there no proper case notes on the night table? Where was the young nurse with the teapot? Where was anybody?

He turned to glance back at the screened bed to make sure that it was still there, that anxiety and overwork had not deluded him. He saw that he had forgotten to close the gap, that he had left the screen open enough to alarm any wakeful patient. Even from where he stood he could see the girl's grey arm, the counterpane mounded by the little brick of mortar beneath it.

He walked back into the space again, the yellow oval of the bedhead light, the green screened rectangle with the iron bars of the bed behind her pillows, the smells of her blood and breath, the excreta between her thighs.

Her eyes were wide upon his own, her lips parted upon her teeth, the lower one gashed raspberry dark where she had bitten it.

He leaned over to hear what she might be whispering. He felt the stir of her breath in his face; it was no longer sweet, and, against his ear he could hear the silly crackle of the phlegm she was too weak to clear. She is dying, he knew, and there is no one else here. No one on duty for her death: and she is dying.

'*Ja?*' he asked. 'Yes, Frau Kleber? What do you want? *Was kann Ich fur Sie tun?*'

'Priest. *Ich mochte einen Pfarrer!*'

'There isn't a priest. A priest we do not have.'

She slurred the word again.

'We have some other doctors,' he told her. 'We have nurses, *Krankenschwestern.*'

She muttered something between her open lips. Her tongue was dry, the fissures between the small papillae of its tip and mid-section had opened up like cracks in summer's mud. She needed more than water; she needed a little glycerine to keep it moist.

'Send for priest!' she said, her voice as peremptory as a child's. 'A pastor for me! *Rufen Sie mir bitte einen Pfarrer!*'

She stopped breathing and suddenly she exhaled and inhaled again on a deep sigh. He took her pulse. It was thready, too sudden and too feeble. It flickered and ceased for a time, for very long or short moments, then it stopped. She exhaled again through her accumulated bronchial phlegm five or six times, the air and the mucus in her lungs only as loud as rustled tissue paper. Her lower jaw sagged and fell. She was still.

Her pulse ceased. Her chest sounds were gone and her darkening eyes were half-open beneath her forehead, her gaze still upon that other view over the tight fabric of the screen.

He believed, he even felt in his muscles, in the sudden weight of himself, in the realised substance of his body, that he ought to kneel for a moment before the parting of her spirit while it was still there present in her swiftly falling flesh; in the membership that was slowly falling away from her as she, unable yet to part with its warmth and familiarity, waited and clung.

He would have kneeled, he persuaded himself, he would have prayed had he been able to keep on seeing her in this fashion. Had he and she continued to stay close together as they had been in those first moments when she had looked at him with such trust and certainty.

But the time in there, in that green space, was more delicate than outside; more unstable. Already all was changing.

Under the contained light, her thin hands supine, their fingers curled half open, the skin of her wrist divided by the black strap of her wrist watch, her wide mouth and drying lips, her viewless eyes, were all hardening to dullness and he found he too was shifting in mood; that the instinct of making a prayer, the impulse to kneel, had gone, that in his own centre a cool hardening had occurred, an ordinariness that freed him from such notions and drew him back into the normal world he so much needed.

He straightened the turn-down of the sheet and folded the tops of the blankets to a pad beneath her chin: he pushed her lower jaw shut so that it should set like that; but could not bring himself to secure it better.

He would have closed her eyes too, if he had not been so angry, so furious that there had been no nurse on duty to attend her; to help him. Nobody to clean her, to grant and fulfil her last need; to be company for him.

Before he switched off the light above the two pillows, the mass of her dark hair, he paused – stayed as by a charm – to look at her once more.

He had to discover again, if he could, that sign he had sometimes seen in the dying; to pick out once more some one particular, small but speaking detail which, though he must already have seen it as she died, was now eluding him.

Standing back against the screens he saw only all that he already had seen, and was about to step forward to put out the bedlight when he noticed again the two open palms of her hands on the rough white counterpane. With each hand's fingers inspread, close together as the ribs of a scallop shell, cupped over emptiness; with their tips only half closed upon their palms, they were the hands of a person who has given something, offered it and then stepped back a little in time.

She had come forward as does a child at a presentation, some small girl chosen to give flowers to royalty; she had held out her hands with the bouquet between them, had curtsied and then withdrawn; disappeared back into the crowd from which for that moment she had emerged.

Seeing her like this, as a party child, half shy, half boastful, in the very best of all her clothes and manners, he could no longer hold back his tears but kneeled beside her hidden body as though it had been Victoria's, praying that leaving him, she might live.

Then he got up and, stooping over her, lifted her hands one at a time to his mouth, touching each palm with his lips before going angrily in search of someone who might explain her coming.

12

As, for the third time, he made his way past the sleeping patients on either side of the ward, cold now with the early winter's night, he was sure he would find someone in Sister Thorpe's office.

Looking this time at none of the tired women in their narrow beds, he stopped by the aquarium. The small black fish, hung with trailing fins and pebble-sweeping tails, were motionless in their lighted rectangle; behind their primitive eyes, incurious, asleep. Only the fragile water snails moved, feeding and gliding on their grey feet past the tendrils of the water-ferns leaving behind them clear paths in the powder of algae lining the inside of the glass.

From one of the ward's beds a sigh reached him, from another, a single snore, a muffled cry; some brief inaudible complaint, the voice blurred and genderless. Further away, a mattress sank into a weaker place on its springs as the sleeper moved to a new posture, then flung out an arm and knocked over her night water.

He heard the flood of it loud in the dimness, the rapid dripping to the pool below; its slowing as he ran from the ward in a fury of anxiety.

The foyer was empty. One of the doors giving onto the compound was moving on its springs in the rising wind; blowing in a little, hesitating, swinging on its arc further in, waiting beneath the yellow light, its shadow uncertain on the outside step; then, latchless, swinging shut again; trembling against its fellow, edge to edge.

He went into Sister's office and sat down on her hard chair. He was about to pick up her telephone to ring the staff room, to get Wantage if he could, or even Dr Whooper, when he noticed a green-bound open book on the centre of the green blotter:

'The weather is bitterly cold,' he read, *'and extremely disagreeable. There is no pleasure in walking or riding and to sit all day over the fire is not particularly agreeable. Sickness is increasing, chiefly coughs and colds and scurvy. We are sending 4 men home with consumption. Thank God we have no cholera . . .*

There were about 700 Frenchmen lying in one heap on the other side of the Mamelon . . . Large lime-covered mounds in the ravine leading to the trenches tell a melancholy tale. We set fire to some large building with our shells in . . .

Three of the 77th have just been carried past my tent, dead; one most frightfully disfigured by a splinter from a shell which entered his forehead and forced both of his eyes out of their sockets . . .'

He was unaware that someone had entered the room and when she spoke, he jumped.

'Must you do that?' he complained. 'A patient, a woman, has just died in the end bed. Not a soul on duty – '

He had been looking at her in the way he had of contemplating himself only, his own feelings. His eyes, peripherally sightless, were wandering over the middle of her body: the grey starched shirt front, its pleats, the empty ribbon where the silver-cheeked medallion had hung.

'Why wasn't I called? And why was no one else on duty?'

'You *were* called: Staff Nurse Edgar developed a high

84

fever. She has influenza and I had to send her home. Her replacement has not yet arrived.'

'It's all very slack. When was I called?'

'I called you half an hour ago, Doctor. Minna told me you had just left your room. I waited and called Doctor Graemes.'

He looked up to her face and saw she might be nearly smiling at him. He stood up to enforce his anger, to retain it as he did the fear which underlay it.

'Miss Graemes? What did you say to her? What are we to do? Why didn't she come straight away? Or *is* she coming?'

'Doctor Graemes felt the injuries were outside our capabilities. She told me to transfer Frau Maria for surgery to the Buffs in Canterbury.'

'Frau Maria?' he repeated. 'Why do you call her that?

'It is her name.'

'Sister, what is going on? Why are you on duty tonight?'

'Staff Nurse Edgar requested my presence.' She smiled at him a little wanly, 'Please know that we are both tired, Doctor Blaydon.'

'I do. I am nervous, Sister. I was too anxious to – I wished to – ' He did not complete it.

'To pray? Well, of course. But do please sit down. I am sorry that these chairs are not more comfortable. There, let me pour you some hot tea. See, it really is hot; Nurse Travis has only just made it – whilst I was talking to Doctor Graemes on the outside line.'

'Doctor Graemes? What did she mean about transferring Frau Kleber to the Buffs Depot? To a Military Hospital?'

'That was *my* notion. Maria is a casualty of war. I wished her to be treated as such.' She smiled. 'Doctor Graemes was not helpful.'

'You mean she didn't want to take her on, to operate?'

'There are some who are all cry and no wool. In the field they discover themselves, their inexperience.'

'But this *is* an emergency hospital.'

'It is an auxiliary hospital only. During *their* raids, the enemy raids on London – ' she was silent for a moment, 'we were quite unable to manage. This is really only a field hospital.'

85

'A field hospital?' He looked at the open journal he had been reading, at the faded print, the neat paragraphs of the cuttings, and touched the given page. 'Is that why you kept this, Sister? What war was that?'

'They're so easily forgotten, aren't they? The Crimea perhaps, or the Franco-Prussian – ' She closed the book and moved it away from the night register.

'Sister, I don't understand your role in all this.'

'I do not think you need to.'

'I meant this military thing of yours.'

'You should not allow your inexperience to make you rude.'

'I'm sorry. But do you imagine you are in the QA's?'

'I imagine nothing.'

He hurried on: 'That this is some other war?'

'There *is* no other war, Doctor. But that is by the by.' She pulled the night register to her and put on a small pair of glasses as she looked at her notes. 'There will have to be a post mortem of course. I have spoken to the city pathologist – and he tells me it will not come to an inquest.'

'An inquest?'

'Please don't get up, Doctor. Nothing has been neglected. I even have tea for you.'

She turned a page, the sleeves of her uniform lavender in contrast to the starched cuffs which were greyish too, even her thin ringless hand, paper-grey. Her face above his shoulder was grave; yet still he felt that in some way, although he troubled her, she was very slightly satisfied, even pleased by him; and because of this he felt his questions dry within him as if they had been inexcusable.

'Could you tell me if they are going to take her to the mortuary tonight, Sister?'

'Yes they are. It is all arranged.'

'But how did she get here? Did *you* admit her?'

'Indirectly, I did.'

'Before she died she told me she came from Germany, from North Germany. A "willage" she said; she even named it though she spoke hardly any English – or at least she said it was near Leipzig.'

'That is quite possible.'

86

'How do you mean?'

'Sometimes our damaged machines, before descending, do accidentally unload a bomb over the English countryside – and there are still many married foreigners living here.'

'But she had only just come from Germany, Sister! In her mind she seemed sure that her home had been bombed in *tonight's* raid.'

'That *was* so for many homes, wasn't it?' Again she paused as though searching for something that would allay his anxiety. 'And *in the mind*, Doctor, so much can happen. For Maria Kleber it would be of no importance whether she and her children were destroyed in England or in her childhood home village in Germany.'

'That's true.' He got up. 'Yes, that's true.' He took his breath. 'She'll be gone in the morning?'

He found he was facing the Sister, that her face, normally quite small, was considerable now with its closeness to his own. He could see every detail of it; the short nasal bones where the overlying skin was lilac thin, where that which lay beneath the lower eyelids was infolded over the edge of the bony sockets before swelling out to cover the lowest section of their globes; where the brows were suggested only as ghostly curves shadowing the eyes; where the whole visage, as if made of a mosaic of tissues was yet held together in the air by some powerful inner force.

'Before you awake, all will have been seen to,' she assured him now. 'And *you* should be finding your bed again.'

'Sister, you aren't normally on night duty too, are you?'

She had sat down and was making an entry in the book. She appeared to be quite small again; her cotton cap grey and crisp on her hair.

'Normally, no.' Her varnished wooden pen, a dipper he noticed, dipped into the ink well and the steel nib moved over the paper. 'Sometimes I'm needed here, out of hours.'

They had brushed one another enough: he had come up against iron, the metal of old age, of acceptance. Anything more he asked would be turned by it, changed into rudeness. He realised that sanctions were not a matter of prerogative, of youth or of years, but only of virtue. Ill-manners were their own habit, their own absurdity.

'Oh well, goodnight, Sister, and thank you for all you've done.' At the door he stopped. 'How, I mean what, did you mean about the prayer? – if you don't mind my asking.'

'I was pleased that you should have thought of it for her. In the army, in the military, you know, after a grievous battle, you will find that the dying of all faiths often do that for themselves if they are able. It can make one feel most inadequate – ashamed, if one cannot, at least, join in.'

'Terrible,' he admitted, remembering. 'Well, goodnight again, Sister.'

He was still reluctant to leave. He had been dismissed unsatisfied, not altogether approved of. Her way, her manner, reminded him of his childhood when he had wanted to take assurance to bed with him and had been denied it. What had he done wrong tonight? In what had he failed?

He said, 'I'll just glance in at the ward, if you like – as I pass?'

He thought she was going to ignore him; but suddenly he looked up and met her gaze, the affectionate smile she gave him.

He closed her door nearly to the jamb and then pushed open one of the doors into the ward and stepped in there to stand once again by the aquarium.

It was not quiet in there; occasional water still dripped from the bed locker to the pool below; the sleepers turned restlessly again- and again upon their mattresses, their breathing loud, their coughing slumbrous and weak.

Down the length of the room on both sides was the stir of life; only at the far end, on the right behind the dark green screens, was there silence.

13

In the morning, the early Saturday set aside for a single list surgical procedure by Doctors Miss Graemes and Mrs Strykes, he was so preoccupied that he had but marginal time in which to think about the previous evening.

Though theatre work excited him, the drama of it, the brittle order it held against so many delicate risks, he longed to have those particular hours to himself; to go over once again all of the previous evening and the early part of the night. To visit Minna with such pleasures still in his mind, and to get her away from her desk with its old jar of willow buds and stroll with her anywhere; even about the compound; or sit somewhere over evaporated milk and tea, recalling the walk beside the marble of the river, the bombers thudding overhead; and, more than all, the talk with Sister Thorpe; and, if he could tell of it so soon, the strangeness of Frau Kleber's death.

But here in the theatre he was able, at least in part, to put back his wishes, to concentrate with curiosity and some amazement on the surgery at which he was assisting. For although he saw everything that was done, heard every syllable spoken, the heat of the small high-ceilinged room, its whiteness, its lights and gasses, the low syllables of the masked team gave it all an underwater remove so that from the yellow swabbing of the backbone to the insertion and withdrawal of the big needles, the resection of the ileum and its suturing to the epithelium of the vulva, he could never afterwards be quite sure that all had fallen out as it appeared.

'There's no need, Maureen,' Ella Strykes told their

patient, 'for us to dally in prep, ducks. If you'll just be brave we can get straight down to cases here on the table.'

As she moved about her business with syringes and needles, the anaesthetist, in her flat cap with her eye glasses jutting over her masked nose, looked like a chef basting a small heifer.

'Now if you'll just pull your pretty knees up to yer navel we'll be able to get at those posterior roots without your feeling more than a little push at your spine.'

Maureen Bason, her shoulder and buttocks covered by her unlaced gown, had been quiet; but now, as she lay on her side with her head bent down towards her knees, she asked,

'Will it hurt, Doctor?'

'No, Maureen. The block is to stop it hurting. There! Another little prick! And now you didn't even feel that, did you?'

'I think I'm a bit cold.'

'Don't worry! We'll have you on yer back in a jiffy, once we've done the other side of your spine.' Mrs Strykes looked up. 'Doctor Blaydon, she's not flexing her femurs too fair. We want full separation of the vertebrae if we're to get between the transverse processes to her nerve roots . . .'

'Yes, Doctor.'

He held the knees as firmly as he could and thought of Minna:

When he'd returned to it his bed had been empty. No note, not a single fine hair on the pillow. He had hoped for that; but it seemed as if she had hardly touched the sheets; for, as he got in between them, there was only the faintest breath of girlhood, of the schoolroom, the ghost of a class-room desk with a pencil-box under the lid, of india-rubber and powdered ink.

'Do you have to do all down the other side, now Doctor Strykes?'

'Well, what do you think, Maureen? *You* wouldn't leave a job half-done now, would yer? Sister! I think a hottie would be advisable. You cold, Maureen?'

'I'm more scared really. That's why my teeth are chattering. Have you got to do many more pricks, Doctor Strykes?'

'Seven up and three to go, and then you'll be floating like a dingo in the Warra.'

'Yes, Doctor.' There was silence except for people breathing. 'Do you put me to sleep, then?'

'Sleep! We send you to heaven, don't we Doctor Graemes?'

'I think we should make a start as soon as it is convenient, Strykes! Bason, can you feel that?'

'No, Doctor.'

'*That*? on your left thigh?'

'No, Doctor. Are you pushing with something?'

'You've caught them all, Ella.'

'Too right! Now, Maureen, just roll over onto your back and we'll waft you away to the Land of Nod.'

'And when I wake up will it all be over? Will I be – ?'

'You'll be like all the other girls, Maureen.'

Wantage said, 'It was frowsty.'

'What was?'

'Tea with Sister Millie.'

'Who's she?'

'The one you call "Balloon".'

'What was frowsty about it?'

'Everything. It was disgusting. She was wearing a black sateen dress, shiny. Her buttocks shone like a show sow's. She had a taffeta rose in her cleavage, a vast pink one. It looked like a –'

'Did you have tea?'

'Rock cakes and Yorkshire parkin in front of his photograph – her husband's.'

'A recent one?'

'Yes, in battle dress. He's a sergeant.'

'Where was it taken? Down at Southampton?'

'By the docks, in front of a bloody great half-inflated barrage balloon.'

'You mean with drooping tail fins?'

'God! I don't know how I – '

'Nurse Lynton,' John mentioned. 'She's sweet! Fresh as melons.'

'Oh hell! Millie was wearing old scent – I don't mean "old" old scent; just the stuff the landladies in seaside hotels wear.' Wantage looked up from the bentwood chair, 'You're "off", as from midday. Aren't you going anywhere?'

'Yes, I'm taking someone to the Coast – to Downchurch, if we can get transport of some kind – for the night.'

'Who? Heather Lynton?'

'No, Miss Frobisher.'

'You mean the kid secretary.'

'Yes, Minna.'

'Is *that* her name! I hope you have fun. How was the Bason job this morning?'

'It went well; but that New Guinea block is pretty frightful, isn't it?'

'Barbaric! What did Graemes use for the vagina?'

'A piece of the ileum; about nine inches complete with the lesser omentum so that it would have its own blood supply.'

'Christ! A piece of intestine! Is Maureen going to tell her fiancé?'

'She can't. She doesn't know; and the Dragon's sitting on her case notes.'

'Did Graemes leave it attached above the sacrum, then?'

'Yes, she tied it off at the top quite neatly. I suppose the levators will hold it more or less vertical.'

'Her husband won't know the difference?'

'I doubt we would,' John said. 'Oh, by the way, when you did my Gynae round for me, was there anyone in the end bed?'

'I don't think so.'

'A German,' John prompted. 'A young German woman?'

'You mean German-speaking? Of course not; they're all detained under 18B – in the Isle of Man or somewhere with that club-footed traitor, that brownshirt bastard.'

Wantage closed his pugnacious jaw tightly and hummed the *Internationale* in a high nasal tenor. 'A German woman? When did you see her? Last night?'

92

'About eleven thirty. She'd just been admitted. She died.'

'You mean she was BID?'

'Not exactly Brought in Dead. She was alive all right until she did die.'

'Who was "on"? Sister Thorpe?'

'Yes.'

'Oh well! That explains it. You must have got tight at the Chatsworth and hallucinated while the Ancient Mariner was pattering on about her past.'

'I suppose so.'

'Don't mention it to Gelda Whooper. She'll think we're even dottier than she does already. You *were* a bit pissed, weren't you?'

'I was half asleep too.'

'Oh well.' Wantage closed his eyes. 'I'm in for a busy night. Give me a call when you get back tomorrow.'

14

In the village of Downchurch the chestnut trees lining the streets were dwarfed; the sea winds, the brine, the flying sands of many winters had scored their trunks and the lumpy cropped limbs which had never been allowed to meet overhead. The houses were small-windowed and small-doored with bare privet-hedged gardens and poor grassed lawns. Wet leaves lay on the pavements and on the tarmac, flattened and dark on the doorsteps of the ancient dwellings.

Only the King Charles' Head had any paint left on its windows and door jambs. Brewer's bottle glass in the saloon windows, the glow of lunchtime through the lighted Victorian frosting of the inner door, and scurries of cardboard, Smith's Crisp packets, Mars and Hershey bar wrappers and paper handkerchiefs on the pavements outside;

signs of the American service men and a few of their girls inside: in their smoother uniforms with their smoother looks, their yellowish unmarked faces under the crew cuts. Tough, heavy-jawed visages frowning with incipient anger, or country boys, innocent, who looked as though they were about to cry out of their round cheeks. The American women were alien too; very made-up with scarlet painted-on lips; their dollish hair under their caps shiny with shampoo and setting lotion, their voices high-pitched and a little frightened.

John and Minna sat huddled in a window-seat and ate the publican's wife's Cornish pasties, flaps of pastry with lumps of boiled potato inside and a leaf or two of onion threaded with brown strings of rationed beef. They drank their drinks – a pint of bitter and a Babycham – with the packeted potato crisps, and spiced the pasties with mustard and bottled sauces: AI, Houses of Parliament, and OK.

It was very noisy all about them; noisy and cheerless. The square blackish tiles on the floor had not been washed for weeks; the service boots of the men, the American variety: over-military, wide tongued, high laced; the British simple and ugly, moved upon a layer of matt polish or grease and cigarette butts, ash and sand tramped in from the dunes. The British, in their coarser, hairy battle-dress stood, rough cheeked and square at one end of the varnished bar beside the leaded grate of the fireplace. They were quiet, watching the WAAFs and ATs getting off with the Americans, girls waxing noisy with their drinks and in their rivalry with their 'sisters' from over the sea.

Everyone, since it was the custom, glued coins onto the nicotined plaster between the black horse-brassed beams. Some of the girls were helped onto bar stools to stick their dimes and ha'pence up there; others were lifted up bodily by the heavy breathing foreigners with the crew cuts.

As closing time approached the company talked louder and drank faster. The Americans grew communicative and boastful, the British more overtly hostile and sullen, holding themselves back from picking quarrels before evening so that they should not be gated on their return to their camps.

Then the landlord shouted, 'Time, gentlemen, please!'

His metallic-haired wife rang the bell and switched off the lights and the company, in groups or in pairs, streeled out onto the pavements, to the waiting trucks and the jeeps.

John and Minna made their way along the sand-edged road to the higher dunes and their chalets where the coast curved out into the leaden sea which divided England from the Continent and the enemy. They crossed through the lower banks, pockmarked with rain and starred with reeds. The wind from Europe blew their tears onto their cheeks and folded and unfolded Minna's colourless hair.

They swung their held hands as they walked and they were quiet, watching their shoes, looking at the drifts and ropes of seaweed and wartime flotsam washed to the foot of the dunes. The tide was far out over the sand and mud; they could see its edge far away past the darker area of the buckled shell-beds beyond the 'invasion' barbed wire and concrete blocks, their rusted posts leaning at all angles, growing sweet green weed on their bolts and staples.

Minna said, 'See? There's a bomber down over there!'

'Where?'

'Right over there in the mud. Its wings look like a bit of wave.'

'Is it one of ours?'

'I don't know.'

'I wish we could get to it.'

'Well you can't. You'd get caught in the wire. There's mines too.'

'I can't even see it properly.'

'You need some new glasses.'

'I know.'

'Let me wipe your eyes.'

'Thank you. Don't you use scent on your handkerchiefs, Minna?'

'I don't use scent nowhere – anywhere. Except in face powder.'

'Why not?'

'Don't like it.'

'Oh.'

'Would you *like* me to use scent?'

'Yes.'

'Well, you can like on then.'

'Why?'

'Because I don't want to look like a doll; that's why. *American*!'

'They looked good.'

'I don't want to smell like one neether. *I*'m not an actress.'

'What do you mean?'

'They aren't natural.'

'You mean the American girls?'

'None of them; boys neether. They're all acting foreign.'

'They *are* foreign.'

'I know; but there's no need to act it as well.'

'Oh *Minna*!'

'Go on then; kiss me again. Ooh, look over there!'

'What is it?'

'It's a sea boot sticking out of the sand. No! *that* way, just below the shally – that one with the brick chimney.'

He thought she would have run over to it as his sister, Melanie, would have done for a rare shell or some nearly invisible button of a mushroom which no one else would have seen. But she didn't; he was left alone as he ran in the still-wet sand to the drier, older wind-pasted drifts at the foot of the dunes. By the sea boot he waited as he would have done for Melanie, out of a childhood chivalry: 'I saw it first!', 'You might at least have waited!'. And, too, he wanted her audience because he was nervous. The boot was quite tall even though the owner of it had stylishly stitched down the top to show the grey lining. It was buried in the dry, wind-smoothed sand only a little way above the ankle with the foot and toe completely concealed.

As though he had come suddenly upon evidence of a crime, the anonymity of this relic frightened him; made him angry. He wanted to make sure that it mattered, to proclaim in some way the unknown stranger's sacrifice to the immense vacuum of the war.

He turned round away from the verandah of the chalet crowning the steep dune. Minna was as far away as ever, a small figure with a background, a freize of rusted posts in concrete and an iron thicket of barbed wire coiled again and again in ever diminishing circles far along the deserted beach, and behind those, as distant as if it were in another part of the world, the grey rim of the sea.

'Oh, do hurry up! Aren't you coming?'

She didn't answer; or if, maddeningly, she had, he couldn't catch the words. Three herring gulls were circling behind her, dark scissored shapes which appeared to be directly over her head, high up, only showing silver when they swooped low against the dun of the far mud on the downed bomber's part of the beach.

'Aren't you coming? Don't you want to see?'

'No-o-oo!' Her voice was so thin it might have come in amongst, or been one with, the cries of the gulls.

He ran angrily towards her.

'Why not? What's the matter? Oh *do* come!'

'You shouldn't touch it; it's his.' Her face was childlike, very private in its self-assurance.

'Whose?'

'His! From off the destroyer.'

'What destroyer? What are you talking about?'

'We shouldn't touch it. It hit a mine and all.'

'Probably.'

She started towards him on her best little shoes, her 'walking out' ones, he thought.

'Are you going to pull it, then?'

'Yes. You coming?'

She took his hand and once again he felt the knots of her knitted glove and, through it, her still-cold fingers in the warmth of his own palm.

'I want to see what's in his box,' she said.

'Is there a box too?'

'It's a little sea-chest.'

'Where?'

'It's part under.'

'But where?'

'It's just nearby. He had – some things in it.'

'Well, of course he did.'

'You won't open it?'

'Of course I will. You said you wanted to see what was in it.'

'I've changed.'

97

'Minna! You're being ridiculous.'

'I'm cold; give us a hug. Ooh! That's ever so nice.'

Her hair, quite unscented, was against his chin. 'You won't pull up his sea-boot, will you? You won't disturb it?'

'Not if you don't want. But I'm going to dig out that box if you'll show me where it is.'

'I will, if you'll promise?'

'Promise what?'

'That you won't open it till we're home.'

'I'm not carting anything back to the Guinea Lane on that blasted bus.'

'I didn't *mean* that. I meant "home" up there in the shally – you said we was spending the night.'

'I meant in the King Charles'. They have a room there. I asked them.'

'I don't like pubs. I couldn't sleep in one of them bedrooms.'

He looked up from where she had directed him to dig under a tangle of amber ribboned seaweed. 'Aren't you going to give me a hand?'

'I don't want sand up my legs.'

'You could just kneel beside me. Then you won't – '

'It will. It allus does.'

'Oh hell! And listen! I'm not breaking into any chalets. You'll just have to – '

'No I don't! And *you* don't have to break into no shally. It's Uncle George's. Me Aunt Nellie's said as we could always go there if we could get, and the key's under Grumpy.'

'Grumpy?'

'They have Snow White and them in the front garden. Uncle George made them out of barbola work – in the peace.'

'God!'

'You shouldn't swear, Doctor. Don't you like Snow White?'

He looked up seeing her short birchy hair framing her face against the sky with the three seabirds still circling some way over it.

'I *hate* Snow White!'

'You aren't half bad-tempered!'

'Yes I *am*. I've got the box up, though.' He rubbed the loose sand off the tight-fitting lid and she leaned over him resting her hand on his shoulder.

'What's it say then? Same as in the sea boot?'

'Yes, in indelible ink, MIDSHIPMAN FOX, RN. Are you sure about your aunt's chalet, Minna?'

'Course! There's tins there; everything. She hoarded up before rationing in case they bombed Addiscombe.'

'Is there a stove? An electric?'

'There's a paraffin one.'

'And bed clothes?' he asked.

'There might be. I think she took 'em back because of the mildew – she doesn't like the seaside.'

'Then why does she – ?'

'*He* does; that's why. Can you manage Mr Fox's chest up the dune? We'll have to go round the front and get in up the wooden steps.'

Back on the road facing the chalets they conferred, dismayed by the ropes and the wet red flags. The newish barrier stretched right up the hill on the left-hand side of the road. The narrow pathways in the sand had all been dug as far as the base of the wooden steps which ran up the dunes to the creosoted palings which enclosed the painted chalets and their pretty curtained windows.

'They hide their mines everywhere,' Minna said. 'It's a wonder they don't float 'em in the air for us to knock our heads on.'

'It's only fifty yards to the steps.'

'Grumpy's up there. Look! They didn't move him. But she isn't there. What have they done with Snow White?'

'Booby-trapped her.'

'They wouldn't do that.'

'Just what they would do – knowing how the Germans get all blubbery over little girls. Hold this, please.'

She took the box. 'You're not going in the minefield?'

'Yes.' He crossed carefully over the rope and stood there looking for footprints in the turned sand, wind-swept

99

hollows where the boots of the Pioneer Corps or the REs
had made their way safely out.

'You're *bad*!' she told him.

'I'm desperate, too.'

'You'll get blown up of a purpose.'

'No, I won't.'

'Yes, you will, an' you won't be like *her* patients.'

'Who? Sister Thorpe's ?'

'Don't go any further, Doctor. *Don't* you!'

'I'm nearly there now.'

She was silent. He forgot about her. He had to find one
more wind-washed footprint and then one more again to
the left or to the right and then he could reach, with one
shoe or the other, the bottom step of the ladderlike flight
to the garden of the chalet.

It was difficult to distinguish between the fortuitous
dimples caused by wind and rain, even by creatures, feather-
boned – whose playground this was in the winter months –
and the weathered original boot prints of the men who had
laid the mines and put up the red stencilled notices and
battered road-repair flags. But if he stepped very lightly by
distributing his weight on his finger tips and toes, by crawling
high, as in Leap Frog, he had a better chance. If he failed
it would be over in a fraction of a second for him; for
Minna? No, it wouldn't. It would be no more over for her
than David's needless death was over for him. Good God!
If he went on, she might be fatally injured too.

He was stuck now. He dared not move. Crouching as he
was, sweat leaking out through his cold skin, he turned back
to look at her, to tell her to move back across the road.

She was pulling a face at him. She had been making it at
his backside even before he turned round. Her eyes were
screwed up past even the slit stage; but he thought that she
could just see him without his being able to be sure; her
tongue was out, pink as a child's, but screwed up into a bud
of contempt. She was holding onto the rope in her knitted
gloves with both hands, her handbag dropped between her
neat 'walking-out' shoes; and the seagulls, five or six in
number now, crying out behind her; their only sounds
in the wind with the distant pouring of the sea.

'I'm stuck!' he called.

No answer; just the face she was making, a mean little gargoyle abutting from the wall of some old church, a rain-spout carved into the air, the face of some low-caste devil.

'I can't go back and I can't go forward,' he called.

'Serves you.'

'I'm frightened they may have put one or two at the foot of the steps.'

'Then you better go to one side then, didn't you?'

'What are you doing?'

She didn't answer.

'Why are you pulling your shoes off?'

'Because me feet are small. Aren't *your* feet smaller than your shoes? Aren't all folks'? Silly!'

'But you're undressing.'

'Course I am. That duffle weighs a ton.'

'You'll freeze.'

'That's *your* look-out.'

'Minna! You can't take everything off!'

'Liking's looking. I'm bird-light in me bra and cami-knickers. No firework wouldn't go off under *me*.'

She was over the rope now, stepping lightly towards him, then beside him on her perfect legs. With her ungloved hand she stroked his sweaty hair.

'Poor old stick-in-the-sand. You can stand up now. Monkey games is over!'

She took two more steps forward, the dark sand mantling her feet; and then, as though she were playing hopscotch, with her left ankle held in her left hand, she skipped across onto the bottom step.

'You fetch me my clothes, please; and Mr Fox's box. Follow your own footsteps both ways and then follow mine – I made the last two heavy a purpose.'

Halfway up the silvery, creosoted stair-ladder, she stopped and turned round again, the seagulls winging away, their cries faint and inhuman.

'An' you needn't be looking out for me any more from down there.'

At the top of the stairway they searched for the keys in the dwarves' fenced-in garden. The painted figures with their seven reduced characters stood on their stumpy legs beside the paths defined by stones and whelk shells. Rosettes of cactus grew in the square beds, patches of sharp grey sea-holly and a rusted grass scattered with the droppings of rabbits. One large stone, a seabird's anvil, was surrounded by broken limpet 'hats' and cockle and green crab shells. The Channel wind keened through the iron interstices of a miniature Eiffel Tower crowning a cairn of pebbled cement in the centre of a basin where the four paths intersected.

'He always wanted a fountain there; but the war stopped 'un. He was going to have had water spouting out the top and some kind of a contraption.'

'What for?'

'To balance coloured balls on it – and a little floodlight focussed so's you could see it at dark.'

'On the Eiffel Tower?'

'He didn't call it that.'

'Oh! That key is *not* under Grumpy!'

'He always said it in French, *Le Tour Eiffel*.'

'A linguist!' John said. 'It's not under Dopey either.'

'And the balls was to have had mirrors in them!'

'A poet, too!'

'Just because you can't turn up the keys, you shouldn't be rude about folk as you've never met.'

'It's better than about people I *have* met.'

'It isn't, either.'

'Why not?'

'Because it means you really don't care for anyone whether you've met them or not. That's what *she* meant.'

'Oh God!'

'Swearing will get you tired.'

'I *am* tired – of Sister Thorpe.'

'Well, you shouldn't be. That's why she showed us; so's we *could* care.'

'I know.'

'Cheer up, gloomy.'

'I've got them. I've found the keys.'

'Where were they?'

'I'm not telling.'

102

'Then I won't tell you what's in the box.'

'You'll have to.' She came up to him and they stood close in the darkening wind. 'You getting tired of me, then?'

'No.'

'Then you *will* show us, won't you?'

'Baked beans is all right,' she said, 'if you make up your mind to them.'

'Without bread? And unheated? You said there was a stove.'

'I never said there was paraffin – with rationing.'

'You said a *paraffin stove*! There isn't even a candle. Couldn't you find just one?'

'In the dark, I can't.'

'You found the sea chest.'

'That belonged to Mr Fox, and he's gone on.'

He took his elbows off the black flap of the gate-legged table, and studied her in the poor light from the window. She was shadowy against the indigo of the far reaches of the night sea. No, she was spectral, her hair was smoke; her whole person so insubstantial that it might at any moment dissolve and become one with the glimmer from the full tide of the waves washing the foot of the dunes.

'They've even turned off the water,' he grumbled. 'We can't wash ourselves or anything.'

'Outside we can go to the toilet. And in the morning we can clean the pans and all in the sea – and then we could open Mr Midshipman's box.'

'Yes, if you like.'

Her hand touched his own. For an instant he thought it was a moth, some delicate-legged insect, even a harvest spider. But they were gone by now, 'harvest men' on their wavering trestles of legs were a thing of the English summer, of slow fields and ripened wheat.

'What are you thinking?' she asked.

'That it wasn't much of a holiday for us, that's all.'

'*Were* you? That's nice!'

The 'moth' moved on the back of his hand again. It pleaded with him; with his exposed skin. Before he could stop himself, he belched.

103

'I'm sorry, Minna.'

'It's those beans! Dad called them 'wind-fruit.''

'He didn't like them?'

'He liked them all right. He liked most things; he did. He liked living. That's why he went to fight.'

'You mean, volunteered?'

'He wanted to keep it and all.'

He found her hand again and held it close to his blue raglan.

'Do you think he minded when he died?'

'*Course* he did – for a bit. Who wouldn't?'

'I meant because he'd hardly got started – done nothing much to help, really.'

'*Nothing much*! It were a lot our dad did. If you only stopped *one* of their dirty great bullets you'd done your lot! He'd tell us.'

John was silent. Her hand tightened within his own.

'He said that; he wrote it in his letter to Mum.' She moved nearer in the darkness. 'Hold us a bit closer, will you?'

'How does that feel?'

'I don't know. I've got the chills tonight. I've had 'em ever since that pub. I don't like pubs, they give me the habdabs.'

'It *was* a bit rowdy.'

'Rowdy! It was worse than the raids. All of them in there, waiting to – get careless.'

'You mean make love?'

'That or start fighting, get akilling – like the bombers.'

They were silent. Below the dunes, a little way out, the waves were washing back on themselves sluggishly. John closed his right hand tight over her shoulder bones.

'What else did your father say?'

'He used to tell us, "I'm not a bleeding sandbag, you know – " '

'Did he?'

'He was often saying it to us; "I'm not *just* a bleeding sandbag, Minna! If I get shot, I'm not just a sandbag. I'm a lot more than a sack of bleeding sand." '

'That's wonderful!'

'It is that.'

Her fingers moved again, curled over the back of his hand, his tense knuckles, and he loosened his grip as she said:

'I don't know how *us*, how we all of us can chuck ourselves around as if we *was*.'

'Sandbags?'

'Not even *them*! No; as if we were nothing – just *nothing*! Here today and all gone tomorrow.'

'No.'

'I don't never think *nothing's* the end; I don't believe that not anything *ever is* the end, do you?'

'I do sometimes. I'm sorry, but I really do.'

She wriggled against him under his containing arm.

'Then that's what you shouldn't. It's not real *bad*; it's not wicked. It's ignorant and – '

He waited.

'I don't know.' Her breath was quiet. 'But we aren't awasted. None of us wasn't ever meant to be *awasted*, however soon we go. Ooh!'

He jumped, 'What's the matter now?'

'*You're* cold too, you feel corpsy!'

'Corpsy! Minna, where on earth do you get such words?'

'I don't know. They just come. Could be the war and all. Have you been down the cinder patch yet?'

'What's that? The mortuary?'

'It isn't half awful! All the bombed bathroom stuff from North London, acres of it stacked there, tubs and lavatories and white wash-basins; and, after the big raids, all the dead bodies. There's some real posh ones from the West End, green marble and golden taps.'

'I thought you meant *bodies*!'

'No, folk say as the whole bodies were pink, that they were all shell-pink.'

'However did *you* get down there?'

'As a witness a time or two. *You* know! When we were short-staffed or between doctors.'

He stood up, '*God*! What a cheerless night this is!'

'Why are you opening the window then? Aren't you cold enough without?'

'I want to hear the sea.'

'I can hear it through. You'll only get them curtains wetted.'

He moved the little table to one side and kneeled by the low sill with the salt wind blowing into the room.

'Shall I get us their bed ready?' she asked.

'Is there a mattress?'

'There's only a wire frame; but I've turned out a feather one from Aunt Nellie's cupboard.'

'Is it dry?'

'The outside is; dry as a bone.'

'What about the feathers?'

'You can't never tell with feathers until you lays on them. They could be a bit wet; but with our clothes on, the damp won't get through till morning.'

He turned round to see her; somewhere by the doorway which led into the small carpeted dressing-tabled bedroom. She was only a shadow, a lighter one against the darkest ones.

'Damn! I'm trying to listen to the sea and you will keep *on* about things. I'm not sleeping in my clothes anyway. I'm off duty tonight.'

She didn't answer. He could hear her moving about in the musty, nearly obscured bedroom. She was singing a little to herself; nasally, as if she needed her adenoids out. He turned back to listen to the sea again.

15

He thought it was about two or three in the morning when they woke up. He felt round on the bedside table for the alarm clock, and then remembered where he was and that he'd left his watch in the staff bathroom at Guinea Lane.

With his stockinged foot he explored the feather mattress; a damp hollow of it.

'This thing smells of hens,' he said loudly. 'Ahoy! You awake, Minna? What time is it?'

'Don't know.'

'Well, look at your watch.'

'I didn't bring it.'

'Blast!'

'I didn't wish it with me – a purpose.'

'Why ever not?'

'Because if you get a watch on your arm there's always too much time or too little.'

'Oh.'

'Being with *you* I wanted there to be only just what's enough, so I left it on our dressing table.'

'Do you want a hug?'

'I want a big 'un.'

'There you are, then.'

'You won't let go, will you?'

'Not ever.'

'Did you say as the mattress smelt henny?'

'Yes, but I don't find it very funny.'

She was laughing stupidly just below his ear; giggling, really.

'It did ought to smell a bit! It was Uncle George's poultry; he saved them up for it – Christmas hens and all – till he'd got enough to stuff it. *She* wouldn't never lie with him in it; me Aunt Nellie said as he never washed the feathers properly.'

'How disgusting!'

'It is, isn't it? When you think of it.'

'I believe you *like* it.'

'It's better than bombs.'

He was staring up into the low charcoaly ceiling: in the sitting room the window was still open. Through the doorway of the bedroom he could make out the shape of the tiled fireplace on the opposite wall below the brick chimney. He could smell the wet sea.

'You didn't work in the air raids, did you, Minna? You couldn't have. You were too young; still at home?'

'At school. I was finishing at the Borough – shorthand and typing. But I *did* see 'em fire-bombing London way.'

107

'I meant casualties; bombed people.'

'Not bombed – no. But one time, at night it was, *she* showed us the wounded and them who were dying.'

'When?'

'She didn't say. Just some old-time war with them . . . enemies.'

'*What* enemies?'

'I don't know. She never said; I think she may have forgotten.'

'But they were soldiers? You saw soldiers?'

'Foreigners. In the ward they were all foreigners in funny uniforms; dark-skinned.'

'Indians? From India?'

'I don't know. They could have been E-gyptians; I only saw them a minute. She didn't want to frighten us with it all; them dying and dirty bandages and blood. There was such a splash of it; seemed as if it was everywhere except back in their bodies where it should have been.'

He moved irritably, angrily:

'If she didn't want to frighten you, what *did* she want?'

'I thought afterwards it was to show us we're all one lot, I think; *all* of us: those men she looked after before we were made, and those as you'll have to look to, and all the people who've gone past, gone ahead – like our Dad. I believe she wanted to show us, as she said, that there's only the living!'

'Only the living!' David, he thought, my brother David; Victoria, Victoria Blount, one with another, one with me and with all the 'foreigners' of the Great War, all the wars, coming out of the dark and the silence, streaming through the bright day and into the shadow, disappearing into the splendour forever.

For a moment, for several, he saw it, he almost held it in the way one holds for an instant the past in the present of some music or perfume.

'Did she *say* that? I mean, did she actually use those words: '*There's only the living*?'

'She said them all right.'

'Where were you?'

'Crossing the back lawn after I'd taken her the message to her ward. She wasn't answering her phone that night.'

'It was at night then? And Sister Thorpe was walking back across the compound with you?'

'No! Sister went back into her office. But it was *her* voice said the words.' She pressed her thin lips against his cheek, holding her scarcely visible face there pressed quite warmly to his own. 'Doctor John, why don't you just love us and not fret all the time?'

'I *am* loving you.'

'Then pull them old feathers over us from my side and we'll go off together till morning.'

He reached over and got hold of a side seam in the slippery ticking. He pulled a bulwark of the mattress up against her thin backbone, and across her duffled shoulders and hips.

'How's that?' he asked. 'Any cosier?'

'Lovely!' She moved closer. 'Is there a word 'blissful'? Is there?

He held her nearer his shivering body. The sea wind, tongued with salt, was blowing over their faces, the mattress warming around them and her breath like a baby's when you leaned into its milky crib. This is something like, he thought, as he slipped into sleep; his arm, his fingers, feeling the pliability of her shoulder, the steps of her ribs and her soft little behind beneath her duffle coat; this is really something like.

By morning the sky had cleared to a deadly blue laced with cloud and the sea was up; the tide retreating niggardly from its bases in the dunes, ragged with torn water and coarse foam. The spiralling fence of the 'invasion' wire was draped now with wide tails and skeins of bladder-wrack and ribbon weed brought up during the night from the coasts of Europe.

They fetched buckets of sea water from the waves' edge, cloudy with sand and chalk, and washed sudslessly in the bathroom with a fissured cake of soap left in the medicine cupboard by Aunt Nellie.

Minna found a metal stove and enough methylated spirit to boil a still bright whistling kettle of milkless tea, and a tin of rice pudding which they ate with a pot of prewar strawberry jam labelled TIPTREE FARMS, and full of whole strawberries.

'What time's the bus leave Downchurch Square?' she asked.

'Twelve o'clock. So, if we're careful, we should be back for supper.'

'Then we still got the whole morning for us?'

'What do you want to do with it?' he asked.

'Open his box, for a start.'

'Then what?'

'Don't know. What's in it could tell us.'

'Get me a poker.'

'You going to smash it?'

'I'm going to try.'

'You might squash what's in it.'

'There's *nothing* in it.'

'Could be something ever so tiny.'

'Such as what?'

'Shells from the South Seas or pearls – seed ones.'

He lifted the pine casket up and shook it widely from side to side, and then, angrily, up and down.

'There you are! Up and down. Down and up and round and round and not a sound – damn all.'

'It rustled.'

'It didn't.'

'It *did*, like leaves.'

'Or five pound notes – *perhaps*,' he said. 'Stand back, I'm going to bash the lid in. There!'

He threw down the poker and walked over to the curtained, hen-housy window.

'*You* look! All you want.'

'Coo! This is a turn for us.'

He tried to conceal a shiver of excitement. 'What is?'

'What he's got here; Mr Fox.'

'What *has* he got?'

'Why, it's more than a month of his sweet rations. All Mr Fox's sweets for the voyage.'

'What sort?'

'Come and see.'

110

'No. I don't want to.'

'All right, sulky.'

'*You* tell me.'

'Well, there's Fox's glacier mints, each one ever so prettily wrapped and twisted in greaseproof paper and a blue polar bear printed and all. And butterscotch, from Scotland, Callard and Bowser in white wrappers, and there's fruit pastilles with pictures on them; pineapple, pears, oranges and lemons – each with two layers of paper, and there's Sharp's toffees in all different colours with *Sharp's the word and Sharp's the toffee* printed on each. Why, they're all like peacetime, only the sea's had 'em.'

'What? What do you mean?'

'The sea's had 'em. It's taken them.'

'You mean dissolved them?'

'Yes, all of them.'

Suddenly eager and hungry he came forward and squatted beside her on the thin drugget.

'But they can't be! Not all of them. Dig down, Minna! Let's both dig down to the bottom. There *must* be a few whole ones – '

'There's never a one. They're just shapes. It's not fair; the sea's had them all.'

'Without even opening them – or the box,' he said. 'The brine must have got under the lid when the ship sank and then worked its way slowly under the wrappers as the box washed about in the waves.'

'Sneaky!' she said.

'Yes.

'Cheated us, didn't it? And Mr Fox, *and* he on his last voyage too.' She kissed him. 'Never mind. I've got my sweet coupons in me handbag. I can get us plenty to suck on the bus ride.'

'No, keep them – for another time.'

'Well then, let's walk along by the waves – before they get to the wire.'

'Carry our shoes, you mean, as if it were summer?'

'Yes, and I'll find us a Fish and Chip in the village. You see if I don't.'

'Do *you* want a kiss?'

111

'I'm not particular.'

'Would you come to the sea again with me?'

'If you asked us, I would.'

'For a good long trip?' he insisted.

She frowned at the box and its scattered sweet wrappers.

'I might – it depends.'

'Everything does,' he said.

16

'You've been away then?' Doctor Gillespie asked a day or two later.

In the umber-dark Admin Room John sat up in his bentwood chair. The Superintendent's uneager face, the boyish hair rubbed away thin from the front of the scalp, wavered against the curtained black-out window.

'Aye! I have too. I'm sorry, I was dozing off.'

'I ken fine. You've done your turn-aboot and your roonds of the Blocks?'

'Yes; everything.'

'And ye're wearied and still on call the night until tomorrow noon?'

John yawned: 'It's my watch, yes.'

'Good, good! Then you can put your emergencies through on the switchboard to the hoose.'

'Sir?'

'Wake up, Man. Get stirring thyssen! There's a braw old game replaying on the wireless the noo.'

'At *your* hoose – house?'

'Where else? And a gentle malt from the distillery in Auchtermuchtie. And it's the Two Queens bodying it out on the good home turf.'

'The two queens?' John got up, the *British Medical*

Journal falling from his lap to the brown carpet. To be woken up so rudely was shock enough without having to start replying in broken English to a bald-headed foreigner.

'I'm not very hot on football I'm afraid – I don't know who the two queens *are*.'

'Queen's Park Rangers and Queen o' the Sooth. Ech! Ech! to be neither hot nor cold, Laddie, on the sport is not the wee-est of your burdens; for in time of war it's as unwholesome for a man to be ignorant of the football fixtures as of the fighting.'

'Yes, sir.'

'Then fetch your plaid from the stand and we'll order your calls put through to the bothie. You've taken your bread and broth since you were in?'

'I've had supper, yes.'

'Fine! fine! For there's little enough in the meal-ark with the women away to the Town.'

'Mrs Gillespie's not at home?'

'Seldom! seldom! Robene's away to her kiln at Chelsea and it's Mistress McVeigh's one night of the week where she'll be pitching the darts doon at the Nag's Head.'

The Doctor paused to regard him kindly in the corridor light. 'Ach! You're fair spent, Doctor Blaydon, tossing your caber all night for the wee lassie, no doubt?'

John met his gaze sadly; all the more sadly for the merriment that still lingered in the boyish eyes.

'We had to keep warm somehow, Sir.'

'*Warm* is it? Do ye no ken that there's nothing so bleeting as thrumming your bobbin all night? And that's not to include the spill of thy seed. Why, Man! You'll be dropping all your teeth before you've a belly to you.' He took his arm. 'Come now over to the hoose for a drop of the malt. I declare the contemplation of your tu-pitude is fetching me the shivers.'

He paused to gaze at John in the darkness. 'And with *that* puir wee poult of a gel! Tk! tk!'

An hour later, slumped in one of the bentwood chairs in the basement of Gillespie's house, John was wondering how his evening had 'happened'. Unwittingly, muddled by the 'malt', he was repeating to himself the small runes and self-questionings which accompany the bewilderment of boredom.

Why is everything so brown? Why is everything this brown colour? Why do I listen to this person on the radio shouting about a pastime I have always hated? Why does Doctor Gillespie like me? Why don't I dislike him more? Why does he look at me so sadly? What does he really want? Why won't he speak English?

'*There* was a braw and feisty joust for you! Are ye not glad I got ye over for it? But your cup, Man! 'Tis empty! Have you sucked up all your malt?'

'It was a very good whisky, Sir.'

'*Good*! It's unique! Containing the wee o' the sheep turf from the scree and the iron water filtered doon from the Reeks of the Auchtermuchtie. Will ye not take another bumper with me?'

'Thank you. I was wondering what you meant about losing all my teeth?'

'Aye! aye! All the knock o' them – from the molars to the wee bittock incisors. He wagged his head. 'Through the *sperm*, Doctor, and the seminal fluid you're pumping out on the lassies.'

'But how does my sperm affect my teeth?'

'Hoots! hoots! Have ye no chemistry? At what Faculty were ye instructed? Your calcium and phosphorous! Where else would they waste but through your orchids – your balls, Man? The testicles banging in your crotch. Have ye no *poetry* in the Sassenach academies?'

'A little; Shakespeare and *Palgrave's Golden Treasury*.'

'But no Rabbie Bu'ns! No runes? No Erse?'

'Do you mean *Robert Burns*? Yes, I've – '

'The Devil! Certain it is you'll not have laid an eyelash to the works of John Blair, nor rhymed his *Wallace* in your slumbers. Ech! ech! I dinna doubt you're dead to a syllable of Dunbar?'

'I've never heard of him. What did Dunbar write?'

'Never heard of *Twa Merrit Wemen and the Wedo*, or *The Thrissil and the Rois*?'

Tedium and whisky were making John reckless: 'The

114

Thrissil and the Rois! I don't even understand the *words*. I don't know what a thrissil *is* – unless it's some kind of a throstle – a song thrush?'

'A warble bird!' Gillespie laughed contemptuously, 'Ye've never noted the national flow'r of Scotland?'

'The bluebell?'

'God save us! The *thistle*, Man. In the English the poem is The *Thistle and the Rose* and was penned to celebrate the marriage o' King Jaimie the Fourth to Mairgaret Tudor!

'Oh.'

'And a black day it was. A black on black day – like the most of such wedlock and trysts.' He drank again from his cup and as sadly refilled it, his eyes on the photograph of a dark woman framed in pitch pine on top of a bookcase.

'They're all the same,' he sighed. 'All crossed with it! Away to their pots and slipware at the firing kilns in the stews o' the city, the red hell-hob of London itself.'

'Mrs Gillespie's in Chelsea?'

'Where else? And who else but my Robene with her crafty wiles and the throbbing wheel from which she throws the dripping clay of her bawbles!'

'I'm sorry, Sir.

'And well you might be, had ye but the thumb of it all. A man left by his wifie! Abandoned continually since the birthing of his wee crested bairn, Dairmid Alexander, in the very hoose he'd wattled for her out of his own blood and bones.'

'You built this place yourself?'

'Built it! Not with the skin of my two hands, but with the briny flux of me brow since I was a lad in breeches. For I came up through concrete and,

> '*My sighing cometh before I eat*
> *And my roarings are poured oot like the waters* – '

Job, Chapter Three, Verse Twenty-four.'

'Job?'

'None other! And for why? Tell me that!'

'I suppose there could be many reasons.'

'And but a single right one! You know your scriptures I hope?'

115

'Not very well.'

'I'm not perplexed! A man who does not follow what football there is in time of war would as likely be ignorant too, o' Holy Writ. Did ye never bottom the reason for Job's complaint?'

'His distrust?'

'Aye, distrust! But not his distrust of the Lord – but of his *spoose*, Laddie – of Mistress Job, the bold wife of his bosom; the feckless companion of his good fortunes and the vexed mistress of his bad. For, mark this in your ignorance, in forty-two chapters of the Book of Job, there is but one single reference to the first Mistress Job – Chapter Two, Verse Nine – and that only to upbraid the quey with the foolery proceeding from her mouth, which, by continual taunting of the good man's faith in God, brought him to the brink of the fathomless abyss in the keep o' Satan.'

'Then what did she say to Job?'

'What did she – Ech! Lad; when the poor sick man was scraping his boils with a potsherd – no doobt squatting in the cinders o' the piggery, did she not fetch herself up and tell him:

'*Dost thou still retain thine integrity? Curse God and dee!*'

He paused. 'And what do ye make of that?'

In the confusion of the peaty drinks he had swallowed and the doctor's increasingly thick brogue, John said,

'I can understand Mrs Job wanting her husband to curse God; but I don't know who 'Dee' was.'

The doctor was breathing heavily through his whiskered nostrils and when John turned to see why he was silent he found that he was glaring at him.

'*Dee*! You ignorant spalp! Mistress Job challenged her good man, the gainer of her bairns and bread, to curse God and *expire*! Aye! Laugh now if you dare? At a brave and suffering spoose whisting his last breath in cursing his Maker – at the behest of his *woman*! Laugh!'

John wished he could, but the night stretched ahead of him with no real prospect of escape, and that only if some emergency arose somewhere in the wards. And now, in the close browness of Gillespie's basement, he wanted only to

116

get to his bed, to reveries of Lynton and endless wonderings about Minna.

'If I may, sir, I'd like a drink?'

'It's in the cag. Help thyself.'

His immediate hurt forgotten the doctor sat hunched forward in his bentwood chair, his posture slack, his glass at an angle in the hand that rested on his knee above the tartan linoleum.

He's away, John thought, he's beginning to enjoy himself; we're getting to the pleasant, stupid stage of the evening where we may totally approve of ourselves and, minimally, of one another. And he decided to 'go with it', to accept Gillespie, even to love him; to find, in everything he said and did, something pleasing and sensible.

Still with his faraway gaze, a lost glance that passed above the mahogany fretwork of a stag at bay, and over the mantelpiece above which, on the wall, a set of bagpipes hung from a picture hook, the Doctor sipped his whisky. Then he sighed and shook his head. John sighed too and drank as deeply from his own sheep-enriched liquor.

Everything was extremely sad. Life was not so much a progression from one phase of meaningless activity to another, as a decline from the glory of childhood through painful adolescence into the dissatisfactions of maturity. The best way to manage lay in following football, reading the Bible – starting with the Book of Job – and in being on the alert for anyone taking up pottery.

Overhead, on the ground floor, a door opened, closed and was succeeded by silence until, perhaps in the kitchen, perhaps in the serving pantry, a pot or casserole fell to the floor.

Unmoving, Gillespie continued to sit in the same attitude, apparently disinterested; wagging his head, sipping at his whisky and not speaking a word.

John sat up:

'I think there's somebody else in the house!'

'Aye.'

'Should there be? I mean, are you expecting anyone? I'm sure I heard someone.'

'No doobt! No doobt!'

117

It could be Mrs Gillespie, John thought. If this is your way of greeting her, no wonder! If all you can do is sit there drinking – I'm not surprised! If she were my wife and she came in late and alone – I'd leap! Why! I'd be in the hall this minute hugging her, kissing her cold cheeks; bustling!

He got up and, simultaneously, the doctor jumped to his feet:

'Nay, laddie, nay!'

He held up a finger to his lips and John stayed quiet. Good God! It could be Gelda Whooper; Wantage had suggested these two were having an affair. Worse, it could be one of the night staff looking for him.

'What do you hear, laddie?'

'Nothing, sir.'

The doctor nodded, 'Aye; never so much as the squeak of a moose – or a clog to the wood. And for why?'

'I've no idea; but I *am* a bit worried; it might be one of the staff looking for me.'

'Ech! Dinna fash yourself. 'Tis but Mistress McVeigh – lost at the darts tourney again and cast all her clouts in the shrubbery.'

'All her clothes? You mean she's naked?'

'Every last one of them, even down to her plasters. Naked as a bairn, and in a wee while she'll be whooing like a lowland heifer for her mate.'

'The bull?'

'Aye! The raging red-eyed bull of her dreams, with a stand on him like the cedar o' Lebanon, and his balls tighter than tu-nips.'

'Does she do this often? Every time she loses a darts match?'

'At darts? Nay, that's but the proximate cause. 'Tis her man, her spouse, Doctor McVeigh, as he styles himself; a self-taught scholar in the Latin and the Greek who instructs the Sixth Form at the Grammar!' Gillespie shook his head. 'And the pity of it is that his learning has all fled from his brow to his balls. For never was there a more earnest seeker

> *After the truth that lies*
> *Atwixt a pair of open thighs.'*

118

'You mean he's unfaithful to her?'

The doctor was rocking himself back and forth in the bentwood chair, and John repeated his question.

'Professor McVeigh is unfaithful to her, to Mistress McVeigh, his wife?'

'To Madgie, aye! Though myself I would not term it 'unfaithful' with Reuben McVeigh in mind. Ye canna call a bantam unfaithful! Ye canna accuse a wee grey rooster who's forever rubbing his crest at all the pert-holed hens and pullets in the run of inconstancy – ! Nay! Reuben McVeigh is but a poor cock-laird whose bittock learning has thrust the two of them into the bedlam of lust and dark.'

'But does his wife take off all her clothes whenever – ?'

'*Whenever*, Doctor, she scents or glims new tidings of Reuben's depravity.' Gillespie paused to wag his head. 'Oh! 'tis *bad*. All of a piece; one death already to his tally, with Reuben meddling in the wedlock of his friends. For it is his custom to find a bad marriage and turn it to a worse! To discover a grief and convert it to a tragedy. For he snuffs out fester quicker than a dog at a wound, and like a dog, the more he muzzles the more he consumes!'

They were silent, Gillespie unbending suddenly from his crouched posture in his chair and throwing his thin frame back against the ochre fabric, his face turned up towards the ceiling.

'Aye! List! There she goes! Away padding up the steps to her lone couch and her prayers and tears – for she will not bide at their hoose this night with him wrapped in the fume of his fornications. 'Twas ever thus in wedlock. Satan lurks in every crack in the fabric of love, fizzing like a petard in the tinder of affection, bright of face and finger to turn bold love to the reeky conflagration of adultery – Och! God! That ever I was breeched!'

He fumbled in his jacket pockets for something, and not finding it, stood up and plunged his hands into the tweed of his trousers. Finally, from his breast pocket he withdrew a large yellow handkerchief and mopping his tears with it, subsided again into his chair, apologising to God and to John for his weakness.

' 'Tis but a wheen of smither, John. 'Tis weeping as a

man must for what might have been. With poor wee Job I ask:

> *Wherefore is light given to him that is in misery*
> *And life unto the bitter soul?'*

'I'm very sorry, Sir. Truly I am.'

'Aye.'

The Doctor resumed his rocking in the brown chair, sipping at his drink and nodding to himself. Then, abruptly, he looked up and with an unblinking eye asked,

'No doubt I have your sumpathy too?'

'My sympathy? Certainly.'

'Then ye may *box* it! Aye, box and ben your sumpathy, for I have as much gain from it as Falstaff had from Honour. Does sympathy salve and make smooth the rough bile of anger? The gall of envy? Or give a body back his own conceit of himself? Never! For 'tis a useless and tinsel emotion as little felt as often expressed.'

John was impatient:

'Oh then I'm corrected. What *do* you want?'

'Your prayers, Doctor. Aye! For *there* is the knockaboot of God with his creatures, the to and fro that clears the eye to glimpse it and the mind to hold it.'

'Does it matter if I don't believe in it? If I don't believe in prayer?'

'How should it? Where's your head if you don't see that the supplication of the sceptic is sweeter to his Maker than all the vigils of the blessed?'

John got up. He looked down at the dazzling pattern of the Black Watch tartan and then at Gillespie whose face was turned towards him.

'Well, I'll try.'

'You *must*, for all your shortcomings and all of mine – and for thy better understanding of the world.' He looked up. 'You can see yourself oot the hoose and to your duties?'

'I think so. Will you be all right? Up the stairs, I mean?'

'I will indeed, and she'll be doon directly. Aye, poor naked Madgie will be doon as soon as you yourself are away, for we two to coddle each other against our sorrows and the dark. Ye ken, laddie? Ye know fine what I mean?'

'Yes.'

John passed up the stairs and out into the bare-treed compound. At the end of the pathway, between its laurel bushes, he paused to savour the wintry air and the chill.

The night was silent, dull; in the distance beyond Batsford the shadowy mass of unlighted London watched and slept.

He turned to look back at the blacked-out house with its pyramidal roof.

How small it was; yet the passageway with the flight of stairs down to the snug, the basement itself and the glimpsed kitchen all seemed nearly limitless. And upstairs the imagined bedrooms extended into vast spaces through which moved, like characters in a dream, the figures of the doctor, his mistress and his faithless wife, Robene.

17

Again he waited for Doctor Graemes by the gate into Guinea Lane. Across the road, through the iron railings of the sewage docks, he could see the gleam of the black metal outworks that turned in the huge circles of the pits, that pumped the air into their contents, that churned the dull emulsion of the distant city's wastes.

He breathed in the night air deeply, quite patiently, exhaling the fumes of Doctor Gillespie's whisky with a righteous sensation and worrying about his health. It seemed sound; physically he felt almost tireless and the sickening pain of David's death was relenting, thinning; like watered dye might one day flow into and coalesce with that other fell pattern, the dark plasma into which Victoria had vanished forever from his sight.

But though he felt 'all right', he sensed that, like a patient with a subclinical haemorrhage, he could suddenly be unwell; might even, in some way, collapse. It was curious that in the times of his measureless relationship with Minna, he knew himself to be strong; whereas when he was with Lynton, all passed too rapidly and he became aware of his own fragility.

She too, he thought, must have noticed this, for one morning when she had come over with the bearers to the theatre block to take a patient back to her ward, she had caught him alone in the recovery room and had looked at him anxiously, her clear eyes crossing ever so slightly as she spoke:

'John, you've really got to be more careful of yourself. You look terrible. No, not terrible; exhausted.'

'Do I really?'

'Darling, if you go on at this pace you'll never last the course: you'll be a wreck at forty.'

'But I only – '

She came closer and whispered to him, her face so near his own, her care so apparent that he was never able to forget the alarm is caused him.

'I know! You "only" run here, run there, run everywhere: over to Gynae, over to theatre; at night out to the Thyroids and the Grannies. And your notes! There's no need to write so much.'

'I enjoy it. I really do.'

'Then out with Wantage and that Sunday drinking crowd from the Mercia. And then off with that little typist you've taken to.'

'You mean Minna Frobisher?'

'Is that her name?' She stepped back, becoming smaller again, her eyes straight beneath the straight starch of her cap from which, on each side, her shining hair escaped. 'Darling, do slow up for everyone's sake!'

Yet, he considered now, how confusing it was, that such care should at all have alarmed him; should have disturbed him so much that he had felt like running away; getting into one of the Services as quickly as possible.

How to understand, to reconcile the contradictions of his

feelings? The fact that the next day, the very next minute, he had felt cossetted by Lynton's concern; recalling with pleasure her every word, finding in them the warmth of his childhood, as if they had been a garment. Why, by them, the Guinea Lane was made safe, habitable.

The dark 'blocks', the asphalt paths, the November nights with their bitter chimneyed air, even the congregations of the aircraft massing for their bombing mission over Europe, were all transformed, viewed with satisfaction; invested with some of the joy of home.

Yes, he considered; even now as I wait here to see Mrs Pobgee die; as I wait yet again for Chlorinda Graemes to fit the frames onto her nose, I do enjoy knowing that melon-fresh, pomegranate fleshed Lynton likes me; that, loving me she may even be planning to marry me. It does make me feel valuable to imagine that anyone so sweet is going to get me 'used' to her: her warmth, her ways of talking and listening. And it does cheer me to think that in the recesses of her mind, like a grub in honey, a plan may be nourished to bring me to maturity in her arms as easily as she does on icy mornings between our beakers of sugared tea in that rough and narrow bed.

But again, why did I suddenly shy at the thought? What was it that passed through my mind like a warning bell? Don't I *want* to get married? Do I shrink and hang back from the cosiness and finality of such vows: money worries, babies and nappies, regular love in well-made beds?

What is the matter with me? Lynton, I am suddenly afraid. Not of you who are so innocent, so ready; for that in you is precisely what I love; but your hunger is deeper than my own. Like your body it goes in and in and into you, to the hollow place you are forever guarding; the cave round which you are wrapped and which you will do anything to fill, to hear a new voice crying. And were I to ask you, you would I know in the future give all of yourself: your interest, your baby-bartered body, your ambitions, and in return ask what? Why! All of *me*. And *that* I wish to reserve to love others; many.

So, please, eager generous Lynton, be whole for me, be whole for yourself, be sporting. Do not come to my bed

123

and box except in the fun we can never quite remember – and always enjoy.

He blew out his cheeks and stood back as Doctor Graemes' shark-grey Jaguar with its slit headlight covers nosed past him and onward into the hospital car park.

His thoughts taking a new course, his stethoscope swinging in his hand, his frosted breath invisible in the night air, he followed it at a distance. He was filled with curiosity about the doctor; how she managed always to maintain her distance, her coolness with him; with everyone: patients, sisters, staff, with Doctor Gillespie, with Gelda Whooper, with Jerry Wantage and, yes again, with *himself*?

Were there such collected people? Was it possible for them to be so sufficient? Did they admonish themselves, 'Stand back, Graemes, don't you get serious about *me*; and do not be intimate, do not even consider that aspect of *you*?'

Or did they not get so far as that? For such self-counselling implied an existing personal knowledge; feelings. If there really was a section of humanity so clean-swept; if, in the human mansion there was one such room, a locked cool conservatory of icy plants, could the unsure, the anxious, the over-heated ever find the key to it? Or failing that, break into it with stones?

Doctor Graemes was coming towards him now, her muffler high round her face; her soft hair, her head, encased in a whitish knitted conical cap with a bobble on top of it.

'Pobgee, you said?'

'Yes.'

'And moribund?'

'I think so, yes. She's fibrillating badly, getting about one ventricular systole every thirty seconds.'

The doctor was silent. Beside him in her white tennis shoes she moved without any sound, the blackish cloak she had put on hanging stiffly from her shoulders.

'We won't talk out here.'

'No.'

Why not? he wondered as they entered the swing doors and paused in the dimly lighted corridor to the ward. The knee-length cloak was made of the same dark navy blue as her more usual school girl's coat with the thick pocket flaps. Her slacks were a dark claret; the muffler, her fuzzy orange one.

'Many people fail to realise that in the lungs the entire blood supply is exposed to the air,' she said.

'Yes.'

'That is why I prefer to discuss matters within. How old is Pobgee?'

'Eighty-three, I believe.'

'You are not sure?'

'I forget exactly which of them is which.'

'There are screens up?'

'Yes. I didn't mean that I can't tell them apart. I meant that – '

'Who is on duty?'

'Sister Balloon – '

'Sister *Balloon*?'

'I'm sorry. I meant Mrs Rogers!'

He was irritated, quite angry. Here was a moment where they might have met in amusement; and instead of smiling or hurrying on down the corridor as if vexed or embarrassed by his slip, she behaved as though no such moment had occurred.

Unlike himself, so greedy to know, to penetrate people's fastnesses by any means, she, socially, seemed totally incurious. The dedication which lay behind and beyond her years of study, her courage in entering the masculine field of surgery, had made her, for the present, impenetrable. And though, despite her authority over him, it was hard for him ever to forget she was a woman, it was often more difficult to remember she was human.

A wave of some deadness that was less than any emotion engulfed and dismayed him when he considered that she might not be 'acting'; that she might genuinely not be subject to the pressures that drove him; worse, that she might not be unique, but one of very many such 'unheated' people.

They moved on now, side by side down the shining corridor of the Thyroid unit to Sister Balloon's office.

In there, the Sister presided over the study of Mrs

Pobgee's case notes. She was very different from Sister Thorpe who was able to be strongly present merely by the quietness of her attention. Sister Balloon 'beamed', or had her features ready to do so with a mixture of obligingness and deference that made people uneasy and curt.

Doctor Graemes ran her eyes down the dying woman's papers. One of her ringless hands dipped into her opened bag on the table and fetched out a smaller black japanned case.

'The immediate cause, Doctor Blaydon?'

Her fingers opened the smaller box. It was lined like a jewel case with dark blue velvet and contained only the immensely intricate 'death' spectacles.

'The immediate cause?' Fascinated by the delicacy of the instrument, its shining wires, its calibrations, its jewelled axles, he could not think what she meant.

'Of death!' Doctor Graemes' fingers picked up the spectacles, her finger tips played over them as needles moved over the ivory surfaces.

'Oh, old age I suppose!'

'I need to know the specific cause, Doctor – in your opinion.'

He thought. He tried to see into Mrs Pogbee's chest, to see beneath its flaccid skin, gemmed with age: scarlet Morgan de Campbell spots, pigmented naevi; one or two spidery angiomata, little warts.

'Heart failure – myocardial degeneration secondary to arteriosclerosis. Also she has a fair degree of bronchiectasis – '

He looked up. Her face pink with approval, Sister Balloon was beaming at him – as if he were her kid brother, he thought: 'Young Albert.'

'I suppose she may have had the whooping cough in adolescence – I mean, pertussis. That would account for the – '

He was thinking of the whistles and grunts that came up the stethoscope as Mrs Pobgee's breath rushed in and out of the ruptured bronchiole walls.

Dr Graemes closed the little case carefully and put a silver fountain pen and a red school notebook on top of it.

'We will go through, I think. You did say the screens were in place, Sister?'

'I've had everything prepared this last six hours, ever since she started rattling.'

'We do *not* want to stress my thyroids on our way through.'

'Oh dear me, no! And I know you don't care for tea, Doctor, so I have a little hot lemon-barley warming on the ring for on your way home – and some of my parkin too – '

Unacknowledged, she was following them as they went soundlessly down the ward between the two rows of beds and their sleepers.

John pushed aside the central, dividing screens of the 'wall' between the Thyroids and Granny's End. There were more screens round Mrs Pobgee's cot with its iron barred side rails, the nearer one lowered so that she might be nursed.

Sister Balloon moved round to the right hand side and John stood at the foot as Doctor Graemes, her cloak black in the dim light, stooped to shine her pen torch into the pupils of the open eyes.

Mrs Pobgee's mouth, thin-lipped, fanged with two or three crumbling orange teeth, was not wide open; the lips were only parted in a convex bow, the corners drooping round her chin, as if she were about to cry. Through this opening in her head, her breath passed in and out, crepitant with the mucus in her trachea. As the little bulb flashed into her retinae, the eyelids closed then opened, and somewhere in her dry mouth, her tongue moved:

'Wha' ? Wha' !'

Sister Balloon's well-shaped unmanicured hands rested on the papery forehead. 'You're all right, Mrs Pobgee, you're all right, my dear.'

'Wha'!'

'It's only the Doctor come to look at your eyes.' She smiled warmly at Doctor Graeme's skiing cap. 'She wants to know what's happening. Don't you, dear?'

'*We* know what's up, we do!' came Mrs Mullen's voice over the screens. 'She's fittin' the death specs on yer nose. That's what!'

'Doctor Bladyon, would you mind quieting that patient?'

Without moving John looked at Sister Balloon.

'Sister?'

She nodded and left them. But in a minute or two she was back, smiling and diffident:

'I've told her to be a good girl and I'll fetch her a cup of drinking chocolate when you've done.'

They neither of them answered her. Dr Graemes, leaning in her ski cap over Mrs Pobgee's rubbery little face, was adjusting the calibrations of the frames with precise movements of her fingers. John was watching her angrily.

'Sister!' He signalled Mrs Rogers to move outside the screens; and amiably, eagerly, she followed him.

'Yes, Doctor?'

'I think it would be as well if you sat with them a little- or just hovered round where they can see you.'

She looked doubtful and he knew that, like himself, she did not want to miss an instant of Doctor Graemes' charade:

'I think they could be troublesome, Sister. I think you *should* stay.'

'Troublesome!' cried Mrs Spark in her high tones. 'Troublesome' he says. We 'eard that, didn't we, ladies? As if we was crabs in a pot.'

'Please, Sister, do go over to her.'

'Crabs in a pot,' repeated the old lady, 'with our claws tied up. Only waitin' to be jumped in the boiler by the likes of *her*.'

'Now, Mrs Spark, make room for me on your bed end, there's a dear.'

'*Room*, for *her*, she says! For *your* bottom, you'd need a ballroom.'

'Sarah Spark, you're to settle down. Doctor is very busy.'

'She's *not*! She's just poking round poor Ellen's eyes with her pesky spectacles.'

Doctor Graemes smelled faintly of a flowery scent; a springy smell; very young. Her face, as she studied and recorded the measurements in her school notebook, was pale with tiredness and concentration. Or was it anger? He was not sure; but he longed suddenly to kiss her pale cheeks, her earnest unserious eyes, to soothe and comfort her.

128

She looked up over the top of the note book and caught his glance. Very quietly she said,

'You are singularly ineffective in dealing with these old women. I really think I shall have to ask for someone more proficient.'

'Kangaroos!' cried Mrs Spark with increased fury. 'You should be on an ostrich farm with kangaroos, you 'eartless huzzy.'

'If you order something,' John said, 'I'll see that it's given.' But she said nothing, packed her instrument into its blue lined case, closed her notebooks and pushed past him rudely.

Soundlessly she stepped back into the ward, and paused there. She stared over at the far corner where Sister Balloon was sitting on Sarah Spark's bed. It was darkish, only the autumnal light of the night-table lamp illumined the three remaining figures propped high on their railed cots.

Doctor Graemes plucked off her skiing cap with an irritable hand. She shook her head and fluffed out her pretty hair.

'Really!' she said into the shadows. 'You people are being very tiresome, very selfish. You are endangering the recovery of my thyroid patients.'

'Come near *me* an' I'll spit in yer face.'

'You will all have to be moved.'

'You needn't think as *I'm* going to die before me time.'

'Sister Rogers, I wish to speak to you in the Duty Room.'

'What you done to our chum? Our matey? What she done to you?'

'It's too bad, Doctor Blaydon . .'

'Never mind, Ellen Pobgee. Never you mind!'

'All of you! You will *all* be moved in the morning.'

'Where you're going,' came Mrs Spark's thin voice for the last time, 'you *will* be wanted. Yiss, you will, Ellen Pobgee.'

He did not go into the office with Graemes. He did not wish to have to know yet what she would prescribe for Sarah Spark, what he might later have to confirm with the Balloon who was a coward too.

129

He waited by the outer doors giving onto the compound, wondering whether she would call him, or more likely, send someone to fetch him.

For seven years, it seemed, he had been hanging about awaiting instructions in anatomy rooms, clinics and hospitals; half idling, half labouring, doing always what he was told to do. For as long, for over two thousand four hundred and fifty-five of his days he had been a beginner at everything he intended, waiting to get started, to assert himself; finally to instruct other people.

Now, as he waited, hunched against the dado on the cold wall, he was filled with the simple thoughts of impatience; the kind that had tormented him during clinical rounds in Dublin when his mind, unfastening itself from whatever was being taught or demonstrated, had seized upon the buttocks of the girl in front of him, tracing with fury her anatomy beneath the skirt; with singular and savage desire.

Attendance, having to wait, he thought, might be the half of all our troubles: indefinite expectation the begetter of our vilest deeds.

When Miss Graemes finally came down towards him in her schoolgirl clothes: her American sneakers, her bobbled skiing cap on her thistledown hair, he would concentrate only upon her hips, her thighs. Ha, he would say to himself, you've got nothing between your legs unless I put it there. Ha to you, and I'm sick of your orders and I'm not going to obey them any more. If you expect me to poison anyone for you or do anything else you demand such as standing about in the car park for your shark of a car to nose in through the snow – '

Her head down she came towards him walking very quietly down the slope of the dull linoleum.

In her ungloved hand she carried the japanned case and her school notebook; no stethoscope. She looked most sweet in her abstraction, her hair fluffing out short from beneath the woollen cap, her pointed face shadowed under the poor lighting; abstracted as a child's.

'I have ordered – ' she began, without even glancing at him.

'I don't care what you've ordered. I'm not giving it.'

She went past him in a little rush of cold, scented air and then halted to stand by the doors as though expecting that as usual he would open them for her.

As he did so, she stepped out ahead of him and spoke over her shoulder.

'Don't be silly.'

'Silly? What the – ?'

'And don't swear. You must do what is ordered.'

'What is ordered? Or what you say? Which?'

'Medicine has no room for sentiment.'

'You mean that *you* haven't.'

He caught up with her as she walked so precisely and containedly towards the car park.

'I should have said, "false sentiment." '

'There is nothing false about fear and you are frightening everybody with your measurements of the dying. You haven't even the sense to wear reassuring clothes. You come in like a vampire. The older patients are terrified of you.'

She turned to face him in the cold. 'It is neither my appearance nor my actions which disturb them, it is their own ignorance. And that cannot be allowed to stand in the way of the research which may help other people.'

'Nor in the way of your ambition, is what you mean.'

'I do mean that, yes.'

He had been going to move ahead of her but now he remained where he was; delighted.

'What have you ordered for Mrs Spark?'

'Four grains of phenobarbitone by injection.'

'I won't give it.'

'It has already been given.'

'Then I shall report it.'

'That will make no difference. If you knew a little more clinical medicine, if you were a little more detached from your feelings, you would know that ethically one is justified in making the choice between her myocardium and her anoxemia, her hysteria. And that does not take into account the pre-operative sedation of my thyroids.'

She stepped away from him. 'Like everyone else, Mrs

131

Spark must take her chance And you need not come any further with me, Doctor Blaydon.'

He remained where he was. He watched her get into her car and disappear as she stooped in its dark interior. Then, before the slit headlights could move over the cindery track and illuminate it, he turned and ran back to Granny's End.

Without seeing anybody he passed down the corridor, along the length of the ward, through the screens and to Mrs Spark's bed.

Wizened and gnomelike she lay on her pillows muttering to herself and singing snatches of old ballads. Her pulse was regular, her heartbeats strong.

18

He slept badly in the narrow bed, lumps in the flock mattress not this night conforming to his body: his mind unable, too, to accommodate Doctor Gillespie's tears, Doctor Graemes' coldness, and the continuing rattle of Ellen Pobgee's breath in his memory.

He wished it had been possible to slide something narrow and flexible down there into her mediastinum quickly, between the vocal chords and deep into the trachea to the bifurcation of the bronchi, and suck the mucus out, so to stop the silly phlegm from flapping about in there. Though it wouldn't have slowed death it would have made it easier, more efficient. For he hated the inefficiency of clinical dying; the misery of organs malfunctioning all over the body as though in the engine room of a ship everything had suddenly gone awry: pipes bursting, steam and oil gushing, wires short-circuiting, turbine blades knocking against casings; the crew panicking.

When Lynton came in with his tea she laughed at him

and plumped down on the foot of his bed, her behind as sweet as a gourd in its crisp blue and white.

'So! I can see it's no good me wasting my time here this morning.'

'Oh, Lynton!'

'If you could see yourself: puffy eyes, puffy lips and, put out your tongue – wherever were you last night? At the Nag's Head?'

'I was working.'

'I'm sure.'

'I was. Don't be so hearty.'

'Thick night for house surgeon. Out with the boys!'

'I tell you – oh Hell!'

She patted his forehead with a Dettolly hand. 'Drink your tea; you've half an hour to breakfast.'

'Don't go.'

'I've got to. The Dragon's playing up something awful this morning.'

'Well, give me a kiss first.'

She leaned. 'Your mouth's terrible – whatever were you drinking?'

'Gillespie's "Whusky".' He drank the cooling tea.

'Did he skirl the pipes for you?'

'Does he? I mean, really?'

'At New Year he does; Hogmanay or whatever they call it. And they say he'll blow it for you know who.'

'Who?'

'*That* one! Doctor Whooper. And they say she's heard more than a wee tune.'

'What? Please, Lynton. Do tell me.'

'What will you give me?'

'*Anything*. Please.'

'Well, Edgar says *that* one's seen more than his chanter. Bag and all, *she* says.'

'Golly! To look at Whooper you wouldn't think – '

'They're always the worst!' She got up. 'Me! I look pure don't I?'

'As risen cream!

'Goodbye now. See you on your "roonds".'

*

133

In the Admin room Wantage was sipping coffee over his empty breakfast plate.

'What's on for brekkers?' John asked.

'Corned beef in batter.'

John scanned the table: 'Looks as though Whooper's been and gone.'

'She'll be back. Some kid in trouble in Fevers; diphtheria, very toxic, not responding.'

'You mean to say she *told* you?'

'I took the house call, so I got all the gen. How was your night?'

'Awful! I say, Jerry, what in hell is Chlorinda Graemes up to with those frames of hers? She's got the grannies all vicious over them.'

'She's got the whole hospital in a lather. They call her Countess Dracula.'

The maid came in with fresh toast, coffee and two slices of tinned beef in a floury batter.

'What exactly *is* she measuring? What has it to do with anything?'

'Soon after death the eyeballs recede a fraction. She wants to know why, thinks there could be a link with the exophthalmos of goitre and needs a good sample for her text book. . . . By the way, has your granny croaked yet?'

'No, but any minute now. What does Chlorinda think the recession is due to?'

'Absorbtion of the post-orbital fat.' Wantage finished his cup of the greenish coffee and stood up. 'We'll be having to get *that* scooped out next; weighed and measured.'

'God, Jerry, I'm eating!'

'Then when we get someone *live* onto the table – a hit and run by the Luftwaffe, or an U.X.B., we can – '

'Oh shut up!'

'I hear Whooper. I'm off. Enjoy your batter.'

Doctor Whooper's hair looked pale green this morning, a bale of hay from which the square face jutted. Her blue coat and skirt shone at the elbows and over the buttocks. She carried the *Daily Mirror* under her right arm and her case notes in her left hand. John wondered if she had been reading the news in the lavatory.

Her eyes scanned him swiftly through the greyish lenses of her glasses as she said, 'Good morning, Blaydon,' and put the newspaper down in front of her covered plate, its black printed headline proclaiming:

TOBRUK RETAKEN

He tried to read the first dark lines of the opening paragraph, upside down. He'd lost count of the number of times the German General, Rommel, and the various British general officers had battled it out over the African coastal fortress.

He was thinking of Minna. She would want to see Tobruk in our hands again; British boots over British bones. Or would she? Minna was unknowable. She didn't mourn; instead she was sure and defiant. He saw her again as that little white-faced girl, furious for a moment – her face screwed up as it had been when he had climbed into the minefield – then smoothed out again into bodily resolve.

Yes, yes, she *was* resolved! Nothing would move her, nothing beat her; not death, nor life.

Dr Whooper's very feminine hand with its long almond-shaped finger nails came over the newsprint; a smell of Dettol, the dark blue sleeve of her dark blue jacket with four cuff buttons firmly stitched to the cloth –

'It's never any use trying to read oopside down, Doctor.'

'No.'

'D'you want it, then?'

'No thank you. . . . Sorry, yes I do. Could you leave it?'

'No, I couldn't.'

You wouldn't, he thought. You are like that; limited liability. You don't give anything of yourself except to your 'children'. You're good on the wards; but you're horrible everywhere else. I suppose you've been hurt by not being pretty. But your patients don't care about that. Children *see* it for certain. They see your big teeth and your washy grey eyes behind your grey glasses and by now, even if they've died, they love them! They love *you*; but I don't. I am not a child, I am some kind of a man and I am drawn to beautiful things: attractive children, trees and storms, fine music and poems, beautiful death and tragedy. *Your* tragedy is not beautiful because it is only disappointing.

'You can have the *Mirror* tomorrow,' she said.

'No thanks, I won't bother.'

'You look sick.'

'I was drinking last night.'

'But you were on call.'

'True; but I was still drinking.'

'In your room?'

'No, with Doctor Gillespie.' He paused to make up a lie or two. 'We played.'

'How interesting.'

'Not cards; the pipes. He played *The Bluebells of Scotland* for me. We got a bit drunk together.'

'That doesn't surprise me.'

Vexed, she got up, tall in her blue coat and skirt.

'I should keep out of that wan, if I were you.'

'Why?'

'Eccentricity is wan thing – '

He watched her pick her stethoscope off the hatstand, shuffle her *Daily Mirror* and her case notes and leave the room.

The middle telephone pealed out on the sideboard, jerking him back into the present. It was the Day Sister in the thyroid unit.

'Doctor Blaydon?'

'Yes.'

'Ellen Pobgee has just died; will *you* call Doctor Graemes, or shall I?'

'I will.'

'And you'll come over to confirm?'

'Yes, shortly.'

There was no hurry. With his foot, he pressed the carpet bell for the kitchens and when Emma came in he ordered fresh coffee, another pot of Golden Shred to take the place of the one Whooper had emptied, and fresh toast. Then he leaned further back in the chair, fitted his behind more snugly into the hollow of the oilcloth seat and ate and drank busily until he had finished nearly everything on the table.

136

It was a conscious decision to behave like this, to be unmoved. Lynton was right; he was getting too deeply into it all, too concerned, running about everywhere at everyone's behest. His case notes, fresh seen after the weekend with Minna, had surprised him: headings, classifications, even fussy red-ink underlinings – and now Mrs Pobgee was dead; Ellen Pobgee, yes, Ellen! Well, what was the hurry? Her body was still warm and wouldn't smell for hours. That was one emergency, one situation he would never hurry over. The newly dead could wait.

He poured another measure of the bitter green coffee into the cup and sipped at it, added sugar and sipped again. He would give Ellen Pobgee's eyes more time to sink back into their sockets, allow the fat a few more minutes to diminish, prescribe for Chlorinda Graemes a few more minutes in which to do whatever she was doing.

And what *might* she be doing? Writing a letter to her mother in Melbourne? For that was what he would be doing as soon as he got a moment; writing to them, to *her*, up in Anglesey, the flat little island in the Irish Sea round which the Nazi U-boats slunk beneath the freezing waves. And Chlorinda Graemes, too, must love somebody; must be striving for someone. She had no husband, no lover that he or anyone else in the Guinea Lane knew of, no woman friend apart from Doctor Strykes with whom she shared only a 'school' relationship of rank and rivalry; and, apparently, no family, no brothers or sisters.

What then would she be writing in her letter to her mother in Australia? He did not know, nor did he wish to invent it for her, since the whole notion of her self-sufficiency was alarming him again, disturbing some level of uncertainty deep within himself. And now, with the image of Ellen Pobgee's old body lying on the railed cot-bed behind the screens in Granny's End, he too, he realised, had reached an end of professional pity, of 'sumpathy' as Doctor Gillespie had called it. And, as for Ellen, of whom he knew so little and so much, her course was run. Yes, her course was run and there was nothing much more to be done for her.

He went over to the sideboard and rang Doctor Graemes' service flat in Batsford on an outside telephone. Then he grabbed his stethoscope from the back of his chair and let himself out through the brown curtained French windows into the hospital compound.

Overhead, above the clouds, the bombers were again massing for another raid on Western Germany. This morning the wrack of the soft-bellied ceiling totally hid them; their throbbings coming through the layers as muffled as the rolling of many drums beaten out of time, so that at intervals a brief and ominous counterpoint was achieved.

Hearing it, quite forgetful of what the War was about, he paused by a bare-branched tree looking up at its twigs with painful affection, his eyes wandering from their frosted ends, beaded with buds, to the low mass of the clouds in which the beating of the bombers seemed trapped like thunder. Vague love of the whole compound, of the chill November air, of the sleeping tree, even of the reverberations of the aircraft stole upon him, circled within him for seconds on end and then, as swiftly as a stooping hawk, centred upon Minna.

How marvellous, he thought, that this sound, this shaking of the heights of invisible air above the clouds should be for him a source of love. Why! Because of her, because of Minna, he loved this whole place, this ugly world and his work in it. Yet there was so very little of Minna; she was so small, physically so poorly endowed and so young. When they walked by the Thames together she had wandered near the water's edge because she liked to see herself reflected, moving under the surface. It was delightful that such shared strangeness should draw them to one another as nearly as if they had shared their earliest days.

. . . We are children together and when we listen to the destroyers flying so heavy above us, I protect her out of a need to cherish something in myself. *She* is not frightened; she is as fearless as a lamb! And out of seeing her as one, as some leggy little creature jumping up and down in the air, comes strength. How marvellous that strength should come from anything so helpless as a lamb. . . .

He shivered, tucking his hands under the hem of his white house coat, thrusting them deep into his trouser pockets to get warmth from his thighs. Oh I do love her, he thought, as he walked on towards the Thyroid Unit, yes I do; she makes my day good.

I don't need to ask her if she does love me. For love always surprises. Why! It is a continual wonderment, a turning of the corner and a cry; a cry of delight at what is revealed.

How else should that thunder of metal that clouds the air more darkly than the most thick of night be heroic, noble? How else should Lynton be so beautiful? Her clean mind, her very flesh. She, too, seems to be stemming from Minna as does the repose in everything; and how else should I see it so clearly? The goodness? Not that alone; but the scale of it all.

Though the hospital is not large, though the wards are not vast, though the world itself is quite small, I can sometimes see that what is happening in them is magnificent; that we move against a backdrop that is in scale only with the gigantic; the infinite.

19

A man was approaching him down the path. He was gaunt-looking and carried a suitcase bound up with a narrow thong of plaited leather.

A patient, obviously, come off the bus and now wandering round stupidly, not knowing where anything was, nor how to get himself admitted, nor what was to happen to him once he was admitted.

'Can I help you?'

'You can indeed!'

'You want the Administration Office, I suppose?'

'Yes, I'm under Doctor Leigh.' he coughed self-consciously putting a signet-ringed hand to his mouth. 'I should say, "Referred by Doctor Leigh" to avoid the old "Ho! ho!"'

John looked at him blankly. He knew, or thought he knew, exactly what the man meant; but he disliked both his familiarity and his lack of respect for his white coat and his stethoscope.

'The old Ho Ho?' he asked.

'*Under* the doctor! Doctor. You know? Large lady, thin physician! Ho ho! Joke over.'

The silence spun itself out. They caught eyes.

'You were referred from St Jude's, I suppose? And you have a letter of admission from Doctor Leigh?'

From the breast pocket of his British Warm the man produced an envelope:

'All present and correct! What does A do now?'

'A?' John asked, disliking more than ever his cocky air.

'Yours truly. *Me*. You *are* a rookie doctor, aren't you? Pardon me. One picks up these things Stateside.'

'Yes, I am.'

'Well then, I ask again. Where should we go now? Where do you wish your little victim to proceed to?'

'Well, you see that low building over there behind the row of sycamores? That's the administration block. Just push your way in and, on your left down the corridor, you'll see the office. There'll be two or three girls working in there; they'll tell you what to do.'

'Thank you, Doc.' He put his once elegant pig-skin case down on the asphalt. The tongued metal plates which were supposed to hold it shut were both sprung open; the near one was held into the leather only by a single brass stud.

'Excuse me, but do you know Doctor Leigh?'

'I work for him sometimes.'

'You *do*?'

'Yes, what's your trouble?'

'Ulsters – in my stomach.'

'Pretty bad?'

'Terrible! Like rats gnawing inside you, biting at your innards, and medication doesn't do any darn good. I've tried everything; magnesium by the truckload, pills, peppermint, lemon-lime, sassafras-flavoured, enough to pave the side-

140

walk to Earl's Court – and now those new brown Dutch ones they got in before the hostilities started. I've – '

'Any bleeding?'

'You can bet on it! That's why Doctor Leigh – '

'When you vomit?'

'Yes, and the other way. My motions are frequently blackish. That's blood – part-digested blood, isn't it?'

'It's what we call "altered blood".'

'Dead give-away, of course – when one knows.'

This fellow was more than cheeky; he was insolent, slick. His slyness awoke the slyness in John.

'You mean?' John asked.

'I mean black blood in the motions; secondary anaemia, Doc; that's all.'

'I see. Now, do you know where to go?'

'Yes, into that low block over there. "Admin", *you* said.'

'I didn't, actually. I said "administration".'

The man smiled: he gave a little shrug of his rubbed British Warm as though he had replied, 'Same thing, isn't it? Really?' and picked up his suitcase in his gloved hand.

'So you're sometimes with Doctor Leigh? That's a bit of luck for me, I guess.' He smiled again and added interrogatively, 'Or is it, Doc?'

'I hope so.'

'Oh, it *is*! Oh, Christ!'

'What's the matter?'

'Just this rat, this goddam rat in – '

He had dropped his suitcase back onto the asphalt path. Grey-faced now he was bending forward subserviently to the pain in the pit of his stomach. Both his gloved hands were pressing against the open lapels of his British Warm, against the silk school tie which had flopped out from his jacket.

'Jesus Christ!' he said, again almost to himself. 'Likewise – ! There's a proprietory in my left hand pocket. Would you – ?'

John pulled out the bottle from the snug velvet-lined pocket of the military coat. 'How many do you take? Can you manage without water?'

'I'm sweating, aren't I? Four to six – chewed. Jesus Christ!

141

I *am* sweating! Look at my glove, Doctor. No, don't say anything. I couldn't hear you till this rat – '

He chewed busily in the cold, his tanned, slightly hollowed cheeks moving up and down the sides of his head.

John looked importantly at his wrist watch. 'I think I'd better take you over myself. What's your name?'

'Bellayr, Christopher Bellayr; my friends call me Kit; but you needn't worry, Doc. I didn't get your name because you didn't give it – I can totter as far as – '

'Blaydon.'

'Doctor Blaydon. I must remember that. On the other hand, I won't have to, will I? Not if you're "under", ho, ho! I should say "with", Doctor Leigh?'

'You can manage then, Mr Bellayr?'

'I should think so. Have to, won't I?'

'I shall see you this evening.'

'When I'm all tucked up in my little – thank you – Doc. *John* Blaydon, wasn't it?'

'John? How did you know that?'

'You told me it, Doctor.'

'Did I?'

'Or maybe I heard it somewhere. Well, till this evening. He picked up his suitcase, the frock of the glove turned back stylishly to reveal the white strap of his wristwatch. 'Oh, *ulsters!*' he added. 'A joke only. Though of course I defer to – '

Laughing to himself he went on his way beneath the heavy clouds.

20

Lynton was awaiting him in the foyer of the Gynae ward. She had on a little scent and a very little make-up; it was impossible not to express his pleasure. He was most pleased to see her, so real and fresh, so natural in the disinfected passageway; also it was very pleasant not to be still in the compound talking to Mr Bellayr.

'What are *you* doing here? I thought you were with the Dragon.'

She touched his hand, gripped it briefly with her own strong fingers. 'You feeling better now?'

'A lot, Lynton.' He looked both ways up and down the corridor.

She smiled up at him. 'Sister Thorpe's in the ward. So be quick!'

He put his arms round her shoulders and thrust himself forward into the softness, her lips soft, softening more in their kisses.

'You're nice,' she said, slightly spoiling it. 'But you know that, don't you?'

He wanted to say, 'No, I don't; not if people say it – like that,' but he didn't want to be ungracious to her: especially after that uneasy encounter in the compound. And suddenly he thought: to hell with Bellayr! I'm damned if I am going to feel cheap on *his* account.

'What's the matter?' she asked, perhaps feeling in him something recoil from her.

'Oh, nothing.'

'*Nothing*? Then why did you pull away?' She pressed against him.

He was quiet in the shadow that had brushed his mind. He pulled away again, slightly out of breath.

'Well, at least you still pant,' she said.

His forehead felt cold with sweat. He wiped it with his hand. 'I'm sorry, Lynton.'

'That's all right. I'm getting used to you. But I've got to run now – back to the Dragon.'

'You're sweet.'

'Like stolen fruit.' She smiled. 'We must watch out, though. I don't know what the Ancient Mariner would have said if she'd caught us.'

'Very little, I should think. Did you say you were going over to the medical unit?'

'Yes, you're still "on" for Doctor Wantage aren't you?'

'Only till lunchtime – if he isn't late getting back from town. Oh! And there's a new patient awaiting you – a peptic ulcer. Pretty dire!'

'Oh that would be Major Bellayr,' she said. 'We know all about him. Doctor Leigh rang up from St Jude's. He wants him on the bypass straight away.'

'*Major* Bellayr! What the – ! Has he really been in the Army?'

'Invalided out – I've got to run. Will you be over to pass the tube?'

'It looks like it. Damn! Why is Wantage always "off" when extra jobs crop up?'

'I'm "off" tonight! Want to take me out for a drink?'

'Yes, where?'

'Anywhere you like. I could be ready by seven.'

'I'll come over for you. Do you mind the Nag's Head?'

She signalled him to silence and turning round he saw Sister Thorpe coming out of the doors to the ward. She was closely followed by Maureen Bason.

He went towards her. 'I'm running late, Sister; but I'm ready for you now.'

Though she smiled at him, she walked past him and went into her office. He found himself looking straight into Maureen Bason's flushed face and was reminded that he had imagined her back in Thyroids with the grannies; forgetting her transfer to Gynae after her 'replacement'.

'You're leaving us, then, Maureen?'

'I'm so excited I could scream. My fiancé's coming for me any minute now. He's taking me to his Mum's, and all the family's to be there in Hammersmith; his sister, Angie, and his brother, Robert. Oh, and he's got a forty-eight from Aldershot and an extra stripe up to full corporal!'

'Wonderful!'

'That means more pay. We might even run to a little honeymoon somewhere – Brighton. Not the posh side, of course; more like Rottingdean. But – '

She lowered her voice; her left hand with its bright engagement ring caught hold of one of his fingers as she leaned closer. 'It will be all right – ? Won't it? I mean, when – ' She stopped.

He could smell her coaly wartime toothpaste and saw the tip of her coated tongue between her teeth.

'Yes, it will be all right on the night.'

'I didn't like to say it.'

'I know.'

'It's just the stitches. I can't help wondering what – '

'What will happen when he pushes?'

'That's it. It does seem funny talking to a man about such things; but you are a doctor, aren't you?'

'Of course I am.' He was seeing her coral pink vulva as if it were her mouth, the lips spread, the puckered entrance to the little bicycle tube of bowel which must serve her as vagina. He saw even its limp blind-end tied with catgut, floating about behind her bladder amongst the coils of her intestines.

'Norm thinks I just had something cut.'

'Does he know you can't have children?'

'We're going to adopt. Norm says all kids are strangers really, so why not get one you like the look of? Oh, and he's proud of me having this done. He says that he's read that society women have *their* hymens cut before the honeymoon – ' She glanced towards Sister Thorpe's door – 'That is, if they've still got them. Norm says – '

'Perhaps we should have got Mr de Fleur to do your replacement then.'

'Why?'

'Well, he did Gracie Fields' hysterectomy and one of the Royal Duchesses.'

'I think I'd rather have a woman do me. Doctor Graemes is nice, isn't she?'

'Quite nice, yes.'

'Don't you like her?'

'She's a good surgeon.' He held out his hand; he half wanted to get away. The thought of Miss Bason in bed in Brighton with Norm worried him, the primitive mechanics of this thing for which men were prepared to kill one another; for which, in a way, wars were fought. 'Goodbye, Maureen. Send us all a postcard from Brighton.'

'A seaside one, Doctor Blaydon?'

'Yes.'

'They're ever so naughty.'

'Choose a good one for me.'

'I will if they haven't all disappeared with the New Zealand butter and the York hams.' She turned and ran back to the ward.

He went into the office: 'Good morning, Sister.'

'Good morning, Doctor. You're looking wan today – in need of tea I suppose – seedy. Will you have an arrowroot with your cup?'

'Thank you.'

'Oh me, oh my! Look at this yellow sugar! Nowadays our empire doesn't seem able to get the demarara out of it, does it?'

She stirred his cup for him, tapped the teaspoon twice on the rim to shake off the drops of tea and replaced it beside the cup in its saucer.

'As we used to say, you're a little "exercised" this morning, aren't you?'

'Yes I am – a little.'

'Well, there's no necessity for you to do your round here just now. Mrs Wilkes' pyelitis is settling down, her B.S.R. is normal and her leucocyte count is nearly so.' She drank carefully but greedily from her full cup. 'I heard you talking with Miss Bason. You did that very nicely I thought. "Three cheers!" I said to myself. My patients – our sex, you know – tend to be very down-to earth and your sex*will* tend to be so very airy fairy with us. I suppose it could be the old nursery rhymes, the Victorian ones.'

'Which ones?'

'I was reminded of:

> *Sugar and spice and all things nice.*
> That's *what little girls are made of.*

Quite untrue as we both well know.'

He laughed. 'Is it, Sister?'

'But of course. We are quite as substantial as men.'

'You mean physically?'

'More in our emotions. We are not so harried. Men are

146

always in *such* a helter-skelter! My Mama used to say that she couldn't imagine how you could all be so very clever; for she didn't know when you ever got the time to *think*!'

'But it used to be women who had the vapours and fainted all over the place.'

'Puff! That was the fashion; and, in its day, most handy. One could get all the attention, be alone with the person of one's choice – and be thought a poet at the same time. Now do take your tea or I shall have to minister to *you*. For you look quite done up.' She sipped again. 'Was it Miss Bason, or some other encounter?'

'A different one.'

'A patient, of course?' She waited for him to reply but he said nothing. 'Well, well! If you don't wish to tell me, you don't.'

'I was trying to *think*, Sister. And now it does seem ridiculous.'

'People may say that of quite grave matters.'

'A man I met just now; a patient, a new one who came in on his own. He seemed a bit lost in the compound – but sure of himself too. In pain as well – perhaps quite brave, but angry about it too. I felt that he might collapse at any moment – emotionally.'

She put her cup back into the saucer with a little clatter; he noticed that she frowned at her clumsiness and that this morning the silver-cheeked medal was back on her pleated bodice.

'And you are not so much concerned on his account as on your own?'

'That could be true.'

'You are afraid, perhaps, not that he will collapse, but that *you* might?' She smiled at him. 'Oh dear me! How we all do dodge the home questions about ourselves. I believe that you are too eager about everything; you must slow down a little, that's all. Now, tell me, have you seen my Miss Frobisher today?'

'No, I haven't.' He knew that she was distracting him and he felt not angry, but vexed at her lightness. If she was so exact, so right; if she did know so much about men, their

147

dissatisfaction, then she should also be more sympathetic. 'Sumpathy', he remembered with fresh irritation.

'Not only that, Sister; but I took an instant dislike to this man; and he's not even going to be my patient.'

'Then you should be careful; vigilant.' She broke her arrowroot biscuit neatly, dipped half of it into her tea before eating it. 'I never trust much to my instincts; they're so often wrong; but that being said, I *am* more wary when my body stirs. Go and face him if you must. I think that if you don't, he will seek out *you*. People are like that; quite often we do scent one another out; the little animal in us all.'

He got up. 'That's a good idea.'

'There are such men; wars throw them up; they sense a challenge – and often their response to rivals has little to do with their real nature.'

'How do you mean?'

'They always have courage; but they can be bad just the same – very bad.'

But bravery is so fine; I mean, it seems it. I keep wondering whether *I* have it.'

'Who knows?' She laughed. 'Who knows? Have you seen? – No, I already asked you that. I am worried about Minna; she was going to have come over for tea with me – and never a word from her!'

'I'll find out. Would it be all right if I did my round with you after tea? We've got to – it looks as though I shall have to pass a deep stomach tube on this Bellayr man.'

'Of course. And after that, I think you should take forty winks on your bed.'

By the door he paused: 'I do like that medal of yours. What exactly is it?'

'It's a very young St Michael. It was given to me by a soldier friend many years ago. It was a family thing of his.'

A lover long ago, he decided.

'Thanks for the tea and the advice.' And the 'sumpathy' he added as he hurried over to the Medical Unit.

21

Minna was not in the office. Her table between the filing cabinets was empty save for her potted meat jar with the twigs of last Easter's pussy willow in it.

'Where is Miss Frobisher?' he asked the senior secretary.

'She's off sick, Doctor Blaydon.'

His heart muscle had not speeded up yet. 'What with? Do you know?'

'Oh, just her winter cough. Doctor Gillespie packed her off to bed.'

'Who's looking after her? Is he, or is it Doctor Whooper?'

'It's Doctor Gillespie.

'Thank you. Have you got Major Bellayr's case notes from St Jude's yet?'

'Yes, the Major brought them in himself. A little irregular; but he says that Doctor Leigh obtained them for him.'

'May I have them? I'll turn them over to Doctor Wantage as soon as he gets back.'

She handed them over the mahogany bar and he grasped them, holding the yellowish folder tightly, not to let it escape him; and to prevent himself from sinking into an anxiety over Minna. When Sister had asked twice about her, he should have known there was something wrong. Typically Minna had gone off without telling him; she could so easily have called him in his machine room, or the Admin brown room. Now she would be in bed, and tonight, this being Sunday, there would be a séance going on in the sitting room below. Her damn silly mother ghosting with her friends; himself unable to be upstairs with Minna because he would be out with Lynton.

149

He flopped into one of the bentwood chairs and opened Major Bellayr's case notes, prepared to be irritated by everything he read.

Where the blazes had the Major got his rank, for instance? He did not look like a regular soldier. His shoulders were not 'separate' from the rest of him; they were not noticeable. He did not look, either, as if he ever drank at all, he had not got a decent drinky face. He looked like a teetotaller.

True, the regular Army was frightful, run by a lot of snobs and fools; but it was not 'common' like the Air Force, nor was it stiffened with the pretentions of the 'Senior Service' as the Royal Navy called itself. The wartime Army got most of the decent, uncalculating men into it; chaps who had not been clever enough to look ahead; who were not such show-offs as the ones in the other Services – apart of course from the commandoes; those schoolboy killers.

So Major Bellayr had been invalided out of the press corps, and he had not been even a war correspondent, just a photographer; and he had moved to America.

In New York he had been what he had termed an 'art photographer; and while there he had developed the symptoms of peptic ulcer when working for a glossy magazine based on Fifth Avenue. He had resigned on the grounds of ill-health and had set up in a private studio in SoHo. He had had three episodes of 'coffee-ground' vomiting; the presence of a gastric ulcer in the classical site above the plyorus had been confirmed by X ray following a barium meal.

He had been married twice: in 1927 to an English girl who was unnamed in the report, and in 1930, in New York, to a girl named Deborah Francis, a journalist, after a 'divorce by mutual consent'. Now, childless, and presumably, again separated, he gave his next of kin to be his 'landlady' in Earl's Court Terrace, London SW12.

It was an uninformative background. Where now was his second wife and why had neither of his young wives had children? And why had each marriage lasted so short a while?

John got up and rang the Dragon over in Medical. Major

150

Bellayr was in bed and had been prepared. Nurse Lynton had set the trolley; they were awaiting him. He looked at his watch. It was only half past eleven and Wantage could well be much later than usual. . . .

Lynton wheeled the trolley behind him as he went up the ward. The Dragon, leaner than ever in the December light, had remained in her office drinking powdered Swiss coffee from America.

Though he did not much care for the Dragon, he did not dislike her. She was an unknown for whom he had feelings only when he thought of her in relation to Lynton of whom he was so possessive that he was alert to anyone who had dealings with her.

It amazed him that the Dragon should have any command of Lynton, could order her about and interfere with her life by changing her hours of duty or days off. Though he could quite comfortably imagine himself doing such things, it seemed outrageous that anyone else should; particularly a woman and a plain one at that.

She looked like a bone in clothes. For him she was so long past the age of boniness, which he thought was about thirty-seven, that in a lazy sort of way he imagined her as a femur or a humerus decked out with nondescript underwear and crowned by a thin, sour-set face.

On her bad days, when only a bed or two was occupied, she would pick a quarrel with herself over some fancied dust or unswept tealeaves and hurl the empty beds one after another down the length of the ward.

And no one minded; not even the probationer who had done the cleaning. In such quiet rage, the Dragon, so tall and loosely jointed in her dark blue and white, her cap awry above her hooked nose, seemed fairy-like and right, a warring spirit.

This afternoon she watched Lynton and himself walk down to the Major's bed and then went back to her room to get on with her *Telegraph* crossword.

John held the green screens open for Lynton and saw that her face was now demure and professional, that she was being contained in her movements.

151

'We meet again,' said Major Bellayr from his pillows.

'Yes. I don't know whether you've been told anything or not – '

'I've been told a few things in my time!' His glance touched and relinquished Lynton.

'What we plan is to attempt to heal your stomach ulcer by a new method which Doctor Leigh is investigating.'

'And what would that be?'

'That would be – ' John stopped. 'That *is* a matter – '

'You don't like the Americanism?' The Major smiled up at Lynton again.

'That is a matter,' John resumed, 'of getting a small stomach tube into you through the gastric cavity, bypassing the ulcer site and entering the duodenum through the pylorus.'

'Sounds fun, doesn't it, Nurse?' The Major had flicked his blond eyebrows up at her in a bid for complicit humour. 'Am I to be the first?'

'Amongst the first fifty or so – yes. Doctor Leigh is getting some quite encouraging results. By means of the tube we are able to feed you liquids adequately without stimulating the gastric mucosa.'

'I'm sure!'

'– Without triggering off the hydrochloric acid from the stomach wall. It gives the ulcerated surface a chance to heal.'

'And very nice too! Provided. . . .' The Major's clear eyes were on John and, as he waited, his gold-ringed right hand beat a little tattoo on the fold of the sheet over his chest.

'Provided what?' John asked.

'Provided it *works*, Doctor Blaydon! Liquids, you mentioned. How long is this ploy liable to last?'

'It depends, of course. About three weeks or a month.'

'Liquids,' the Major's left hand joined in the tattoo, 'through a toob don't sound too good to a citizen who enjoys his food.'

'Well, the diet isn't exactly tasty; but at least you don't feel hungry.'

'Oh ho! Everybody laugh!' The Major's fine-boned fingers

lay still and spread on the sheet. 'Excuse *me*! But I don't eat for hunger – I eat for pleasure, for gratification.'

'I understand that; but if you don't mind, I think we should start.'

'Seems to me that – '

'Show Major Bellayr the tube, please Nurse. Now, Major, it's only a matter of swallowing a bit of this at a time, and, as you see, it's quite thin. When it touches your soft palate and the back of the throat it may make you gag for a moment. But – '

The Major stretched out his ringed hand. 'Any objection if I look at this gismo before you throttle me with it? Christ! It's *some* length – what's *that*?'

'A small weighted end-piece to show up on the X-ray so that we'll know we're in the duodenum.'

'And what's this slime on everything?'

'That is glycerine.'

The Major waved the kidney dish away.

'I think I should warn you that I'm very body-conscious; I don't believe I'm the right kind of guy for this noo guinea-pig medicine.' He paused to smile flashily at Lynton. 'That is, if you don't mind!'

John glanced at Lynton. She disliked rude patients and behind her self-control she had a quick temper.

'Perhaps Major Bellayr would like to take his discharge?' She replaced the kidney tray on the trolley and with her eyes on the Major's face spoke to John. 'Shall I notify Sister?'

'Would you like to be discharged?' John asked him.

The Major sat up against his pillows, his faintly tanned face expressionless and smooth,

'Ah, the lady speaks and she means it! Bluff called and all that. The Major to his discharge, suggests she, in that cool accent!' He whistled suddenly and leaned back again, 'Jeese! Hold it will you! This rat. This son-of-a-bitch rat-'

His face blanched to flesh yellow, his blue eyes remained fixed on the Nurse's face as his hands came up to press against the pit of his stomach. Lynton flushed: the blood crept up from her starched collar over her neck and jaw to her cheeks.

153

'Ah!' said the Major after a moment, 'It's letting go and the lady wins. She's made up our minds for us, I guess? So let's get cracking – though I do warn you that where other guys gag, *I* puke.'

'Very well. Now we're going to have to take away your pillows for a bit so that you can lie absolutely flat. . . .'

Wantage was in the brown room drinking dark tan tea from a beaker on a plastic tray. He looked up as John came in:

'How did it go? Your turn-aboot?'

'Oh, all right – no panics. My granny croaked and you've got a new patient in Medical – a sort of semi-American – at least he's been there long enough to collect a nasal drawl.'

'What's the pathology?'

'Peptic ulcer, pretty big. Quite a few haematemeses. Dear old Leigh sent him in via St Jude's Outpatients. He wants to try him on the gastric bypass. I slipped one in.'

'Thanks. Why didn't you slip in a little hydrocyanic acid at the same time?'

'He's not American, Jerry.'

'He'll be an anti-second fronter – a Republican wart.'

'He may be; but he's British – Cockney behind the American, minor public school on the top; frightened and a bully too.'

'What's his name?'

'Major Bellayr.'

'*Major*! He ought to be in one of *their* military hospitals.'

'No; invalided out – review board. He was a press photographer in our Army. Had his own studio in New York at one time.'

'What kind of studio?'

'Portraits mainly, I gather.'

'Christ! Why *did*n't you poison him? He'll be a Fascist and a pervert – a pornographer. I know the type.'

'I thought *you*'d prefer to do it.' John opened the door. 'I'm off now. I'm taking Lynton out for a drink. But first I'm going to go and see Minna. She's sick.'

'Christ! A hard-core Americanised bastard! I never thought we'd get one here at Guinea Lane.'

154

22

He hurried across the compound in the unlit dark; a few fiery pinhole points in the canvas of heaven, the air stilled with the December cold, and the horizon, over beyond the staff housing, pale and blank.

By the back door of Mrs Frobisher's house, he paused. It would look a little familiar to bring her out there; she was rather a common woman; he knew from Minna that she was very house-proud and hygienic; she would set a little guard against him if he brought her through to her back kitchen on a séance night . . . Also, it was lowering his dignity as a doctor; she would think less of him from the start.

Swinging his arms he walked round the asphalt perimeter path past the cement ponds and their standing ibises to the main gate with its twin unlighted globes.

He glanced across the road at the sewage docks. Through the black railings he could just make out the mixers as, dully, they turned above the circular sludge pits; huge clocks buried in the ground with only the minute hand slowly revolving. A thin scent of soapy water and blunted sewage lay lightly in the air; a smell as innocent as bathrooms, making humanity seem very childlike and good.

His glance wandered past the powerhouse chimneys; past more distant housing, ancient spires, bare oaks and elms, close-boughed fir trees, to where London itself cobbled the horizon with black rectangles and domes.

Waiting, he thought, the whole city awaiting in silence, a change that is bound to come. All the people in that just-visible city are sitting out Time; *this* time; not sullenly, not happily, but with the certainty with which people await a birth; as confidently as children await joy.

He knocked on the door of the small two-storey house and it opened almost immediately.

'Oh, thank you. I wondered if I might see Minna – I hear she's unwell.'

'It's Doctor Blaydon, isn't it? Come in, Doctor. Minna's told me about you. She's upstairs.'

He followed her into the lighted sitting room. The furniture seemed almost to jump at him in the sudden transition to the bright electric lights.

'I'm expecting company, so you must excuse me.'

'Of course.'

'I suppose you'd like tea, would you?'

'Well – '

'It's no trouble. The kettle's on – and we're not short of coupons this month.'

She had very definite brown eyes, he noticed, not a bit like Minna's. She seemed only to have eyes; for her face was a parchmenty white and the colour of her hair was indeterminate. Whatever shade it had once been, it had faded and she had left it like that. She seemed customarily tired.

'There's this chair,' she suggested, 'or the couch. I'll just tell Minna you're here. She'll want to – '

In her dusty velvet housecoat and the incongruous high heeled shoes she wore with it, she left him on the sofa opposite the upright piano, closing the door behind her.

A small 'candled' gas fire was glowing in the tiled fireplace. There was an overhead light in a fringed shade, and two standard lamps. The black piano was open and over its yellow keys there was a piece of sheet music on the bracket which, without getting up, he couldn't read. On the mantelpiece there was only the plaster figure of a little boy in yellow breeches and buckled shoes.

At the far end of the room there stood an oval dining table with a set of vertical and uncomfortable-looking chairs ranged round it. In front of one chair there was a square white blotter with a school exercise book and two yellow pencils; facing the opposite chair was a heart-shaped planch-ette board, its metal wheels reflected on the table surface.

He looked round the entire room for photographs. He hoped to see family pictures: Minna as a little girl; plump perhaps, with the rounded cheeks and stomach of child-hood; snaps of her in early adolescence: sulky, furious, sullen with indistinct longings. Pictures of the sister who had given her the vanity bag; Elsie? Would she be of the same mould or better developed? Saliva dried up in his mouth at the thought of Elsie's, of Minna's body filled out, an amphora of hips, gently curved, small breasts behind white silk.

And her father, dead in the desert surrounding Tobruk! Why was there no picture of him? He would have liked to know whether the certainty, the directness, came from Edgar Frobisher.

Mrs Frobisher came in with a fine wooden tray of tea, a Sheraton tray, he noticed; perhaps from some 'good' family where either she or Minna's grandmother had been in service.

She put the tray on the coffee table, poured the tea and sat down opposite him on the piano stool.

'Every December, Doctor,' she said. 'Regular as clock-work she comes down with her chest. That's Minna! Well, I'm sure I don't know. Do you take sugar, Doctor?'

'Yes, please. Is she asthmatic? I mean, does she have asthma?'

'Asthma; no. She *is* nervy; but she doesn't have asthma. She did wet the bed a year or two; but she never bit her nails.' She sighed. 'I'm sure I don't know.'

'And Doctor Gillespie? He's looking in on her?'

'Who? Doctor Gillespie? Oh yes, he's in and out.'

'He hasn't told you much, then?'

'Not him! One of the silent ones is doctor. But then.' She put her cup down, hardly tasted. 'Well, we'd best go up. I've got friends coming – our little get-together. If you was staying for a bit you might hear the piano – but I know how busy you doctors always are.'

Lynton, he thought. Yes, I shall be busy with her tonight.

157

She's reliable, is Lynton; always in a good mood except with Major Bellayr.

He got up. 'Do you sing hymns? I mean, is it a religious gathering?'

'*Hymns*! I should say not! Ah, they don't like hymns; none of them don't care for them. This way, Doctor. The reason we meet Sundays is because it's the only evening we're all free; and even then – '

'Yes, I can see it would be difficult. I don't like hymns either.'

'Well, you're in good company then. *Our* spirit guides can't abide them, not one of them. Someone to see you, Minna. I'll get out a chair for you, Doctor. Shall I take your work, dear?'

'No, I want it.'

'You can't very well do it with visitors, now, can you?'

'Doctor John isn't a visitor.'

Mrs Frobisher put a hand to her dull hair and looked in the dressing table mirror. 'There goes the bell; it will be Ruby Webb, come to run through the music. I'll leave you to let yourself out then, Doctor Blaydon.' For a moment she gazed at him steadily, then added, 'Unless you want to look in on us on your way through?'

'Thank you, but I've got to meet – I've got someone to see at seven.'

'You young people! Never rest, do you?' She glanced at her daughter. 'Well, I'm sure I don't know.'

The bedroom door closed behind her and John took Minna's hand. The fingers of her left hand, soft as sea anenomes, curled round the little finger side of his palm:

'Now, how can I take your pulse if you do that?'

'I don't want you counting it. You're off in your mind, aren't you? It's Nurse Lynton, isn't it?'

'Yes.'

'She your favourite, then?'

'I don't know.'

'She better not be.'

'What are you making?'

'Jewels. You could sit on our bed.'

He looked at the homely tray and the cardboard boxes

full of bits of metal: finger-ring blanks, glistening fragments of 'paste', tiny mirrors, thin chains.

'Have you been doing this long? What do you make?'

'Only winters and when my chest plays up. Rings and necklaces mostly; service brooches and identity bracelets a time or two.'

He picked up a box of small shields, insignia: the Royal Artillery, the King's Own Yorkshire, the Royal Electrical and Mechanical Engineers, the Oxford and Buckinghamshire Light Infantry, the Royal West Kents.

'Do you fancy any of them there?' she asked, coughing.

'I don't know.' He let them trickle back into the box.

'You don't know much this evening, do you? Ooh, I'm not half wheezy.'

'Sister Thorpe was asking after you, she was rather upset.'

When she had finished a fresh bout of coughing, her face red with the blood forced up into it, she added, 'She told you I never came to tea and she said as you was to look me up, didn't she?'

'Why didn't you tell anyone you were ill? Why didn't you ring *me*?'

'I couldn't be bothered with them I love. I only told Mrs Stacks in the office to tell the Doctor – and Mum.'

He was looking at one of the brooches, the Royal Army Medical Corps – silver snakes round a silver stick.

'But you love *her* – and you told her.'

'She's my mother, that's all. What else did *she* say?'

'Sister Thorpe? She said that you often slipped over there for tea and that – '

'I meant what she *told* you; I meant what she said you was to do?'

She was threading a chain through the clasp of an ugly chromium pendant. He saw her very pale fingertips touching, exploring the minute 'bead' that opened and closed the circle. How soft they were! They were softer than the most pallid green grapes from the Mediterranean. Why! to have one's hands touched by those, one's body anywhere, would be ravishing, exquisite.

'She told me, she advised me, to do something straight away.'

'For a patient, was it?'

'Yes, what else would it be? Are you still on about poor Lynton?'

'Poor?' she asked.

'She *is* poor. We all are, in a way.'

'I'm not. Why you so angry?'

'I'm not angry.'

'Frightened then?' She picked up a Major's 'pip', a little brass crown. 'You come in ever so scared.'

He said nothing.

'Is it Mum?'

'No.'

'You didn't see nothing in our parlour? Mum or Ruby Webb didn't say nothing as would pickle you a minute?'

'*Pickle* me?'

'Well, what is it then? Not that lot downstairs: their silly spirits?'

'It wasn't anything like that.'

He was looking at her with what he hoped was not too obvious a longing; to have her all along the length of himself, her pale little face beneath his, those anemone hands, her grapy fingertips stroking the back of his neck, his shoulders.

Downstairs, the piano started to play quietly; Mrs Webb, in a hat he imagined, playing '*Somewhere over the Rainbow*'.

'You're right,' he said. 'They *are* silly; the spirits or whatever they are.'

'Course they are. Else why would they come back here when they're always on about how nice it is where they're at?'

'If you were a spirit, would you come back?'

'I *am* a spirit!'

'But not *just*,' he insisted. 'You have got fingers!'

'I can do a lot with them, too.'

'I wish you'd show me.'

'I am showing you; but you mean something else, don't you?'

He nodded.

She looked across the tinsel tray at him; her gaze very gentle, he thought.

'Do you ever feel you could make *anything*?' she asked. 'Anything you've ever seen, like the Taj Mahal in the Hippodrome?'

'I do, sometimes.'

'Funny, isn't it? And them in their other world. Fancy coming back *here*! Wherever that lot are they must be ever so dull if they want to talk to Ruby Webb.'

'*And* to your mother.'

'Mum lost our dad – she's still in shock, isn't she? Do you mind the piano music? *I* quite like it.'

'I do too; especially sentimental songs like that.'

Minna picked up a pair of tweezers and placed an oval agate between the claws of a ring. 'Where you taking her tonight?'

'Who, Lynton?'

'*Her*!'

'Oh, the Nag's Head.'

'Not into where we was?'

'No, not the Chatsworth.'

'You can if you want, if it helps you.'

'You don't like Lynton. Do you hate her?'

'I don't hate no one except the bombers sometimes – the men as drives them.'

'Do you hate the Americans more than the Germans, or us – the British?'

She didn't answer for a while. He watched greedily as, with the tweezers, she squeezed the claws of the bezel together over the piece of frosty agate. She was frowning with concentration:

'The pilots, navigators and such; all the crews as go up in them and the under-generals who send them are hasty folk, is all. They're pushing our world ahead of us, before time. But that fat Churchill; he's just a cry-baby.'

He took her hand and held it amid the rings on her tray. In the silence welling up from the sitting room, the cessation of the piano music, he studied her, the thin nightdress over the ribby chest, a coil of one of her own chains round her neck, curved as it crossed over the clavicles.

'Would you ever like to get married?' he asked.

'Who to?'

161

'To anyone.'

'Not specially.'

He saw that the movement of her fingers had hesitated only fractionally and, until he thought that she might have been controlling them, was for a moment angry.

'Aren't you lonely, with no one of your own?'

'Course I am. Everyone is.' She looked up. 'But you've no cause to be cruel.'

'Do you like *me*?'

She slipped the ring, with its frosty little stone, over her middle finger.

'Yes.'

'I mean, do you like me a lot?'

'For ever I do.'

'That's good.'

'What is?' she asked.

'You are right. I *am* a bit scared at the moment; I *was*. I mean.'

She patted her bed. 'You could get right on the bed with me, like at Downchurch. You could move this old tray out the way to the book chest – that one there, under the window – and get under the eider with us.'

He lay down beside her and she wriggled lower beneath the sheets. 'Could you be taking my germs? Us kissing like this?'

'Probably.'

'Doctor Gillespie says it's not all that catching.' She sighed. 'It's lovely to be warm hugged; it's blissful.'

'Yes it is, but – '

'I could go to sleep straight now.'

'I wanted to ask you something, Minna.'

She lay without moving; so still that he grew alarmed at the course her thoughts might be taking. Whereas with Lynton he could make guesses enough to satisfy himself –

Minna sat up a little, propping herself on her left elbow, looking level into his eyes.

'You want the monkey business too. You can get that from her.' She smiled. 'Satisfied?'

'No, of course not.'

'Well, put out the light and hold us closer.'

162

23

Doctor Gillespie caught him as he was crossing the empty compound on his way back from Lynton's bed-sitter in Sister Balloon's house. A little snow had fallen during the evening, the silver gleam of it giving grey light back to the clouds and definition to the black boles of the sycamores and elms.

Though he had heard footsteps in the distance, muffled by the snow, not fading off in a different direction, he had not given them much attention for he was thinking about Lynton, the Eden he had just been thrust out of when she had left him to go on night duty. But the dismissal, after all, was only temporary; for that garden was never far away; one could always return to its bounds and, in the pain of every love-affair, even re-enter it.

He paused for a moment; someone was in a hurry. The distant footfalls of whoever was out there on the far side of the compound were rapid.

He waited by one of the circular pools, narrowing his eyes to see better through the stillness and gloom. He was out of breath, not physically but in the pleasurable mess of his emotions. To have passed such an evening; first with Minna and then with Lynton had made him exultant. *He* was no poor fish: *Whoosh!*

At the Nag's Head a porter from one of the hospitals had given Lynton a gold and black packet of smuggled cigarettes from Malta, and she had passed them on to him. He lighted one now, pulling the Turkish smoke deep into his lungs, waiting for whoever it was, hoping it wasn't some 'emurgency' Wantage was unable to manage on his own.

'Why, man!' Doctor Gillespie began as soon as he had

reached him. 'Why didna ye bide when ye heard me hasting after?'

'I'm sorry, Sir. I was in a hurry to get to my room.'

'Aye! Your sprint was all in the ding of your clogs.' He put a finger to his lips. 'But whist! I want a talk with you. Will you not come away to the hoose for a smoke and a drink?'

'I will; but I am a bit tired.'

'Tired?' The Doctor put a finger to his pulse. 'Ye're wanthriven, John! Spent all your spunk on one of your flisk mahoys doon at the pub, no doobt?'

John drew on his cigarette. It was pointless to ask what a 'flisk mahoy' was; the explanation would be more obscure than the expression; but perhaps he would be able to find out something more definite about Minna if he asked the Doctor before he had much more to drink.

'How may I help you, Doctor Gillespie?'

The Superintendent put a hand on his elbow and turned him around in the thin snow.

'To the hoose! Dinna dawdle in the cold. It is not fitting to gab it out by the village.' He exhaled a fumey breath. 'Robene has *rin*. Aye, Robene's away from the clean peathag of wedlock to the dirty midden of that potter, Dougal. She's rin!'

'– Run, Sir? Has Mrs Gillespie left you for good?'

'For good or for evil, Robene has misguggled the couch of all her vows and fled to stew with that devil's buckie in Chelsea.'

'Gone off with the potter? With Dougal? That's terrible!' His companion was silent and he felt constrained to say more; 'That's sad. That's very sad for you. I'm sorry, indeed I am.'

The doctor put an arm round his shoulders:

'Sad is it? *Sad*!! What's in *that* word? So wee and brief to express such sorrow as forbodes the mind as a toll in the dark o' the storm.' He paused and resumed, ' "Sad" you say? Aye, *sad*! Such a cutty syllable for to skirl oot the grief of a man cut to the heart. But come away, climb down with me. We'll warm the hoose whiles I have a favour to ask ye.'

He pulled a chain of keys from his trousers' pocket and,

breathing loudly, his sighs mingling with his sobs, unlocked the front door of his not very large house.

'Make it fast!' he ordered, switching on a light. 'So, we'll not be bothered by any of your gilpies till we have done.'

'You're not expecting anyone else tonight?'

'Never a shadow of a body this Christmas. Never so much as a hare till Hogmanay and the young year's in.'

John followed him down the steep stairway to the basement.

'I wondered perhaps – whether Mrs McVeigh – ?'

'No doobt! No doobt! This way, and go canny on the stair. Madgie McVeigh can knock if she calls – and if she's been dunned at the darts again and cast all her clouts in the laurels she can *shuver* till you draw the bolts for her. Aye, *shuver*!'

'Shiver? Will she mind *me* opening the door, do you think?'

'*Mind*! She'll be that glad to get out the cold she'd buss the devil himself to be in.'

He sat down on the edge of his bentwood chair and reached for the spigot of the cag, pouring a good measure of the pale spirit into his 'yilli-caup', a wooden goblet picturing St Andrews' Golf Clubhouse on the calix.

'I take it you've mouthed your sunkets this night?'

'Sunkets? I'm not sure.'

'Victuals, Man. For there's little enough to pick in the meal-ark.' He paused to groan, 'Och, God!

> . . . 'He is chastened with pain upon his bed,
> and the multitude of his bones with strong pain.
> So that his life abhorreth bread and his
> soul dainty meat' . . .

There's *Job* for you!'

He swallowed and was silent, staring at the photograph of his wife on top of the pinewood bookcase. Stealthily, without shifting his gaze, he sent his hand out to the cup, brought it to his lips, tilted it until it was empty and then replaced it on the brown tablecloth.

John got up and went over to the small cask to fill his own to the top. He drank a little of it greedily, glanced at his companion and then refilled the cup to the rim. He felt as though he were taking a small part in someone else's dream; that in the stagnation of the doctor's evident pain he could do what he liked with impunity; lift up the cag, remove the bung and drain it; or, if he got angry, pour the contents over its owner's head; and if he got very angry, pick up the photograph of Robene Gillespie and spit in its face.

He was hungry; these impulsive thoughts were the consequence of drinking too much and eating too little; of devouring sweet Lynton too often.

Where, he wondered, was Doctor Gillespie's meal-ark? What did it look like? Where was he most likely to keep it? And what, if anything, did it contain? Oatmeal? Sheep's intestines? Brains? Blood? Or all of these in the form of haggis? Wherever it was, if he could but escape up the ladder to find it, he would eat whatever was in it.

Still the doctor ignored him. He sat eagerly forward on the chocolate fabric of the chair as though he were confronting something, or perhaps, like a child in a slow cart, urging it faster forward. Yes, that could be it, he decided. Gillespie was seeking out his grief, his mourning; running into it so that he might unhand it; deprive it of its power.

If that was so, should he himself say something? Should he make another remark or should he stay quiet?

His eyes seeming a little sunken under the jut of his scandy brows, the doctor was now muttering something to himself; a rune perhaps, some fragment of Scots poetry or even a psalm. His bony fingers, a heraldic ring over the knuckle of the little one, began to tread out the measure of the verse on the arm of the chair.

For John, the sunken eyes, gazing at so distant, so invisible an object as grief, were Ellen Pobgee's. She who had gone out to meet and pass by the bell that had 'tolled in the dark 'o the storm'. But whose were the fingers that tapped out their tattoo of melancholy on the bentwood birch? They were the Major's fingers, the lightly tanned phalanges of 'Kit' Bellayr, the military man rapping out anger on the fold of the sheet whilst his eyes were on

166

Lynton; while Lynton, in the most extraordinary way, had blushed back at him.

My God! he decided. He's not having *her*. If necessary I shall swap with Wantage. I shall go Medical and *he* can do all the Surgery. Besides I like Medicine; it's gentler, more tender than Surgery. Some of those silky brusque carpenters of flesh don't know half the time what they *are* doing. Without the chemists they would be lost. They just stroke a cut, tie a knot and look close at something and say to themselves, 'Oh, there it is! I'll take it this way – that's safe enough.'

They are right most of the time, thank heaven! But just the same I shall change with Wantage next week. I can do with the experience and at the same time I shall be able to keep an eye on that swine with his cold, rude eyes. He won't be able to take my Lynton away from me. I knew the moment I met that man in the compound that he was a rival of some kind. Sister Thorpe said that we do scent one another out; and I did, I bristled, the follicles down my back stood up. And there was Lynton on the way back from the Nag's Head, half teasing me about him – and only *half* teasing. She said he makes her feel exciting; and evidently she finds him a little pathetic too – a dangerous combination. If she feels like that about him already what will it be like when he's convalescent?

Gillespie, he noticed now, had closed his eyes, was swaying slightly on his chair as, long ago in the Yorkshire kitchen on the night of Victoria's murder, her mother, Enid Blount, had swayed on the rocker. How dreadful, he thought, that such a terror, such a gesticulation, should rise from the past, every hair of memory in place, and signal us out of the dark that lies behind the warmest light.

He stood up. He would, he really would, have to rouse Doctor Gillespie; he would have to pat and reassure him, stir him back to the present. For he himself now needed the good doctor's company against the sudden tumult of his own thoughts.

He said, 'I believe you were going to ask me something, Doctor Gillespie?'

'Aye, I was too – what's in the cag? Is there a dram yet?'

167

'I think there's plenty.'

'There's no providence in *thinking*. Dinna be so gare-brained. Shake it, Man, shake it!'

'Myself I need food more than another drink.' He shook the cag. 'There's a good bit left. Shall I fill you a goblet?'

'Brim it, and thank you – but you're looking haggard about the chaps. Climb upstairs to the kitchen and take a snap of gruel from the cauldron above the hearth – and there's a crust in the meal-ark.'

'Thank you. Where do you keep the meal-ark?'

'In the closet – where else?

Halfway to the staircase John hesitated.

'I was wondering what it was you were going to ask me?'

The doctor was quiet, lost again. He had resumed his rocking motion on the bentwood chair, his steep head moving with his shoulders, the cup at his lips swaying evenly so that any drop that spilled at the bounds of his arc flowed into his mouth.

'You said, Doctor, that you had a favour to ask? I wish you would ask it because I have to be going!'

'No doobt! No doobt!'

'I mean *now*, sir.'

'Aye! Get away to seek the cap of thy rest so be thy skull will wear it.' He rocked deeper and was granted a moister overflow from his cup. 'But first bide a while more with me!'

He paused to point across the Snug at a battered green travelling chest decorated with bands of metal and tin stars.

'Lift yon lid and pull oot the boot-hose from the top tray. But dinna dunch it!'

John did as he was told, sliding the rusted iron tongues over their hasps and lifting up the lid to rest against the wall. The shallow tray inside was covered up to a depth of six inches with countless copper coins: 'bun' pennies; thick, almost black fourpenny pieces, old ha'pence and farthings; whilst here and there amid the dullness, sovereigns gleamed like yellow quartz in arable.

In the centre of the tray was an immensely large worsted stocking, almost a boot in thickness and size. It was tightly tied across its neck with a black leather thong.

168

'Dinna glim the treasure, but hand over the boot-hose – and gently; then make fast the chest.'

The doctor put down his empty cup on the linoleum and with shaking fingers struggled to untie the boot lace from the neck of the stocking. The 'sole' of it, John now saw, was well rubbed, dully glossy with some substance that had dried into the thick knitting of the wool.

'Och! This lace is dour as sin; and for less than's in my trunk I would deck that Dougal's neck with it. Ech! ech! 'Tis no marvel that the traitor Judas suspended himself by his crupper in the *Potter's* field!'

'Can I help, sir? There's a better light over here.'

'You may *not*! It was my old luckie Dad's hose with the mire of the shippon still upon it, polished bright by the uncivil rasp of the age.'

He struggled again with his boot lace.

'Ech! I jerked it fine so as to foil even the tooth of my own despair.'

John was still thinking about the cowdung in the web of the hose. To keep one's grandfather's stocking with the homestead's dirt in it was not so very curious a sentiment. Such a keepsake, after all, was more intimate, more specific than any pressed flower, any fading picture or stuffed grouse.

By now Gillespie had succeeded in undoing the bootlace and was sitting back in his bentwood chair with his memento lying like a very flat cat across his trousered thighs.

'And now there is no looking back. We must draw it out – and gently.' He paused, his eyes wandering to the ceiling and then to the boot-hose on his lap and finally, with a fixed resolve, to John's own face.

'*You* draw it out for me, laddie. You push it in to your hand and see for yourself Satan's pretty persuasion to a broken man.'

John was nervous. Were there dangerous spiders, in the Highlands?

'Is it something from Scotland, from Auchtermuchtie?'

The Doctor rose to his feet. 'From Scotland?' he shouted, 'From Auchtermuchtie? You blithering cull! Do you really believe I've had no place else for my marketing?'

169

'I only thought that like so many of your things it would be something from – '

'Are you such a cloth-head that you would think me confined to the place – to Auchtermuchtie? Would you have had me *raised* in Scotland?'

'Why, yes certainly.'

'Man, Man!' The Doctor wagged his head in sorrow. 'Do you think that since the good Lord had the foresight to make His creature a Scot that He would of necessity entrap him there? To tread sole the dark moors and bogs barefoot like a starvit hound?'

Gillespie regarded him more reproachfully than ever: 'Nay, nay! We left that country at a tender age.'

John swigged the last of his whisky. He was really angry now to feel so practised upon. The doctor's 'rich' Scotland had begun to supplant for him the cheerless country about which he had only read, and he had begun to grow fond of it, to see virtue in the hardship of its geography, a gaunt independence in its language.

'But there *are* a lot of Scottish people in Scotland! God allows a great many of them to remain there.'

' 'Tis but too true. One of the mysteries of the Lord's providence!' He smiled more cheerfully as he drained his cup. 'But then consider all the folk who were *never* breeched in Scotland. More! Consider all the wee babies who *dee* there before they scan their lot, and the many too who straight escape the day they ken the fullness of their misfortune!'

'That's true!'

'And think of all the battles they've waged and roared up yon in the echoing glens and bare reaches of the heather. Consider the black rage of my wee Robene and think, too, on poor Mary, Queen of the Scots, who came sane and hale from France; but fled her Scotland as distraught as Bess o' Bedlam. Now, fill our horns and search out the consequence of my own perfidy. See! I'll gape wide the hose for ye; so think what you're doing. Take care now.'

The doctor was a man good in his suffering. John was confident that he would let nothing untoward happen to him, so he thrust his hand deep into the leg of the open stocking.

There was something bulky in the bottom, in the close foot of it; a compact unyielding object, cold to the touch. He sought for a grip on it and was drawing it out when there was a deafening report and the boot-hose disintegrated between Gillespie's hands. In the sudden silence succeeding the explosion, grains of gunpowder and shreds of worsted floated down through the blue smoke that was filling the basement.

'God!' shouted the doctor. 'Ye've holed the tartan!'

John was dumbfounded. He was in a world of stillness, in the tranquillity of a dream which he was still sharing with the dreamer. His head felt quite separate from the rest of him, suspended in some echoing place in which, through the drifting cordite fumes, his companion faced him palely, his long index finger pointing at the gun.

'I bade three not to rough the firearm!'

'I need to sit down, dammit!'

'Foregather yourself. Squat doon in thy chair and take a sup of the malt.'

'I can't hear you properly. I think my ears are damaged.'

He supped at the cup that the doctor had handed him, 'I think you ought to sit down. You look very pale – you could be in shock. I hope *your* heart's strong.'

' 'Tis a match for your wrath!'

His knees shaking, Gillespie lowered himself back into his bentwood chair.

Again they sat quietly; John still holding the heavy revolver in his left hand, resting the weight of it on his knee. Beside his foot, the Black Watch tartan of the linoleum was pierced and starred at an intersection of the green lines; a neat entry wound from which a little smoke still rose.

'I think you should have warned me I was handling a gun.'

'You do?'

'And loaded! Why, the damn thing's still loaded!'

'Aye, it is. There are five good, sture bullets in the chamber yet.'

'You don't seem worried. It doesn't seem to worry you?'

'Worrit! A man who's but slipped death by a quillet is not about to meddle with the hobgoblins of his head.' He paused to drink and then resumed, 'We are drawn, Johnnie, one to another, by that which was designed to waste us. Aye! We are given the gift of more golden time to number yet our steps in the fair dream of day.'

Still dazed, John held his tongue. What the doctor had said sounded fine; mysterious. His voice had been thin and genderless, even oracular; but what, he wondered now in the smoke and the silence, whatever *was* Gillespie really trying to tell him? What was he expected to do next?

'We had a narrow escape, I agree; but I'm still very hungry. What do you want me to do?'

'To do? Why, take it! Take it away and safekeep not so much the gun as thy fellow in misfortune, Diarmid Fairburn Gillespie. But first empty out the hot bullets from the magazine, and when ye bide lone in your chamber, hide well the colt in a safe place; for 'tis no gutter-blood gun in thy keep but a douce weapon, very finely engineered and chased – for I wouldna have quenched myself with less.'

He raised his gaze from the linoleum: 'And now, with the Lord's purpose filled gang away to thy bed and find what gruel you may in the kitchen above.'

John handed him the five cartridges and got up:

'I was hoping you might tell me what is wrong with Minna Frobisher. Her mother believes she's got a chronic chest condition?'

' 'Tis so. She bids fair to have an infirmity of her lungs. And since you fancy her, mayhap have lost your poor heart to such a wee quey – ?'

'I have. I may have.'

'Then 'tis love; for naught else could be so daft; you'd better beseech thy Maker, and hers, to heal her fast, or she'll not bide long in this troubled vale.'

'But that's *terrible!*' The revolver shook in John's hand. 'Are you sure of it?'

'Never *sure*, Johnnie; never black certain in the shifting bounds of the skill we aspire to. Though there's no tubercle in her sputum yet; and her pictures are nigh clear; there's

172

a history in her kin and a whisper to her breath, a tint in her cloth that concerns me sore.'

'Then she has a good chance?'

'I'll not prognosticate. Get yourself to bed and don't churn your head over what is in the keep of the seeing God. The two of us will consult again at a better time.'

John went up the ladder-like stairway to the little hall, brushed past the Doctor's plaid on the hatstand and went into the kitchen.

24

It was cottagey in there. At one time there had been an effort by someone, Robene Gillespie perhaps, to make the large room cosy and at the same time generous, for it had been furnished with wide cupboards and substantial chairs.

In the tiled hearth beside the steel-hinged oven, a 'gree-shoch' smouldered in its cloak of ash, while above it an iron cauldron hung from a beam, its contents mingling steam with the smoke of the turf.

On the deal table, scrubbed to the grain, stood a Stafford-shire pitcher with a Highland couple in relief upon its surface. Holding her hand above the bonnet of her groom, his bride lifted a corner of her skirt to show her black shoes and tartan stockings. Above them were the blue needles of Douglas fir twigs and some teazel heads, dusted with the Jack Frost and tinsel of a previous Christmas.

Several more Preston Pans figures of noted Scots folk stood on the Welsh dresser among the ironstone dinner plates, and glued to the back of each was a bunch of dried white ling or bell heather.

Heather, the moors, Yorkshire! He shook off the attendant images that had come crowding to fill his emptiness and realised again that it had been several hours since he had eaten anything and then it had been only a pub sandwich which, in his hunger for Lynton, he had hardly tasted. So now he must help himself to whatever the doctor's housekeeping offered.

With the handle of a ladle he lifted the lid from the cauldron and looked into it. Whatever was simmering in there was impossible to see clearly; but it smelled good and he spooned a wash of it into a soup plate from the dresser and then recovered the pot against the soot falling from the chimney.

On his plate lay bits of pink rabbit flesh in a gravy of oatmeal and leek leaves. So all he needed was some bread and a little margarine or butter from the Doctor's ration; and it was possible that Mrs. Gillespie, before she had 'rin', might have had something of the kind in the meal-ark, if that was where they had kept such things. Or had she gone with those, as well, to her Chelsea potter?

He sipped at his broth, wondering about Robene and her relationship with the doctor. What a cold thought this was; that the man's 'wifie' might have deprived him even of his fat ration. In a way it was as cruel as the separation. But then, if like his own Victoria, she had been taken from him, and by her own wish, why should Robene scruple to deprive him of a pot of butter?

Their love had been a joint possession too, a pot purloined from the storehouse of their marriage, a little porcelain container perhaps painted with flowers, its lid perforated so that the scent, drifting through it, might permeate their house and their whole time together.

How terrible for the doctor to have to go on living in the once shared house, when at every end and turn he must be so reminded of Robene; when even such things as those thistled lids of the tureens on the dresser must recall the pressure of her fingers, and the door knobs the thin oil of her palms.

Worse still, he thought, that in the larger house of the doctor's body, in its tissues, in the impulses that passed through the axons of neurones to the cells of memory,

174

Robene Gillespie must not partially linger, but still be completely present.

And yet, *now* she was gone! It was a frightful, it was a horrendous situation! No wonder the doctor drank and watched football. No wonder he found his old gun so tempting!

Should anyone make off with his Minna or with Lynton – he himself would simply give up, he decided; he would die inside. For as long as he had mourned Victoria or his brother, David, or perhaps for just very slightly less time, he would hang inside himself like an empty suit in a locked cupboard; lifeless, inconsolable.

But to feel unconsoled you had first to imagine yourself being consoled. And was not the doctor already considering this? Actually enjoying it with Mistress MacVeigh for one? And perhaps with Gelda Whooper for another? If this were not so, where were all the casseroles, ginger jars, platters, jugs and mugs of Robene's crafting?

He looked round the kitchen; at the mantelpiece, with its dusty stuffed 'muir-poot' or grouse, the dresser, the tops of the pitch-pine cupboards; but there was not a pot or a pitcher, a pickling crock or thick-walled ewer to be seen.

Had the doctor, in a fit of northern fury, destroyed them all? Taken them down one at a time to his snug and jumped on them? Or had Mistress McVeigh, in her jealousy of Robene, thrown them into the shrubbery after her clothes following a defeat at the dartboard? Was she now, passionate as she sounded, taking over the kitchen, the meal-ark, as well as the bedroom?

And where *was* the meal-ark? he wondered. And, come to that, where was the revolver?

Good God! What a fool he was; he had left the gun with the doctor who by now must be so drunk that he might at any moment be tempted to use it.

He was about to run down to the basement when he was reminded of his dizziness. Really, he must be in a poor state, very low, if he could ramble on like this without doing more than pour his broth and then forget it.

There was no light in the larder at the end of the kitchen, only an empty socket above the slate shelves on which were

175

ranged so few supplies that he wondered if it really had been raided by Mrs Gillespie. He counted three bottles of whitish gooseberries on the top shelf, five cans of tomato soup, three of matchbox sized tins of *Edwards' Dessicated Soup*, two of Scotch Broth, one of Chicken with Chopped Mushroom Stalks, and six of *Meldrum's Rabbit Stew*.

On the bottom shelf at the far end was the meal-ark, an oak chest with barrel hoops. He lifted the lid and looked into the rectangular opening. It was less scented, he thought, than a manger where the horse had eaten all his fodder; but he put in his hand and after some fumbling pulled out a brown paper bag labelled:

CANDLE ENDS
For use in case of enemy action
Not to serve as kindling

Beneath this he found a wedge of orange-coloured cheese with a blue coating of mould on its sides and beside it, tightly swathed in cloth and greaseproof paper, something oblong which dented to the fingers. He dropped it back at once, fearing it might prove even more smelly than an old haggis, and was groping about for bread, when he at last drew out a quartern loaf of wholemeal which he immediately tore open with his fingers and dipped into his plateful of stew.

He ate it hastily, staring ahead of him through the shallow curtain of green and yellow glass beads which fringed the lampshade above the table. In the grate the greenshoch smouldered soundlessly beneath its furry ash and, from the passageway with its open door leading down to the sanctum, came not one snore nor even the sound of the doctor's breathing as he lay sprawled on his chair. All that broke the silence was the ticking of the Balmoral clock above the mantelpiece, its brass pendulum winking monotonously at each end of its arc.

He was just thinking it would be a good moment to slip down to the basement and collect the gun before the doctor woke, when there was such a loud rap at the front door that he dropped the remainder of the loaf into his soup.

His heart thudding, he went out into the passage and was

176

hesitating by the front door when someone again pounded at the knocker so violently that flakes of brown paint fell onto the coconut matting.

Hesitating no longer, he went down to the basement, grabbed the gun from beside the cag and ran back to the front door. There he paused and shouted above the knocking to know who was out there.

'Who else?' came the reply, 'You feckless dolt! Who else but the cod of thy couch, thy tittie? And if you dinna straight draw the irons from the door-cheek I'll paik thee such a scaithe as would jag the Devil hisself.'

The voice, thick with anger, was so menacing that John raised the empty gun before opening the little wooden panel over the 'squint'.

It admitted the smell of whisky and stale tobacco and revealed the face of a woman with burning eyes and a scanty downswept moustache.

'Ye're not me Billie,' she shouted, pushing her face closer to the grille. 'Why are ye hereabouts, ye rintherout donnut? If thee dinna clang the bolts this minute I'll have yer ba's for a baccy pouch.'

'I will, in a minute. But first I just want to know how you did at the darts tonight – that is, if you are Mistress McVeigh?'

'Darts is it? *Darts*! I'll rubbit yer tailze and stow your ba's with a kitchen gulley, you grinning fool.' And she pounded again at the knocker.

At the bottom of the stairway the doctor appeared:

'Is that Madgie again, willywhaing outbye?'

John waited for the knocking to cease and then turned to Gillespie.

'I think it must be, and I'm afraid that she's lost at the darts.'

'Aye.'

'I mean, sir, that she's probably naked.'

'Good, good! Let her chill awhile on the slate.'

'She's very cold, I think, shivering!'

'No doobt! No doobt! And sharp as a hawk.' The Doctor paused as the front door thundered afresh. 'Ach! What a tempest she blows. Ye'd better pull the bolts before her plasters peel.'

'Yes, sir; but if she's got nothing on?'

'Man, man! Ye've seen more lassies in thy golden years than the green blades a goosie grazes in the high of summer; and Madgie, though a bittock hairy round her parts, is no different from the motley of her sex! So draw now the bolts and let the poor carline into the hoose.' He put his finger to his lips; 'And whist! Never a syllable about the hagbut – about the gun.'

As the doctor returned to the snug, John dropped the gun into his pocket, then he pulled back the bolts and Mistress McVeigh stamped naked into the little hall.

With never a glance at him, she went to the hat-tree, pulled the plaid off the hook and draped it round her so deftly that he caught only a glimpse of the mustard plaster above her buttocks.

Before he quitted the house for his room in the Geriatric Unit he glanced through the kitchen door. Her face down, her red plaid about her shoulders, Mistress Madgie was finishing up the rabbit stew.

Back in his bed, shivering in the sickly aftermath of the whisky and the fright he had suffered, he grew angry when he thought about the doctor.

In his own eyes, Fairburn Gillespie's misfortunes, like those of Job, were as much a distinction as his earlier prosperity had been; yes, anything untoward also served to mark him as the Lord's especial creature. Whatever his vicissitudes he was able to view the good and the bad both, as signs of divine favour, and still have the pleasure of rejoicing in the one while complaining of the other.

25

A few weeks later, it must have been about two or three, Wantage told him at breakfast that he was transferring Major Bellayr to the Surgical side.

John was chewing his breakfast toast, looking out through the French window at the blackness in the snow which had come down overnight. Every fallen leaf, every grounded branch in the compound, every dog print, cat pug or nurse's scurry was pitch black, and a little area round each, black too. The boles of the bare trees were greenish black, and their boughs and twigs grey-black save for a chalk stripe of snow on their upper sides.

On sullen foot, Christmas was coming to Southern England; to blacked-out London, to its smoking factories, its barrage balloons; to the Home Counties, the airfields, the Nissen huts, the gun emplacements, and the soldiers swarming everywhere.

He dipped the toast into his coffee and let it soften.

'What did you say? No, wait! Major Bellayr, you said?'

'He isn't healing. Old Leigh thinks he's got what he calls a bother, a neurosis that's keeping the ulcer open.'

'Why doesn't he discharge him on diet and sedatives?'

'As usual, I suppose; sorry for him! Says he's to go to Surgery; your team.'

'My team? de Fleur doesn't touch general surgery. Oh Christ! You mean Strykes and Graemes?'

'Yes, they're willing to have a go; but Graemes wants to fatten him a bit first.' Jerry got up. 'Anyway, I'm having him wheeled over to Male Surgery this morning. You'd better pop in and reassure him. He's a panic merchant and he's guessed there's been a change of plan.'

'Haven't you told him yet?'

'His eyes are bolting out of his head as it is. If I trigger a haematemesis I might not be able to shift him over to you.'

'You know I hate him.'

'And Lynton likes him – he's going to miss *her*. Well, I must be off. See you at lunch.'

'You mean little chimp.'

'*God rest you merry gentlemen*,' sang Wantage,

'*Let nothing you dismay.*'

His voice faded as the door closed behind him and he made his way down the corridor, past the office and out into the hospital compound. John sat on at the table.

What, after all, did he *know* about Major Bellayr? That he was about thirty-seven years old: a journalist and a some-time portrait – and child-photographer; twice divorced. He had lived in the North of England and in New York's Soho; but now, as next-of kin he had only his landlady in Earl's Court Terrace.

And what was *she* like? John's thoughts clinched to a nearer concern: Well, he had better lay off Lynton! Already she is sorry for him with his greedy eyes, his unknowable past. She doesn't realise that he's not our kind; that the more he talks about himself the less he discloses. And that is what alarms: he chooses to share only enough to make his claim on the soiled part of oneself; the baby who wants his own dirt, the schoolboy who treasures his scorn; the blind man with the fingers. He connives.

And as for his army camouflage, it sickens. *I* would have liked to be a real soldier, to be in the thick of it, away from peace for a bit; away from women for a time, perhaps for ever. I'm tired of always being on the stretch to impress one or other of them; I am tired, too, of being nothing but a student; for that is what I am: a 'rookie' doctor, a rookie!

I must join up, I have to, I shall get some letters off to the Admiralty, to the War Office . . .

He had finished his coffee. He had planned looking in on Minna before starting his rounds, kissing her and assuring her of his concern as she sat downstairs in her rabbit-skin bedroom slippers and her father's old dressing gown; but Sister Thorpe had sensitised him to Major Bellayr's pressing expectancy, so he decided that Minna would have to wait. He would allow just sufficient time for the Major to be wheeled over to the Surgical Unit and then he would look in on him and tell him of the change in treatment.

He rang through to Doctor Graemes' service flat in Batsford: the patient was to be weighed daily and to have all the usual pre-operative laboratory checks. He was to be kept well sedated pending a partial gastrectomy and gastrojejeunostomy in a week's time – just before the Christmas holidays.

Christmas, he realised, as he crossed the compound. How strange to be passing it for the first time away from the family; how extraordinary to be having it here in this place which until a few weeks ago he had not known even to exist.

The Guinea Lane: a scatter of buildings, a desolate encampment beneath its gun-laden sky, beneath its clouds which so often screened metal barrels, brass shell casings, cylinder blocks, whole engines, shrapnel, aluminium propellers, tons of rivets and metal sheeting, pounds of flesh and gallons of blood and urine.

All passing high in the skies of Southern England.

The Dragon had allotted a private room to Major Bellayr. It was one of a pair in the Surgical Unit.

'He's very upset,' she told John, 'said he could not "stand" to be with other patients right now.'

'I suppose you haven't told him that he's down for surgery?'

'It's hardly my place! I thought you could take him in the consent form?'

'Very well; but you will make the rounds with me as usual?'

'Yes.'

'Then we'll leave him till the last.' He hesitated as the Major's buzzer sounded. 'No, we'll see him first – you needn't wait long, Sister.'

How bright it was in the small room; the reading light full on, the grey-white luminescence from the frozen grass of the compound striking in through the window to the pale walls and ceiling.

Still faintly tanned, his short hair dull, his eyes blank as he looked first at the Sister and then at John, the Major sat propped high against the black bars of the bedhead:

'What, one would like to know, *what* the hell is going on?' he began, staring between them. 'One has been in this goddam place three weeks to the day, living on pulp, deprived of one's creature comforts, one's women – and one is no better at the end of it – one is worse.' He paused, his long hands flat on the turn down of the sheet.

'Well?' He waited. 'So? Nobody articulates this ack emma.' He looked down at his hands. 'The point being that *I* am worse.'

He waited again, his eyes now on the Dragon.

'Well, Sister?'

His elbows out, his hands linked behind his head, he lay back against his pillows and gazed stagily up at the ceiling. Sister said, 'Doctor Blaydon has come in to discuss this with you, Major.'

'One knows, of course, that one is merely a patient in this place, and that as such one is subject to – That between the staff and their playdough there is a great gulf fixed. One also knows that there is a war on for our pal Tommy Atkins in which we, belatedly, have decided to participate.' He leaned forward:

'But let's cut the cackle, shall we? And the jolly red tape, and ask again what the *hell* goes on in this – ' He stopped for a moment; and, though he continued to speak to the Sister, he had shifted his gaze to John's face.

'I know *you*, Doctor Blaydon! We met earlier when I was an unsuspecting noo boy – out there.' He gestured towards the window. 'Is that not so?'

'We have met, yes.'

'And, if nobody minds my saying so, *Doctor Blaydon is wet behind the ears!*' He looked at the Dragon. 'Now, as an older, more mature female, would you not agree, Sister?'

John turned to her. 'I know you're busy, Sister, and I have the case notes and consent form; so you needn't wait.'

She smiled at him and left them. The Major's eyes had

182

not followed her to the door, they had remained fixed on a point somewhere just above John's forehead and his face was expressionless.

'Good idea that,' he said. 'Get the women out of the way. Yes, I like that. I do indeed. The world would be a much cleaner place – but, tell me, what was that I heard about a consent form? Or did my ears deceive me?'

'It's only the usual consent form we ask all patients to sign before undergoing surgery.'

'Surgery?'

'You see, we've decided that since you weren't responding to – '

'And very nice too.' The Major leaned forward eagerly, smoothing back his blond hair and rubbing his hands. 'Some action at last! Patient's body suitably weakened by slops and slime over a period of three weeks; sexually malnourished too; save, of course, for what all guys and little gals can do for themselves. Oh ho! And then the old One Two! the cut and bloody well do something for the sonofabitch. Oh, very nice, Master Doctor!'

He gestured; 'Hand over that document and grab me something to sign with. This guy wants out. I don't deny it; this person, no longer so young as he was, but young enough, wants O-U-T. He wants a lot of things, beginning with his creature comforts, and effective, non-heroic treatment. So, lead on Macduff! There; how's that for a genuine signature?'

'Thank you.'

John took the folder and waited. There was now a small pain in his own midriff, a gentle but fundamental pressure. He was surprised by the Major's agility; he was like some jumpy animal, an ebullient terrier; some larger canine that snapped and barked amidst its gambollings, snarled and showed its serried teeth so swiftly that you could not be sure that you had seen them at all.

Certainly there was something very confusing about him, a quality of mind, a shifting of view and vocabulary that suggested he was not merely two people, the one momentarily watching over the other's shoulder before the players changed roles, but many; a whole troupe, a legion. And

183

with this display of many selves, as with a stage that is too busy, a crowd-scene ill directed, he was worse than confusing and frightening; he was tedious too.

'And when, one would like to know, is this little pantomime at which I am to be the – human sacrifice for the merry season and all that – to take place. In a word; date please?'

'We have no exact date. But it will be about a week from now and that will give you time to – '

'Recuperate, limber up? As the young virgin said to the chimney sweep, "I can't wait!" Oh ho!'

His expressionless face more placid than ever he asked, 'And you, one supposes, will be present, Doc Blaydon?'

'I expect so.'

'What! What! Don't be so modest. You will be doing your stuff, as they say Stateside, dicing up the – whatever.'

'I shall be assisting, yes.'

'Bravo! bravo!'

The Major flapped his tanned hands on the sheet, first the left and then the right as though he were playing pat-a-cake. His smile vanished and in its absence his face sharpened; a visible honing of the tissues, as though some overriding emotion or the absence of it, had swiftly flensed his features down to their bony armature; illness now apparent in the hollows beneath his cheekbones, the sick painting under his eyes. ˇ

'One hopes,' he added more quietly, '*I* hope that you will not get – carried away.'

'Carried – ?'

A bell was ringing somewhere across the compound, the single clamour of a telephone coming across the snow from one of the offices in an adjacent block. Nearer at hand, a peal of laughter rang out from one of the nurses in the main ward.

'I'm not sure what you mean by that.'

'Oh, spare my blushes! People *do*, you know – in *anything*! Anger, curiosity, and – dare I say it? – *love*, as I see it. But – on the table, with no one there but us chickens – oh so easy!'

His face remained clean swept. 'Well, well, you and the

184

other gentlemen – *not* Doctor Leigh unfortunately – because one would trust him never to – but hence, of course, a physician and *not* a brother of the knife!' His eyes widened as he paused, as, again, his two hands, one after another, patted out a tattoo on the sheet. 'So now, tell all! Which of the medical men atttending this somewhat unusual – *who* is operating upon me?'

'It will be Doctor Graemes.'

'I know him not.' He had smiled, 'And the anaesthetist? Who do we have to take me away? For that *is* important, you know. Stateside they are very advanced in the painless sciences.' He waited interrogatively, his eyes on John steady.

'Doctor Strykes will give the anaesthetic.'

'Ah!' He thought for a moment. 'And these gentlemen are already organised, have been rounded up to operate upon me in, perhaps, the coming week? I must let my honey-jar of a landlady know. Also – ' He had smiled again, 'Yes? You have something further to tell me?'

'Only that Doctor Graemes and Doctor Strykes are not men.'

'Not men? Oh great! Young and tender rookies perhaps? Castrates of the Ward?'

'No, they are women.'

'Women?'

The Major's hand moved abruptly forward from the edge of the sheet to the white cotton counterpane overlying his thighs. As though a withdrawal of the blood in his skin had occurred, a negative blush, his face blanched swiftly, yellowing into an almost colourless tissue.

'Females?'

His tongue tip touched the corners of his lips, his jaw closed tightly, opened again to let his tongue once more creep out as if it were a mouse, and touch the edges of his mouth all over, delicately again, from one end to the other.

'You've got to be joking.'

'I'm not.'

He sat up vigorously. 'You cannot be serious! You aren't telling me that two *women* are to – tell me that you're joshing?'

185

'I'm not, Major Bellayr; but both the Surgeon, Miss Graemes, and the anaesthetist, Mrs Strykes, are highly qualified and experienced in their fields; here in England as well as in Australia.'

'*Australian*? Did I hear the word? – This is – '

He fell back against the pillows so naturally that it appeared theatrical and he closed his eyes as he whispered:

'A fugue. There ain't no such thing as a net. This is some damn order of coin-cidence. Ah ha! but they left a hole!' He sat up. '*You*!' he ordered. 'Come here, Billy Boy!'

'You don't speak to me like that.'

'Come right here if you don't want me to come and get you.'

'Yes, what is it?'

'What do you know about me? *Give!*'

'I know only what is in your case notes.'

'Oh yes!' Again he touched his lips delicately all round with the tip of his pathetic tongue. 'You don't, by any long shot, happen to know that I don't go for ladies in any real sense? You don't – nobody whispered to you along the line, that Major Kit Bellayr – Hey, man! Women have periods. You know that. Their hands shake: they don't keep their cool. They drop pots. They get slippery – *Periods*, Doctor!'

His mouth gaped with distaste.

'You wouldn't want anyone carving you up with their nerves all bo-jangles of Harlem! And *Australian* – ! Coffee-fingered with pink palms. Christ almighty!' He closed his eyes and was silent.

'I think you should try to control yourself, Major Bellayr. If you cannot we shall have to consider transferring you to a different hospital.'

The Major opened his eyes:

'A funny farm! That's rich. *This* is the nut house; this goddam ramshackle flea market run by a bunch of little girls, old spinsters, and fuddy-duddy didn't-make-it-in-the-big-league physicians.'

He paused, licking his lips with greater intention:

'So *you*, Rookie Blaydon, don't know nothing?' The Major stared at him.

'As I told you, I know only your case history: that you

once lived in England, that you've been divorced twice, that you were a photographer – child studies; that – '

'No, don't tell me yet. Don't tell me. *Nothing!*'

'Major Bellayr. I'm going to order you a sedative by injection. It will help us all if we can have you less tense.'

'A sed – Christ! He jokes again. He jokes at this pass.' He was sitting up again looking past John as though he had removed him from whatever he was looking at. 'Women! On *me*. *My* body? Wait!' He swung his blue-pyjamaed legs over the mattress. He thrust his feet out to find the hospital bedroom slippers on the piece of drugget beside the bed. He swore to himself when he couldn't find them.

'I take my discharge. Where is that sheet? That damned death warrant consent form? Give it! *You!* *Give*, you creep, you fumbling little greenhorn. Stand back, stand back!'

John stepped back away from the bed towards the closed door. He was shivering, watchful; unable to move further, amazed by the Major's face as it now turned to look at him directly. For it appeared to have no bounds; it filled his vision in the way a body of water fills a space where there is nothing especial for it to reflect.

The gaze, though directed at him, was fixed upon nothing, the eyes limitless too in the depth upon depth, not of their terror but of their need of it. In the silence, they continued to hold his own as expressionlessly as a reptile's, before, quite suddenly and with no warning, their owner fell forward into his arms, brown blood and acid running from his mouth.

26

He went to be at the Frobisher's that evening. He had been uncertain whether to ask Lynton out to dinner somewhere along by the river in Stourmond, or to sit with Minna amongst the furnishings of her mother's recent séance: but soon he had settled for the Frobishers. For he was afraid; his indecision a consequence of the unease which, like a noisesome smell, had risen from his confrontation with the Major that morning; the 'mix-up' as he later termed it, when talking to Wantage.

Why should anything that *he*, that particular man, had said, have the power to disturb him? And what had the Major said? That he, John was a greenhorn, a part of the outmoded system which he served; that in some way he was personally corrupt as well. No, he had not said that; he had not even inexactly said it; but somehow it had been present in the words he had used; in the quick images he had slid into the fury of his complaint.

Evidently he considered Medicine as suspect as it was ineffectual; for him the hospital was worse than dated, it was a cover for dishonesty, decadence; cruelty in the surgeons, incompetence in the physicians, and, for the men and women who staffed it, a ground in which they might visit their mutual distrust of one another on their patients.

'Women! Females!' he had said with certainty; speaking as if he knew of some rotten thing that was unarguable; so personal a fact that over the years, it had affected his body, causing it first to ulcerate and then to bleed.

Females, women, virgins, little girls were to him a danger. He spoke against them, he tried to laugh about them, to make a jest of them; but when he found he could not escape them, rid himself of some hope through them, all his subterfuges fell from him to reveal the real reason for his scorn: his indifference.

'They're sending me into the sanatorium at Cold Harbour,' Minna told him as they sat together in her father's big armchair. 'Leastways, *he* is.'

'Doctor Gillespie?'

'Yes.'

'When?'

'He says as how it's got worse, my lungs. And it will be just after Christmas, soon as there's a bed.'

'I didn't mean when are you going in; but when did he tell you?'

She smiled. 'You interested, then? Been talking of me?'

'Gillespie should have told *me*! I can't understand why he didn't.'

She sighed. 'You're not very warm tonight! Does my breath smell or something?'

'Only of itself.'

'Well, kiss us. What does it smell of?'

'Haystacks.'

She was looking across at the sheet music on the open piano. 'I don't half love you, Doctor John. When you're not there I follow you as if I'm a dog at your shoes, which you don't never seem to polish. I say to myself, 'He's going into Theatre and now he's off to eat arrowroots with Sister Thorpe. No, he isn't; he's sitting down in Admin for his coffee, and now he's dodging off to see that Nurse Lynton.' Do you ever do that when you're not with me?'

'I did until you got ill. I used to think of you sitting in the office with that little jar of willow on your desk. Sometimes I imagined you in your bed or even in the bathroom.'

'You like that? Me, in there?'

'Yes, it's exciting, it's secret. It's *you* – one person! It couldn't be as much anybody else – I suppose that disgusts you?'

'You're a boy, is all. I was a bit of a boy like that, when I was turned eleven. But it's gone now.'

'Don't you ever want to be loved – in your body?'

'Not the way as when I was eleven. Now it's a lot of dreams.' She took his hand. 'Am I too heavy for you?'

'What kind of dreams?'

'Of myself mostly. I was a garden; trees in summer and fields all stitched in silk; I was everything with light on it, silver grass heads and the sky a blue hole over me – and sometimes with faces looking down and I'm sharing the looking in a funny sort of way.'

'Whose faces?'

'Young men's mostly.'

'But if you're with them, looking at yourself? When you

189

imagine all that, don't you want someone *real* to be with you?'

'Of course I do – sometimes; but I don't never seem to want the rest of it all clear to myself; not what *might* be – not the way I did when I was young.'

'But you *are* young.'

'Not as young as when I didn't know I was.'

'You *are* disappointing to me.'

'Because of the dreams?'

'Oh, partly.'

'Don't vex yourself. They could go; they could turn, if anyone wanted. But I don't think I'd ever get through the badness of times if dreams was to stop forever. There's been evenings when I've said, "If I'd known what today was going to be like: skinning my knee, people shouting; and the *cold*! I'd never have got out of bed to it." What I see is more than dreams though. But you get like it too, sometimes? You must do or we wouldn't be so close!'

'I did today. He got in amongst me.'

'Was it that new patient?'

'The whole place, the Guinea Lane, shrank like something on a stick when you hold it to the fire.'

'That Major again! What got him so pickled?'

'I had to tell him he was up for surgery. He got very angry and insulting. He seems to hate everything, women especially.'

She was still. 'People hate what they've hurt. Perhaps he's a cruel one.'

'That's what I'm beginning to think. That he's been a swine to one of his wives. He's had two, one an English one a long time ago and one a girl in America; and he's divorced them both. Now he's talking about his 'honey jar' landlady in Surbiton or somewhere.'

'The Major's a greedy guts. It's what happens when you stop letting life be in the air a bit, like a play. I think I could be ever so grabby if I got well.'

'Have you got a headache *now*?'

'A bit. I was thinking it would be better for us upstairs. Keep your hand on my head.'

He stroked the soft line of hair above her forehead:

'Major Bellayr seems to have nothing – to *be* nothing. I don't know why we're bothering to save him. This morning he gave me the hell of a fright.'

'What did he say?'

'He made me feel a fool – worse, dirty.'

'Did you want to fight him?'

'More as if I wanted to blot him out, snuff him out like a smoking candle.'

She snuggled closer to him, her thin breasts against his jacket in the big armchair. 'A candle? Is that how you see him?'

'He seems empty, limitless, a desert that could swallow things up; whole companies marching into it and disappearing like the armies in North Africa; like your father's battalion.'

She sat up. 'Well, that means as you shouldn't.'

'What does?'

'You shouldn't see things the way he wants you to. I think the Major's one of them who sees us *all* bad, when we're only part. That's what she says, anyway; Sister Thorpe.'

'What does she say?'

'She says as some are "all cry and no wool".'

'That's true.'

'Well now you should go and ask *her* about it.'

'I think I will.'

'And you could tell us some more of your story about the North. The girl – the one you loved – as was killed. Tell what she was like.'

'I will if you don't keep asking about her.'

'I promise.'

He kissed her. 'When you're in the sanatorium, you'll still love me as much?'

'It will be more.'

'Then put out the light and I'll tell you.'

'Victoria? Victoria Blount?'

Sitting quite still in the chair they remained quiet, the last word she had spoken and then repeated, seeming to echo continually in the silence. The air was cold in the dark parlour, the gas fire hissed blue and orange in the blackness of the surrounding grate.

'And up North?' Minna asked. 'You still loved Victoria up there in Yorkshire?'

'More than ever.'

'You didn't fall out?'

'I don't think even once. We didn't see any danger there. At least – '

He stopped. It was the sense of threat that made for quarrels; the pressure of even the slightest menace, feathery as gas, shortened tolerance, poisoned generosity. He was remembering the bickering, the unease, the clumsy mating between Victoria's mother and George Harkess.

He was remembering too Victoria's meeting with her murderer somewhere on the flinty road down into the dale.

On every trip with her, whether collecing bilberries on the slopes of the sheep-hung moors where larks rose one upon another in ribby song, wading in the iron-stained streams for rusty pebbles, or lying silent in the red blossomed heather and bracken in the whiteness of the sun, there had been an undertone, a chord, fitful as the wind which came and went along the reaches of the dale always.

Always until the picnic in the Stump Cross Caverns.

Then they *had* sensed danger. Then, they had fallen out as though the running chord had changed as do bells from far away when the wind blows in the summer: a gust of it, rude and boisterous, bringing change into the accustomed quietness of everything, so that for one of the first few times, one of the last, they had looked at one another as slyly as though they had eaten of Eden, neither of them saying that with that note, all else, too, had changed; the rock faces, the rushing streams, the dark blood-purple of the heather; and when they had crawled into it, the quality of the very music of the cave.

'Then there was something that caught at you?' Minna said now.

'It was hardly anything at first. It wasn't anything more than what is so often between people – lovers.'

'So you don't want to tell us it?'

'Not now.'

'It's too near for you, is it?'

'Yes, it is still, sometimes.'

'It can get bad when they really come together; what you dream and where you are. I don't know if it's this room, with all their silly carryings-on and their spirit guides; but I've got the frights too – You could hold us a lot tighter than you are. You could – '

George Harkess, he was thinking, and his pursuit of Victoria's mother. He saw his heavy face, the roll of his moustache, the old and silly legs as he had stood in his shirt tails beside the double bed on which Enid was screaming out her humiliation at having been discovered by John, by so young a boy, her daughter's follower.

'Please carry me upstairs out of this, so we can get back into my bed again,' Minna begged. 'It's that chill and dark down here and Mum won't be in for hours.'

'Are you sure?'

'I doubt she'd mind anyway; she knows me!'

'Then I will,' he agreed. 'That would be just right for us.'

To be with Minna would seal away that other night of fifteen years ago, of the couple in the upper room at Nettlebed Farm. It would muffle the sounds for him; stop the music of the water dripping down from the stalactites into their still pools; stop, too, the wind moving gently as a woman in unseen extensions of the cavern: the splashing of the shoes of Victoria's man approaching them in the candlelight, swearing, laughing to himself in the darkness.

It would hold him in his present, in the sweetness of Minna.

He tucked the pink eiderdown deeper round her. He picked her up light as a moorland bird and carried her up the narrow staircase to her room and slid her into her sheets before getting in himself.

27

'Ye were over to Minna then?' Doctor Gillespie asked him later in the admin room. 'I trust ye contained your passions the while? For ye ken fine the tubercle's a greedy bacillus and fires up even a wan quey like yon lass to outgate herself.'

'Miss Frobisher didn't outgate anything, Sir, whatever that means. She's too unhappy and so am I! Is she much worse that you're sending her into Cold Harbour?'

'Minna is wuss in her left apex and must have the lung collapsed awhile.'

'An APT? For how long?'

'Why, till 'tis whole and haled. She has no phthisis as yet but in the bitter cold of the season and the melling of her mother with the ghosty hobgoblins of her own head, the daughter should mend faster down the Sanatorium.'

'She'll get better food there?'

'She'll fare better on the victuals and healsome wares they're shipping in from America: the orange syrops and poodered egg.'

'That is good.'

The doctor put an arm round his shoulders:

'Ech, ech! Ye're wan-thriven again. Come over and ben the hoose; and should she bide here this night, my tittie will give you a sup of onion broth.'

'Your tittie? You mean Mistress McVeigh?'

'Who else, man? Who else but the dryer of my tears, the blancher of my sorrows since my wild Robene, waxing so hot with her dreams, sundered us to couch with that hempie potter in Chelsea?'

'I don't mean to be rude, sir; but isn't it possible that

194

your wife didn't care for your having Mistress McNeigh as a 'tittie' – at intervals, I mean?'

'At *intervals*! What are you coming at? Madgie has always been my wee tittie, raised in the selfsame crib of love, supping the same sweet milk of childhood; and now, in our dry years we are turned comforters one to another. Why, laddie! What else would be the custom and purpose of a blood-sister?'

'A blood – ? Is Mistress McVeigh your sister? "Tittie" sounds – '

'Take a care to your words, Doctor! Had you but the smatter of the Gaelic in your mother tongue you would not smirch your witness with such reekie notions. For what man, knowing the poet Job would dare try scathing God, for,

Who can open the doors of his face?
His teeth are terrible round aboot . . .
The sword of him that layeth at him cannot hold;
The spear, the dart, nor the habergeon. . '

'Well, I'm sorry,' John said. 'But I think it was an understandable mistake.'

'Aye! All such grippy vice is easy for men to understand whiles the virtues are ever strange.' The doctor paused to look more reproachful:

'And there I was in good faith confiding in you about my poor sackless tittie, Madge, and thou sitting down with thy scomfish thoughts and slakey brew of adulterous incest – for even you, with your fair sense, would not be troubled by the rompy games of bairns?'

'I never exactly thought of incest. I didn't even realise that Mistress McVeigh *was* your sister.'

'Hoot! Dinna haggle over your moral errors.' The doctor leaned forward and rapped him on the knee.

'Ye heard just now what wee Job said about the habergeon?'

'Is that a primitive kind of gun?'

'Nay! 'Tis a short haber of chain mail. But tell me, has Doctor Wantage made you an offer yet – for my gear?'

'Your gear?'

'The hagbut! The fine gun I loaned you to mind a while.'

'Jerry did borrow it. But do you want me to sell it to him?'

'In time; in God's good time. No haste! For he's a jinker, is Doctor Wantage, and sight unseen, though he's a fancy for firearms, he's not about to offer me the worth of it.'

'But you were going to – You were thinking of killing yourself with it, Doctor Gillespie.'

'True! true! And can you come up with a better reason for a man to exact a bonny price?' He paused and leaned closer to John, his face sharpened with suspicion:

'I'm thinking that wee Wantage could be a bit of a Jew, ye ken? He's so canny with his shekels.'

'I don't know whether he's Jewish or not. He was born in Bangkok of native parents.'

'I'm not straightened to learn it. Ech! no!' He grew thoughtful. 'So the wee Wantage has never mentioned a figure!'

'Not to me.'

'And you have not heard him at practice with the bullets I left in your keep?'

'I didn't give them to him. I didn't like to, after – '

'Man! man! You're oversentimental!' The doctor wiped his eyes with his yellow silk handkerchief. 'I'm thinking that since he hasn't come at me yet, I'll raise the price higher before I lower it less. With Christmas upon us all, it is but just that the heathen should be shaved.'

28

John was wary of Sister Thorpe. He thought of Minna's advice that he should go to her because she was 'different' and might set his mind at rest about Major Bellayr; but because he knew that she might not, that, as with many wise people, she might first disturb him more, he still hesitated.

He had not 'forgiven' her for the several things he thought she might have brought about when he was new to Guinea Lane: the 'shewing' of Frau Kleber on the night of the air raid: that desolate talk he had shared with the dying woman in the end bed, before she had disappeared as inexplicably as she had come, leaving him with yet another incommunicable secret in his life.

Nor had he forgotten Minna's matter-of-fact account of finding that particular ward full of bleeding soldiers at some time in the recent past when she herself had been new to the hospital.

These and other less complete mystifications which he associated with the Sister, brought back all of his unease with his mother's second sight; her predictions, her written memoirs, her conjuring up of his brother David's childhood body into his own church three days after his death.

Yet he was drawn to Sister Thorpe. Though she shared some quality with his mother, the Sister was, in a way, clearer. One's mother, he thought, could never be wholly freed of the dirt of one's childhood. No matter how fine she might be, she was pressed in with all manner of soils of the body and mind, from excretion to sexuality and, consequently could hardly walk easily and unhampered in the reaches of the later mind.

Sister Thorpe, perhaps, was a sport of Time; a person

less personal even than a grandmother; an embodiment, a presence leaping out of the ancestral past without any claim upon one of blood or heredity, with only that interest and affection which, supposedly, was the prerogative of God for His creatures.

So really, he decided, he had no need to forgive the Sister for anything. She had not given him to life, her suffering was her own affair and no stumbling block to his love for her.

For he did love her; she had helped him to relish old people, to see them as a child sees venerable trees; cloisters of the birds, provinces of leaves and boughs, gateways into magical pasts.

And now he hurried, almost running, across the dark snow-lit compound to catch the Sister before she went off duty.

The ready warmth of the unit hit him as soon as he was through the double doors into the varnished corridor; a whiff of disinfectant and scented soap from the Gynae Ward. And he saw that, here, the decorations had started early. Above the doors to the ward the nurses had tacked up a green shield of crimson-berried holly; and, through the glass inserts of the doors, he could see the first of the large cardboard bells, red and gold; the looped paper streamers hanging below the yellow ceiling.

Sister was at her desk in the small office, an open book, a history he thought, in front of her resting on the big Day Register. She was tired, he saw, a little trembly; for, as she looked up at him, turning her capped head to see him, her small face wobbled minutely as a baby's who has not yet sufficient muscle to hold the skull steady on the narrow pedestal of its neck.

'Well! You *are* in haste this evening!'

'It's very cold, Sister; really snappy out there.'

'And it's not your supper time yet?'

'No, I wanted to see you before I went off duty.'

'So here I am. You caught me reading about my friends in the Crimea at their Christmas festivities nearly a hundred years ago. Would you like to hear this journal's entry of December 28, 1855?'

'Where were they then?'

'In the Crimea, camped below the Mackenzie Heights.' She replaced her metal-rimmed glasses and with her finger traced the open page to where she wanted to read:

'Here we are: every discomfort and deprivation, you notice; but no rationing!

The grand dinner on Xmas Day went off pretty well. Of course several fellows were 'screwed', myself not amongst the number though the champagne and sherry were pretty bad.

'Just look at the programme for the dinner!' she went on: 'Soups, hare and pea; fish: whiting and mullet, five or six entrées, joints of roast beef, boiled legs of mutton, roast leg of pork, goose and turkey. And then, Game: hare. Pastry: plum pudding, plum tart, rice pudding, jam tarts, cakes, etcetera! And all served with champagne, porter, ale, sherry, port, whisky, rum, gin, brandy, and more. I believe they did not eat very much of any one thing; but think of the preparation and clearing! He says:

'The plum pudding was very greasy and squashy. Mine is 50 times as good, I know.' She glanced at him and then back to the page as she continued:

'The weather is bitterly cold and extremely disagreeable. There is no pleasure in walking or riding, and to sit all day over the fire is not particularly agreeable. Sickness is increasing, chiefly coughs and colds and scurvy. We are sending 4 men home with consumption. . . . Thank God, we have no cholera. . . .'

Her forefinger rested on the book: 'You'll have guessed, of course, that the writer is a medical officer? He was an acting assistant surgeon, no less.'

'I know, I've read it before – on the night Frau Kleber died. Do you mind if we don't go on with it?'

'I'm sorry.' She closed the book so briskly that he suspected she had been using it only as a play to reach whatever was troubling him.

'But what *is* the matter? Or who, I should ask? That same man of the other day?'

'Yes, Major Bellayr. He – I can hardly tell you. He's been transferred to our side for surgery and he really gets in amongst me. He's so objectionable; I dread touching him; even *seeing* him, speaking to him.'

'Could you be more exact?'

'That's what I can't be. *It's everything*! His face, his insolence – arrogance, I should say – even hatred.'

'Of you, Doctor?'

'Yes, I think so; I'm nearly sure of it; but it's more than that. It seems to be a scorn for the whole world, all life! Even this war is nothing to him – no more than *he* would expect of us. And of course he's the kind of trickster who only appears to be in the fight when really he's smiling at the chaos of it all.'

She was looking at him with real interest as he added: 'And about women he's disgusting, frightening.'

She was looking down at her journal:

'And that is what disturbs you most?'

'Not that exactly.'

'What then?'

'It's my anger, Sister.'

She looked up: 'That's a little sudden! Anger with the Major or with women?'

'With both. No, I'm not sure. Perhaps we, perhaps some people are born angry. I believe I was – and it seems to have nothing to do with my will. I don't *want* to be raging. Sometimes when I think I'm getting better, getting away from it, as if it was something stalking me through the snow; a fox – ' He hesitated, seeing that leach of snow with something behind it.

'A wolf?' she suggested.

'Yes, that. I stop to make sure and again I see its tracks not far away, alongside mine; or even, and this is horrible, ahead of them. Then I know that it hasn't given up, never will.'

She was very still, not quite real in her starch and age. She tucked at a pleat of her bodice:

'And you connect this fury with us? – with women?'

200

'I do.'

She laughed a little: 'And since your Major is less than civil about us?'

' "Civil!" Don't laugh at me; and please don't call him "my" major. You should hear him. You wouldn't use words like "civil"; though I suppose, in the armies you've been with, the battles you've served in, the warring of all those men, you *have* heard him. But that's not it. Whatever *is* the real cause, the fear or the hope that we men have in us through women, through passion or sex – whatever *that* really is, only disguises itself in physical, in romantic passion. Really, it's something quite other. It can never be satisfied, not by any marriage or mistress, not even when it destroys itself or someone else, as Victoria was destroyed. My God! When you are in love, Sister, there are times when you *want* to be tested, when you want someone to threaten, so that rather than be cheated you may move yourself into some other temper, the plane of rage. That's true, it really is. I've heard men on about their daughters: they say, "If anyone were to hurt my girl there'd be nothing that I would not do." And then they smile.'

She had turned away to look down at her memoirs again: an etching of a young Victorian officer. Beneath the canvas of a high tent he lay sprawled in a chair, stretching out his breeched and booted legs beneath a spray of mistletoe on the lamp above his pomaded head.

'There are many such men. I have heard things from refugees, terrible whispers of certain camps in Germany, of slavery and persecution, torture.' She sighed. 'It's so very difficult to talk usefully without being personal.'

'I want to be personal.'

'Doctor Blaydon, we talk of fear of the unknown, for we prefer not to admit that it is the known which alarms us. And in this instance, of course, the known is in yourself.'

He fancied she had smiled at him, had said something to jolt him; but had not the attention for her to be sure, as he continued:

'I forgot to tell you – I got lost in detail. My real fear is that this evil, the power to do what he has done – all of it – is in *me*. The difference is all in the doing; that I have *not* done such things. It is on the other side of the act itself that the real unknown lies.' He paused, 'Sister, he's gone into that unknown, beyond anger and shame. He couldn't even be bothered to harm people now.'

'Now?'

'They don't exist for him any more. They're the doors you slam or the dogs you kick.'

Certainly she was smiling at him as she had done when they first met, with the same unplaceable amusement:

'And *you* know this?'

'Somehow I do; but you mean, don't you, that I'm still young enough to go on being cruel? And that's true. I have been, to my family, my friends. I've been extremely cruel to several girls in the past.'

'Then, if you will allow it to be, it is over; for it is only in what we privately enjoy of it that the past has any sway over us.'

'I can't see that.'

What could he wish, he asked himself, to retain of his past love, of Victoria, that was not most painful in the impossibility of its completion?

Had she but gone away, had she but left him for a time to journey to some other place, as in this war so many people so continually did, becoming no more than partial images, remembered breaths in the air –

Or if, somewhere, at some time he should hear her breathe again, that excited breath! Ah then. But, dead she never could, they could never share it, never could ever again.

His fitful grief, his undying resentment for what had been denied, that dream that was beyond breathing: he saw it now in its truth and in glimpsing it, was able to tell the Sister:

'I'm afraid you are right.'

She was standing now, ready to go: 'That's good. Perhaps soon you will be glad that you are young while there's time for it – glad of the darkness too.' She moved towards the door. 'Ah, as we would say in my day, "You don't half like that", do you?'

'I'm not sure what you mean.'

'That you half like being told off and half do not – but about your Major, and I *shall* say it, for you have made him yours – you should distance yourself from what is in him and from your own shadows. Then you'll be bigger; no longer in any danger from the wolf.'

She pulled her blue cape more tightly round her shoulders, straightened her cap and picked up her book, *The Campaign in the Crimea*.

'There is some good tea in the Thermos flask and some biscuits in the tin. If you'd care to stay here awhile?'

In the next minute she was gone.

29

Major Bellayr's stomach, thin as a pink balloon, floated above the jaws of the long-handled forceps between the edges of the ventral incision. The organ was distended with a little flatus, a scentless gas that overlay the hydrochloric acid within the saucer of the Greater Curvature. Beside it, similarly captured, a coil of the jejunum lay like a puce garden hose. Above both of them, nearer the patient's head, the dome of the diaphragm swelled and contracted, pumping in time with the lungs inhaling the ether and oxygen of the anaesthetic.

Miss Graemes, her eyes pretty above her mask, said,

'Get your fingers under, please, under the pylorus.'

She spoke little at any time and, in surgery, her words were few indeed, so it was a comfort to hear them; for, during her thyroidectomies he often had the chill feeling he was not there, not assisting at all; that he was one of her less reliable instruments; a necessary, unwanted obstacle between the surgeon and her goal; an artery forceps that would not hold, worse, one that would not unclip at the second pressure.

His gloved fingers explored the warm pool of the Major's belly; everything so subtle so delicate, no hard edges to which the anemones had clung in his boyhood in Anglesey. He could make out the head of the pancreas, lumpy as cottage cheese, the under-surface of the liver and, behind it, the firm peritoneal-clad vertebral musculature.

'Well?' Miss Graemes asked.

'We're in no hurry,' added Mrs Strykes, 'but we *would* like our calories this side of two o'clock.'

'I think there's an adhesion or something; I can't get behind the fundus.'

'There's a history of perforation, then?'

'No, Doctor.'

She was silent, turning her head to study her viewing screen of the X-ray: the Major's last barium meal. The ulcer crater showed clearly in the pyloric portion of the gastric cavity. The surgery of choice was to excise that area of the stomach with its contained ulcer and then join the remainder directly to the jejunum, thus bypassing the duodenum while still allowing it to function.

The Major was not quite silent; he breathed as regularly as does the ocean on quiet nights, his exhalations filling the silences of the operating theatre.

He is peaceful for once, John thought: he cannot speak, watch all this, make, for the present, any more of his one-line comments.

30

The Major was dying; behind the windows of the oxygen tent he sat stiffly, rigid with the energy of the moribund, of those in the last surge of strength, as he begged for final release.

He raised his yellow hands and scraped at the thin perspex with his finger nails. His mouth opened and closed, his words came clearly through the fabric.

It interested John to see that his once yellow hair, yellowish gold in that last sight he believed he had had of him on the beach at Worthing, was tonight not even the greyed gilt of the patient he had first met on the Guinea Lane compound. His cheeks were hollowed out in the swift post-operative weight loss: his eyelids were thinned as lizards', as those of the avian predators – the gyr falcons and their eyasses fluffy in the nest – they had pulled back from the sclera of the eyeballs, the thick bilious whites giving him a screaming look that since he could not loudly scream, was comical in its exaggeration of anxiety: not clownish, for it was an extreme of comedy; there was nothing half-solemn about it as there is in the business of the circus.

John was inflexible; a rock inside him could not be moved. He was as righteous as though clothed in the rank of court martial, the cap of tribunal.

'Give!' the Major mouthed. 'Something! Christ's sake!'

John did not trouble to reply to him. He only went on looking. He was not even surprised at his own coolness in the face of such anguish. His position was unassailable; he was not allowed to give more analgesics than he had already prescribed. The bounds of pain, of continuing life, of chemical relief were laid down. Only those in final authority could change them; and in inquests all records were examined. A house surgeon could always be held culpable for exceeding his orders. It was his duty to comply.

He had dismissed the Night Sister ten minutes earlier and was standing beside the Major's bed under the lampshade hung by one of the probationers with mistletoe. Inside the windows between the gap in the drawn curtains he could see a strip of the blackout and hear the fading rumble of a few aircraft making for their especial targets in Europe, in the Christmas lull of the bombing.

He leaned forward and spoke distinctly:

'It was you who killed my girl in Yorkshire.'

'Christ! Doctor! A pill! Anything.'

'And in Yorkshire, in Huddersfield. You disappeared in that town – after the murder.'

'Murder?' The Major's face closed in thought. There had been a cessation, brief, in his pain and he was able to consider:

'I've done murder?'

'You have.'

'Is this a grudge? Women's orders?'

'No. You've harmed women.'

'They looked for it.'

'In New York. You used art photography as a lure to get women.'

'They were easy.'

'You preyed on children too.'

'Their folks liked the money. Kids are vainer then; sexier; and energy they have!'

His face shortened as he closed his jaws in the onset of more pain. The sweat he had been proud of had diminished, his forehead was dry, his wrinkles smoothed out as he drew down his white eyebrows over his closed eyes. Between the lapels of his hospital nightshirt his ribs stood out of the whiskered skin, the sunken troughs over the lung tissue.

A tea trolley was being wheeled down the corridor, the cups and teaspoons rattling, the sound of the probationer's heels knocking smartly on the linoleum.

'Why knock me? Back there it's industry – only the start.'

John leaned forward. Suddenly he wanted to get into the tent and feel his hands on the loose skin of the Major's neck.

'You picked on my Victoria, you saw her, spoke to her in our Dale. I don't know what else you did; but you ended her voice – '

'I told you from the start; you're crazy.' His eyes wandered. 'It's going to be business; cruises arranged to good kid country – good brothel country. At that age they've got faces for the camera. Most kids got faces.'

John stood up. 'Faces! Shut your eyes before we have to do it for you, and you'll see faces.'

206

'Hey, don't go, don't leave me. Remember your oath?'
'I don't hear you.'
'*Doctor!*'

He closed the door behind him with only the normal pressure of the tongue into the groove. Inside his chest he felt satisfied; so full and contained that the organs within him were visible to him as vessels of life, as vases upon a shining table.

He walked lightly out through the doors and into the compound, the cold air of it. How good it was, fruitful, to have done such a thing; to have waited and then waited again, with so much unexpressed hatred, to end such recurrent pain destroying so many possibilities of joy, to have been revenged.

Vengeance! To have captured the cause of his fury and dealt with it: to have reason at last to recover; to be sure, to be nearly certain in his whole self that it was enough, that it would last; to believe that it might; to hope that for a time he would be reconciled.

31

He fetched Doctor Gillespie. He could have telephoned from the Sister's office; but what he had to say must not be overheard. Besides, he needed the doctor in some way which it was hard to specify; he needed him more than he needed Sister Thorpe. She was so very commonsensical and though she overleapt questions easily her answers were flat, even a little exhausted, not so much with the experience of her years as with her 'other world' certainty. In Doctor Gillespie there was more warmth; more comfort in his counsel, because it came of a nearer, more masculine confusion. Also he knew about Victoria, about the moors, the unsolved murder. True, in that first interview he had said only,

'Blaydon? That would be *John* Blaydon, would it not, Doctor? Aye! I heard the most of it at the time.'

But those few words, that little, had proved more powerful than hours of open discussion. Like a secret shared it had been a key in their relationship from the start, an understanding all the more potent for never being mentioned; an odd delight to John and perhaps to the doctor as well.

He thought of all this as he passed through the snowy compound hurrying along the glimmering asphalt paths past the cement birds – burdened now with snowy plumage – and the iced pools and the frozen shrubs towards the Superintendent's house. Else, if Gillespie had not taken a kind of comfort in his remembrance of that heavy childhood, why would he have confided his own affairs so fully and so soon?

Yet never had the doctor been even a trace vulgar in his affection, in any display of his knowledge. Though often he must, in his own humiliation, have wanted to say such things as, 'You'd ken fine with that wee girl's loss in your heart!' or 'With the lass taken, you'd *know*'; he'd never so much as 'looked' such things.

Out of breath, John thumped the black iron knocker against its seat on the pine-grained door and waited for the doctor to ascend from his comfortless snug in the basement.

He looked up at the strawberry sky from which a few dark flakes still wandered down through the air. Though London was blacked out, never a cranny showing from a myriad house lights, a moon shone from somewhere over the snow clouds, and tonight it was as warm as the peacetime amethyst he remembered over every town and village in England when the ceiling was low over the countryside.

Mistress Madge slid open the wicket 'squint' for an instant. He saw her black-browed eyes through the little bars before, with no word, she drew the bolts and let him into the hall.

She looked him up and down from under the golliwog of

208

her hair and clicked her tongue in the same manner as her brother:

'Tk, tk! What are you aglow with *this* night?'

'Aglow?'

'Afire, John, you're ablink with your tidings. Hot as a cheese-winder from the mill.'

'It's the damned – '

He stopped. He and Mistress Madge were good friends. Ever since that night when she had run in upon him with only a mustard plaster on her bony body, she had accepted him, cared for him in a rough way. But tonight he did not want even her scant words to delay him.

'It's someone dying,' he told her. 'I need your brother.'

'He's not here. He's with that uncouth lass in Fevers.'

'Doctor Whooper?'

'Aye.'

'Well, could I ring up the unit and get him over to the surgical ward, do you think?'

'It's your affair.'

'Is Doctor Gillespie – ? I mean, is it a consultation with Doctor Whooper?'

'A *consultation*!' Mistress Madge thumped him so hard on his chest that he took a step backwards. 'With that one beribboned like a heathen maypole? A barnyard banging behind the hallan, more like!'

'I'd better call him up, all the same. It's very urgent.'

'Then call him! Well it is for you to hold Fairburn Gillespie from knocking out his nail in some drossy closet with that basin-faced kale-worm.'

'If you think – ' John began, trying to banish Madge's vivid imagery. 'I hardly like to interrupt the doctor; but I have to.'

'With that maggotty Robene gone away to her spumey lover in Chelsea, he kens not where to turn for his comfort. For the Good Lord is a chancy master, forever larking with his suitors. Go you and prick me froward brother's crest with a call to duty whiles I spoon out the broth you're to swallow before you leave the hoose.'

'I was with Gelda Whooper over in Fevers in a bittock

209

conference when you called,' Gillespie told him as they read through the Major's case notes in Sister Rogers' office.

'I was sorry to have to call you, sir, but Major Bellayr – '

'A rare one she is, that Gelda, douce indeed! What would be *thy* opinion of the lassie?'

'I haven't thought. She's a bit plain but – Sir, about Major Bellayr?'

'Plain! She's a bonny bit thorn. I would not compare her with a bush of roses visited by every fly in the kingdom. But for a green thorn decked out once a year and privy to the singing thrush – ' The Doctor paused, staring intently at the day register. 'But for why are you so dooms down-hearted about the poor Major? If he's deeing, ease him; if he's to bide, tend him.'

'There's more to it than that.'

'No doubt! 'Tis ever the way. What do you fancy?'

'It isn't fancy; I don't think it is. It sounds mad, but I believe, I'm just about sure that he's the man who murdered my girl, Victoria, in Yorkshire all those years ago.'

'Aye. 'Tis your right to think so.'

'It was he who followed us into the cave and wouldn't leave. Just as he does now with Nurse Lynton, he played with us both; with our uncertainty. Then later he took her away – '

The doctor nodded. 'I ken fine. I remember the case.'

'And from that came my sickness, Doctor Gillespie. I don't talk about it much; but since that black division in my life, that filthy trickery! A promise of such love, such understanding! So complete' – he broke off.

'It *must* be him. In Worthing, on the beach, I heard some girls he was meeting talking about him, about someone they called "Kit" though he was calling himself Desmond then. And there's his way of talking; he says "Lead on MacDuff" – and the murderer said that – Oh! There are hundreds of significant things – '

'And you have charged him with it and he has confessed?'

'No, sir. He denies it.'

'Aye, he would.'

'But it all fits in – everything. Oh, thank God you understand! Oh, I knew you would.'

210

'The more particularly would he deny it were he innocent.'

'What?'

'John, John! Where's your grudge? You're burning up with it!'

'And why *shouldn't* I be? Now that I have him where I wanted him after fifteen years of waiting, of giving up hope and then always expecting it again. For that's how it is with me: a cry for justice and a revenge that I knew was there somewhere. Then to be cheated of it – cruelly!'

' "Cruelly", you say? Cruel on whose part?'

'Why, on *his* – or God's.'

'Aye! Then you need the Major sore.'

'Need him?'

'Indeed. How else would a man sit down with his life and not give his faults a face other than his own? We are ever at war with ourselves, John, and with no garbed enemy to counter and no good God to sweetheart us, we can never be reconciled.'

'You think I'm mistaken?'

' 'Tis likely. You've dwelled over long with thy fury. Like a brave horse bowed in his collar with his pulling, you belabour him with such sharp blows and kicks that he dances at shadows and throws you both in the mire.'

'But that man in there is merciless – beyond it in all that he does – and therefore fearless – not even evil since he has no feelings for anyone in the world!'

Gillespie laughed. What's this? You'd prefer the evil then?'

'I would. I can sense its absence and it chills me as no ordinary wickedness could. I feel there's nothing to limit him, that there's nothing he hasn't thought of, hasn't done, wouldn't do.'

The doctor straightened himself; he looked steadily at John and then turned towards the door.

'We must haste to the poor carle straight and give him all the ease we may with our quiet and skill.'

'He is in the private room, sir. I have him on oxygen and all the Omnopon he's allowed. But he's terrified – ' John hesitated.

211

'Of what? Of what is he terrified?'

'Nothing, sir. I'm afraid he may have a post operative bleed. The ulcer was adherent to the pancreas; we couldn't detach it. Despite the packed blood and drips he's on, he's too weak for further surgery at present; and even then we don't know what the best procedure would be.'

Further down the corridor an electric bell was ringing continuously: a thin irritating noise that never varied in tone.

A young nurse, her cap awry on her hair, hurried out from between the swing doors of the ward and into the Sister's office.

Gillespie paused by the door into the Major's room.

'The laddie in here is deathly feared of *what*?' he demanded.

'Of dying alone, sir.'

'And you prevaricated! For *you* were afeared of telling me.'

The nurse came out of the Sister's room and ran up to them:

'There's something wrong with the Major's bell, Sir. He was calling for Doctor Blaydon earlier; but he seemed to give up, to settle; and Sister can't come for a few minutes – she's dressing a drainage.'

'Thank you, Nurse.'

'Is there anything else, Doctor?'

'There is. When we have gone you may bide with the Major. He's to be on continuous watch till the morn.'

They pushed open the door and went into the highly lighted room.

The Major lay back on his piled pillows, his now bright yellow face outraged as he gazed up at the roof of his private tent.

The cable of the bell ran taut between both his hands, ending in the black bell-push itself which was thrust into his open mouth like a baby's dummy, wedged between his jaws by him in his last agony – and still shrilling down the corridor.

212

Gillespie lifted up the hem of the tent and pulled out the bell coated with froth and bile – and the ringing ceased.

He passed it to John who put it in the hand-basin.

'We were too late, Doctor Blaydon. Whoever this lost, straughted man may be, he's parted this world for a clearer! Nurse, leave him be awhile to make good his peace. Dinna fashion his limbs nor any part of him this half-hour.'

'No, Doctor.'

They closed the door on her, for she was inclined to straighten the room a little and perhaps, out of her youth and kindness, to stay with the Major.

With John lagging uneasily behind him the doctor walked fast along the linoleum, down the three steps and out into the compound,

'You'll come down the hoose a bit? Take a drink to stop your stoits.'

'My stoits?'

'Your staggers; for you are fair whipped down with the bitterness of vengeance. Ach! 'Tis a bilious cud to set your teeth to knocking.'

'I am unhappy, that's true; but I was so sure. And I'm still not sure.'

'And never will be! Of that thou canst be sure.'

Ahead of him Gillespie paused by a group of cement birds pillowed with the snow that had fallen in the night. 'But come up, Doctor. Dinna lag behind me like a wet lurcher.'

'I feel I've done wrong. I know I have.'

'And will again.' The doctor put an arm briefly round his shoulders and then withdrew it. 'For 'tis a truth that evil stalks not in the world but creeps in the sweetest courses of the human heart; in all our best dispositions it bides as the twist in the yarn, as the knot in the woodgrain. In hope it is ambition; in ambition it is greed; in greed, the fist; in the fist, murder, and in murder, the pit.'

He halted and in the dark stared at John. 'What! Would you have this strangler, if strangler he was, haste *you* to your pit as first he ran to his? Never, John, never!'

They had reached the front door now and the doctor gestured him inside.

'Run down the stair whiles I bid my tittie, Madgie, fetch out and cut for us a piece of my salt bacon from Auchtermuchtie.'

'Thank you, Sir. You're very kind.'

John hurried down to the snug and helped himself to a cup of whisky from the cag.

He sat on the bentwood chair and drank it slowly to start with and then finished it at a gulp.

32

The next day as they scrubbed up beside one another, Miss Graemes was crystal cold about the Major's death: so withdrawn and monosyllabic that it was strange to him to see the same prettily shaped eyes above her mask, the same gentle body beneath her surgical gown.

'You did not keep me fully advised.'

'I'm sorry.'

'And now there's to be a post mortem.'

'When, Doctor?'

'This afternoon. When you have attended it, you will report back to me.'

'Is it at the Cinder Patch?'

'It's at the Borough Mortuary in Batsford.'

Behind them, Mrs Strykes, busy with the anaesthetic, looked across:

'And he'd better watch his tongue or he'll be in the excrement – we don't want another balls-up at the inquest.'

'Are you sure that patient's under?'

'She's deeper than a dongo. We can say what we like.'

'Have I to attend the inquest as well?' John asked.

'Certainly.'

'I meant – on my own. I was only assisting.'

'Only assisting!' said Doctor Strykes. 'You 'ad yer dabs deep in the poor sod's guts – but doun't worry; we'll brief yer.'

'Doctor Graemes, I want to know whether I'm to represent the hospital at the inquest as well as the post mortem?'

'This is not the time to discuss it.'

'No, wait till you've 'ad yer tea and buns, then we'll tell you what you're to say.'

Over the patient's head Mrs Strykes was smiling at him with the greatest warmth and disinterest. He did not know which of the two of them he would have liked to shake first; the physically delightful, virginal surgeon or the querulous divorced anaesthetist.

Pearl Cleary, the Theatre Sister, her two assistant nurses, efficient and sure of themselves, were graceful. They, too, could put him in his place if he made mistakes or was rude; but there was not the same hostility. He felt they saw the comedy of his manhood rather than the threat of it. The other two, each in her own way, he thought, were in new ill-fitting modes. Unsure of their powers as yet, they knew less how to behave to his sex than to their own.

At the end of the day's 'list', a single thyroidectomy, he walked with Doctor Graemes to her car. He was dismayed at the prospect of bussing into Batsford that afternoon for the Major's autopsy; angry at the thought of the inquest that must follow it a day or so later. It had never occurred to him that the Surgeon would back down and leave him to give the medical evidence alone. It would have been unpleasant enough even if the surgery had not been in doubt; but with the memory of the haste that had set in, the inept cobbling round the adherent ulcer, he felt guilty and frightened. From what Mrs Strykes had said it was apparent that the Coroner had proved awkward over some previous post-surgical death.

Then, too, there was additional fear, a double reach of it through his touching of the Major's flesh when he had been 'away'; when whatever he was, whoever he was, had been absent from his body in the theatre. For he knew he could

215

not have borne such intimacy had the man been conscious. Used as he was to the sudden exposure of strangers' bodies, to allowing his hands and mind to play over familiar surfaces whilst they, the owners, looked away, waiting in hope or dread for what he might discover; with the Major and a few others he had had to overcome so great a repugnance that he almost felt surprised he had not been accused of it – as of some misdemeanour.

Even during the operation, with his gloved fingers sliding over the hidden places in the Major's abdomen, he had felt like a nervous burglar exploring, in triumph and fear, some coveted space.

And that was not all: though he was at pains not to think about it, to dodge it if he might, there were times when the day of the inquest on David's death had burst into his mind like the waters of an inundation. For that remembered interval, that very particular event, was no more a recollection than was every instant of the night of Victoria's taking in Danbey Dale.

For him, recollection, like love, was initially a gentle matter, stealing through his senses as a perfume; but there was this other kind of memory, the affective kind, the sensory re-living of passionate experience which could be an explosion, destroying the present and blotting out the future.

And now, as they stood by Dr Graemes' car he was silent, trying to hide his trembling as he passed through fear into anger, and with it found strength to repeat his question,

'Will the Coroner be satisfied, do you think, Doctor?'

Through her orange muffler drawn close above her chin, her breath filtered out into the chilly air:

'If *you* are competent, why should he not be?'

'Because I was only assisting. I mean, I did not do the actual repair.'

'I should think not!' Her eyes regarded him coolly. 'You take over the Medical side after Christmas, I believe?'

'Yes.'

'It would be well for you to remember that.' She pulled one of her bare hands out of her navy blue pocket and opened the car door with a jingle of keys. 'You are going to need my reference.'

'That sounds – '

'Yes?'

'It doesn't only sound it; it *is* threatening.'

'I quite agree.' She gave her keys a little shake. 'Doctor Blaydon, you are an apprentice; you are here not just to learn your job, but to learn to obey your superiors.'

Oafish in the face of such certitude, he said baldly, 'I don't have to obey threats.'

'How you choose to view discipline is your affair. How I choose to express it is mine.' Again she rattled her keys, holding them out provocatively over the ground frost.

'I think you're damned unfair.'

'You should not swear, you know. To say the least, it is unprofessional.'

'That's because you're woman, isn't it?'

'No, Doctor. It is because I am a person.'

He did not answer but stood there obediently, as if seeing himself from outside; a young man in a starched white coat standing on frosted cinders helping a pretty, slender woman into a motor car. Who was to know how furious he was? How much more angry than if she had been another man? Why, she was threatening him, humiliating him; and 'unsportingly' so when she, by her nature, was so much stronger. How dared she? How did she dare?

With a man he would have coveted only his skill, his greater experience, ability; and this in order to excel; and that so that he might be esteemed by people; by women.

Here she was possessing not only the skill he wanted, but her whole self which he more than wanted or needed; whose acknowledgement he demanded.

Reluctant, he walked away from her over the frozen cinders to the end of the parking space, to a gap in the ropes and posts.

Always he disliked leaving her, hated it as if leaving a winter fireside: for something in her chill blazed for him, warmed him and touched their work together to excitement; significance.

He had heard the driver's side door close, the click of it,

imagined her gym shoed feet touching the pedals: the clutch, the accelerator.

The interior of the Jaguar, he knew, was scented by her, very slightly it had trapped the shampoo she used or the sandalwood bath salts she allowed herself – of which on early morning rounds she left a light trail in the wards, a purer, more teasing vapour along the corridors.

Now he heard the starter motor whine beneath the bonnet. Once, twice, three times, then more petulantly again and again. And he stopped outside the lot; waited by some leggy cement bird or other, an emu or a stork.

She was angry, pushing the button repeatedly without pause, bleeding her battery and, as it was dusk, leaving her head and side lights still on, not saving the current they used to help turn the flywheel and the crankshaft.

He turned back and stood by the ropes so that he might watch through the increasing thickness of the November light.

She got out and pulled up the near side flap of the bonnet; stood against the yellowish clouds of the horizon peering into the darkness of the engine.

After a minute she looked back at him, her face a sallow disc within her shadowy hair. She was quite still, her muffler drawn close round her neck as she stared towards him where he waited, equally motionless.

She said, 'She doesn't appear to want to start.' And when he didn't reply, added, 'That *is* Doctor Blaydon?'

He realised then that she was just a very little short-sighted and, standing his ground, smiled inside himself.

'Out of petrol?' he asked.

'Possibly.'

He had switched off her headlights and was standing beside her at the front of the grey shape of the car. 'I don't think you can be. If anything you've overflooded her. Can't you smell it?'

'But don't they all stink of that when one opens the hood?'

'Have you got your pen torch handy?' It was still warm from her breast pocket as he took it. 'Thank you. There! You see, you've got petrol slipping down the side of your

218

carburettor. Your choke must have jammed, or you left it out too long.'

'I understood that in cold weather – '

He handed her back her torch. 'It's still possible to overdo it. Sitting there grinding away with your starter and your choke full out and your lights left on. Don't you know anything about engines?'

She laughed. 'Of course not. That is the kind of thing one does leave to the men.'

'All we're fit for?'

'I mean only that you seem to enjoy it; that for some reason – ' She didn't continue, was silent sufficiently long for him to turn and meet her impatient gaze as she added, 'How tiring you are! Can you never understand that it's a matter of choice only – has nothing to do with one's conditioning? Had I chosen to clutter my mind with the mechanics of the internal combustion engine I would have done so – '

'Yes?'

'My concerns lay elsewhere.' Again she laughed. 'So what should I do now, do you think?'

'Get in and start her. I think she'll fire up by now.'

She got back in and pressed the button. The engine spat for a moment and then turned as she revved it hard. She lowered the window, and he leaned down to hear her, smelling the tantalising scent of the moist breath which so short a second before had been deep in her lungs next to her blood.

'Thank you, Doctor Blaydon, And about tomorrow's Post Mortem – it will do you no harm to follow through a surgical failure for which you were even less responsible than I was myself.'

Before he could reply she rolled the window up again and let in the clutch.

Kicking the cinders hard he walked back through the gaining dark.

33

The gates to the Blackford Mortuary were padlocked with a zinc chain through heavy staples. He rattled at it until the hasp slipped open, then pulled wide one of the gates giving onto the 'Cinder-Patch' and went in.

On each side of the dark pathway were the rounded white shapes of the bathroom fittings Minna had seen: metal tubs, rain-filled and tap-stained, the enamel starred by bomb splinters; vertical urinals from blitzed hotels and suburban railway stations, water closets, white cabinets, galvanised tanks, copper geysers and electric heaters; wash basins with their taps still in them; slabs of grey veined marble, cracked mirrors and pier glasses; cisterns and chairs, mounds of dirty white sanitary bricks.

As he walked along the cinders in his blue raglan, the bag he had needlessly brought with him heavy in his hand, his eyes wandering over the repeated shapes of the bombed bathrooms, over the rain-spattered enamels, the lavatories with their seats up or down, their outlet pipes unconnected to anything, the leaning mirrors reflecting the clouded sky, he was suddenly transported to an instant in his boyhood: walking down a quiet London street.

There had been a doctor's plate beside a pillared front door; the brass, freshly polished by some servant, so that it shone at him out of the ingrained soot of the wall.

'Never,' he had vowed in that moment to himself. 'Never shall I ever be a doctor.' And, as if through that orange winking plate, some spell had been cast upon him as he said these words, he *was* a doctor; not only a doctor; but one who might be quite similar to the man who lived in the house behind the brass plate. Nor was he young; he was a middle-aged medical man coming in beneath a winter's sky to a meal of cold beef and hot cabbage after a morning's work.

How, he wondered now, how could such a shift have happened? He had been only eleven or twelve years old; there was no thought of his being a doctor, no discussion of it in the family; and yet, for some moments, he had been another person in the middle of another life: one that filled him with dread.

He paused on the cindered path, putting his bag down with a crunch, his gaze wandering past the barrage balloons to the far chimneyed horizon where a few seagulls wandered over some other reach of the dump. Had that other moment, that viewing of another man's life, been prophetic? Had he been recoiling against a destiny of which some part of his mind was already aware? And what would he have done to change his course had he, in those few seconds, known *this* reality? Himself on his way through a city at war to open a newly dead body for whose demise he could be held in part responsible?

He lowered his gaze to search for the mortuary. He yawned and shook himself, he jerked his attention back to his surroundings, thinking only that he needed something he did not possess, had not until now specifically required: some grace of endurance.

A man was coming towards him, tall and misshapen; innocent looking, carrying a bulging black case. He had come out of a large corrugated iron building, a shed like an aircraft hanger with metal doors that were straight to the pitch of the roof.

John waited for him impatiently for he saw he was despicable. His rough cap, unpolished boots, slovenly gait as if he could not yet direct his heavy body, signalled simplicity; idiocy.

'Good morning. Is Doctor Tarn here yet? The Pathologist?'

The man spoke slowly, smiling amiably,

'Doc-tor?'

'Yes. And you are – who are you? What is your name?'

'Bert-ram. They call me Bert.'

'Good. Well, where do we go, Bert?'

'Doc-tor?'

'Yes, I told you: Doctor Blaydon. Now, is Doctor Tarn here yet? Is there anybody else here? I'm supposed to meet the Pathologist, the other specialist. You understand?'

Bert pointed, 'In there.'

'Where? Oh, he's arrived, has he?'

The square featureless building, its sheets of metal badly bolted, rattled in the wind.

'How do we get in?'

They walked side by side to a cleared crescentic area in front of the doors, where Bert paused. As if in imitation of John, he put his long black case down on the cinders and, turning round to face the now distant gates, he waved his arms at the scattered acres of bathroom fittings.

'Pretty! Here is pretty!'

'Yes, I suppose it is, in a way.'

Bert smiled. He had a pale orange coloured face and green eyes.

'Like? You like it?'

'It's quite nice; but it's raining. Doctor Tarn will be waiting.'

'Rain fills all. Music.' Bert picked up his case. 'Follow!'

At a better pace he led the way along the front of the building to a corner where again he paused waiting like an anxious host for his guest to catch up with him. Then he opened a small door, a sheet of corrugated iron flush with the jambs, and showed John in.

It was at first dark in the draughty, rumbling, rattling space; an ochre-brown darkness with sudden streaks of grey light entering from the roof and sides where the sheets of metal had been badly fitted.

The wind too, moved in there, blowing from the East Coast of England over the city spread along the Thames valley as far as the Estuary and the Medway towns, hooing in the semi-darkness, swinging the lights, touching John's face and smelling of something.

He stood still. Near to, he could not see the floor clearly; in the distance it was the indeterminate colour of cement, a neutral surface splashed as might have been stagnant water with the light of two bulbs slung across girders below the roof.

Behind him, Bert moved forward, planting his boots down on the invisible floor with a knocking sound as he moved away towards the two yellow pools; and, watching him, trying to stay with him, John was for a moment suffused with memory again, so much so that his place in the makeshift building was gone and he was back in Yorkshire, in the Stump Cross cavern.

As though there had been a pause in his consciousness, as though his mind had yawned at some undeclared knowledge, he felt his facial skin shrink upon the bones, his scalp prickle, his testicles draw back into his groin. He was squatting behind the poor fire they had lighted, Victoria silent beside him, both of them aware that many little things, small events, had now taken substance and that someone was moving towards them, his shod feet knocking the limestone, brushing hidden pools of water.

A stone fell, bounded against rock into water; the person approaching them swore. There was just the dull sound of the stone hitting the cave floor, the innocent splash of the water, then the short word spoken slowly by the man's mouth.

Near John, a little behind him on his unrolled mackintosh, Victoria gasped. He felt for her hand, the thin coolness of it, the trembling; but it was not there. It should have been beside her hip on the wrinkled mackintosh, or on her skirted lap; he was sure he knew where it was, could usually find it as easily as he could find his own. But now it had been moved out of his reach. He fumbled for it, his own fingers desperate, full of ideas as to where hers might be.

Her hip, too, had been moved; her thighs, her whole body. The mackintosh they were sharing was empty; it reached quite far over the top of the buttress on which he had spread it. By leaning back, his eyes still on the person who was approaching, by stretching out his arm, he was able to explore its furthest reaches, the very part where she had sat, to its unbuttoned edge; and there was no one else on it. Victoria's body had been removed; there was no part

223

of her left. He had heard her breath, the swiftness of it, only in his mind.

Bert was standing under the bulbs, his shadow thrown back over the floor more huge and misshapen than himself. He was patient, his old cap rough against the lights, his uneven shoulders and oversized head set in ape-like benevolence as he waited for John to come up to him.

'Where is Doctor Tarn. Where is – ?'

'Doctor is coming.'

John walked forward. Beyond the dull penumbra of the lights he could make out a dissection table with a body on it; beyond that, the wall of the building with three or four more people lying motionless on the floor.

'You said the doctor was here. Where are – '

'You read.'

'Where the devil are the lights? This is absurd – We can't – It's disgraceful.'

Bert leaned closer:

'*You* read!'

'Read what? Where?'

'I find a good light; you read his name.'

Bert moved over towards a small office with an inside window and suddenly flooded the centre of the building with light.

His big toes tied together with a luggage label, Major Bellayr lay on the dissection trolley a few feet away from the wall where four others lay naked on the floor.

There was a wide Windsor chair and a clerk's wooden stool beside the table and a bath tub with several white enamel buckets standing beside it.

Bert wheeled the trolley under the central light and held up the label tied to the Major's toes.

'Is right?' he asked. 'Jack?'

'*Jack?*'

In his anger and surprise John had repeated the name aloud. 'Jack Noone' the man in the cave had called himself; he had said it contemptuously as if he did not care whether they believed him or not.

'Let me *see* that!'

224

Bert's stained hand, large as though gloved, pushed him gently away.

'Card has to stay. You read it on Jack.'

'Damn!'

Bert patted the Major's left knee. With his childlike smile, so certain of approval, he asked again:

'Is he right? Is Jack all right?'

'Yes, this is Major Christopher Bellayr. He is the man we have to examine.'

Bert looked at the length of the yellow figure: at the pale ivory feet with the nails untrimmed; the jaundiced thighs and almost white penis resting innocently upon them: the brilliant apricot abdomen with its linear incision, the silver stubble of the sutures: the closed face so cold with silence.

'Good Jack!' he said. And this time he patted the flat stomach.

A car drew up outside and Bert fussed with the trolley, moving it a little this way and a little that, to get it under the fullest centre of the big light: 'Doctor likes to see poor Jack bright.'

His head was bent tenderly over the Major's face, his big hands hesitant as to how he might adjust the set neck. His concern, so total and unselfconscious was like that of a mother for her child, a baby in its pram that she was going to leave for a few minutes.

Doctor Tarn was brisk; black-coated, short-built and whiskery; he greeted John in a military fashion.

'Sorry if I kept you, Doctor. No doubt you've had a chat with our Bertram! Kept you thoroughly entertained I daresay.'

'Now, what have we here? Thank you, Bertram; hang it in the office and bring me my dressing gown and slippers.'

He glanced at John without winking.

'Bertram likes to view the whole rather grisly procedure as a kind of bedtime story with trimmings. He's one of Nature's eunuchs – unmarried, no children or dependents – and, I'm inclined to think, the war's been a Godsend to him – literally! Given him a never-ending family to mind. Ah! Thank you, Bertram. Clean gloves of course, and the thickest – Pop my box of tools on the big chair and hand

225

me the scalpel and the cutters. But, first, the Surgeon's notes.'

He parted his lips beneath his brushy moustache with a kissing sound as he skimmed the post-operative dossier.

'Phrupp! phrupp! Dear me! Those ladies again! What have they been up to this time? Nothing experimental, I hope. Well, shortly we shall see.' He looked up. 'You want to garb up for this party or will you trust *me*?'

'I'd much rather leave it to you.'

'Had enough, I daresay?'

'Yes.'

'Pretty grim, was it? And you're fairly new at it I suppose? You young men come and go so fast we hardly ever get to know you, do we, Bertram?'

Bertram nodded contentedly. He was crooning to himself, humming an air very low in his deep chest.

'But then,' went on Doctor Tarn as he ran his scalpel up the median raphe of the abdomen, 'I don't suppose you're all that keen to know *us*? Lordy! Lordy! What a carnage! What a field day these ladies have had! Just look at this, Doctor – '

His black rubbered hands had shifted the transverse colon to one side, moved away the apron of the greater omentum and coils of small intestine to reveal the head of the pancreas nestled in the horseshoe of the duodenum.

The pancreas was shot with blood, richly starred with huge browning magenta haemorrhages centred in the ulcer burrowing from the stomach wall. In the depths of the cavity, more blood, mingled with the 'water' of ascites, washed about over the renal fat and into the bowl of the pelvis round the rectum, the bladder and the seminal vesicles which sat up through it from beside the prostate like the ears of some furry little animal.

'I would like, I really would like a few of these gentry to come and see the *end* results of some of their efforts in the theatre.' He made a kissing sound again, '*Phrup*! They never do, you know; *never*! Always detail off some – I was going to have said "greenhorn", but that is an Americanism – some young houseman to keep score and carry their – '

He broke off. 'But let's, for the sake of thoroughness,

open the chest and see if we can't possibly mitigate things a little with a fatty heart or a fibrous lung. For, after all, those ladies are rather new to it all – and haven't yet learned to – pass by on the other side when they encounter a pathologist anywhere but in Court. There!'

He had clipped racily through the rib cage up towards the neck and now folded it back like a red and heraldic shield over the Major's peaceful face.

'Nothing!' His surgical scissor points flitted along the course of each coronary, laying it open like a yellow rubber tube. 'Quite a healthy fellow in his – What was it?'

'Claimed to be thirty-seven.'

'Well, led quite a clean life – dietetically at any rate. But we can't, unhappily, lessen the damages for our enterprising colleagues up on the Hill. Just look at this roaringly healthy liver! No matter where one slices it – apart from the poor chap's post-operative jaundice – Are you all right, Doctor?'

'I think so.'

'The stink getting to you? Or is it my merry comments?'

'The stench, Sir. I *like* your comments.'

'Fine! I rather cultivate them. I mean, one has to have an attitude – patter if you like – or the job might – Really I find the only thing is to be interested, to care very much about it, like Bertram here. Isn't that so, Bertram?'

Bert's green eyes did not move from Doctor Tarn's face; they were as fixed as a cat's upon its master.

'I make Jack together again? I put him back now?'

'Thank you, Bertram.' Doctor Tarn turned to John.

'Well, you may tell her that I'm not going to be difficult – our Lady of the Thyroids. There's a war on – and a lot of untoward mortality. But, between ourselves, if she was going to jump in she *could* have caught a few more of those little arteries, to say nothing of the – What happened exactly? Did she panic?'

'We both did, sir.'

'Ah, they *are* so – Trouble is that their natural courage is all being expended on holding their place at present. We shall just have to wait until they have accepted *themselves* in the professions, in the world; learned how to idle in it as

227

we do. *Then* we shall see something quite extraordinary, quite delightful.' He took off his heavy gloves:

'Well, I'm going to our palatial ablutions at the other end of this hasty pudding of a place. Can I give you a lift anywhere?'

'It's very kind of you, sir, but I'm going to take the morning off and have coffee somewhere.'

'Good idea! I wish I could join you. Oh, Bertram! How many of those others are for *me*?'

Bert paused in his stitching. The shield of the Major's chest was back in place; and now the edges of the long abdominal incision were being carefully knitted together by his big gloved hands.

'Joe, Mag-gie, Jill and Dan.'

'All four then! When were they delivered?'

'Joe and Maggie came after breakfast. Jill and Dan-yel for tea-break.'

'Today, from St Jude's?'

'All today. St Jude and Jasper.'

'Well, I'll be back about three o'clock and make up the reports at the same time.'

Doctor Tarn hurried into the washroom and emerged very shortly looking exactly the same, as pink and sanitary as he had on his arrival.

As he put on his black overcoat in the office, he said:

'Another thing, Doctor. In order to be *able* to idle, one needs surplus energy. And that, unfortunately, is what they lack. You follow?'

'Not quite. You mean the women?'

'Our fairer colleagues: the tortoise and the hare! *He* was male, obviously, and could afford to sit about between spurts – because of his greater capacity; but she, poor little creature, had to keep going the whole time: plod, plod, plod!'

John was at first delighted. 'Oh yes, that's good. But then – the tortoise *did* win.'

'She did indeed! Indeed she did! But *what* a slow race!'

He looked at his watch and went over to Bert.

'Our Major looks most presentable again, Bertram. What are you going to give him? *Men of Harlech*?'

228

Bert rested his hands on the Major's thorax. He looked very grave.

'For Jack I play *Sweet Chariot*.'

'He'll like that; yes, nice choice!'

'He was sad to leave, Doctor Tarn.'

'Very likely.'

'And his chariot swings low for to gather Jack.'

'And why not? You're a good fellow, Bertram. Don't know what the war effort would do without you.' He pulled on his motoring gauntlets:

'I've got a lecture over the other side of the river: lot of little tortoises – first year nurses. Sure you don't want a lift to the village, or are you going to hear Bertram's 'cello piece?'

'Is *that* what it is? I was wondering.'

'Given him years ago by someone. He's a natural and he likes to play his friends out.'

'How strange!'

'I thought so once. But now it would seem a deal odder if, because of the war, no one *bothered*.'

'Yes.'

'Well, thanks for your help. I suppose we shall be losing you too? Which is it to be, the Army?'

'Not if the Navy will have me.'

'Remember, the sooner you apply the better. I gather it's most people's first choice.'

Doctor Tarn bustled off with his case of tools whose place had now been taken on the chair by Bert's 'cello case.

Over the following weekend John determined that he would not report the Pathologist's findings to Chlorinda Graemes. It would be pleasurable to make her suffer a little, to force her to come out into the open by saying nothing; by making her await Doctor Tarn's written report.

As it was, on the next Monday morning, she asked him about it at a most unfavourable moment when she and he, with Ella Strykes, were having morning coffee in the Recovery Room midway through that day's list.

'You did attend the post-mortem on Friday, Doctor Blaydon?'

'Post-mortem? Oh, you mean on Major Bellayr?'

She waited coolly, drinking her coffee in little sips, very upright on the chromium stool.

'Been more than one in your little black book then?' Ella Strykes asked. 'Or is it you don't want to tell? Screwed it up for us all?'

'Probably.' He was watching the ivory face of Miss Graemes, her pale lips as she sipped and turned to look at him.

'Well?' she asked. 'Did you?'

'Did I what?'

He wanted her to say it, to be forced into the crudity of her colleague; to see her thoroughly ruffled, as though in love-making someone had tumbled her roughly.

'Did you screw it up?' she said clearly. 'Make a balls of it, Doctor Blaydon?'

He put his coffee cup down on the white radiator.

'No I didn't, Doctor Graemes. It was all perfectly straight-forward – apart from the surgery, of course.'

'And the findings? Aside from old multiple peritoneal adhesions?'

He was going to have told her about the mess. He was poised to do so, when with a smile she added,

'And, of course, the unavoidable pancreatic haemorrhage.'

34

Lynton's mother, Lois, was ill and she had been given compassionate leave to nurse her over at their home in Watford.

'I shall miss you over Christmas,' she had said as they

waited for the 'bus in Guinea Lane. 'A wartime Christmas is no fun at home.'

'It won't be fun here without you.'

'You're sweet!' She fitted herself against him in the cold. 'Miss me a lot, will you?'

'I don't know.'

'Beast.'

He hugged her to atone for his honesty. He had spoken truthfully because he was angry. He really did not know how much he would miss her. Did one miss a weight? Her affection, her expectation of him had become heavy: he felt as though he were carrying a little girl on his back: fat and merry.

'You upset about something?' she asked.

'Everything really – Christmas in this place.'

'You've never been right since you lost the Major, have you?'

'I suppose not.' He stood very still, watching his breath condense in the cold air. Beyond the black railings, the sewage docks were pumping softly. 'What do you mean? Since I *lost* him?'

'Did I say that? I think you miss him, that's all.'

'I *don't!*'

She was silent. He saw that her face had frozen: the little girl was no longer merry – only plump. They stood estranged, saying nothing to one another.

Miss him, the Major, he thought, perhaps I do. She is so simple that she could be right. Oh God! I wish the 'bus would come. Parting is not sweet sorrow, it's only embarrassing.

'You'll have fun,' she tried, 'you'll be in the concert, won't you?'

'If I get desperate enough.'

'You need *me*.'

Oh I do, he decided; but only as a background.

'Perhaps you don't; with all the others after you. *They'll* be glad I'm away for it.'

'I can't be bothered with them.'

'Fibber!'

He laughed, and the sound was sad, rueful.

231

'Men,' she said, 'never satisfied. Back in Watford there are only boys and cripples left. Oh, I'm sorry!'

He wondered what she was sorry about. But only for a moment. Making love with her had given him familiarity with some parts of her mind, her responses, which in other women were closed to him.

'I don't think of Minna as a cripple.'

'No, she's just – not strong.'

'Not physically strong,' he corrrected.

'Poor child! Are you seeing her before she goes into Cold Harbour?'

'I'm taking her out to dinner somewhere.'

'You are kind.'

He stood on one leg and then on the other. He did not actually lift his shoes from the blank pavement; he just changed his weight-bearing to relieve his intense irritation. It would be hateful to quarrel openly when Lynton was leaving him; particularly since he was glad.

'I believe you want me to go.'

He said nothing. In the distance there were sea-birds flying over the sewage farm. Heavens, he thought, I hope they don't eat that.

'You do, don't you?'

Minna's gulls had circled her like something come from Heaven. Anything out of the other world was remote; in a way, unfriendly. It never quite touched.

'Oh I do,' he said thinking that, as usual, she had reproached him with not loving her. Suddenly merry again, she laughed.

The Major's seagulls had flown over the Cinder Patch in the furthest reaches of his vision. Little shapes and patches floating about below the barrage balloons, they had not been able to come any nearer.

She laughed and said, 'You are the limit!'

'What did I say?'

'Only that you *do* want me to go.'

He kissed her cold face, loving her merriment because it eased him of guilt.

'I wrote to the Admiralty yesterday.'

'Oh.'

He could feel her climbing down from his shoulders.

'So that is what it is.'

'I feel useless.'

'That is not true. You're doing a fine job.'

'What? Fumbling about with cripples and old people? When young ones like us are being cut to pieces, blown up, blinded, burned alive?'

'Why be in such a hurry? They'll call you up soon enough.'

Through the clear air, scented with human wastes, he could hear the gulls calling; their knowing, always poignant cries.

'Ever since you lost – ' she began. 'Ever since Major Bellayr died, you've been different.'

'Have I?'

He had not certainly noticed it in himself; but now that she had suggested it again, he did. Why had not the Major's death been more satisfying? Was it because he was not sure that he had been Victoria's murderer? Or was it that even if he had been, the crime still floated meaninglessly between heaven and earth.

'It was the post-mortem,' he told her, believing that was sufficient truth in their relationship. 'We had bungled the surgery; it seemed as though – '

'You shouldn't brood. You did your best; and anyway, Chlorinda Graemes! *She* was responsible. You said so yourself.'

'Nobody could have done anything. Our mistake was in opening him in the first place. I mean, a laparotomy would have been enough; a look around and leave well alone.'

She did not reply. She squeezed his forearm briefly and smiled down the road where the green bus was grunting up the hill.

He knew that what he had just said was not untrue; but was renewed in his anger by his inability to express even to himself his real sense of grievance; suspicion of some hidden factor that had betrayed them all; that, in a larger sense, had brought about the whole interminable war.

'Yes.' On an impulse, a need to reassure them both, he held her close against his blue raglan; 'Darling Lynton!'

The conductor was standing beside the driver turning

233

the handle that changed the route indicator. The words GUINEA LANE rolled up into the roof and disappeared, to be followed and replaced by WATFORD.

They kissed restrainedly. Her nose was wet and a little of its clear mucus clung to his cheek as she climbed up the steps to the top deck.

In a moment she was up there behind the top window glass, smiling resignedly as she was born away from him.

35

Because of the night's chill Doctor Gillespie would not allow him to take Minna out to dinner. So, well-mufflered, he took her along the familiar gravelly path beside the Thames for a Christmas tea in Stourmond.

Very quiet, silent almost, the river's polished surface slid beneath the mist that, like some stealthy adversary, seemed always to retreat ahead of them, to close in behind: and, as does the presence of something felt to be mysterious, alien, the pervasive dimness of the fog clinging to the rushes and the upper branches of the willows and alders, made all else more significant.

A solitary rower, sculling fast against the opposite bank, as though he were a painting executed by some unknown artist, glided upon his reflection with a chilling reserve; the slap of his oars, as they feathered the surface of the water on the return stroke only adding to his silence and isolation.

Nearer at hand, water birds: coot and teal, called briefly; not, it seemed, to one another, but only for themselves as though proclaiming their defiance of a world they had found to be hostile.

Minna coughed quietly, her face, between woollen muffler and knitted cap, a chip of pallor against the steel of

the river. He held her gloved hand tightly against his breast,
supporting her light body on his forearm, jealously.

'You're quiet,' she told him. 'Is it with her gone?'

'Partly.'

'I'll be gone too; soon.'

'I know.'

They listened to their footsteps on the moist pebbles.
Up river, out of sight, a barge chugged somewhere out of
Stourmond; they heard the thudding of its engine retreating,
coming nearer, retreating again, alternating in the thick air.

'You think I'm gone *now*,' she said. 'I know.'

'Yes, I do; in a way.'

'Have to share me, don't you, with my illness?'

He held fast to her gloved hand; he would have liked to
squeeze it as a fruit until all the juice was in a cup from
which he might drink.

'Yes.'

'Will it be worse because you never loved us, that way?'

'What way?'

'You're naughty, you are. You only want me to *say* it.'

'Yes.'

'Well, I won't. Yes I will: that you never got on top of
us – in bed.'

'I might have come from underneath.'

She was silent with interest:

'Can you? I never thought of that. Wouldn't it be – ?
How would you put your – ?' She tussocked into her muffler.
'Or will it be better for you?'

'No.'

She repeated it to herself; he thought in order to be quite
clear about it:

'It won't be better for you when I'm gone; it will be worse
because *we* never made love.' She skipped beside him. 'That
means you'll miss me more than her.'

'I shouldn't be too sure. It's a great – '

'Great what?'

'Pull.'

'How is it a great pull?'

'It's something you think over a lot; again and again.'

'When you're bored?'

235

'Yes, and when you're not bored. When you're anything, in fact.'

'I'm missing a lot, then, amn't I?'

'You certainly are.'

'If I could get a baby without; would I still be?'

'Missing as much? I don't know.'

'My baby, with all the – ' She walked in silence.

'All the what?'

'Trimmings. They're different from us, babies; foreigners really; the way they all talk the same even if they're Chinese. Ooh I *do* wish – '

'Well, why don't we?'

'Have a baby?'

'Yes.'

'Me going into Cold Harbour pregnant!' She looked round at him, up at his face and then over at the leafless hawthorn hedge beside the towpath. 'It's ever so wet, everything. We couldn't.'

'No, we couldn't. Anyway, there's your cough – and – '

'And what?'

'It's no fun the first time.'

'Then I'll just have to go on as I am, won't I?'

You will, he added to himself; you poor little thing. How much you have. At nearly every end and turn you surprise and delight me with your clearness which is like mountains in the distance. And I do not know where in your body those white ranges lie.

'Don't be sad,' she bade him.

'I'm not.'

'Mawkish, then. That's what me Aunt Nellie calls it. She says, "Now, George, don't you be mawkish." '

'When? When does she say it?'

'When he's looking out at ships, mostly.'

'Not when he's gardening, putting up the Eiffel Tower – I mean the "Tour Eiffel"?'

'No. When he's watching out to the ships.' She halted to look at him. 'You haven't half got a long memory – regular elephant.'

'Yes.'

'Will you remember all this? Everything?'

236

'Yes.'

'The way you remember her?'

'Who? Lynton?'

'No, Victoria; the other one as you never had.'

'You don't think – ' He let her gloved hand fall to her side between them. 'You don't imagine the only reason I loved her was because – '

'I wondered, is all.' She spoke in a small voice, looking down at the full river's edge where were some drowned plants, spindly but green. 'But you're over her, lately?'

'I think I am. Not "over" exactly, but she's gone so much further away that we don't need that any more.' He took her hand up again. 'How did you know?'

'You said, "*loved* her".'

'So I did.'

They walked on loudly; their shoes crunching the gravel, Minna coughing a little, the river mists thickening and growing acrid with the addition of the smoke from the chimneys of Stourmond. It was starting to rain.

'Was you going to get us our teas in one of them ladies' places?' she suggested as they walked towards the hill into the town.

'Yes, at least I think I was; if you mean the cafés?'

'Cafs is all right; I meant places like the Pilgrims' or the Maids of Honour in Melsom Street. *You* know, where the servers all wear cretonne smocks and have their hair straight brushed.'

'Don't you like them?'

'They make good sticky buns and Eccles cakes; but they talk so high – even to themselves.'

'You mean, above your head?'

'No, silly. I mean "superior". *You* ought to know that!'

'Why should I?'

'Because whenever they get some fellow or some officer dragged in there by his auntie or his girl friend, their voices go so high they might as well be up with the peacocks at Kew.'

He smiled at her and was silent. She walked along beside him so lightly on his arm; as light as everything in winter's lease: its blanched colours, its twigs stripped to next year's buds, its rivers' fat edge spent to the smallest of fishes.

'I was going to have got·you everything you fancied.'

'What, then? What things?'

'Apricot jam and toast, tea cakes, crumpets, cream puffs, apricot tarts and a plate of whatever assorted cakes they have.'

'You aren't half funny, Doctor John.'

Her laugh turned into a cough and he held her loosely, patting her duffled back.

'Funny in what way?' he asked when she had recovered.

'Only that all *them* things are what *you* like.'

'Well, what do *you* want?'

'Apricot crumpets,' she replied scornfully, 'apricot toast, assorted apricot cakes – and apricot tea.'

He shook her.

'I didn't say *that*.'

'Sounded like you did.'

'Go on; tell me what you *do* want.'

'Celery sticks in cut glass. Dates in a box with camels and palms on it, American baked beans on toast, custard tarts and a square teapot for me to pour it for us.'

'I'll get you them.'

'Will you?' She skipped again and got out of breath. 'Will you really? Where?'

'In an hotel.'

'A hotel!'

'Yes, the Garter.'

'But that's ever so posh. The Garter's huge. None of my friends except gawky Elspeth Berbeck-Hunter has ever been in it and her only to do with Chinese potato research for the Land Army. Do you think they'll serve us?'

'Why shouldn't they?'

'You aren't in uniform yet, is why; and I'm only in my mousecoat and muffler.'

'Just hold yourself haughtily and I'll snap out commands – as though I were a Guards' officer on leave.'

She laughed. 'It's always so busy, the Garter. It's head-quarters for *our* war effort – oh my!'

'What's the joke?'

'I can't explain. You haven't half brought us to the Queen Bee's hive. *You* could get in trouble, Doctor John; stung to death for a drone.'

'A drone? I'm not lazy – I work hard.'

'Poor little drones don't none of them work so busy as them in women's war. *They* are those as run the men as are running it all in these parts. There's Lady Constance Terrell of the Mission to Seamen, Countess Drogheda of Dig for Victory, and Mrs Louise de Flower who's in charge of Infestation and Mrs Kreuze of Venereal Disease and the Women's Institute and – '

'All the better for us. Wherever there are enough women there's bound to be plenty of tea – even High Tea.'

'You won't leave us, will you?'

'Only for a few minutes, and only in somewhere cosy.'

They walked hand in hand through heavier rain past the entrance gate and up the tawny gravelled drive. On either side of them were black laurel bushes, large leaved, glossy with rain and soot.

In front, the grey stone-blocked building towered up to its fat balustrade, dwarfing even the planes of the trees flanking it. Water from the badly guttered roof dripped onto the camouflaged cars and the caps of the military chauffeurs strolling about smoking cigarettes under the cedars. It clanked down the square drainpipes into the grilles of the ground wastes and coursed thinly down the thousands of panes of the storeyed windows.

On each of the grey painted pillars flanking the outer pair of entrance doors were circular brass bell mounts larger than soup plates lettered in relief DAY BELL and NIGHT BELL, while through the carpeted foyer with its door mats, bayonet cactuses and dying fern trees, could be seen the second pair of doors beyond which human figures moved slowly beneath a warm golden light.

John grasped the brass knob of the Day Bell and pulled it out to its furthest extent. Then he did the same to the Night Bell and they waited to listen for the ringing to come up from the distant caverns of the basement.

'Whatever made you do that?'

'*They* did. Those words.'

239

'It doesn't say "Pull". Ooh! you are reckless.'

'It says "Pull" on the knobs.'

'We'll get caught now.'

'We will if we wait.' He took her arm. 'Just walk in slowly with your nose slightly pointed upwards as you go through the doors. Don't smile at anyone we meet: look as though you've just come out of the lavatory.'

'Look at this doormat – it might have come off the *Queen Mary*. It's bigger than our best carpet.'

'And the red lettering isn't just painted on. It goes all the way through like peppermint rock: GARTER HOTEL.'

'It's a bit sad in here, isn't it? Them ferns and spikey plants are all a'dying. They don't look after them.'

'They don't have to. Hotels get them from a special warehouse near the sea.'

'Where?'

'Cornwall, Bodmin Moor. They send in an order every few years:

'Please forward six dying fern trees in tubs and five more diseased bayonet cactuses. Present stock exhausted. Signed, the Management.'

He pushed at one of the inner doors giving into a vast carpeted space.

'This door's got one of those air brake things on it. Help me shove.'

They pushed together and stumbled into the foyer.

Minna smoothed her hair. She was trying not to cough.

'Aren't you scared?'

'Don't say things that you *have* to whisper. Speak loudly, and if a waiter or anyone comes up to you, look as though – '

'What are bayonet cactuses?'

'Those ones we just passed? Each leaf has a long thorn at the tip.'

'Where do they come from? Do you think anyone's noticed us?'

'Melbourne, Australia; like Doctor Graemes and Mrs Strykes. No, they haven't noticed us. Just walk straight

240

ahead with me. Do you want to go to the cloakroom while I find our tea?'

'Only if you'll come with us as far as the door.' She grasped his arm. 'Ooh look! There's one of them!'

By the reception area a woman in army uniform was talking to a sharp-featured man with a bald head. She turned suddenly and looked at them. She had round blue eyes and bulbs of golden hair above her ears. Below her khaki tie and shirt her bosom swelled out with no division for her separate breasts. In a shimmering row to her belt, brass buttons studded the slope.

Her shoulders were squared, her neck erect, and her back poker-straight. Encased in olive stockings her calves narrowed to her shining military shoes. She ran her eyes up and down Minna, skated her gaze over John, and, with a final word to the Manager, strode off toward the lifts.

Minna said, 'I don't half need a bathroom.'

'Well, walk as though you meant it. If you get much more droopy they'll shove you into a tub with the fern trees. Think of that ATS Controller, or whatever she was.'

'Poor thing.'

They had entered a wide burgundy corridor where fluted black wood columns flanked openings into dining and writing rooms, dance floors, assembly areas and lecture halls. At the far end, oily glass signs signalled

LADIES

GENTLEMEN

'There!' John said. 'Meet you here in five minutes. Why did you say "poor thing"?'

'Buskers *is* poor things.'

'Buskers?'

'Trampling along off the kerb with her corns and accordion. They ought to let her put her feet up with some crochet.'

She disappeared.

They sat in front of a coal fire in the Music Salon and drank their tea cheerlessly over the crowded table. The otherwise empty room was furnished with a burgundy red carpet, small

241

tables, dark oak chairs and a grand piano surrounded by spiky music stands.

The day's last grey light filtered in through the rainy window, and, beyond the archway, uniformed women passed suddenly and silently on the thick carpeting of the corridor.

Minna ran her eyes over the 'spread' before them, at the plate of petits fours, at the silver dish of baked beans and its triangles of toast drooping into the tomato sauce, at the boxed dates and the celery:

'Whatever did you tell the kitchen? – to get all this for us?'

'I didn't tell the kitchen, *she* did: Captain Rounside. I button-holed her on her way to a meeting or something and told her the truth – more or less.'

Minna slid a date stone onto her plate.

'But what?'

'Oh, you know: poor little orphan; TB. Father shot, fighting the Boche in the desert. This, our last Christmas together. Sanatorium. Self: volunteered Royal Navy – Oh, please don't cry!'

'But it's not true. It's none of it true!'

'It is, except the orphan bit. *Now* what's the matter?'

'But that is the only true part: I *am* an orphan since Mum went dead with Dad.' Over her handkerchief she stared at him. 'You aren't half cruel, Doctor John.'

'It got us our tea, didn't it?'

She glanced at the square white teapot, dwarfed by the silver dishes.

'One cup each! And I don't want *this*!' She passed him the box of Christmas dates. '*You* can keep 'em to eat in your Officers' Mess whiles I spit blood in the sanatorium.'

'Minna, I'm sorry; I didn't mean – '

'Didn't mean! You despise us is all. You see us cheap, leading cheap lives and dying poor deaths at the end of it. Well, we're *not*!'

'I didn't. I don't. Your father's death was heroic – '

She stood up. Her duffle coat behind her on the back of the chair, her crumpled white dress hanging from her shoulders. Her face blanched in the winter's light, she stared at him for a moment.

'How dares you, Doctor John? You don't never use that word again.'

'What word? What do you mean?'

'Calling my dad a hero as if you was blooming suet-pudding Churchill!'

'Please, Minna, sit down.'

'I won't sit down! Who do you think you are with your airs? My dad was something your lot couldn't never be if you don't watch out. And he *didn't* die heroic; he died for things as he didn't hardly believe.'

She leaned over and picked up the box of dates again.

'And that's why we shan't have these neether. There! Onto the slag with them and let them fry with the snobs. I only wished them at all because they grew in the desert where he laid down. But you couldn't never acredit *that* in a person with no schooling; a woman who hasn't got a thought in her head beyond getting a man to monkey with her – well, you can just take me back to my mouse house afore the undertaker gets there to measure me up and "do" me mum.'

He was still, silently watching the frilly white edge of the date paper curl and brown like the lining of a little coffin. Then he jumped up and thrust his hand into the flames and drew it out.

'Good God, Minna, what have you – ?'

He stared at her, shivering. Tall suddenly in her narrow dress, against the green pannelling she shone out like a Christmas rose from its mat of leaves. All this time, he thought, and never until now did I realise that she is; that she really *is*. And in all the life I've had so far, this is what I've sought: this sweetness, this fury, this rage of rightness, and now there, there beside the chair, all of it, in her.

A passion of longing, of a hunger he had not known since boyhood, shook him as he stared at her and she looked back at him. He fell to his knees and took both of her hands, feeling the bones of them as if they were something just plummeted out of the air, the flesh cool as wings.

243

'Minna! Please, please! Oh most dear. I promise I will never, that I shall never – '

The anger had left her, the tears dried on her face. She lifted her shoulders:

'*Bayonet* cactus! You tease too superior sometimes; but it's all right! I just – You don't know, is all: brought up wrong by your folks. But don't kneel, Doctor. Just hug us a bit for closeness and we'll get home for a proper supper.'

He was bewildered by her matter-of-factness. Could she not see what had happened to him?'

'Minna, I love you. I want you; I mean, to myself – all to myself. Oh please! I can't, we can't. We can't just go back to your home.'

She freed her hands and he got up to stand over her where she now sat in the tall chair. She looked at him steadily as does a very young child when, in silence, with its full attention, it questions some other person's presence.

'You're a funny fellow, you are! I knew as you loved us a long time back. With me going away, I was hoping you might tell us.'

'I have. But I can't tell: I didn't know it was possible to *see* anyone so clearly – since Victoria. And it is true. I *have* loved you from the first when you came into the Admin room that morning to bring me coffee. But now it has changed; it's *more*. It's – '

'Well, kiss us then.' She stood up. 'Why don't you? I'm not that fragile. And love is always more; if it isn't, it won't never do for me.'

They clung in the cold room scented with the fire smoke; swaying by the tea table; hearing for a time the distant voices of people in other parts of the hotel. Her mouth, her whole spare flesh, was open to him, familiar but strange; and, for the little girl he had thought her to be, amazing in the readiness of its consent; as if she had been most practised in such loving.

'We better give over,' she said as they were getting back their breath. 'I don't half feel shaky. Where are you going to – ? Where shall we?'

'Ah! There you are!'

244

They turned towards the archway to face Captain Rounside. Her back to the corridor, her legs slightly apart, she was standing there watching them with patient disinterest.

'Just the bods I was looking for! Perfect!' She smiled tightly, 'Don't fret about the necking. I wasn't here long and I'm completely unflappable; but completely. There's a war on and smooching's gone public – as with the Frogs.'

'But now, if you're all set – don't need to visit the ablutions or anything? – I've got to take you in charge. On, don't be alarmed; it's simply orders of the day – a lecture in the King Ludwig Theatre which is looking too damn empty just now.

'So, if you're quite ready, my dear; your lipstick in line? It's at the double for instruction in wartime cookery followed by tea and buns.'

For a moment her eyes took in their neglected meal. 'You'll be ready for tiffin by the time it's over. This way! this way!'

She stood to one side: 'Straight along the main corridor; first right by the Regimental drums and then on into the Stalls. If you don't get lost you'll be just in time for it.'

They started to obey her; but halfway along the second corridor John remembered that he had left the bill unpaid and hurried back to the Strauss Room. The Captain was still in there, talking to another uniformed lady of lower rank, but with an even straighter back.

'Just what we needed to swell the numbers, Armitage. A couple of proles – at least *she* is – who will soon be pupating by the look of it. I found them in here trying to do it standing up – never a good idea; so I volunteered them along to the Woolton cookery talk. 'Yes?' She looked at John: 'Couldn't you find it? Oh, your tea bill! That's on the War House. We'll settle it.'

'That's very kind of you.'

'Not at all. Now, mind you sit through our demo. You'll find it most instructive – practical too.'

'What exactly is it on?'

'Victorious cooking.' She glanced at her junior. 'For young marrieds, just the ticket, isn't it, Armitage?'

'We aren't married.'

245

'Aha! You'll soon remedy that – and in any case, bobbined or spliced, we all have to eat.'

'Who is giving the lecture? Is it an army cook?'

'Good Lord, no! One of our ABCA luminaries – a real dab hand; Doctor Gillespie.'

'Doctor *Gillespie*?'

'You know her?'

'Yes; I mean I know *him*.'

'No, no! Not old "Gawbles". This is his ex. – Robene Gillespie. She has a doctorate in Home Economics.'

'Oh.'

'She got it in a cow college in Poughkeepsie or somewhere. And now you'd better trot or you'll miss the meringues.'

She turned to her colleague. 'All set, Armitage?'

36

John ran down the corridors and into the Ludwig Theatre.

Although he was moving fast he felt he was stationary with happiness and excitement. The wide corridors slid past him like the walls of Alice's tunnel; and just as everything in his mind travelled beneath the light of his attention: Minna's body, her eyes, herself in a white dress, herself naked and secret; the box of dates purpling in the fire, the smoke-scented music room, the corridors with the wine of carpet and black pillared walls; so did his body drop delightedly through the hotel passageway with its sporting prints, Anna Zinkeisen drawings, white Victorian busts and festoons of bright Christmas holly.

He could scarcely believe that in so short an interval of time he would be seeing Minna again; sitting beside her, talking to her. In the few yards he was crossing he found a change of view as startling as is the transformation of a dark countryside when golden sunlight falls suddenly upon it.

And in this interval how marvellous was Captain Rounside, her flesh-filled skin encased in buttons, her swelling undefined breasts, her fluting authoritative voice; a lay figure conducting them into another part of the forest.

He saw Minna at once, her face turned to him; the smile she gave as he hastened down the aisle and took his seat beside her.

'Did you get it settled with the waitress?'

'*They*'re paying for it!'

'You mean Old Bossie?'

'She said it was on the War Office.'

Her hand came over the red plush arm of the seat. 'It's our lucky day then?' She sighed. 'It's so lovely in here. I feel all – Oh, I don't know.'

He gripped her fingers. 'I can hardly breathe.'

They sat quiet stroking each other's hands, only that small part of themselves touching; their eyes wandering over one another's faces and then off to the sides to see all else that they might; like animals at a drinking place so safe, he thought, that between sips they dared look about them with joy.

'From what she said I thought it would be deserted. But there's quite a few here – though you're the only man.'

He looked behind him and then across both aisles. The Dress Circle was empty; to the right there were a few seats filled by women in tweeds or khaki talking in the clipped, easy manner of old school friends:

'Quite a fun party, that! Thanks to the Black Market!

'Oh Sophie, how could you? He was absolutely rank with garlic.'

'Robene Gillespie! They say she's *different*!'

'This Dougal creature, I've heard, is a poppet. . . '

'No, darling, a *puppet*! Ah! here he comes. Oh Gawd!'

Someone, the assistant in dark trousers and a plaid shirt, had come quietly onto the stage carrying a black cockerel in a glass case which he placed in the centre of the long, white-clothed table midway between bowls, copper dishes and colandars and a thicket of wine and liqueur bottles.

247

Further up stage he adjusted the valves on the gas cylinders to the stoves, twiddled the burner knobs and lifted the lids of steaming saucepans to stir their contents before settling himself self-consciously on a tall stool.

The women filling the six or seven rows of the centre stalls were of a different drawing from the group across the aisle: their clothes older, their cardigans droopier, their coiffures tired and hasty. Some were knitting in khaki or air force blue wool and most had notebooks and pencils sticking out of their handbags.

In the comfortable phrases of the suburbs they talked quietly:

'I told Valerie – she's my married – I said, 'Val, if you haven't got the breast milk, it's not a bit of good worrying; put him on Cow and Pasture. 'Cow and Pasture!' says she, 'That always turns his nappies green.'

'If this doctor woman's been in America, mark my words! She'll be all choc'late cake and cookies with choc'late substitute.'

'Whatever can that feller up there want with that bird?'

'It's a cockerel, isn't it?'

Across the aisle, too, there was speculation:

'I do hate men who creep about the place.'

'Why do you suppose he's sitting sideways? Is it the pallid brow act?'

'It could be submission, darling. Dougal downed!'

Minna squeezed John's hand. 'I could listen to them all night, couldn't you?'

'No.'

'Suppose it was a woman they was discussing?'

'Then I could, of course.'

Now, as the lights in the auditorium had dimmed and those on the stage brightened, Dougal stood up and bowed to a tall slightly built woman who swept clicking down the boards to the footlights.

Dressed from head to foot in black, she had bright black hair swept back from her forehead to hang down to her waist. A short velvet jacket, the lapels studded with jet,

248

covered the top of a low-cut velvet sheath that reached to her ankles and her pointed medieval slippers.

As she moved she tinkled and clicked with the knocking of her necklaces, her loose belt and elbow bracelets: all of them, as John saw later, strung of coral fillets, fishes' teeth and the knuckle bones of little animals. Her face, small and white, was that of a bad tempered child, black-browed and frowning. As she smiled her thin-lipped mouth was frilled with two rows of little teeth.

For a moment she stood motionless, looking particularly at the noisier group on the right. Then she curtseyed and ran a hand over her hair.

'You are wondering,' she began in a high voice, 'about my rooster and my assistant – probably in that order.'

'Oh I say!'

'People *do*,' she insisted. 'Dougal dear, do remove his cupola and display Abraham – everyone's longing for a better look. There. You see, all of you, that, though stuffed, Abe is still a proud and glossy rooster. And why? Because in life he always contrived to be *well-fed*.'

A sigh of anticipation passed through the stalls and beside John and Minna the audience stopped knitting, their handbags and notebooks forgotten in their laps.

Across the aisle, the better dressed group, the wives or daughters of officers, girls not too long returned from distant colonies, readied themselves for a confrontation.

Robene Gillespie, her ossuaries clicking and clattering as she held up a hand, turned to face them:

'So now let's introduce my dogsbody, my *cavaliere servente*, Dougal Dunbar.'

Dougal bowed.

'Dougal pots and does hair, and does them both very nicely.'

With another quick smile for him she walked back to the table and took up an egg beater and a large white bowl.

'While Dougal grates the parsnips, lightly marinated in essence of coconut – No, I'm not cheating; the essence can still be found – for a Baton Rouge Flan, *we* are going to set meringues.'

'Coconut flan? Why bother?'

'A slightly *outré* pudding, I daresay,' Robene agreed, 'but not to be despised when we gals are wondering what to place before our jaded providers when they need to feel petted.' She smiled down at the civilians.

'I am talking to the homemakers; you down there *understand*, you ladies of the larder, gooseberry bottlers, do-it-yourself girls. For *your* pleasure I have something lighter than open pies, something more feminine – *meringues*!'

'Gooseberry bottlers! What a nerve! When she's finally thrown old Gawbles.'

Robene turned to Dougal. 'Meringues with this difference! That they will be made without egg whites but *with* albumen. Be a honey and show them, darling. There! You can see, can't you, that Dougal is holding up one *egg*? And that is all we have with us, Honest Injun.' She paused. 'And from where, you are wondering, from where *do* we get the albumen? For without that slippery gooey stuff there would *be* no meringues, now, would there?'

'No, no meringues,' they murmured.

'Oh, you are a shy lot! Heavens to Betsy! When I was in the States, where to be a woman is such a high wire act, I used to tell myself that my friends back home were still slopping about in the same old British way; but now I find you all just as uptight as the gals in Baltimore or Maine. So wouldn't anyone like to join me on stage for a little Christmas courage?'

She drained her glass and signalled Dougal again. 'Darling, the Amontillado! So where *do* we get the albumen, do you suppose? No, not from poor Abraham – because that never was his function – nor from his offspring – not from poultry at all; but from gee-gees, the *horses*!'

'Gee-gees! How barbaric!'

'Sinister. . . .'

Robene glanced at Dougal who handed her a bottle of yellow fluid. She pulled out the red rubber stopper: 'Some people, I know, make a religion of horses; but we don't, we make *meringues* of them.'

In silence she poured the liquid into the bowl. 'There! We feather this golden serum into our granulated sugar; we fold it in; and if there are those who prefer something that

250

has passed, rather slowly, through the entrails of a fowl, to this saffron liquid that only yesterday could have been powering a stallion on the plains – '

'Or a knacker's yard.'

Robene paused: 'Oh my! Someone *is* hurting. I do know that, as women, we gals are supposed to have all kinds of hang-ups about equines: but personally the Shetland given to me when I was too little to handle him was more than enough. You wouldn't credit it – a real male, choc-a-bloc with misdirected energy – Far more fun served up as meringues! But enough! Dougal, the OBJ please!'

She raised the small screw-topped jar he had handed her. 'Oh Be Joyful, or cream! One of my private war aims – cream all round.'

She waited, smiling; but nobody laughed. Minna took John's hand.

'She's angry, and she isn't half swigging the sherry.' In the silence Minna's voice had been too loud and Robene returned to the footlights:

'You two, yakking down there in the stalls! Do please come up and join us in a Christmas tot.'

John stood up and Robene clapped her hands together as he made his way down the aisle and onto the stage.

'If only some of the home-bodies would follow suit. Now, please go that way past Abraham and Dougal will see to you. Is no one else going to join us?'

As she handed John the wine, Dougal's shadowy eyes met his, slid away and then boldly returned his stare.

He was not discomfited to find that she was a girl. The surprise had come earlier while he was believing her a man; it had lain in her delicate features, her long hands, her chancy diffidence.

Now as he looked at her, sensing her coldness, he felt as angry as he had with Chlorinda Graemes. Over the wine in his glass he delighted in her silky cheeks and the soft line of her eyebrows.

'Is your sherry all right?' she asked.

'Was I making a face?'

'I've no idea.'

251

She lifted her chin, her eyes again shifting over to where Robene stood beside the cockerel.

'Dougal, give him a Fortnum's biscuit. He's an Englishman and they need food every two hours.'

Dougal held out an open tin. He saw the familiar shapes in the grey corrugated compartments.

'No, thank you.'

She waited patiently. With as good a grace as a waitress, she continued to hold out the tin.

'Thank you, I *will* take a few for my fiancée.'

As his hand wandered among the divisions, seeking the choicest, she said something angrily.

'What did you say?' he asked.

'Nothing.'

'But you did!' He was at ease, suddenly good-tempered again. 'You said "Poor her", didn't you?'

'No, I did not.'

'I heard you. You whispered, "Poor her"!'

'She's so thin.' Putting the tin on the table she replaced the lid and handed him a tea plate.

'Thank you.'

As he made his way up the aisle, watching the golden tower of the biscuits wavering on the little plate, he heard Robene's high childish voice, continuing with her 'War Aims:'.

'South Sea sponges with the sand still in them. Vicarage Murder Mysteries. Edinburgh Rock. . . .'

37

It was the end of a season; with the lights of Christmas bright in the wards, the grass drab in the compound and the starlings passing at five when already it had gone dusk, he knew that for him it was term, that he had come full circle. He knew, too, that it was because Minna had gone.

Standing out in some corner of the compound beneath trees harsh in their bareness, he watched the flights of the starlings; first a few, fifteen or twenty, questing the air as they hurtled silently above the hospital; then a large curling flock, dark beads against the unlit sky, grains of life shifting within their own moving pattern in motions so complex they were restful, in numbers so generous they reassured.

These to be followed by yet another wavering, directed, covey of thousands; and these again to be succeeded by yet more; the stragglers, such ones as, by distraction of the wet fields or their sickness, had left late; but who still made their way through the cold light with fortitude.

Last of all, the oldest birds in little numbers, flying less easily, with diminished skills, to the place where all their fellows had gone to rest for the night: some grove of close-boughed fir trees in a park or cemetery, some settlement of not too steep roofs where many chimneys warmed the slates.

He wondered how the absence of one person from a place could so change a city, even an entire country, as to make it hateful. For, while Victoria had lived, all Yorkshire had been dear to him. Even Middlesborough, smoking and smelting, pouring dirty flame into the clouds from its Bessemers, had been beautiful. The moors, nearly tenantless, studded with stony villages and rocks, pierced by watered valleys, had held such a glory for him that he had wanted never to leave them.

And now, with Minna gone, the Guinea Lane by which he had come to feel safe, to awaken in comfort, was alien. The buildings, the asphalt paths, the cement birds by their pools, the low chimneys, the linoleum corridors, varnished boards and brown dadoes, hollies, had all taken on a strange and hard identity; as though an invisible but softening light had been extinguished; as if some bright source allowing all a melting quality had ceased to flow. And with its cessation he too, he realised, had ceased either to accept or to consent to much of himself.

He walked the wards without purpose or pleasure, talked to the patients without interest, examined and wrote down his findings without pride. With no further need to appear unmoved, he watched people get better, part recover or die without the continuing fear that he was at heart a cruel and selfish person.

And he was angry, would have enjoyed a set-to with any one of the staff from the Dragon to Whooper, to Mrs Strykes, to Sister Thorpe or Fairburn Gillespie himself: more than all, a show-down with Chlorinda Graemes.

With her he did not visualise a clatter, not even any rudeness; but something of a circling, enjoyable all of it; the hurts of clever argument; and, as she was a woman, the intimacy of such quarrelling. Ultimately, he saw victory over her by the uses of his wit and so an assurance that he was, must be, superior to her in some one respect. For so far she had proved the better in all that was measurable.

He knew that such quarrels were futile, could not get him back Minna; but he felt they might ease his pain, his loss of himself when he had just begun to feel a little good, purposeful. With Minna gone this sense had vanished. He was more than alone, he was desolate.

The Saturday of the concert was cold and vaporous. No snow fell, no rain; the thin clouds seemed motionless over the hospital and as soon as he had finished his evening ward rounds John went angrily in search of Doctor Graemes to collect a reference from her.

He found her outside the Thyroid Unit. In a heavy black overcoat, her hair free above her turned back collar, she looked paler than normal. In one blanched ringless hand she carried a file of case notes in a red folder.

'Yes?' She glanced up at him without hostility, with just slightly less indifference than usual. 'You were looking for me?'

'I wondered if you had written my reference yet? You were going to have given it to me last week.'

'That is correct.'

She really did look at him for some moments out of her extraordinary eyes with the green ring round the periphery of each iris like a circlet of jade.

'Well, may I have it?'

'If you will hold my file – it is in my pocket – please do *not* drop my papers.' She pulled an envelope from the inside pocket of the black overcoat.

With her fluffy hair, already beaded with mist, and her mannish overcoat, it was strange to see her slipping her hand in towards her left breast.

He looked at the off-white envelope she had handed him; it was made of the thinnest wartime pulp and seemed to contain only a single sheet of notepaper.

'Is this it?'

'Such as it is, yes.'

'Do you mind if I read it?'

'That is up to you.'

> *The Guinea Lane Hospital, E.M.S.*
> *Hullshold,*
> *Middlesex*

From Miss Chlorinda Graemes, F.R.C.S.

Doctor John Blaydon has been my assistant in the capacity of House Surgeon at the above hospital for the quarter ending December the 31st 1942.

> *Signed, Chlorinda Graemes.*

'Oh!'

'My file, please.'

He handed it to her.

'I think you might have said something more, Doctor.'

'I have given the facts. They are accurate, aren't they?'

'But – '

'Had I given *all* the facts you might have had more reason to complain.'

'But this is my first house job. Everyone else has given me excellent references; Doctor Leigh, Mr. de Fleur, Doctor Hepton-Mallett.'

'You are joining the Royal Army Medical Corps, aren't you?'

'Yes, I am; next month.'

'Then I should have thought they will find my reference adequate.'

'Adequate! What do you mean, dammit?'

She smiled. Beneath her delightful eyes, two delicate

255

pouches of skin bellied out, giving her a most feminine and flirtatious look of merriment.

'You should not swear, you know.'

'I still want to know what you mean by 'adequate' Doctor Graemes?' She had a dimple high on her left cheek.

'Armies, the world over, are rather rough and ready, you know. It is not as though you were going on to Guy's or to Bart's.'

She stood there on the asphalt, beside a stork made of cement. Her pale face was quite serious again, expressionless really, as if she had retreated from him into her other world, her continual preoccupation with her research, her career.

He was going to have said, 'I hate you,' to her; but seeing her disinterest, as removed, as unheld as his own, he said nothing.

In seconds she would be gone; he would turn, she would step forward, back into her life again; he into his.

He looked at the envelope again, stuffed it into the pocket of his house coat and said, 'Hell!'

Beside him, she laughed, a thread of song such as a song-thrush gives to itself when it is resting. He felt his mind, his whole body flush with rage. He moved closer to her:

'You shouldn't laugh at people you've just insulted.'

Her upper lip twisted and he realised that she was witty:

'Well, really, Doctor Blaydon!'

'It's not just "well really", Miss Graemes. It is unfair and I think, insolent. What the blazes do you mean by your "well really"? And what's the matter with you as a woman? Why are you always so cruel and hard-bitten? Why can't you – ?'

'How very childish you men are.' She stepped back a little, nearer to the cement stork by the standing water, her soft hair alight with the wind.

'Childish! Childish?' He tasted and tested the word to himself. How did she know that he was childish, that Wantage and Fairburn Gillespie were too?'

'It is childish to expect praise all the time for every one of your little achievements.'

'I don't expect praise; I only expect to be noticed – myself, I mean.'

'How would it be if *we* expected not only to be noticed for ourselves all the time; but to be praised for everything *we* carry out?'

'It would be nice; I would love it, and I'm not *only* a child.'

As was her habit she looked not past him but back into herself again before she spoke:

'It is even more childish to expect a sexual response in every situation, especially when there is so much to be done.'

'Well then, I *am* a child, a boy-one, because I do expect that to be there underneath – a little flirtation with life.'

She was unmoved, 'And were I a man?' she asked him. 'What then? Would you want this nonsense every few minutes?'

Smarting, he swore again.

'Try to see, Doctor Blaydon, that all that kind of thing is self-indulgence – in its way, insulting.'

'All that kind of thing! You mean us being human, don't you? Nothing venial, but just recognition, the touching of each other, the excitement, really. That's what you're so dead against?'

She smiled at him, her eyelids crinkled with amusement. 'You know, Doctor Blaydon, you are a great loss to the profession.'

He waited for her to go on, alert for the hurt he was sure she nursed, but against the grey sky and its cold light she was silent. And, as carefully as he could, he went on, 'Without that, you're missing the whole point, the fun, in a way. I don't mean actual surgery, all it entails as a science; because that *is* serious. But the patients, the people! You're not Joan of Arc, you know.'

'Joan of Arc! How ridiculous. What a loss you are, Doctor Blaydon; not to this profession but to the stage.' She shivered with the cold. 'I'm sorry if my reference has disappointed you; but these matters, too, are serious. And were your dedication to Medicine matched by that which you claim for "people", I might respect it more.'

He thought back furiously, recalling first her constant distance from Maureen Bason, her absence from the inquest on 'Kit' Bellayr, her maddening prescience of the findings with which he had sought to discomfort her.

'How narrow you are!' he broke out. 'Can't you see that all I'm saying is that instead of being a great woman, your studied professionalism is making you behave like a failed *man*!'

Silently she stepped away from him, then said, again, as if to herself;

'That is quite enough of that, I think.'

While the day still held her near him, he looked at her thoughtful face, the unsadness of it, and knew that he would never forget that particular moment, one of the uncountable number he had already known. To seal it, to make it tangible, he was going to have touched her, to have taken her hand; but already she had moved and was level with him so that he saw only her fragile profile against the dead winter's grass of the compound. He turned abruptly and went over to the Gynae ward to see Sister Thorpe.

Her office was cold: the electric fire, a copper disc with its single 'candle' unplugged from the wall, her Thermos flask empty beside her unwashed cup and saucer.

Graemes wants it both ways, he decided. When she mucked up the gastrectomy, she was the master sex, unaccountable for her actions; but when it was a question of the inquest, in an unspoken way, she let me suffer and do duty for her incompetence. Had I argued about this with her – she and that horrible Strykes would have turned on me and told me to 'be a man.'

Sister Thorpe's Crimean Journal lay open on her desk. Awaiting her in the way one awaits someone who might be long delayed, he scanned it:

. . . *Our batteries have received very little injury this bombardment; not one gun touched in the 21-gun battery. The five-gun and eight-gun batteries have suffered most, a magazine blew up in the latter.*

It is not pleasant to find your friends dying all round you and to pass the grave one day of a man whom you saw in perfect health the day before.

Life is very uncertain here, in no place I suppose more so.

*Our regiment has got off well though we have our hospital
hut nearly filled with wounded men.*
We have had no officers killed . . .'

She would not come, he was sure of it. Where was the
welcome tea?

Where the familiar restraint of the affection he had come
to rely upon?

The office had shrunk this morning. It was no more than
itself, and not well built; flimsy walls, the jambs of the
windows not plastered up to the fly-ridden cracks running
the length of them. On her desk stood some paper-grey
chrysanthemums, vigorous with the half-life of their species.

Tomorrow he would bring Minna whatever else he could
find in Stourmond when he changed buses. He would bring
her a load of magazines: gloss-papered frivolous sheaves
with all kinds of advertisements in them: a shop of pictures
and print, a secret shop with many counters, crushed with
girls buying advice about different parts of their bodies from
their toe-nails to their hair; and all manner of aids to make
them stranger and even more alluring.

He had taken Dymphna magazines and flowers in Dublin,
when she had had her 'surgical miscarriage'. He remembered the smell of the blood and the milk climbing over the
flowers in that naked room into which she seemed to have
been thrown down like the little girl's doll he had found
under a chair in the waiting-room.

Minna's was a bed in perhaps a similar room out at Cold
Harbour. Or were sanatoria, longer tenanted, more
absorbent? Allowing the walls and furniture of each room
time to accept its tenant and return an emanation that was
cosy?

Each time he visited Minna – and even the Army would
not stop him until he got overseas – he would take her
something to fit in with her: things that would be an exten-
sion of herself: a tortoiseshell comb for her hair which she
would grow longer in order to hold the comb, a two-inch
arrow of silver filigree to wear in her bed jacket, a spidery
chain joining the two halves; a light scent made only from
the petals and corollas of white flowers, and a tube of

lipstick, cyclamen, that she would put on and he, with his finger, nearly remove before kissing her: a book of poems chosen by his sister, Melanie, of the kind that would make her fond and passionate for him.

He looked at his watch. Though Sister was probably in the ward with her patients he did not want to go in there. It meant too much acting; it was a strain he could not allow himself with his departure so near – with the concert this evening.

All those women in their beds, in the thick domesticity they had made of the long, badly-built room with its paper streamers and cardboard bells hanging below the rafters and the ceiling, its drying Christmas tree at the far end, dropping dark needles onto the crimson paper surrounding the tub, its branches stuffy now with each nurse's contribution to the decoration.

Each nurse! All save sweet Lynton who, as they both had guessed, had never returned, volunteering for the grey cotton uniform of the Queen Alexandra's Nursing Institute and possibly by now in training for North Africa and service with the Eighth Army.

No, he could not face the Gynae Ward when so very soon, for him, there would be no more women about the place in the 'rough and ready' Army. All he could face, all he did want to see, was Sister's aquarium: the containment, the monotony and the association it had for him with his very first day in the hospital, the charge he had been given of the women's ward.

'So you came along to say goodbye to us! How very thoughtful of you.'

He turned and spoke without looking at her; noting only that her voice was old, not girlish any longer, though so softly modulated.

'But I'm not going yet. I only – '

'Ah, but *I* am!'

'You are? Where to, Sister?'

He was quite unmoved; he knew that he had not been smiling at her but at the thought that she, the old thing, was finally pulling herself out of it all.

She sat down at her desk and he noticed with greedy

260

interest that she was trembling again, her movements all less precise. Her cockle white cap was not quite straight on her head; and, now that he came to look more closely, the linings of her lower eyelids were very slightly everted as though her misted irises had been underlined in red ink.

'Where to, you ask? Ah, that *is* of interest.' She straightened her dark green blotter. 'Has there been no 'shave' of my plans?'

'Shave?'

'Whisper. It was a word we used a deal in the old days – over postings usually.' She straightened the straight blotter again; her hands not quite steady. 'I have no very definite plan for service as yet; and that is a comfort, don't you think?'

'I'm not sure.' He was still looking at her impersonally, with the hostility he quite often felt for those who were failing.

She was a little like the last of the starlings, those enfeebled flyers who had lingered too late in the wet fields.

'*Free!*' she announced with a quaver of laughter. 'Free as the wind. But this will never do. Put on my kettle, there's a good fellow. It's just inside my glory hole – my pantry. There, behind that door. That's right; thank you. Now, won't you sit down and relate any "shaves" that have come *your* way?'

'I've heard very little. I certainly didn't know that you were leaving.'

'Puff! I am of no great moment here. I thought you might have had word of Minna' – She glanced out through the window – 'up in Cold Harbour in this *nasty* weather.'

'I'm going to see her tomorrow.'

'How very delightful. Oh, I *am* pleased. Let us celebrate; I can hear my kettle lifting its hat with excitement. Just heat the pot and pour the water onto three teaspoonsful of the leaves and then put back the cosy and we shall drink to each other – So you really are to visit Minna with a most appropriate gift?'

'Sister?' He was surprised and embarrassed, angry; for he had not bought anything yet: did not know quite how much he dared to spend with Aldershot so near.

'Oh, 'tis no "shave" that reached me,' she admitted. 'I meant only the gift of yourself, Doctor John; so pray, don't be difficult.'

She looked at the tray he had put on the table.

'There! That is nicely set. I will pour for you and perhaps you would open that tin and give us both an osborne and a ginger snap.'

He handed her the tin and she took one biscuit, eating it eagerly, a dust of crumbs falling from her lips onto the blotter.

'You have never called me that before,' he told her.

'Doctor John?' Have I not? Perhaps it is because this is a parting of our ways.'

Behind his eyelids a gland filled; he felt the ducts prickle.

She touched his hand on the tray cloth. He saw the stain of her age resting across the back of his own hand.

'*She* does so like to say it, does she not? Most catching!'

'Yes.' He held her hand and looked into her red-inked eyes. 'Sister, where *are* you going?'

'To my caravan, in Storrington, below the Downs. It's not very mobile any longer and it is lagered outside my home which is a tied cottage I bought years and years ago when I came back from the Congo.'

He released her fingers and she at once took another biscuit, eating it with even more crumbs than before.

'It does so excite me to be going back there for a time. There's nothing like leave of absence approaching, to fill one with plans, is there?'

'But, who will – '

'Who will look after me? Why, my tenants! I had the foresight to install a little family of paupers in my cottage after their coastal hovel was bombed. Now they are as hale as berries and Mrs Fergusson will cosset me for as long as may be.'

She paused to take another biscuit and refill her own cup. 'And, would you credit it, should my hips become too tiresome in January, she will turn Alison out into *my* van, and I shall have *her* bed in the cottage? So you see – ' She waited, studying his face.

'I see that you've been very generous to the Fergussons.'

'Very calculating, some might say. But that's enough of me. Apart from seeing Minna, what are *your* plans?'

'The Army, I suppose.'

'Lucky you! You *will* enjoy that – after *this*. Nice healthy soldiers to look after and the excitement of action every now and again. Oh, I did feel so – I was so very useful in those days and that is such a good notion, isn't it?'

He got up. 'Is that why you never married, Sister? If you don't mind my asking.'

'I'm not sure. It scarcely seemed needful when we were busy, and a little too demanding when we were not.' She stared up at him shyly, 'But for you – *well*!'

'*Well*? What does that mean?'

'Why, that you *should*, of course. But then, as Doctor Gillespie would say, "Dinna fash thyself ower it. For 'tis all in the haft o' the seeing Lord".'

'Why do you think I should, particularly?'

She laughed at him and for an instant her laugh was the laugh of a girl with some others in the fields of August.

'You want me to be personal, Doctor?'

'Yes.'

'Vain fellow! Well, we took several votes on it.'

'Who did?'

'We did, the women of Guinea Lane – and it was decided each time that you should.'

38

During Christmas Eve supper Doctor Whooper said:

'So you're to perform tonight, Blaydon? What are you going to coom up with for us all? Black yer face and sing comic songs?'

'I don't sing.'

'Conjuring tricks?'

'I don't know any.'

'Oh, lay off him, Whooper. He's unhappy.' Wantage's face was blank with sincerity.

Whooper raised a forkful of bully beef to her mouth.She looked first at Wantage and then at her full fork. 'You two!'

'What *are* you doing?' Jerry asked him.

'You could *croon* – do loov songs – ' Whooper suggested wiping her lips on her napkin. She drank busily at her beer. 'You could give uz all the *Indian Loov Call*. The nursing staff would loov that. It goes, 'When I'm calling you-hoohoo – hooo! Ever so tooching.'

'Oh shut up, please! I'm not sure I'm doing anything.'

'All overcoom are you? Shyness and temperament?'

'In fact, I am.'

'Then why don't you run down to the Nag's and get something strong inside yer – if you're too fancy for the hospital beer.'

'He's broke,' Wantage said. 'Saving up.'

Whooper belched and refilled her glass with Bass.

'Who for? *You*?'

John took the quart bottle from beside her and drank from it.

She watched him wipe his mouth on the back of his hand.

'Cheeky, aren't yer? That's *my* Bass. Get one of yer ow from t'case. There! Fetch it over here and Wantage will open it with his little toolie. You two aren't half slow sucks. *I* thought you'd be good doers when it came to Christmas, the pair of you.' She drank again slowly from her glass, with evident pleasure. She wiped her lips and looked expression-lessly at John through her grey lensed glasses.

'Who are you saving oop for then?'

'For Minna.'

'Oops! That's wan up on Wantage, any road.' She leaned forward towards him, her square face only a foot away so that he could smell her beer as comfortingly as that of some fellow down at the pub. 'Do you want to know summat? I had hopes for you when it was Nurse Lynton; but *Frobisher* – Oops!'

John got up.

264

'She happens to be very sick, Whooper.'

'Sick! That sort's always poorly. If it's not wan thing it's anoother. What's the matter? Aren't you two going to partake of the mince pies?'

'We've got dates.'

'With each other, Wantage? Coom Christmas Eve? But as we say oop North, it taks all sorts to mak' a world.'

'Sorry to leave you on your own again,' John told her as they got up to go. 'But I suppose you're used to it.'

She smiled at him. He could not see her eyes, but the corners beyond her horn rims creased momentarily and her teeth showed.

'Know what I think? They should have left her out on't slab at birth.'

'You mean, Minna?'

'Fancy eatin' your heart out for a con-soomptive!'

'Oh come on, John; she's drunk.'

They walked out through the main gate beneath the unlighted globes of the entrance posts, down the road on the paving whitened by the semi moon and alongside the sharp railings of the Sewage Docks.

Jerry snuffed the air:

'Rich tonight, isn't it? London's been doing itself well.'

'It'll be even riper after the Christmas port and sherry. God! wasn't Whooper foul tonight?'

'Hurt, that's all.'

'Because we don't take her out?'

'Probably.'

'Us! She *must* be hard up.'

'Speak for yourself. *I* do all right.'

'Sturdy,' John suggested. 'Compact.'

'You bet:

> *Long and thin goes too far in,*
> *It does not please the ladies.*
> *Short and thick it does the trick*
> *Brings out all the babies.'*

'Where did you get that one?'

265

'Whooper. She rattled it off just before you came in for your skilly.'

'That's the trouble with Northerners. Just as you're getting used to their ill-manners, Christmas and Hogmanay turn up, and they become friendly.'

'You are sharp tonight,'

'Wouldn't *you* be?'

Wantage was singing to himself, but paused:

'Couldn't be bothered. Anyway, I rather like the Gelda. She doesn't faze *me*.'

'I like her too.'

'No one would know it.'

'I've only just discovered it myself. She's fatherly – makes me feel safe. With Minna gone, I mean it, Jerry; I need her.'

'So does Gillespie, she's all he's got.'

John stopped dead outside the pub: he stood still on the worn pavement listening to the singing starting up in the carpeted warmth of the Nag's Head.

'What's the matter now?' Wantage asked.

'I was going to have said something very important. But I've forgotten what it was.'

'Oh, come on in, John. The place is full of talent – topping up for the concert – *Are* you going to do anything?'

'I'm going to do a woman I saw in Harrods; in the Food Halls last Christmas. She's very upper class, a Mrs Hall-Tipping. She makes a lot of horrible little cakes with carrots in them. She has bags of make-up on and flutters her eyelids and twitches at a mauve chiffon scarf'. He paused.

'She's not quite sure who she is. One minute she thinks she's back at school in the sixth form teaching domestic science to the Juniors; then she decides she's forty and married – an educated, patriotic matron; next, she remembers that her husband is a bore and that *she* is still attractive and that he's working away at the Ministry of Information for Brendan Bracken – '

'Sounds good. But how does she manage such quick changes?'

'The drink. She keeps sipping at the sherry, chablis and Cherry Heering. I was rather reminded of the whole thing by something that happened the other day. In the end she just flumps down on her stool and decides the world was made for women.'

'That's crazy.'

'Well it may be; but it's a happy thought for Christmas. *She* says that God forgot to complete Adam after the rib resection, or that he didn't get enough of the apple – something like that.'

'It sounds good.'

'It is. All I need is to get just enough to drink before I go on stage and then a steady supply on my demonstration table. Where is the meeting, by the way?'

'In the Fever Block Auditorium.'

'Didn't know they had one.'

'You're not very organised, are you? Do you need a hand with your costume or anything?'

'Thank you. How long have we before the show starts?'

'Oh, an hour and a half, about.'

'Great! Hey, Jerry, you won't mention this once we get inside?'

'Mention it! I'll tell the world.'

'You little bugger.'

'It will be a draw. And the funds are for the Bombed-Out – good Party Line.'

Jerry told Edgar first, and she, sitting away from the mahogany bar in the best red plush alcove beside the coke fire, her marble-topped table spread with bottles, spam sandwiches and potato crisps in crumpled bags, told a gaggle of the others; nurses John had never seen before.

Some were from unfamiliar units of the Guinea Lane, some from other hospitals in nearby suburbs. They were standing about the table in the warm light of the candled sconces; all of them glowing with the sense of their leisure and their drinks; some in uniform, crisp-cuffed and tight-waisted, others in coloured winter dresses glimpsed through the parting of their unbuttoned overcoats.

They were smoking their rationed cigarettes, telling brief stories, listening with silent interest to each other or suddenly breaking out into the happiest laughter. Around

267

them, jealously aware of the smoky air the women scented, of their exclusiveness in the confidence their numbers gave them, the young doctors, the uniformed men on Christmas leave and the dusty civilian patrons, watched and waited.

Edgar caught John's eye. Older than the others; still dissatisfied beneath her present joy, she winked at him.

'Missing her?' she asked loudly through a gap in her nurses.

'Yes – a lot.'

'Shouldn't have let her go, should you? . . .' She solicited the group. 'Should he?'

'No,' they said.

'Who are we talking about?'

'Him! Doctor Blaydon. Him, who's in our concert up at the Guinea tonight.'

They looked at him. Like gazelles he thought; as like as a herd of them, all the same and all unique; and so damn wary. But how delightful to see all those gently fierce eyes upon one for a moment; a moment in the forest.

'Who did he let go?'

'Yes, who?'

'Played her cards wrong,' Edgar said, still watching him, 'gave him her all. Same old story.'

They closed ranks a little, most of them. One or two, a dark girl with a dark brow moved nearer the fire, out of the circle, and looked at him with heavy speculation. Through his beer, his second pint, he saw her instantly as a square-shouldered mother with a perambulator outside a shop, whiskery faced and masculine.

'*She was poor but she was honest,*' sang Edgar.

This was very warming. They were all so strange, and, without having to act it, so foreign to him. He thought of Minna; he had not felt so pleased with everything since she had left.

'You haven't told us who.'

'No, who did he let down?'

'What was her name?'

'Was she in Fevers?'

'Was she in Theatre?'

268

'She wasn't staff at all,' John told them.

'Not staff? Why not?'

'Who, then?'

They drew away: the cluster of gazelle pricked ears beneath the greening trees. One or two hooves hit the forest floor; knocked their warning.

'She *was* staff too,' said Edgar. 'And a good 'un.'

'But who was she?'

'Tell!'

'Heather Lynton.'

God! he thought. They don't realise. He had just sufficient discretion to keep quiet.

'Heather?'

'He let Heather *go*?'

'The QAs poor thing! Troop ship to Tripoli.'

'Heart-broken she was,' said Edgar. 'And does he care? Fat lot!'

'*Mean!*' they said and the younger ones took it up.

'Mean! Mean! Mean!'

Edgar stood up. She had a tall glass in her hand; a tankard of some mixture pretending to be Pimm's Cup.

'Know what?' she asked.

'No,' they said. 'Tell us!'

'He cares so bloody little, he's dressing up as some floosie or other tonight for the concert.' She tossed off most of her drink. 'Let's help him get ready! *He* thinks all he has to do to be a woman is to dash on some lipstick and a nice smile and mince on to the stage, signalling. He'll have seen his mother run a comb through her hair and set out for the big world, I wouldn't wonder. Well, we shall just have to show him how it's *really* done.'

'Yes, let's!'

'After all,' said Edgar coming up to him. 'What's he know about a poor girl's struggles with her face? Her feminity? What's he know about *our* struggle – never mind bloody Hitler's.'

'Mascara,' said another. 'Night starvation; the monthly Curse, dilatation and curettage, prolapse – all for one night of love.'

John looked round for Wantage; for an ally; but everyone

nearly everyone, was laughing. They were forming a perimeter wall. So he stood his ground contentedly.

How bold Edgar was. She had taken over the saloon bar and the probationers, even some of the staff nurses who, with five or more years of authority behind them, were more than usually dignified.

Now at the bar, gawky and quite charming, she cajoled Mrs Shaw, the landlord's wife:

'Oh come on, Doris; lend us the boudoir for a bit. No cigarettes I promise; and no men and no larking! Be a sport! It's all in a good cause.' She turned round.

'You coming quietly, Doctor? Or do we have to truss you up?'

He was pushed up the private stairway behind the Bar, to a carpeted landing and in to Mrs Shaw's 'boudoir', a strange ante-room to the bedroom she shared with Mr Shaw who weighed twenty-five stone. With its flounced kidney-shaped dressing table and satin-covered love seat and chairs, it seemed furnished for a young girl – perhaps the girl who should have been wearing the puffed-sleeved and youthful dresses that were Mrs Shaw's idea of clothes for an evening behind the bar.

'Nobody,' said Edgar, 'is to move anything. Elsie, get your hands off that bear! Doris is very particular about it. Bob bought it for her in Switzerland their last holiday before the War. It's hand-carved by one of them Geneva watch-makers in his spare time – though what the silly devil wanted, carving bloody great German bears after working all day on finicky watches; but that's men for you: always busy doing something they should have finished with when they were kids.'

She stood back amongst her courtiers, her probationers and staff nurses, and looked at John's face in the lighted triple mirror of Mrs Shaw's dressing table.

'You're all right about the eyes,' she said, 'though you could do with a pluck to the eyebrows. Your hair's all right – Eton crop – and if it wasn't we could give you a scarf. What kind of woman do you want to be? Down in the bar I said 'floosie', but I don't think that's right, is it?'

270

'No, a Harrodsy type. Upper-middle class; quite dressy, affected and rather flirtatious.'

'It's your nose,' Edgar said. 'Isn't it, girls? He hasn't half got a bloomin' beak on him – I don't know how we're going to camouflage that.'

She ran her hands over his cheeks and chin.

'Here! You shaved today, you lazy devil? Come and have a feel, Elsie. Don't be shy, dear. You've shaved fellows round naughtier things than noses. Someone look in the bathroom – it's through the bedroom – and get a razor. We're going to groom you, Doctor. Can't have you walking on stage all pretty but for a blue chin.'

'Well, please don't cut me. I've got a date tomorrow.'

'Not with Lynton though – no, not likely. Poor Heather with all her hopes, on some coffin of a troopship in the Mediterranean. We ought to bob him for that, didn't we?'

'Mean!' they giggled. 'Ever so mean he's been.'

'I've promised, no larking about up here. Elsie, leave that bear alone. If you want to get your hands on a man there's one on this chair. But you better hurry up because he's changing fast. There! We'll powder over the foundation, and give him an ever so delicate complexion. Did you say Bishop's Wife, Doctor?'

'No, that was someone else.'

'*I* did. I thought she would be the sort you'd find in the Food Halls.'

'All wrong,' John said. 'My woman was quite daring. A Bishop's wife can never – '

'You be quiet for a minute! Think yourself into your brassière and knickers while we get something onto your eyelids.' Edgar stood back.

'Nice eyes! Yes! I do say, hasn't he? Ever so liquid and passionate. Anyone want to touch up his lashes?'

'I do.'

'Let *me*! I've only done the shaving so far.'

'You can't all – Oh, very well, Norma. You put on the mascara and Beryl can smooth on the rouge. Close your eyes, dear. Let yourself go. No one's going to hurt you, are they?'

'Noo, Nooo,' they chorused, closing in on him as he

leaned back in Doris Shaw's comfortable chair and closed his eyes, listening as though in some sunlit hammock to the mystery of their voices in a green wood.

'Wish I'd been given his lashes. They hardly need a thing.'

'Curly, aren't they? Lucky thing!'

'Are his ears clean? That's where a lot of girls fall down. There was this friend of mine at a service dance and, after supper, all the men got in a corner by the bar, the way they do to compare notes as they call it, though it's gossip really, and she heard her partner say, 'Elspeth? Oh she's very fetching; but her ears are like piccalilli pots.'

'*Piccalilli* pots! What a thing to say!'

'You couldn't never forget it, could you?'

Fingers stroked him gently beneath his eyelids, a breath, scented with lipstick, toothpaste and gin, a very young breath touched his cheeks and made its way up his nostrils. His ears were tweaked, his neck muscles stroked; and all the while a gentle, bubbling comment was kept up.

'Oh my! She isn't half coming on! What we going to dress her in? Do you think Doris – ?'

'Wake up!' ordered Edgar 'Want to take a look at yourself, Doctor? Stand back everybody. Now what you going to call yourself?'

'Hall-Tipping. It's hyphenated.'

'But what Christian name? Beryl, give her a touch more lipstick. You've got to have a Christian name.'

'Sylvia! Sylvia Hall-Tipping,' Norma suggested.

'No, she's too dark for that. She wants something short, like "Ruth" or "Anne".'

'Why not Phyllis?'

'Phyllida?'

'No; gorgeous she may.be. But – '

'Darling!' One of them put her cheek close to his, smiling into the big centre looking glass. He felt the warmth of it, scented the sweet wormwood of the gin.

'You're quite delightful, d'you know that? *I*'m going to call you "Claire"!'

They stared at each other's reflection: the dark face with the strong nose, the heavy eyes; hers dreaming, her lips parted with pleasure.

'It's my turn now.'

'Bags I do his hair.'

'*Her* hair, Valerie.'

'However does it feel?'

'Oh, do tell us.'

'Are you in the part? Is it a help?'

'Most certainly. I feel – '

'Go on!'

'Desirable,' he said. 'Well, almost.'

'Ooh! "Desirable", he says.'

'Give him a drink, Edgar. Go on, please, Doctor.'

'Well, it's hard to say exactly. But I feel precious. No, don't laugh.'

'We're not.'

'I mean I feel very special, as if I was going to be discovered: my legs, my arms, my thighs – even my breasts. At the same time I'm not certain, never am, that I'll be a success – that anyone will want me.'

'Shaky then?'

'In two minds?'

'Sort of; though I'm sure men do want me, I'm never certain it will be now.'

'That's like it, isn't it, Edgar? Go on, Doctor Blaydon.'

'I can't. Only that they don't see me enough as *me*, to treat me – suitably!'

'You must be a blooming pansy to know all that,' Edgar told him.

He rounded on her:

'Then we all are, all except the football babies – because that's how *we* feel too!'

'You shouldn't have stopped him, Edgar. Please, Claire, tell us one more.'

'Yes, just once.'

'O.K., it's this: I not only know that I *am* very special, I'm also pretty sure that I know much more than any grunting, staring man – '

'He's right.'

'*She*'s right, you mean.'

'Clever you.'

273

They fussed around him so trustingly that he was amazed at himself for ever having doubted his own opinions.

'Someone, give me that drink, please, and I'll tell you one last thing: with all these clothes on me and all you round me, I suddenly saw that if *I* am going to have to mould my whole life round some man he had better be worth it.'

'That's it!' they cried. 'What do you want to drink then?'

'A Babycham.'

Minna, he said to himself as he drank it, if you were in this little glass, to start with I would only touch my lips to the meniscus of the wine.

39

Still in his 'get-up', in the tweed coat and skirt too short in the sleeve and the hem, a floppy pre-war blouse which he had not troubled to stuff with a cushion, having settled on Edgar's advice to be 'one of the rangy sort'; still in his flimsy pink scarf, silk stockings and high heels and all his make-up, he sat in a bentwood chair of the ochre brown Admin room enjoying the quiet and Whooper's beer.

Though he could not remember all he had said, all the sudden alcoholic illuminations with which he had spiked his act, he knew he had been a remarkable success, that Claire Hall-Tipping had stolen the concert and that now he himself was the rage not only of 'The Guinea', but of both the other hospitals too, Jasper and Jude's.

He half wished he had deferred his letter to the Army; that he might stay on for another three months or so to be near Minna. Why, even Mrs Strykes and Chlorinda Graemes might respect him now; might understand that though he occasionally fluffed his knots, he was talented and amusing.

But then, there was still tomorrow to get through: Christmas Day, the ward-merriment, the King's speech, the rumble of bombers moving to other aerodromes for a resumption of the destruction of Western Europe; the silences that fell always in the intervals of seasonal singing: the last beery evening either in the hospital or at one of the pubs, before, on Boxing Day, he could at last get out to Cold Harbour with his presents.

He groped for the quart bottle of Bass beside his chair, poured it into his glass, turning it to impress a fresh section of the rim with Claire Hall-Tipping's lipstick. He crossed his ankles in a ladylike way, enjoying the rustle of the silk, the feel of the genuine lingerie supplied by Norma and Elsie.

He had rejected the black because it matched his pubic hair and made his thighs look strappy. The ivory, edged with some kind of crochet or Mechelin, or what Edgar had called 'Swan and Edgar's one-and-elevenpenny's', had toned down his whiskers and plumped out his groin.

He felt physically delightful; good, quite good, in his mind too; and decided that as soon as he had made some real money he would move permanently into silk vests and pants, silk pyjamas, shirts, sheets: silk everything.

'Hoggin' my Bass, are yer?' Whooper asked from the doorway. 'Well, you're welcome, after the show you put on.'

He sat up, crossed his left ankle over the top of his right knee and craned round at her.

She was in quite a pretty dress. Her hair was done; still new-hay green, it shone smooth round the square face.

'You liked it, did you?'

'You were good, Blaydon, real bonny; it's a wonder you got away intact. We thought you'd get mobbed if you'd coom down centre aisle.'

'Who did? I mean, who thought I'd get mobbed – the staff? The nurses?'

'*Them* mooffets! Little milk-and-water misses. No, Lad! Me and Fairburn and t'Matron.'

275

'Oh!'

'*Oh*', she mimicked. 'That all yer got to say to me?'

'I like your dress.'

She came further into the room; wandered over to the sideboard and pulled another quart bottle from the brewer's case.

'Nice, isn't it?' She sat down opposite him, 'Shoov us over the bottle opener. Thanks moochly! There it goes: boobley, boobley, boobley!'

She drank from her full glass, and with the froth sitting thick on her lip looked at him speculatively:

'So you got yourself safely away from t'nusses, did you? With your vir-tue intact!'

'They smuggled me out the back door.'

'Who did?'

'Staff Nurse Edgar, mainly.'

'*That* wan! You were lucky.'

'Was I?'

'Mebbe you weren't. Who's to know?'

'As a man?' he asked.

She glanced indolently up and down his length – from his high heels to his eyelashes.

'A *man*? You must be right boozed if you've forgotten what you're wearing.' She drank. 'Do you fancy my beer, do yer?'

'I do. It's just what I needed.'

'And me dress? Foonily enough, I got it down Harrods only last week.' She twitched up the hem to show a puffball of thigh, a stocking top stretched tight to a suspender. 'Here! Did you really see that wan in the Food Halls?'

'Of course I did.'

'Eeh, well I never! You didn't fancy her though, did yer?'

'No.'

'Not your cup o' tea? Your type? Was she too skinny or summat?'

She got up and stood over him. 'Shall I fill you up?'

'Thanks.'

'Well, go on then. Was she?'

'My type? I really don't know. I didn't think of her as a woman at the time.'

276

'Tha didn't?' She sounded most surprised. 'Why ever not?'

'I saw her as an act; an attitude. She was being a "part", a person in the War Effort, several different people.'

She looked down at him, smiling:

'You're a queer wan and no mistake. How do you see *me*, I'd like to know?'

'Tall,' he said, 'short-tempered, efficient; lonely – '

'That's enough!'

'You *did* ask.'

She took his hand and looked at it, peering through her thick lenses.

'You didn't daub your finger nails then? You left soom of thyssen as nature made thee?'

'Plenty.'

'Well, get off yer bottom, then. Stand oop and get uz a few quarts. We don't want to be swoppin' it here where anywan can barge in.'

'Where do you want to go?'

'This way. My flut.'

'Your what?'

'Flut; my apartment. You haven't ever seen round it have you? It's pretty posh and all com-plete.'

She put an arm through his.

'Ever so moodling this is, the pair of uz in twin sets and you plastered with cosmetics and me in professionals.'

'These high heels are the devil,' he said.

'They'll coom with practice. Everything does if tha tries hard enough.'

She unlocked the dark-stained door with a steady hand.

'Eeeh! Whatever would our moothers think if they could see uz now? You and me preparing to have a bit of foon together – Christmas Eve, nineteen hundred and forty-two.'

He slid his arm around her waist.

'Get the bottles, luv. Then come on over to t'divan.' She closed the door and together they wandered across the carpet.

Beside the divan she stopped, holding him close. She took off her grey glasses and placed them carefully on an occasional table beneath a small stone statue: a nude.

'Tell us something, will you?'

277

'What?'

She was suddenly shy, leaning away from him, and then in close, so that her face with its long flint-blue eyes was only a few inches from his own.

He waited. 'Well, go on! What do you want to know?'

'Joost – are you proper, are you?'

'Proper?'

'All complete?'

'I think so.'

'I didn't mean *that*. I'd have coom out with it. I mean undies? Have you got 'em on, the lot?'

'You could soon find out.'

'I could that.'

'But first I want to ask *you* something?'

'Go on then – Mind, I don't mak' no promise to answer.'

'Are you going to marry Gillespie?'

'Who? Fairburn?'

'Yes.'

'Well, I'll tell you; I'm that desperate I joost might. Poor old luv-a-dook!'

'That's good. That's wonderful.'

'Tha thinks so?'

'Aye, I do.'

'Coom off it! *You're* no Yorkist.'

'I am that; raised in Beddington I was.'

'And tha thinks as Fairburn and I – '

He thought she was overcome by shyness again and looked into her simple face. She smiled slowly, pressing her long thighs against him and kissed him squarely on the lips.

'Never mind that now. *I* reckon as it's Fairburn's turn for a *woman* to wed and me to find out some oother side of meself.'

40

The night was sour on him. He lay in the blouse and the skirt on the bed in the machine room hearing the distant sounds of London's Railways and road traffic drifting over in the risen wind: the scraping of the sycamore boughs against the bricks and the blacked-out window pane.

His body had gone mad, unable to dispose of the complex chemicals he had poured into it, it had become obtrusive: each part of it, every organ, proclaiming its unease, so that he could not concentrate on the interesting confusion of his mind.

Whooper had worn lavender water:

'*Me grandmother, Bessie, was never without it. You like it then? Or do you reckon it's too old for uz?*'

How could he tell her, when the scent of it was mixed with everything else? Their beer, the dry gin and the fried fat of the potato crisps they had shared; the cold sausages.

'*Your Bay Rum's clean. Where'd you find it? Boots in the High Street? I'd like a bottle for Fairburn's Christmas box – or Hogmanay.*'

Minna never wore scent; but she would once she had sniffed the special white-petalled kind he was bringing her.

'*I don't mind telling you you're a bit of a surprise packet: a joomping cracker! But then you're young, aren't you? Energetic!*'

And *you* were a little too passive: but that may suit Gillespie; it could be 'joost right' for him with his discs and his femoral hernia.

Now he switched on the bedside light and groped about the box for his glass of water.

It was empty. He had drained it as soon as he had stumbled in from Whooper's 'flut'.

Shivering, he crossed the bare boards of the floor and made his way along the corridor to the staff bathroom. With customary disappointment he inspected his made-up face in the mirror and scrubbed his teeth vigorously.

'Wan of the gloomies, aren't yer? What they used to call melancholic'.

Lynton had liked his gloom. Whenever he had been feeling really sad she had told him how handsome he looked; 'devastating'.

Minna had never questioned his looks. He had no idea what she thought of him physically.

Good God! It was Christmas Day already! He had loved and drunk his way into it, if you could really call it love; the spurts of pleasure he had felt for Whooper; the aftermath of gratitude and distaste for himself.

How cold the night had become. The air in the bathroom did not stir, it lay in layers of chill invisibility contiguous with that in the corridor, the hospital compound: the deep freezing acres overlying London and England.

'You're a talker, aren't you? I'd bite me cheeks sometimes listening to you and Wantage gaffin' on.'

Then you should have shown it. I should have liked you better; *one* Chlorinda Graemes is enough.

'But you're a sport, aren't yer? Won't let on to anywan about tonight? For I don't fancy many fellers even come Christmas. And with Fairburn coming to the boil –'

Gillespie! He would *have* to see him. There was no possible way of avoiding it. He longed to talk to him about Minna: to be sure that when he was gone he would visit her, keep an eye on her treatment, take her little presents from the local shops in Stourmond.

But before he could request that or any such thing, he had to conceal from the Doctor his meeting with Robene, the extraordinary moments with Dougal, her lover.

How could he be absolutely sure that the Doctor knew nothing of that afternoon at the Garter Hotel? How could he be certain that he knew all of it? For with friends it had to be one or the other; complete concealment of all that shamed them; or, for one's own self-respect and in the last resort, total revelation.

And now, after tonight, after the evening that had run into Christmas Day, there was not only that; there was Whooper, Gillespie's 'bittock thorn with a thristle singing in its boughs'.

He slouched back along the dark corridor to the machine room and, as he opened the door, the telephone rang.

41

Obeying the Superintendent's order to 'come by' dressed as he was, he crossed the compound in Claire Hall-Tipping's tweeds, his blue raglan worn loosely over them, the front unbuttoned, her chiffon scarf playing round his ears in the night wind.

Against the sky, clear now as a mountain lake, the sycamores and elms rattled their branches. No light showed, no Christmas moon; only, in the depths of the dome of heaven the chill fire of the stars.

He hurried unhappily towards Gillespie's house. Once he had wondered what he would have to do in order to be noticed by Doctor Whooper. Now he knew it had only been necessary for him to notice her; and this, to his discomfort, he had done. Amid the freckles and hair of Gelda's gentle surfaces and warmth he had stumbled into the sweetness she had so stubbornly concealed in blue serge and glasses; in rudeness and sexual contempt. . .

And now in her sudden acceptance of him she had made him in part responsible for her: anxious that she should not have to contain her anger, that she should be cared for; loved. Arrogance, of course, such as a man could hardly escape, to suppose that only a woman's recognition of *him* could be the master key to any concern for her.

But how could he help it if this was the coinage? That by the loan of their beauty they exacted your care.

In his unease he felt, lackadaisical, at a standstill. He had not troubled to wash himself and still smelled of the drinks he had shared with Gelda, of the potato chips, of the greasy sausages and of her lavender water.

Minna might die of his carelessness. That was true: insufficient constancy, limited love, was carelessness, and that caused accidents.

So he thought, and, wishing to make it reasonable to suppose that his easy betrayal of the doctor might in some way threaten Minna, whom also he had cheated, he said to himself: what else is this war but the consequence of a gigantic accident which, in its turn, is the result of everyone's failure to be selfless enough.

He rapped at the door with the doctor's black iron knocker and wondered with idle interest, who would open it – his tittie, Madge, with her pitchy eyes squinting through the wicket first and, with a withheld smile, letting him in, or would it be old Gillespie himself?

And what, this time, did the doctor want of him? And what did he care? Apart from the reference he had already written, he had nothing further to give him. And he himself had nothing further to give to Gillespie; only his laughter, his amusement at him, the memory of some once small affection.

Betrayed on all sides, Fairburn Gillespie was feebler than the dying, more absurd. Why! The 'wife of his bosom', Robene, had left him not for some younger colleague; *she* had not eloped with a man at all; but gone off with a girl. And Dairmid Alexander, the one 'wee crested bairn' of their marriage, an ingrate who would not even pass Christmas with his father, had turned coward and, so he had heard, fled to play out the war in neutral Dublin.

And now Gelda Whooper, his chosen, his 'bittock thorn'

282

was privy no longer to the singing thrush alone, but to every 'fly in the borough and land'.

'There's no call for you to be poonding on the iron when the door is on the latch.'

John turned round. The doctor, clearly shadowed in the aqueous light of the sky, was standing between the laurels and the foot of the steps looking gloomily up at him.

Wondering again what he might want so early on a Christmas morning, John said nothing as the older man took a step nearer, his face still fixed upon his own:

'I came roond to meet you as I considered you might better waste the spume of the liquors you swallowed at the concert were you to stirk a pace or two in the frost of night.'

'Thank you, sir, but I'm cold.'

'In that gawsie gear a Hottentot would shuver.'

'I'd have changed; but you seemed to want me in a hurry.'

'Och, dinna skim your tongue with picqueerings; but come down the snug – and make fast the door against the air raid wardens: they're out in force this night to fatten the fines and thin the cost of their Christs' mass follies.'

In the lighted hallway he scanned him again: 'Ech! ech! 'Tis no 'maze you have not the heart for the football with the worriecow that's in you.'

John pulled off his chiffon scarf:

'Worriecow! I was sure you'd enjoyed the concert?'

'Aye.'

'I saw you laughing at my Mrs Hall-Tipping.'

'It was canty enough at the time.'

'*At the time*! Dammit! You and Doctor Whooper were in fits of laughter.'

'Miss Whooper you say?'

'And Matron,' John added quickly.

Gillespie led the way down the open stairway and took his station in front of the bagpipes above the mantelpiece:

' 'Tis of Gelda herself that I wished to talk with you this Christmas morn.'

'Then, may I take a drink?'

' 'Tis there in the cag. Ye may draw me a tot for company.'

283

'I rather wanted to see you too, Doctor; but not about Whooper. Not that I don't like her; I do. I think she's a fine person and I'm sure she would make. . . It's Minna who's on my mind. Naturally, she's a fearful worry to me.'

'Aye.' The doctor upended his goblet, tilting it until all but his chin and the rubbed top of his forehead were concealed by it. Then he set the vessel on the mantelpiece, looked deep into it and, at a funeral pace, made his way to the cag for a refill.

'Aye! There's no vantage in wampishing the tongue to whisterpoop the truth, John; and the truth is – ' He paused to drink, wiped his lips and fell silent.

'Wampishing,' 'whisterpoop,' 'worriecow,' John repeated to himself. Such a pomposity of words could only mean that the doctor was not merely *thinking* of marrying Whooper; but that he was already secretly engaged to her. No, not engaged, *betrothed*! And that was a great deal more Scottish and serious.

Standing there on the linoleum beneath the bagpipes, the doctor did indeed look serious, and it came to John that he must know everything and was playing with him.

As though to fulfil this fear, Gillespie placed a hand on each of the bentwood chair's arms and leaned close in towards him:

'John I have to warn ye. I have to tell you that which will be no pleasure to your ears.'

'I can't tell you how sorry – ' John smiled up at him.

'Sorry you will be if you fail to heed my advice: Never bed with a child-woman! Dinna link thy life and love or lippen with a bairn-lass. Ye're in great fault this very winter of fettling yourself with a wee wetter who'll smelt thee in the heat of her maggotty whims until you part either with your truth or with your head.'

Struggling to break free, John pushed himself forward:

'If you are speaking of Minna Frobisher – and I'm sure you are – then you are quite wrong. Minna is very different; she is – '

'Nay, Doctor, Nay! not differing at all; but touched like all the rest; decked out in squeaky innocence and as beribboned with charm and bells as their smocks in summer.'

284

He leaned further forward and, bringing his mournful eyes to within six inches of John's own, he raised and shook his left hand in time to his words:

'Though 'tis well enough to toy and jink with the scent and seed of them, to loose their baby passions when daisies are thick to the wall or the hay fresh in the stack, 'tis a strong fetter you forge for yourself when you seal your vows to such infant-women in *wedlock!*'

He stood up, passed his hand over his brows and continued to fix John with his eyes. 'And now you may speak out *thy* mind to me.'

'Thank you, I think I will.' John gulped at his whisky, rose from his chair then changed his mind and sat down again. Unwilling to consider the doctor's words, affronted by them, he still felt the need to placate the man.

'Life is so hard for *you*, Doctor, and I've an idea that may – '

'What are you coming at?'

'It's only this; that I've seen how things are with you and Robene – with Mrs Gillespie – '

'Ye may name her Robene; for that she is and aye will remain – the daft quey.'

'Yes, Robene. I do want you to know that I understand even about the – about the perversion. I mean your wife's affair with Dougal.'

'Perversion! What a slickery word, John! Where is your proper understanding? *Regression* is what it is with my wild Robene. She's away like a kittle seal to the dugs of its dam; 'tis the running back of the lost child who cannot dare be a full woman. This is the very crux and catch of that snare I was warning you about – for all of its truth and pain.' He paused and then resumed, 'For come the time when you couple with such a child and get bairns from her, you find, with Job, that:

> *She is hardened against her young ones*
> *As though they were not hers. . . .'*

'You mean Robene's neglect of your son, of Dairmid?'

'Indeed! Though in your ignorance of Holy Writ, you will

not know that wee Job was referring to no woman born; but to the leggy ostrich of the Eastern desert:

> *Which leaveth her eggs in the earth,*
> *And warmeth them in the dust,*
> *What time she lifteth up herself on high,*
> *And scorneth the horse and his rider. . . .*

'You hear? The witless bird takes flight on her bony legs, leaving her chick to the horny hoof of the horse.' He paused. 'You ken what I'm telling you?'

'I'm not absolutely sure,' John admitted. 'Though I do know that your wife doesn't care for horses – '

'*Horses!*' The Doctor thumped the mantelpiece: 'Man! Where is your mind? Dinna be so Sassenach-dull and literal. Have you not e'en the nipple of poetry in you? The chick the ostrich abandons is her own unborn nature; it is her refusal to turn woman; for in the nursing of the bairn she brings *two* folk to maturity: the babe itself and the green lass who bore and nourishes him.'

'That is marvellous.'

'You say that, yet you bid fair to tallow the wick of your own future with just such soft wax as was the misguggling of my own.'

'You mean that by marrying Minna – that is, if I do?'

The Doctor looked up to the raftered ceiling and then down at the tartaned floor. His lips moved to release the almost inaudible words:

> *Lo now, his strength is in his loins,*
> *And his force is in the navel of his belly.'*

'Job again, Sir?'

But Gillespie continued more loudly:

> *His bones are as strong pieces of brass.*
> *His bones are like bars of iron.'*

'That's very striking; but what has it got to do with me – or Minna?'

Sorrowfully, Gillespie noticed him again:

'Ech! ech! With the Bible swept from the schools, where is the education, the allegorical understanding that was

286

given to the least of our shepherd boys in the days that are gone?'

'It's not that – '

'Though Job talks of Behemoth, he intends only the complete person, the fitting mate.'

'Oh, that's perfectly clear; but – ?'

Nothing was clear. He had been considering how best he could persuade Gillespie to cut his losses and marry Gelda Whooper; but now he wondered which of the nursing staff the old fellow had in mind for *him*!

It was likely that Sister Thorpe had discussed this, might even have told him that the women of Guinea Lane, determining that he should marry, had gone on to select a bride for him as well.

They could see through him, he knew, these women. In his traffickings with the wards he had not been able to hide from them his delight in their minds and bodies, his hunger for them all. No degree of professionalism could cover it; and the very openness of the secret was a relief, a joy; a crossing place, into their true company. And now he was pleased to think of their concern for him; to be sure that their love had survived their discernment; might well have been strengthened by it.

He found his way back to his chair and, closing his eyes, began to list the nurses he had taken out during his first tentative weeks at the hospital.

He sat up abruptly. The clue had been in the doctor's use of the word 'abandons'; his similes from the Book of Job.

Lynton, of course! It could be none other; the forthright tongue, the roomy pelvis and brassy bones could belong to no one else; and evidently these qualities had registered as vividly in Gillespie's eyes as in his own.

'Well, laddie, what have you to say for yourself. What answer do you vouchsafe me?'

'Only this: that it *is* Minna I love. She's as right for me as Victoria would have been if that man Bellayr – or someone like him – '

'Aye, the type of the time. Rude spirits all.'

The older man fell silent and in John something awoke.

287

'They're like awful dreams, the impossible is in them. They are monsters who will kill as I would kick a door shut.'

Gillespie's face was stern:

'Aye! Uncherished, uncomforted bairns, who grow to be more scornful of mankind than they are of God.'

'And now, for me, there's Minna,' John continued.

'*Minna*! Are you not heeding me?'

'I didn't hear you. Talk of God tires me. I was thinking of Minna.'

'Will you not *listen* when I bid it? I have that to say to you which could free you forever from the whims of that wee wetter.'

John stood up, 'Doctor, that is . . . disgusting – an insult to my taste and to her.' He paused. 'And as for listening to you. I've been doing nothing but listen when really I only came over here to suggest something to *you* – to help you in your own sorrow since your wife left you. I mean *your* chance of happiness in Gelda Whooper.'

'Gelda Whooper!' Gillespie stumbled over to him. 'Me, Dairmid Fairburn Gillespie to wed another child-woman? A bairn-lass who sups up her liquor like a lad. Put my life in a niffer for another wetter? And that when already 'tis gone dark on me; when even now the light of my days is motty with dusk!'

He paused, swaying. 'John Blaydon, ye're a mocker and a son of a mocker. You know full well 'tis *you* I had in mind for the Whooper lass, for with you she'd have time to grow to the full of her. Strong in the loins and the palms of her hands, sweet in her navel, practical in her jaw, *she* could bring you the fulfilment the Lord intended.'

'*Me* with Whooper!' John took a pace forward. 'You astound me, sir; amaze! To be so wise for others and, as often, so blind to yourself. Have you really no idea why your wife, why Robene left you – probably years ago, in spirit? Well, since you asked me to speak out, I will; I'll tell you. She left you because she was sick of playing nurse-maid to you with your childish games of ball and soldiers and your little bottles of drink – '

'Speak on, man. There's some truth in your tongue.'

'And then you set yourself up to disparage women, to

288

wag your fingers at them: at Robene and Whooper and *Minna*, and scorn them for *their* immaturity – calling them "bairn lasses"! Well, I'll take my chance on Minna, but as for Whooper, you'd better marry her quick, for I've just been to bed with her and her mind was on *you*.'

The Doctor jumped out of his chair, but stopped short in front of him. 'Man, man, you're a ruffler. You're a mischievous carle, as twisty as a turnpike stair.' He put a hand on John's shoulder. 'Even so, I cannot help but rejoice in thy impudence. For 'tis clear to me this Christmas morn you are healed of your morbid holding to the tatters of the past. Therefore with the poet Job I lift my face to the blue above and say,

> *I know that thou can'st do anything*
> *And that no thought can be withholden from thee.'*

He dropped his arms and, looking brightly, asked,

'Was she? Was my honey a hellie-cat with you in the graith of her hunger? Did she hauff and plunder the loins of you like the bright gales of Auchtermuchtie roughing the pines of winter? And then, full as a bairn at the breast, did she couch a hogshead beside you on the yellow straw? Did she?'

John stood back. 'She did sleep, Sir; we both did. But I'm not sure of all those other things.' A yawn was rising in him and he held it back unsuccessfully. Seeing the disappointment in the eyes of his friend, he added,

'But she did seemed excited, very eager.'

'She *did*? By what? What poppled and piked her in particular?'

'I think it was the underwear. It seemed to – ' He paused, trying to remember.

'Yes, laddie?'

'To delight her in some way, to reassure her. *I* felt safer, too.'

Gillespie stood very still for a moment and then paced back to his place before the empty hearth.

'Aye.' He drew out the syllable a second time, 'Aye, 'twas ever so with the jink of the kilt. You could not have done better in a threshie-coat.' He paused. 'But, John, you

289

must pretty her sheaf. You took Miss Whooper in your cups and now would hand her on to me.'

'We weren't drunk. It was merriness. No; more than that, a small celebration in the dark of the war. Like Minna she's so brave and good and Minna's away and I was missing her. I tell you, Sir, we're not lost without them, but we are unfound.'

'There's a truth in that.' Gillespie came forward. 'But John, since you are cracking your tongue this night, give me your opinion: do you think that the lass would take me on in the tumbledown that I am in?'

'She said she would – as good as. She's pretty desperate, Sir.

'Ech, ech! There wasn't the need for that last. But thank you. You're a fine wee fellow.'

42

Boxing Day shone fine; a clean arched sky dusted with whisps of cloud at a great height; the sun close-plating the barrage balloons and the surface of the river as it slid out of Stourmond and on down between its sheer banks and lawned mansions to the wharves of Hammersmith.

Breathless with anticipation, light with it, John hurried along the towpath between the frost-striped hawthorn and rustling reeds; the air of the riverside rich in his nose with the scent of old water and rotting flotsam.

In his trouser pockets he carried silver: half-crowns knocking florins, shillings, sixpences and wafer-thin three-penny bits. All of these clattering and jinkling with the heavy coppers and halfpence of his loose change.

Beneath his raglan, in his wallet in the left hand breast pocket of his Donegal jacket, were the folded notes of his month's pay and the Christmas present sent down from Anglesey by his mother and father. Enough, all of it when put together, to buy everything he wanted for Minna on this his first visit out to the Cold Harbour.

As he walked he saw her strangely, almost behind his eyes, as if a slide of her whole self, a vaporous image, rested between the river and his retinae, her face misted and smiling amongst the black spokes of the alders; her body, its small breasts and childish hips wrapped in the metal of the water; quite still; the flesh, the white skin motionless with the patina of the moving surface flowing all about.

He longed to see her; was dried with his hunger for the quietness of her voice, her steady eyes, almost colourless hair falling about her ears, her physical presence and the marvel of her understanding. But above and more than all, he thirsted for her assurance that he had not foundered, that if ever she really had, she still did love him.

How absurd, how mistaken poor old Gillespie had been. He who must once have set out just like this in some other place, in the glens or granite of Scotland to meet and claim Robene Hannay in her kilt and manty; and how the gaining of his bairn-lassie had soiled his perceptions, his judgement of women; how old it had made him, how far removed from the right instinct of youth.

Walking up the hill into the town and on past the laurels of the Garth Hotel, John forsaw himself telling Minna everything of the doctor's last counsel to him, everything except his remarks about her; unless perhaps in the interests of honesty, he told her those too. Championing her in his mind; holding her close beside him on the sanatorium bed, her little face cradled on his shoulder he might explain how the old fellow had got her thoroughly mixed up with his recollection of his courtship of Robene; even with her own childish ailments and nail biting.

But 'maggotty whims' was going to be difficult to explain no matter how brave and honest the context in which he placed it. And at this, outside a jeweller's small shop, its window meshed with steel, he suddenly remembered Minna's response to his honesty about her father's death in the Libyan desert. He saw again her flesh-white face; the box of Algerian dates purpling and bursting in the fire, and her white dress hanging from her shoulders.

It would be wiser, at least on this first visit, not to venture on to that part of the old man's advice. And, if it came to that, it might be kinder, happier, not to touch either upon Gelda Whooper's excitement over Mrs Hall-Tipping's lingerie; sensible, as well, to play down Edgar's management of his make-up; the enthusiasm of the other nurses in Doris Shaw's boudoir.

When Minna was better, was stronger in herself; had settled into a sunnier convalescence, then it would be quite time to amuse and entertain her with an account of the whole of that Christmas Eve and Night's dialogue; but in the meantime he must remember that she had been living too; had a whole new story to tell, even though it could only be of anxious things: of sputum tests and X-rays, of manometers and pills, of medical jokes and nurses' capers, of games on the wireless, of the rumours and flirtations of the wards.

In the shop which he had now entered he looked down through the glass counter top as into a pool.

The rings glistened in their trays and cuboid velvet-lined boxes. They had not changed at all: though the War had diminished nearly everything else – most merchandise, the jewellery lay out unchanged in all its cheapness or expense; and his eyes wandered with pleasure over this glimpse of another time.

He did not know what size of ring Minna would take: he knew it would have to be narrow, a thin fillet to slip over the third finger of her left hand, to slide down over the grapy tip and the middle joint to the two clefts above the knuckle; and he knew that it would be only temporary; since all his family were provided with such serious rings, or stones for them, from old ones of his mother's – ones he had played with in the big bed during the illnesses of his infancy.

Particularly he remembered a heavy golden hoop with five sized diamonds in it. Picking it out of its compartment in the big box, he had known even then that it was valuable; not, at first, in the sense of money but as seaside holidays were valuable; as Puffin Island was valuable in the ocean with waters drenching its rocks and its thin grass glistening in the white Welsh sunlight.

If one of these diamonds was left, even one of the pair of the smallest, it would be his; but if Melanie had been given it then his mother would find something else; a link between himself and those shadowy days of her own excited meetings with his father in Birkenhead at the end of the previous century.

He had not certainly been going to give Minna a ring before he left for the Army. He had never really considered doing so.

With some daring he had wanted to give Victoria a ring years and years ago after that first wedding; he had wanted to give Dymphna a ring in Dublin; but not until she had said that she loved him. Since she never had; since she had been careful never even to imply it in all their talk in all the five years he had sought her, he had ceased to think of finger rings with anything but a distaste so strong that it had nearly become hatred.

A ring, he had thought; a circle about space; and in that space, nothing.

But now, as the shop girl waited for him to speak, as his eyes wandered over crusted emeralds, platinum, pinchbeck, minute diamonds wedged into cut metal facets and the dullness of gold, exhilaration filled him.

'I'll have that one,' he told her, 'with the blue stone.'

Her hand hovered beneath his eyes over the trays. The nails were varnished and a little diamond between twists shone upon her ring finger.

'This one, sir?'

'Oh, that's a sapphire, isn't it? I want that plain one in the silver. It's glass, I suppose?'

'We call it "paste".'

'Yes of course. It *is* silver, though?'

Her fingers closed upon the tray and she lifted it out and slid it onto the counter top. She moved back towards the doorway which led into her parents' house and switched on some brighter lights.

'It's marked inside; there.'

293

'How much is it?'

Her finger and thumb picked at the little label.

'Would you wish any inscription? My dad, my father, could get a short word in there if you was to want it.'

'There isn't time.'

What word would he have wanted? What one word? He would never ever know.

'You haven't told me how much it is and that label's in code of some sort.'

'It's three, sir.'

'Three pounds?'

'Three guineas.'

'Guineas!'

'Yes, sir.'

'That's all right, I can afford it easily. It's just that I met her at the Guinea Lane. I mean that's where we actually met.'

'Shall I wrap it for you?'

'It's only temporary, of course. As soon as I can get hold of it she's going to have a real diamond, in gold, like yours.'

'Yes, sir.'

'You *are* engaged, aren't you?'

'I am.'

'You don't seem very thrilled about it. I mean I'm just hoping that my girl will be a bit more excited even though it is only paste.'

'He's away. He's with the Eighth Army and there's heavy fighting – I've had his ring on my hand for months and now they're saying we're going to fight them all the way up Italy.'

'I'm sorry. I didn't mean to be rude. But – '

'I don't mind.' She smiled. 'I hope things will be better for her. It gets you down, browned off, just waiting all the time.'

'We'll win, don't worry. It won't be long now.'

'I was saying that two years ago!' She handed him the little wrapped package. 'Well, good luck anyway . . .'

As he opened the door the trembler bell affixed to the top of it rang out. As he went down the road towards the other shops and the chemist's where he was going to buy her the scent, he heard its thin janglings echoing.

43

In the green 'bus he put all his parcels except the scent and the pale grapes into the railed luggage compartment by the steps spiralling up to the top deck. Then he climbed up there himself to find a seat and smoke one of his hoarded Gold Flakes.

In the Army he would do better for tobacco and after the monotony of the Guinea Lane menus, the food would be excellent.

The 'bus was very crowded; even the top deck seats were bulging and black with old people: dusty ladies with shopping bags, scrawny old men in shabby clothes; a few soldiers with red faces and whiskery sideburns.

Near the back of the 'bus he found an empty seat behind the stairway barrier and put down his bag of grapes and two or three magazines beside them.

He was tempted to sample the grapes, to test them. The doctor had passed them on to him from a patient with greenhouses where they grew:

'He preserves each bunch by suspending it from a bottle of water sweetened with charcoal,' he had explained, and they were unwrinkled still, positively sharp, less tender than Minna's finger tips, but perhaps if she kept the fruit in her hospital locker, or found a sunny window-sill, it might turn golden. In any case she would be pleased; she would know that each fruit, rounded, translucent, potentially sweet, was an offering. She would know as well that the printed 'shops' he had brought for her in the women's magazines, the advertisements, the pretty frivolities, were proofs, too, of his care, places that he wanted to know about because they were one part of her pleasure, an aspect of her strangeness.

But she might not know this. He did not believe she could ever realise how much in awe he was of her. For how should she ever know that her lost hairs in a brush, wavering when he blew upon them, fine as gossamer, filled him with desire, with a wonder childlike in its immensity?

His Irish girl, Dymphna, had once said she was afraid she had put him off by telling him that she had vomited with fear in a railway carriage when confronted by a stranger. His sister had confided that she usually felt quite unattractive inside herself and that she was half sure no man would ever find her lovely.

From such confidences over the times of his hoping and fearing for himself at the hands of love he had constructed an alternate sense of women: a mode of ordinariness, of personality, linked to that of his own sex; thinking that if ever he learned permanently to believe in it, he might be happier with them. That in their turn women might come to accept him as a creature no less aspiring, no less bewildered, than themselves.

But today, as on most days, though even more positively than usual, he was quite unable to slow his excitement, the pulsing of his vanity, the doubts and joys with which it filled him.

Now, as the 'bus moved forward again after a halt, he made room on his seat for another passenger, putting the brown paper sack of grapes on top of the two magazines on his lap.

With the exception of a couple of soldiers sucking on their cigarettes and looking hungrily down at the pavements in the hope of seeing a girl down there without a perambulator or a uniform, the passengers on the top deck were full of cheer. And today such satisfaction did not seem ridiculous in them with their poor prospects of ever falling in love or of living longer than a few more tatterdemalion years.

He even wished that the old man now sharing his seat had been at one with them in their merriness at riding a 'bus on Boxing Day in the middle of an interminable World War.

But his companion was continually coughing. His feebly shaven, hollowed cheeks were puffed out with his exertions and then fallen in as he fought to draw more air into his ruptured lungs. Then, when a respite relieved him, when the reflex centre in his brain-stem suddenly settled for a few minutes, he looked about him sadly, even, it seemed, hopelessly.

'Couldn't get meself a place on the lower deck,' he told John. 'Them stairs always get to me. And there's the smoking when you do get up here.'

John started to put out his cigarette on the ashtray behind the next seat.

'No, don't bother, sir. One gasper don't make no difference in this jungle.'

He really would have to make up his mind to cut down on it for Minna's sake, he realised. Certainly this afternoon if he wanted a couple at the Cold Harbour he would have to go outside to smoke them or stand out in a corridor. Perhaps, on so glorious a December day there would be a verandah and French windows opening onto it.

'Excuse me, Sir, but I think I seen you a time or two down at the Nag's Head. Aren't you one of the young doctors up at the Guinea Lane?'

'Yes I am; but I'm leaving the hospital very soon. In fact I've already left. I'm joining the RAMC next month.'

In his preoccupation with Minna, her little breathing chest, the very sweetness of her coughing, it was all he could think of to prevent a consultation. And even before he had finished speaking he knew he had not been adroit enough.

The loneliness of chronic illness, the persistence of it, its slow smothering of optimism, made its people obdurate; and the patient beside him was a seasoned fighter, a veteran of situations. He sensed it in his silence as the old man paused to work out a strategy; one that would gain for him the interest of the young doctor, the advice that might, with the wonders of modern science, lead to the alleviation, even to the cure of his distemper.

'I was sure as I'd seen you a time or two with the other young gentlemen down at the Nag's Head of a weekend?'

'I suppose you may have done, though I don't often go there.'

'And once you're in the Army Medical you'll be dealing with all kinds of folk – all sorts of illness?'

'Mostly young people,' John suggested. 'Mostly conscripts, eighteen and upwards.'

'No time for the older people then? Of course not, I do say.'

John turned to look at him frankly:

'Oh of course, once the war is over, we'll do the best we can for everybody.'

His companion got out a large blue handkerchief and let himself go in a bout of dramatic coughing while John looked fixedly out of the window, unwilling, since he was a doctor, to pat his back.

As soon as he could do so, the old man spoke again:

'*My* war wasn't never over; not where me sponges were concerned.'

'That *is* bad luck. Rotten!'

Soon, John knew, the invalid was going to say something which could not be ignored. By his 'sponges' he had meant his lungs and now in his rest from coughing he was still hoping that John would be sufficiently unwary to ask about them.

'Touch of the Boche gas, you see, Doctor: chlorine. And that meant bronchitis and ticker trouble and all the rest of it.'

'Exactly. And you're getting regular treatment, naturally?'

'Regular treatment?'

'Yes.'

'I *was*, but not now. He's left; called up like you.'

Minna would have to stay under the care of old Gillespie once she had healed, once she was on top of her lesion. Was Fairburn really up-to-date? Did he keep up with the journals?

'But your doctor must have had a partner,' he said now. 'He must have left someone in charge of things?'

'He did! A fellow dragged out of retirement, older than myself and tired.' He caught John by the elbow. 'Do you

know what, Doctor? Old Phelps doesn't undo your shirt button any more. He takes one look at you when you come in – No, he doesn't, I'm a liar! He leaves the 'certsificates' and prescriptions in a heap on the surgery table. The mixture as before.'

'Very slack.'

Outmanoeuvred John cast round for a different opening, one that would lead into a wider discussion.

'And you live alone, do you, Mr – ?'

'King, Bob King. Only this past Autumn since Batsy left me, the wife.'

'You mean that she, that your wife died?'

'Died! No, she got breathless; my Batsy got so breathless that they moved her to the Heath. The Council found her a ground floor place: no stairs, no climbing.'

'You must be lonely without her.'

'It's Ladies only up at the Heath – or we could have gone in there together. Now we'll have to bide our time till the Armistice same as everyone else.'

'Then you do miss her? You miss your wife, Batsy?'

'Of course I do, Doctor; after more than forty years and together through the Kaiser's War as well as this lot.'

They were silent for a time, nodding together involuntarily with the movement of the 'bus. Light and dark alternated as the sunlight flashing through the shadows of the roadside trees patterned their faces.

'Are you on your way out to the Heath now, Mr King?'

'I'm taking Jemima out to her, our budgie. He takes turn and turn about with us since Batsy went in there.'

John craned over his shoulder to look into the well of the aisle.

'Where is she? Where is Jemima?'

'She's down below in her cage with the parcels. I wasn't going to bring her up into this lot. She's a tidy little body, is Jemima; likes everything just so: clean water in her trough, millet sprays when I can get 'em, a sanded floor and good air.'

He coughed again.

The 'bus rolled on and out past the last villas of Stourmond and into the frosted countryside of rural Middlesex;

the turned arable and smooth pastures scattered with stands
of poplar, with oak trees and groves of ivied elms.

The Palouse
1984–1986